RETRIBUTION

A TEAM REAPER THRILLER

BRENT TOWNS

WOLFPACK
PUBLISHING
— EST 2013 —

Published in the United States by Wolfpack Publishing, Las Vegas.

Wolfpack Publishing
6032 Wheat Penny Avenue
Las Vegas, NV 89122

wolfpackpublishing.com

Paperback ISBN 978-1-64119-514-0
Ebook ISBN 978-1-64119-513-3

Library of Congress Control Number: 2019932476

OTHER TEAM REAPER THRILLERS

RETRIBUTION

Retribution
(rɛtrɪ bjuːʃən)
noun
1. *the act of punishing or taking vengeance for wrongdoing, sin, or injury*
2. *punishment or vengeance*
Collins English Dictionary.

"*Judges, lawyers, and politicians have a license to steal. We don't need one.*"
– Carlo Gambino

"*I never lie because I don't fear anyone. You only lie when you're afraid.*"
– John Gotti

"*Sometimes I feel like God…when I order someone killed – they die the same day.*"
– Pablo Escobar

CHAPTER 1

THE MOTOROLA BUZZED in his coat pocket. Reaching in, the man retrieved it and looked at the backlit screen. It said: **Private**.

He raised it to his ear. "Hello?"

A gravelly voice asked, "Are they there?"

"Yes."

"Good."

The line went dead.

―――――

West Virginia

They came out of the dark with military precision, like wraiths from a dense mist. Dressed in black, armed with suppressed SA 80s out of Great Britain, loaded with 5.56mm NATO rounds.

Professionals. A three-man splinter, part of a team of six

with special skills. They each wore tactical vests and night vision.

The point-man took to his knee beside a large maple. He paused and brought the SA 80 up to his shoulder and sighted through the night scope, and the weapon coughed once.

He felt the light pressure of the second man's hand on his left shoulder. Then he was up and continuing his stealthy advance on the caretaker's cottage. Their target.

The second team had the house. The initial task was to cut the phone and power before entry. In and out. No noise, no fuss, no survivors. All in a night's work.

————

"Sure as shit beats Colombia, huh, Reaper?" Chip Roberts commented as he watched the second Yankee batter go down swinging in the bottom of the 6th inning.

Thirty-two-year-old John 'Reaper' Kane nodded. He'd hated Colombia. A green hellhole filled with snakes, bugs, and unbearable heat, not to mention the revolutionaries and drug cartels.

He and Chip had spent three weeks down there as part of a four-man team of Force Recon Marines (MARSOC). Their mission objective was to interrupt the supply of drugs being sent north to the States, without getting caught, by the cartels or the Colombian government. It was one of many they'd been on over the years.

When they'd returned Stateside, Chip took on the catch-phrase, 'Better than Colombia'.

Shit! Anywhere was better than Colombia.

But that had been four years ago. Now they were out of

the service and working as personal security experts for the Gilbert Foundation.

The Foundation was run by Mike Gilbert, out of Charleston. A one-time marine colonel, Gilbert had gone into the private security business after leaving the corps.

The current job had the two friends watching over a husband and wife in a large house out in the West Virginia countryside. It was a foundation house used by them on previous protection details. The 'protectees' were upstairs asleep.

This time around, Mike Gilbert was doing a favor for an old friend in the marshal service. Kane and Chip's subjects were witnesses in the trial of a notorious mobster out of New York.

Both men had been out there for a week and were bored with the inaction of the job. Two more days, and it would be over.

"What you think, Reaper?" Chip asked. He gave his friend a wide, toothy grin.

"I think it's time for another coffee," Kane said, and hauled himself to his feet from the sofa, beside Chip.

Kane was six-four in his socks, broad-shouldered, and powerful. When he stood up, it felt as though every inch had a kink in it. He ran a hand through his black hair and started to make towards the kitchen.

"You want to get me one while you're there?"

"Sure."

Out in the kitchen, Kane picked up their cups from the draining rack and turned them over, ready to take the bitter, black liquid. Reaching across the counter to pull the sugar bowl towards him, his jacket fell open far enough to reveal a shoulder holster with the Heckler and Koch USP nestled in it. He changed his mind and pushed the bowl away.

Once he'd finished pouring their brews, Kane paused and stared out the large kitchen window, his pale-blue eyes taking in the state of darkness. It was hard to see past his reflection, but he was aware of the line of large Sugar Maples lurking beyond the yard.

Kane returned to the living room with the coffees and passed one to Chip. The red-head blew a cooling breath across it first before he took a sip. He screwed up his face and grumbled, "Fuck, man. Are you trying to kill me? Where's the damned sugar?"

Kane smiled. "You're getting too soft, Chip. Toughen up."

"Haven't you heard? We ain't in the corps no more, buddy. I get some comforts."

Kane turned to look at the television. "What's the score?"

"Yankees up by two."

Kane sat back down, careful not to spill his coffee, then sipped at the steaming liquid. "Damn it. You're right. This stuff is getting worse every time I taste it."

"I told you."

"Yeah."

Kane froze. "What was that?"

"What?" Chip asked, not taking his eyes from the television.

"I heard a noise."

Chip muted the television.

"There," Kane said.

"It was one of the horses," Chip said. "Bennett will take care of it. After all, it's his job."

Chip turned the volume back up.

He was probably right, Kane thought; Bennett would

see to it. Besides, the safe house was a horse ranch. And Bennett was the caretaker.

Kane settled back on the sofa and took another sip of coffee. It had to be nothing. No one knew where they were.

———

When the horses in the corral made a fuss, Randall Bennett was reading all about how some energy company had set up a huge solar panel field in the Namib Desert, and how it would supply half the country's power once it came online sometime in the next year.

They had a picture of it spread over two pages in the technology magazine he'd picked up at the local store earlier in the day.

He shook his head in disbelief. "Christ, what next?"

Hearing the disturbance with the horses, he paused for a moment, laying the periodical in his lap, and looking up, focused his eyes on the far, white-painted wall of the cottage. He raised his glasses to the top of his head and waited.

The horses made more noise.

Bennett leaned forward and laid the magazine on the glass-topped coffee table. Beside it was a 9mm Smith and Wesson M&P semi-automatic handgun which he scooped up and then rose to his feet.

From habit, Bennett dropped out the magazine to check it, then slapped it back home. Before he'd joined the Gilbert Foundation, he'd been an MP for the U.S. Army. Now in his late fifties, he saw this as semi-retirement. A job that put a roof over his head, without all the dangers the other had offered. All he had to do was look after the place and the horses.

Just because the job was more laid back didn't mean he wasn't ready if trouble came calling. Why last week he'd had to unblock the latrine. Not a pretty job at all.

Bennett walked across to the doorway, flicked on the light-switch for outside, and opened the heavy, timber door. The handgun was held down beside his thigh as he walked out onto the veranda and stared into the blackness beyond.

The corral was over by a huge double barn near the stables. He could just make out the animals as they milled within it.

Practiced brown eyes scanned the darkness as he sought the cause of the horses' angst.

"Can't see shit in this light," he growled and stepped down onto the gravel driveway.

He began to walk towards the corral when he realized the dog wasn't anywhere to be seen.

"Rory?" he called in a low voice.

Nothing.

He frowned. The dog was always around. First thing of a morning, or last thing of a night. It didn't matter. The black lab would be there.

Bennett's grip tightened on the Smith and Wesson. "Rory?"

Nothing.

He stopped when the hairs on the back of his neck stood up. Bennett was half-way between the corral and the cottage. Something wasn't right. Maybe he should walk over to the house and find Kane and Chip.

"Stop being a baby," he muttered and kept going.

By the time Bennett reached the corral, the horses had quietened down. He took a quick look around but found nothing out of the ordinary.

It wasn't until he had started back that he almost fell over the dog. He bent down and felt the animal, noting the dampness of its coat. Bennett's hand came away tacky.

The realization hit him like a runaway train. "Christ, Randall, you're screwed."

He came to his feet and brought the Smith and Wesson up to the firing position. No sooner had he done so when a suppressed SA 80 coughed twice.

Bennett was slammed back by the twin hammer-blows and fell in an untidy heap beside the dog.

A shadow appeared out of the darkness, stood over the fallen man and placed another bullet in Bennett's head.

"Target down."

————

Everything went black! Lights, television, everything.

"Reaper!" there was urgency in Chip's voice.

Kane was already off the sofa as his military training kicked in. "Yep. We got trouble. Cover the front door. I'll take the back. Nobody gets up those stairs."

"They'll have NVGs," Chip pointed out as he took off his coat and withdrew his Para P14-45 and worked the slide for a .45 caliber round to be rammed home into the breach.

"We'll wait for them to get inside before we spring our little surprise."

"Roger that."

The surprise was the backup power supply, made for just such an event. Night vision goggles weren't worth shit when the lights were on. In fact, the glare would blind the wearers.

The difference between the normal power and the

backup system was that when the switch was turned on, every light in the house lit up.

Chip took up position behind the sofa while Kane went back into the kitchen where he waited within arm's reach of the backup switch. He just hoped the bastards wouldn't use flashbangs.

With his H&K in his right hand, Kane reached into his pants pocket with his left and took out a company issue cell. He hit speed-dial one and put it up to his ear.

"I'm sorry, but the number you have dialed has been disconnected."

"Fuck!"

He stuffed the phone back into his pocket and waited.

Kane figured they'd breach at the same time. That's what he'd do. Hell, he'd use the damned flashbangs too.

He thought about going for one of the M4 Colts in the gun safe but dismissed the idea. The space within the house was too confined, so the handguns would have to do.

The back door opened in a smooth, silent sweep. Kane hugged the wall and waited. A shadow filled the dark void of the doorway, stepped inside, and swept the room looking for targets.

Come on, another step.

The intruder obliged and took it.

Kane flicked the switch.

"Arghh!" the intruder shouted, blinded by the sudden flare of light.

Kane stepped away from the wall and shot the man twice in the chest. The sound almost deafened him in the enclosed area of the kitchen as the report bounced off the tiled surfaces.

The man in the combat gear lurched back, and Kane saw that he was wearing a tactical vest. There was no way the .45 caliber rounds from his handgun would pierce that.

He shifted his aim and fired twice more. Both bullets punched into the man's face just below the NVGs. With a spray of bright red blood, the intruder went down and didn't move.

Behind him, Kane heard Chip's weapon bark twice, and then twice more.

There was more movement at the back door, and another figure appeared. This one had discarded the NVGs and started to blaze away with his SA 80 as soon as a target came into view.

Bullets riddled the kitchen. They punched into walls, shattered tiles, cups, and plates, smashed into the fridge and splintered the bench behind which Kane had taken cover.

Debris rained all over the tiled floor. Kane leaned around the end of the counter and fired twice at the gunman. His shots flew wide and plowed into the door frame behind the shooter.

Meanwhile, the sound of automatic fire sounded from the living room where Chip was heavily engaged with those who'd come via the front door. Bullets smashed through the drywall and sprayed plaster chips and dust across the kitchen.

The sofa that Chip had hidden behind was riddled with holes, much of the stuffing seeming to float through the air as it was blown out.

Chip rose and fired three shots at the nearest intruder and then dropped back down. He heard the man shout and took satisfaction in knowing he'd hit his target.

Chip fired twice more. He'd tried for three, but the Para was empty.

Before he'd even dropped back down, the empty magazine had been released, and another clip rammed home. An instant later Chip was back in the fight.

The sofa was once again sprayed with a hail of bullets and Chip felt one tug at his shirt. He responded with a barrage of four shots. He hit another of the intruders, but an additional two had forced their way inside.

"Damn it!" he cursed out loud as the sofa jumped under further heavy impacts.

A burning sensation seared Chip's right leg. He looked down and saw the red stain already starting to appear on his pants. Another scored his ribs, while a third opened a deep gouge in his left forearm.

"Reaper, I'm hit! I'm pinned down!"

Kane heard the shout. "Hang on, buddy; I'm coming!" He added in a low voice, "Just as soon as I kill this son of a bitch."

He heard Chip's Para fire more shots and then his voice again as it shouted, "Reaper! I've got an asshole who's made it up the stairs!"

Kane bit back a curse and loosed a couple of shots at the gunman in the kitchen. His response was another storm of lead from the SA 80.

"I've had about enough of this shit!" Kane grated and stood up from behind the counter.

With a bellow, he emptied the magazine at the man before him. Six shots. Two hit the man's body armor, another the gun in his hands, a fourth drove through the upper part of the right arm, and the last two tore a gruesome wound through his throat that spurted arterial blood across the damaged walls.

Kane dropped the second clip out of the H&K and rammed home his third and final one. Twelve rounds and that was it.

Suppressed gunfire sounded from upstairs followed by a woman's scream.

"Damn it!" Kane snarled and hurried forward.

He picked up an SA 80 and dropped the magazine out and checked the loads. He slammed it back in and brought the weapon to his shoulder.

As he passed through the living room, he sprayed the last intruder with what was left in the weapon's magazine.

The bullets stitched a diagonal pattern across the fighter's tactical vest. The hits stopped at his throat when the magazine emptied. He was left unbalanced, his arms windmilling wildly.

Without any hesitation, Kane dropped the SA 80 and drew the H&K. It came up to firing position, and he squeezed twice. The slugs ruined the shooter's face.

"Chip, are you OK?"

"Fucker got me again," Chip groaned. "Save the targets."

With the H&K still raised, Kane took the steps two at a time. When he reached the landing, he could see along the hall to the master bedroom. The door was open. Halfway along was the body of the man. His torso was riddled with bullet holes, his pajama shirt torn and blood-stained. A large pool had also formed on the carpet beneath the body.

Another high-pitched scream echoed along the hall, and further gunfire erupted. This time it was not suppressed: a handgun.

"Shit," Kane snarled and raced along the hall.

He was almost to the doorway when the shooter appeared. Surprise registered on the killer's face. Kane drove the muzzle of the gun forward so that it smashed into his mouth. As it made contact, he squeezed the trigger.

The intruder's head snapped back, and blood sprayed

from the rear of it in a fine mist. Kane shoved his way past, the killer's body falling backward through the doorway.

Kane stepped over the fallen man's boots and hurried across to the bed where the woman lay in her bloodstained pink pajamas. She'd been shot twice in the chest.

He checked for a pulse but found none. He cursed under his breath.

Both of their 'protectees' were dead. Six attackers were down, but so was Chip. And he had no damned idea if there were any more of the bastards still out there in the dark.

Back downstairs, Kane found Chip still behind the shot-up sofa. There were no more shooters, so he hurried to the fallen man's side. "How you doing, buddy?"

"Hurts like a bitch. How's things upstairs?"

Kane gave him a look that told the wounded man all he needed to know.

"Shit!" he swore in a bitterness-laced voice.

Kane patted him on the shoulder. "I have to do a sweep, Chip. We need to know if there are any more of them and see if Bennett is OK."

Chip nodded. "Go. I'll be fine. I've been hurt worse."

Kane took his handgun, checked it, and stuffed it back in his hand. "I won't be long."

"Watch your ass."

First up, Kane checked the three downed intruders in the living room. All were dead. Then he went through to the shattered kitchen and checked the two there. Same result. He did, however, find a map on one of them.

Kane moved to the gun safe and worked quickly. He selected one of the M4 Colts and retrieved a tactical vest from the bottom of the safe. Finding three extra box magazines for the carbine, he checked that they were fully loaded with 30 rounds each and stuffed them in the vest's larger pouches.

His H&K was placed in a holster on his left side, and three full clips of .45 caliber ammunition were put in the pouches above it.

He took up the pair of NVGs discarded by the second intruder and walked out into the night.

Once outside, it took him twenty minutes of careful searching to secure the area and locate Bennett's body, shot twice in the chest, next to the dog.

Something inside Kane troubled him. The phone call and the map. He reached into his pocket for the cell and tried Gilbert again.

It was the same as before. "I'm sorry, but the number you have dialed has been disconnected."

A sense of unease came over Kane and then his anger built. "You bastard."

———

By the time he reached Chip, his wounded friend had turned a pasty grey color and was beginning to shake. Chip looked up at Kane and gave him a wan smile. "Bastard must've got me worse than I thought, Reaper."

"Hang in there, Chip, I'll call for a meat wagon."

Chip shook his head. "I don't think it'll make it in time, Reaper. I can feel the blood running out my back."

Kane leaned forward. "This might hurt."

He rolled Chip to get a good look at his back. His friend was right. There was a large hole from which blood ran freely. With medical help at least thirty minutes away, Chip was certain to bleed out before it arrived.

"I'll get the kit and see if I can stop the bleeding. If we can get that hole plugged, you'll be fine."

"Don't waste your time, amigo," Chip said softly. "Listen. You know as well as I do that those bastards had to have someone tell them where we were, don't you?"

Kane nodded. "I tried to ring Mike, and I kept getting told his number was disconnected."

"You figure it was him?" Chip asked and then coughed a deep, wet cough.

"It looks that way. These guys were professionals, Chip. Ex-operators like us. Going by the hardware they were using, I'd say they were Brits. Fly in, do the job, and fly out the same night. I found a map on one of them. Showed the layout of the whole place."

"Reaper?" Chip's voice was weaker.

"Yeah?"

"Take care."

Chip slipped silently away. His breathing grew shallow and then stopped altogether.

"I'll take care, buddy."

———

Kane called 911 on Chip's cell and waited for the operator to answer. He then threw it on the floor beside his friend. He figured he had somewhere between twenty and thirty minutes before someone showed. In that time, he aimed to be a long way away from there.

He walked around the back of the house to where the Chevy Tahoe was and put the M4 in the rear of the vehicle then climbed in. He dropped the visor and found the spare keys. He tried the ignition, and the SUV started first try. He turned on the headlights, slipped it into drive, and, with a minimum amount of wheelspin, took off.

Kane's face was illuminated by the dash lights, and his determined expression was visible.

He wanted answers and knew where to get them. It would take two hours to get to Gilbert's home just outside of Charleston. Someone would pay.

CHAPTER 2

CHARLESTON

A trembling hand poured another large whiskey into the tumbler. The ice was long gone. Now, it was just a matter of refill after refill. Some of it splashed onto the expensive, polished-hardwood desk. Mike Gilbert cursed his clumsiness.

The cell on the desk rang and caused the big, thin-haired man to jump. He reached out with a ham-sized fist and picked it up.

"Hello?"

"Is it done?"

"I don't know."

"What do you mean, you don't know?"

"I haven't heard from them."

"Well fucking call, them. How hard can it be?"

"I tried. They won't pick up."

The line went eerily silent.

Then: "Do you like life, Mr. Gilbert?"

"I like it just fine."

"Well, find out what the fuck has happened! This is your mess. You hired them. You said it was simple."

"You can't blame me."

"I already am. And if this has all turned to shit, I'll kill you, your family, even your fucking dog. Do you understand me?"

"I understand."

The line went dead.

"I don't have a dog."

————

Two minutes after the phone call ended, another cell rang.

"Hello?"

"Something's gone wrong. Do it now."

The call disconnected.

————

After the connection was broken, Gilbert sat in silence for a minute or so before saying in a casual voice, "You killed them, didn't you?"

There was movement as Kane filled the doorway to the lavishly furnished study. He stepped inside, the H&K, now complete with a silencer, in his right hand. His voice held an icy edge to it when he said, "Every last one of them. Who were they? Brits?"

Gilbert nodded and took a sip from the glass in front of him. He placed it back on the desk and said, "Yes. I thought so when I never heard. I guess I underestimated you all."

"Who was your friend on the phone?"

"Colin O'Brien."

Kane nodded. "He's the feller we were guarding them against? The Irish Mob Boss?"

Gilbert nodded.

Kane's face grew grim. "Why, Mike?"

"They had something over him."

"Not them, Mike. You betrayed us. Why?"

Gilbert stared at the H&K in Kane's hand. He sighed. "Money. The company is all but broke. Damn it, Reaper! No one from this company was meant to get hurt."

Kane's voice became like granite. "Why don't you tell Chip or Bennett? That's right; you can't. They're fucking dead!"

Gilbert flinched. He bowed his head. "I'm sorry, Reaper."

"How much did he pay you?"

"What?"

"O'Brien. How much?"

"Two million."

Silence.

Gilbert looked at Kane. "They know about your sister, Reaper. Hell, they know everything about all of us."

Kane's face screwed up into a mask of rage. "You son of a bitch. You gave them our files, didn't you?"

"I had no choice. It was either do that or ..."

"Where can I find him?" Kane snapped.

"What?"

"Come on, Mike, where can I find the bastard?"

"You can't just go after him. He's too well protected. You wouldn't get within twelve feet of him."

Kane raised the H&K and shot Gilbert in the right shoulder.

Gilbert lurched in his seat and cried out, "What the fuck, Reaper? You shot me!"

"Where, Mike? The next one goes between your eyes."

"He'll kill me if I tell you."

"I'll kill you if you don't," Kane promised.

A thin bead of sweat formed on Gilbert's brow as the pain from his wound increased and his fear intensified.

"He's got a restaurant on Fifth Avenue. It's where he makes all his deals. Likes to take his clients up to the rooftop to impress them."

"It's a high-rise?"

"Yes. It's vacant except for the top floor. That's converted to the restaurant. You're crazy if you think you can get to him."

"You've left me no choice."

The crunch of tires on gravel in the driveway was audible from the study. Kane noticed the look of alarm on Gilbert's pain-filled face.

"You expecting someone?"

Gilbert shook his head. Then realization hit home. "The bastard didn't waste any time."

"You mean whoever it is, is here for you?"

"The son of a bitch is Irish. He's mean, he's bad-tempered, and he don't much like mistakes. He must've had someone close at hand just in case."

Kane moved to a position beside the window and peeled back the curtain a crack to look out. A large black SUV was parked in the drive, and two men were climbing out. One was a huge man with broad shoulders while the other was slim and tall.

"There's two of them," Kane said.

"Is one of them a big feller?"

"Yeah."

Despite everything, Gilbert chuckled. "That's Bannon. He's O'Brien's enforcer. I guess he means business."

"So do I," Kane grated.

"Get out of here, Reaper," Gilbert ordered him. "They're here for me. After all I've done, I guess I deserve it. Go make your sister safe."

"Thanks to you, she won't be safe until O'Brien's dead."

"Then go do it."

Kane heard the doorbell ring.

"Last chance, Reaper."

Kane cursed. "I came here to kill you, Mick."

"I know –'

The H&K came up and coughed twice. Twin eruptions spurted red on Gilbert's chest as he jerked in his seat from the impact. A third shot smashed into his head.

The doorbell rang a second time as Kane slipped silently from the house.

———

"Hello?"

"He's dead."

"Good."

"We didn't do it. Someone beat us here."

Silence.

"What do you want us to do?"

"Kill the girl."

"She can't hurt us."

"Kill her anyway."

———

2 days later

. . .

"Hello?"

"She's gone."

Silence.

"What now?"

"Her brother must still be alive. My contact says the count came up one body short."

"Do you think he killed Gilbert?"

"Yes."

"What do you want us to do?"

"Come back to New York. I'll see if he can be found."

The line went dead.

———

Maine

It looked like an early fifties hunting lodge at first glance. Surrounded by tall pines, it sat in a secluded cove on the rocky fringes of Moosehead Lake.

Really, it was a home for the sick and terminally ill.

Kane watched his sister in silence. The slow steady rise and fall of her chest, the peaceful look on her face. In addition, the steady beep of the heart monitor as it ticked along registered all sixty plus beats per minute. It was always the same, never changing.

There was movement beside him, and an older man in his fifties said, "She looks so peaceful, John."

"I just wish she'd wake up, Doc."

"How long's it been now?"

"Five years."

Melanie Kane was twenty-eight. She'd been a bubbly twenty-three-year-old with her whole life ahead of her when a car wreck had killed her parents and left her in a coma.

Kane had been on deployment when he'd been notified. His immediate reaction had been one of stunned silence. Half of his family, gone in the blink of an eye.

The details at first were sketchy. However, when he arrived stateside, he found out that his father had suffered a heart attack while driving and swerved in front of an oncoming truck.

His parents had died instantly while his sister had suffered brain trauma and never woken up.

The doctors were at a loss why. The results of all the scans that she'd undergone over the years showed no reason for her not to wake up.

Ever since, she'd been institutionalized.

"Are you sure this is OK, Doc? It's short notice, and these guys could find her."

David 'Doc' Harper patted him on the shoulder. "She'll be fine, John. She's registered under a different name. No one but me knows who she really is. Besides, I owe you. I'm glad you called."

Harper was referring to a time, four years before when he was a doctor with the 33rd Medical Battalion posted in the Congo on a U.N. humanitarian mission. Kane had been there too, though not officially. He and his team were running covert operations against the rebels, who at the time, were killing civilians hand over fist. A call went out about a large contingent of them closing in on a party of U.N. medical staff in a small village. Kane's team was the only help within thirty miles, and they'd been directed there.

By nightfall on the day of their arrival, they were surrounded.

Under the cover of darkness, the recon marines had slipped out and carved a broad path through the besiegers in almost total silence. When the sun rose the next morning, the rebels had hightailed it and left their dead behind.

"I'll check in weekly, Doc. Money's not an issue now that it's fixed to be paid automatically."

"Hell, John, even if you had no money, I'd take care of her. It's the least I can do. I've just got something else to do, and I'll be right back."

Harper left the room, and Kane moved over to stand beside his sister's bed. He picked up her right hand and held it in his own.

"I'm sorry I won't be able to visit so often, Mel. But there's something I need to do to keep you safe. Then I'll have to disappear for a while. Don't worry none, though. Doc Harper will take good care of you."

Kane leaned forward and kissed her forehead. He straightened up and ran a hand through her hair. "You keep fighting, Mel. I love you."

Ten minutes after he'd left, Doc Harper returned to the room to find Melanie Kane on her own.

———

New York, 1 week later

Kane kept surveillance on the place for four nights before deciding to make his move. O'Brien had five men with him at any one time. When he arrived at the restaurant, two of his thugs stayed on the door. The remaining three accompanied him to the top floor, one of whom was his hired man, Bannon.

This was Kane's dilemma. The elevator would be a death trap. More than likely they'd have CCTV cameras in it and see his approach. He could always parachute onto the rooftop, which meant that he'd only have to get down from up there. Both were bad ideas.

That left the third, and more likely option. Kane had observed that every night, once O'Brien and his entourage were dropped off, the driver would park under a street lamp thirty meters away from the building. After finishing in the small hours, O'Brien and his escort would make their way down to the car. Not once did he see the car drive to meet them.

On the fifth night, Kane put his plan into action. He'd walked by the building's entrance earlier, and as he'd passed under the street light, drawn his silenced H&K and shot out the globe while still on the move.

Then he returned at midnight to await the arrival of Colin O'Brien.

———

O'Brien and his entourage were late. Much later than usual, and when they did arrive, they had an extra man with them. Not that it mattered to Kane much. If he had to take down an extra man to get to the mob boss, then so be it.

Then he noticed it. When they were about to go inside, Bannon and the new guy turned enough to reveal the gun in Bannon's hand, pressed into the newcomer's back.

"Shit!" he swore. This changed everything. There was no way he was about to sit idly by and allow them to kill an innocent. But who said he was innocent? He could be a rival. A drug seller.

"Or innocent, Reaper," he said out loud.

Kane stared at the entrance. For some reason, there was only one man left on the door. He mulled over a new plan in his mind. "Come on, Reaper. You know how to think on your feet. You're trained for it."

When he spoke next, his voice was laced with sarcasm. "Got it! Frontal assault!"

Kane climbed out of the SUV and walked along the footpath, his rubber-soled boots almost silent on the concrete surface.

When he reached O'Brien's car shrouded in darkness due to the absence of the street light, Kane tapped on the tinted side window. With a whirr, it came down, and a face stared out at him.

"What?"

Pop! Pop!

The man's head snapped back, and he fell across the center console and onto the passenger seat.

Kane lowered the H&K and moved towards the guard on the door.

He kept to the shadows as much as he could until the last minute when he emerged twenty feet from the lone guard.

Without any hesitation, Kane walked up to the man and stopped in front of him.

The man stared at him and snapped, "What the fuck you want, boyo?"

He had a scarred face and a week's worth of stubble on his jaw. Kane stared into his blue eyes and said, "I want to see your boss."

"Fuck off!"

The thug reached out to push Kane away. Mistake!

There was a flurry of movement, and before the mob man knew what was happening, he had an H&K pressed hard up under his chin. Alarm spread across his face as he waited for his life to end.

"I'll say it again. I want to see your boss, please!"

————

The room was cold and poorly lit. The solid, grey concrete walls gave off no warmth, and the floor sloped gently to the center where a chair had been placed over a grate. Convenient when it came to cleaning up after Colin O'Brien was finished with those unlucky enough to see its interior.

The group came down the steps, and once inside the room the Irishman snapped, "Get the bastard sat down, and we'll see what he knows."

O'Brien wasn't a big man by any stretch. His hair was dyed black, and his face showed his age to be in his mid-fifties.

Bannon forced the struggling man onto the seat and held a gun to his head as one of the other men secured him to the metal legs.

Apart from O'Brien, Bannon, and the guard from the door, there were two mob men in the room. One was the man who'd accompanied the enforcer to kill Gilbert, and the other looked a lot like the mob boss himself.

Once the job was done, O'Brien said, "Right, let's see what this copper prick has to say for himself. What were you doing in my warehouse, detective?"

There was no response from the man on the seat. He sat there. His head slumped forward onto his chest. O'Brien nodded to Bannon, and the big enforcer grabbed a handful of brown hair and wrenched the man's head back with merciless brutality.

The seated man gasped, and pain registered on his bruised face.

"I asked you a question, Detective Lemming," O'Brien snarled.

The detective gave him the best defiant look he could muster and said, "Screw you, asshole."

The man who'd tied him up suddenly lashed out with a right fist and struck him in the mouth. The sound was akin to an ax biting into wood. Blood flowed freely, and Lemming spat out a tooth.

"The warehouse, Detective," O'Brien reminded him.

Lemming ignored him and looked across at the man who resembled the mob boss. He gave him a bloody grin. "You proud of your pa, boy? Going to become an asshole like him too?"

Another blow smashed into Lemming's face. This one crushed his nose with a sickening crunch, and more blood joined that flowing from the detective's mouth.

O'Brien's son slid his right hand inside his coat and came out with a Colt Double Eagle. He stalked over to the policeman and placed it against the side of his head.

"You were there searching for our shipment, weren't you? Someone snitched. Who was it?"

Lemming spat blood on the floor.

The gun in the younger O'Brien's fist crashed, and the detective's head snapped sideways. The .45 caliber slug exploded from the other side, dragging blood and bone fragments with it.

"Christ, Sean, what did you go and do that for?" Colin O'Brien snarled at his son. "I wasn't fucking finished with him!"

"He weren't going to say nothing," Sean shot back at his father.

"You got to keep a rein on that temper of yours, boy," Bannon said stoically. "Before it gets you in a lot of trouble."

"Shut your gob," Sean snarled at the big enforcer. "Your job is to do what you're told."

Bannon's face remained passive at the barb directed at him.

"Enough!" O'Brien shouted. He focused his anger on his son. "This is your mess. Clean it up! Roy, go and get the plastic."

"Sure, boss," said the mobster who'd tied Lemming up, and he started for the concrete stairwell.

He'd no sooner climbed the first step when there was a pop, pop sound, and he slumped to the floor.

"By Jaysus?" O'Brien gasped.

Kane appeared, pushing the front door guard ahead of him at arm's reach. The silenced H&K was in his right hand, ready to fire again.

The tall, thin mobster who'd been with Bannon at Gilbert's, tried for his gun. Kane identified the threat and shifted his aim. He put a bullet in the man's chest.

"Son of a bastard?" Sean O'Brien snarled and brought his Colt up.

Kane shot him twice, once in the arm and then in the leg. Sean screamed in pain as blood spurted from the wounds.

Once more, Kane shifted his aim and shot Bannon in the top of his thigh. The leg crumpled under the big man, and he choked off a screech of pain as he fell to the hard floor.

Then the H&K settled on the face of Colin O'Brien.

The mobster never even flinched.

"Who the fuck are you?" he growled at Kane. "Did Isaac Kirov send you to kill me?"

Kane didn't answer at first. Instead, he glanced at the still form in the chair. His teeth ground together, and his jaw clenched as anger flooded through him. On the floor, Sean moaned as waves of pain swept through him. Bannon, however, remained silent.

Finally, he said, "My name is John Kane."

Recognition registered on O'Brien's face. "You got big balls, Kane. I'll give you that. But where do we go from here?"

"A good friend of mine died because of you," Kane grated. "And after it was done, you decided to clean up the mess that was left behind so it couldn't be traced back to you."

"Nothing personal."

"You made it personal when you acquired information about me and my sister."

"Ah, yes. Where is the lovely Melanie, by the way? Just so it makes it easier to find her after we drop you in the East River along with Detective Lemming here."

"She's safe. You on the other hand ..."

O'Brien's face screwed up in a mask of rage. "Go on, do it! You come here to my place of business and threaten my life! Fucking asshole! But just you remember this after you kill me, my son will hunt you and your sister to the ends of the earth. And when he finds you, he'll chop you both up into little pieces and feed you to the fish in New York Harbour!"

Kane glanced at Sean and crooked his head in the direction of the wounded O'Brien. "Is that your son?"

Before O'Brien could answer, Sean snarled through the pain of his wounds, "Bet your ass I am."

Kane shot him; one well-placed round through the forehead.

"Sean!" O'Brien screeched. *"You rotten bastard! You're dead! Dead! De ..."*

The H&K fired again and cut off O'Brien's hysterical screams. The bullet slammed into his chest. Kane fired a second time, and O'Brien went down in an untidy heap. The gun then switched to the fallen Bannon. Kane said, "It's up to you whether you live or die, you choose."

"I'll take life."

"Am I ever going to see you again?"

Bannon looked at his fallen employer. "That's doubtful."

"Then I'll leave."

Kane disappeared up the steps, and once he was gone, Bannon dragged himself to O'Brien's side. He checked for the man's pulse. Then he looked at the stairwell where Kane had gone. He said in a low voice, "You should have made sure."

CHAPTER 3

*RETRIBUTION ARIZONA, **6 months later***

The Greyhound bus shuddered to a halt beside an old Pepsi sign still displayed on the rusted framework of a rundown gas station. Another sign below it was damaged and read *Arno's*. The dark-haired driver turned and stared at the man making his way along the aisle towards the front of the bus.

"Mister, are you sure you want to get off here? Retribution ain't your average stop along the line."

Kane paused by the man before he disembarked and said, "It'll be fine."

"Hell, I'll take you to the next town if you want. It is only another thirty miles. The company can wear it."

"This'll do. Can I get my pack from underneath?"

The driver shook his head in resignation. "Up to you."

He opened the door, and a blast of hot air infiltrated the bus. The driver and Kane climbed out, gravel crunching under his boots as they touched down.

The driver flipped open the underneath compartment

and grabbed Kane's pack. "Here you are, mister. Good luck."

He nodded and watched the driver clamber back aboard, glad to be out of the heat. Within a few more heartbeats, the bus roared away in a cloud of dust.

Kane looked at the sign, which like the gas station, sat on the outskirts of town. It read: ***Retribution: Gateway to the border.***

Behind Kane was no more than a harsh, saguaro-covered landscape, dotted with large boulders, and miles of desert sand. In front of him lay Retribution. It looked large enough. Maybe he'd be able to find work here for a while.

"Howdy, stranger."

Kane turned to see a broad-shouldered man, dressed in grease-stained bib overalls, emerge from the gas station's open front door. He nodded.

"You all get off the bus?"

"Yeah."

"Staying long in town?"

"Maybe."

"You looking for work?"

"Maybe."

"There's a job going here if you want it."

Kane glanced around and saw one car. "Don't seem like you're snowed under."

The man nodded. "Ever since the mine closed, things have slowed some. But cars and gas ain't all I do."

"What else?"

"Run deliveries. Handyman maintenance, stuff like that."

"Uh huh."

"You got a name?"

"Kane."

"That it?"

"Yeah."

"My name is Elmore. Elmore Druce."

"Name on the sign says Arno's."

"Shit, that sign is older than me. Arno up and quit years ago. The place has had three owners since then, and not one has decided to change the sign."

Kane figured Druce to be in his middle thirties, although it was hard to tell under the walnut-colored skin, the week's growth of stubble, and the mop of unkempt black hair.

Kane asked, "Can I think about it?"

"About what?"

"The job."

"Sure. If you want it the place opens at six."

A thought popped into Kane's head. "You got law in this town?"

"Yeah, got a sheriff and two deputies," Druce replied. Then his expression changed. "You ain't wanted, are you? Not that it matters in a place like Retribution."

Kane indicated the sign. "How far to the border?"

"About fifteen miles."

"Is there somewhere in town I can get a room?"

"Chester's at the other end of the main street is a budget motel. Won't cost too much and they tell me they change the sheets once a month."

His smile disappeared when Kane stared at him stoically.

"There is another motel in the center of town and one on Second Street. They'll cost you a might more than Chester's place. Or you can try Molly Miller's boarding house."

"Motel will be fine."

Kane started to walk away when Druce called after him. "Remember, Kane. Be here by six if you want the job."

————

Retribution had all the signs of a town in the throes of a slow, painful death. Potholes in the main street's asphalt, paint peeling from storefront signs, the local bowling alley boarded up. Yet for a dying town, it still seemed to have some life.

A white Chevrolet 4X4 with red and blue lights and the words Border Patrol on the side passed him, headed south.

Kane kept on along the sidewalk. He passed a laundromat, a general store, post office, hardware, café/diner, one of the motels Druce had mentioned, plus a dozen other specialty shops spread out along each side of the thoroughfare.

"Hey, you little prick, get your ass back here!"

The shout brought Kane back to the here and now. Ahead of him he saw a kid, perhaps no older than thirteen, run across the road, followed by four larger boys.

"If you run, you'll only make it worse for yourself. We was only going to teach you a lesson. Now we're going to cut you."

Kane watched as the kid disappeared into an alley between two brick buildings about twenty feet in front of where he stood. He saw the look of absolute terror on the boy's face and knew he had to intervene before the kid got hurt.

As he walked forward the leader of the group glared at him and snapped, "If you know what's good for you, stranger, you'll keep walking."

Then they too disappeared into the alley.

Followed by Kane.

The alley had once gone all the way through to the rear of the block. But over the years the amount of rubbish and debris that had been dumped in it had built up, creating a dead end. The kid had himself boxed in.

"Got you now, Jimmy," Kane heard the leader of the group say. "Your mamma ain't going to help you this time."

Through a gap in the wall of four pursuers, Kane saw the desperation on the young boy's face.

"You're scaring the boy. Let him be."

They turned as one and looked at Kane. Their leader walked a few paces towards him, his right hand holding a large-bladed knife.

"I thought I told you to keep walking," the punk said, his voice dripping with menace.

Kane figured him to be maybe seventeen, big for his age and well-muscled. His face still held the scars of pubescent acne which made him seem even more intimidating.

"Maybe you should put that knife down before someone gets hurt."

The young man glanced at the others with him and grinned. "Maybe I should stick him instead, huh, boys?"

"Yeah, stick him, Bolt," one of the others said.

Bolt nodded. "Maybe I will."

Kane was conscious of the H&K stuck down the back of his pants. However, he'd rather not go down that path if it was avoidable. Besides, the kid was only a punk. Take one down, and the rest would run. He placed his pack on the ground.

"Last chance ... Bolt, is it?"

"Yeah."

"OK ... Bolt. Here's what is going to happen. You and

your friends are going to walk out of this alley and leave this kid be."

Bolt snorted. "And if we don't?"

"I'll take that knife, and at least one of you will wind up in the emergency department."

"You got a big mouth, asshole," Bolt snarled and closed the distance between himself and Kane.

Kane waited until the last second to move. Bolt thrust the knife forward, aiming to drive it deep into Kane's guts. With the weapon, no more than six inches from disemboweling him, Kane's armed services training kicked in.

His left hand clamped onto Bolt's right wrist and stopped any further progress. He twisted it savagely until he heard the wrist break, and a high-pitched shriek escaped from Bolt's throat. The knife dropped from his hand and clattered on the asphalt at his feet.

Kane kept hold of the damaged wrist and dragged Bolt forward. He brought up his clenched right fist and smashed him in the face. The nose gave a sickening crunch, and blood ran thickly from the twin orifices. Kane hit him again and felt the jawbones on the left side give. Bolt's eyes rolled back into his head, and he slumped to his knees.

Kane let go of Bolt's ruined wrist, and the unconscious young man fell to his side and didn't move.

"Any of you fellers want to join your friend in the emergency room?"

No one moved.

Kane motioned to the kid. "Come on, time you were gone."

As the kid passed him, he said to Kane, "Gee, thanks, mister."

"Get out of here, kid."

He heard footsteps retreat along the alley and stared at

the three confused figures before him. "I'm leaving now. If you fellers feel the urge to follow me, think of your friend."

"Barrett ain't going to like this, man," one of them snarled.

Kane looked at the thinnest of them and asked, "Who's Barrett?"

"He's Bolt's older brother. He'll come looking for you and pop a cap in your ass."

"He sounds like a mighty scary feller."

"You best believe it. Retribution is his town."

Kane nodded. "Tell him that he might want to be more welcoming towards strangers."

"You hang around, and you'll get to tell him that yourself."

"Uh huh," Kane grunted dismissively and turned around and walked towards the front of the alley.

Once Kane was gone the thin young man said to the others with him, "Dink, get Bolt to the Emergency. Davy, follow this asshole and see where he goes. I'll go and tell Barrett what happened. When he perches, call me on my cell. The bastard will be dead before nightfall."

————

When Kane emerged from the alley, he looked left and right but couldn't see the kid anywhere. So, he turned left and kept on along the sidewalk.

The center of town was at the main crossroads. He stood briefly on the corner outside the town hall. Diagonally opposite him was the courthouse. The Sheriff's Office was opposite that, and on the other corner was a car dealership with five cars in the lot.

Kane was about to step down onto the asphalt to cross

the street when a siren gave a quick whoop! A sheriff's cruiser pulled up in front of him on the wrong side of the road. The window came down, and a solid man wearing a uniform and mirrored Aviator sunglasses looked up at him.

The first words out of his mouth were, "Stranger in town?"

Kane looked around the intersection. An orange Ford pickup drove by, and a beat-up Chrysler came back the other way. Across the street on the sidewalk, a girl, perhaps seventeen, walked along and looked in his direction. She wore denim shorts cut off a hair below her buttocks and a tight, white, singlet top. Her long, black hair spilled down her back.

"I asked you a question, mister."

"Yeah," Kane said and dropped his gaze to the man in the car. "Sheriff?"

"Deputy. Deputy Art Cleaver," Cleaver said and looked him up and down. "Come in on the bus?"

"Yeah."

"You staying or passing through?"

"Ain't sure yet."

Cleaver took off his glasses and pointed one end at Kane. "Let me give you some advice. Keep going. Ain't nothing in Retribution for you."

"Must be something."

"What's that?"

"Feller offered me a job," Kane told him.

Cleaver frowned. "Who did?"

"Druce, down at the gas station."

A look of concern came over Cleaver's face but quickly disappeared. "All right then. If you got yourself a job, I guess that's OK. But if you step out of line, I'll run you out of town so fast your head'll spin."

"I'll remember that."

"Make sure you do."

The glasses went back on Cleaver's face, and the window whirred as it returned to the closed position, keeping out the heat of the day. Then, with a small screech of tires, Cleaver was gone.

Kane began to think that the bus driver's offer might have been the better choice rather than stopping in Retribution.

––––––––

"Damn it, Marylou, how many times do you have to be told? No testing the fucking product."

"I'm sorry, Barrett, it wo –"

The crack of knuckles on bone filled the room. "Shut up! All you have to do is get it ready for distribution. Just put it in the little packets. Christ, are you dumb or something?"

Barrett Miller took out the handgun tucked into his pants and placed it against the side of Marylou's head. She trembled with fear and tears ran from her pale-blue eyes.

"Next time I'll put a bullet in your head and take you out into the desert for the vultures to pick clean. Understand?"

"Y – Yes."

He shoved her away from him so hard she stumbled. She caught herself and moved back to work with the other four women.

Barrett tucked the nickel-plated Smith and Wesson 1911 back into his pants and signaled to one of his men in the far corner.

The drug dealer was a tall man, maybe six-feet-five.

Broad across the chest and the black singlet top he wore showed the jailhouse tattoos on each well-muscled arm. His eyes were dark, cold and distant, his hair black and his jaw square.

The gang operated out of a house in the backlots of Retribution. The sheriff's office had raided the house on several occasions but failed to find anything each time, thanks to an insider they paid well.

Whenever a tipoff came in, Barrett and his crew were well organized and quickly dissembled any evidence of illegal activity and stashed it in a subterranean room beneath the basement. Along with money and weapons.

Once the cocaine was cut and bagged, a third party was brought in to deliver the goods to the sellers in Phoenix and collect any money that was owed.

"What you want, Barrett?"

"Keep an eye on Marylou for me, Buck. If she starts testing the product again, I want you to take her out in the desert and put a goddamn bullet in her head."

The man's deeply-tanned face remained stoic, and he nodded.

"I got to go to Sonora in a couple of days to see Montoya and deliver his money to him," Barrett continued. "There is, however, another shipment coming across tonight. The crew in Phoenix want a double batch this time around. The Cardinals have a game this weekend. That'll give the girls three days to get it cut and bagged."

"That's a lot of work, Barrett," Buck pointed out.

Barrett shrugged. "Give them some incentive. Tell them if it don't get done on time, I'll take them with me to Sonora next time I go, and they can visit *El Hombre*."

El Hombre! Juan Jesus Montoya, of the Montoya

Cartel. A dangerous man if there ever was one. Especially if you erred on his wrong side.

The cartel boss lived in a fortified villa outside the small town of Acuña, ten miles on the Mexican side of the border. He surrounded himself with armed men who had been hand-picked for the job. Most were either ex-military or *policía*. Some were just plain killers.

Barrett had known him to venture onto American soil only once before. A trusted business associate had skimmed an extra five-million off the profits. Montoya came across with his *sicario* and paid the man a visit.

They returned before dawn the next day, leaving behind one of the worst crime scenes Arizona law enforcement officers had ever seen.

Buck knew it was pointless to protest further so let it go.

A door opened, and the thin young man who'd been with Bolt entered.

"About damned time, Alton," Barrett snapped. "Where's Bolt? He was meant to be here an hour ago."

Alton's expression was grim. "We had ourselves a slight problem, Barrett."

A dark cloud descended over Barrett's face. He hated problems. They always seemed to breed more problems.

He said in a low voice, "Tell me."

By the time Alton was finished, Barrett had become eerily calm. "Where is he now?"

"I'm waiting for Davy to call once he perches."

The phone rang.

Alton picked up and put it to his ear. He waited in silence for a few seconds and hung up. He looked at Barrett. "Chester's Motel."

———

The bell above the door jingled when Kane entered the motel's reception area, signaling his arrival at the empty wooden counter.

When Kane had first swung into the motel's driveway, the garishness of the bright-yellow building hit him between the eyes like a 5.56 NATO round. Then he saw the sign that said: *Pool*. When he looked around for it, he saw only a fenced area where giant cacti had grown within.

"Looks like the oasis is a desert," he murmured.

The motel was all on one level. It spread in a long L-shape, with the main reception area at the front. The neglected lot had two cars in it. One, a Ford Taurus with Arizona plates, and the other was a beat-up Buick that Kane figured would be lucky to make it out of its park.

As he got closer, he noticed that large flakes of the yellow paint were peeling off and tufts of grass grew out of the cracks in the concrete walkway in front of the rooms so bad that a cleaning trolley would have trouble getting by them.

The sign on the door had read: *Budget Rooms*.

Kane reached the counter and was about to pick up the pitted bell to ring when an unkempt, middle-aged man dressed in jeans and a stained white singlet emerged from the back room.

"Howdy, stranger, what can I do you all for?" he smiled and revealed a row of discolored teeth. "The name's Chester."

"A room would be good. Preferably a clean one."

"Sure, sure. Clean's all we got. If you sign the register, I'll rustle up a key."

He signed his Christian name only while Chester turned away to the keyboard. When the man turned back, he looked down at the ledger. "Is that it?"

"That's all you'll get, apart from the money for the room. How much?"

"Eighty."

"For the week?"

"Per night."

Kane raised his eyebrows and reached into his pocket. He took out a roll of bills and peeled off two twenties. He tossed them on the scarred countertop. Kane stared at Chester and said, "You'll get the rest if I like the room."

Chester almost protested but instead scooped up the money as though it were about to be taken back. He nodded. "The rooms are fine. You'll see. It's number nine."

Kane took the key, walked out of the reception area and paused. His time in charge of recon missions had taught him to be aware of his surroundings. He took in everything around him; the parking lot and its derelict asphalt, the large, now-defunct furniture store across the street, a graffitied dumpster outside the loading dock, and the punk beside it, trying not to be seen.

Kane stared at him for a good thirty seconds before it got the better of the gang member who walked away. He watched him go, then made his way along the parking lot in front of the rooms to avoid the grass, past a line of yellow doors until he found his number.

The key slid smoothly into the door-lock, but when Kane tried to turn it, it wouldn't move. He jiggled it a touch, but there was still no movement. He stepped back and looked at the number. Nine. Then something caught his eye. There was a hole in the wood above the number. He stepped back further and looked at the door to his left. Number five.

He worked out the problem. A screw had come free, and the number had turned.

Kane found his room number and this time the key worked. He turned the doorknob and pushed the door inward.

The trapped heat from the room rushed out and smacked him in the face. It released the built-up-over-time smells of stale tobacco smoke and another odor that Kane couldn't nail down. He stepped inside and found the carpet stained with indeterminate matters. The mirror had a large crack in it, and the bench where the microwave and glasses sat was delaminated and had dropped woodchips.

He checked the bathroom and found it a similar state of disrepair. There was a copper-green stain in the shower, and the toilet still had the previous occupier's stains on the bowl. He peeled the covers back on the double bed and hissed in disgust. The once-white sheets were stained. Now he knew that the grass on the path would not get in the way of a cleaning trolley – they obviously didn't have one.

Far from happy, Kane stalked outside and pointed himself in the direction of the reception. He pushed in through the door and stopped at the counter. He picked up the bell and rang it until Chester appeared.

"What's up?"

"The room."

"What's wrong with it?"

"How about what the hell is right with it?" Kane growled. "I'll give you an hour to sort that shit out, and I'll be back. If you ain't done, I'll kick your ass until it is. Where can I get a beer?"

Chester opened his mouth to protest at the way he'd been spoken to. Before a sound could emerge, Kane snapped, "The next words past your lips better be, Yes, sir or I'll drag you down to the room and use you for a rag. Understand?"

The motel owner's mouth clamped shut, and he nodded.

"Good. Beer?"

"There's a bar one block over and down to your right. It's called Drew's Cactus Rose."

Kane cocked a quizzical eyebrow.

"Don't ask."

Chester peered over Kane's shoulder, and his expression changed. "Oh, shit!"

Kane turned and saw five men walking into the parking lot. The man at their center was a full head taller than the rest.

"Who are they?"

"Barrett Miller and his crew. They ain't due for another couple of days?"

"What do you mean?"

"I have to pay them insurance."

"Insurance from what?"

"From them. Damn it, I ain't got the cash."

"Don't worry," Kane told him. "They're here for me."

"Huh?"

"I put his brother in the emergency room. You don't have a baseball bat or something I could borrow?"

Chester ducked below the counter and came up holding a wooden bat. He passed it across to Kane and said, "Won't do you any good. He's more likely to shoot you."

Kane tested the bat's weight then reached behind his back and took the H&K from inside his pants. "That's what I'm trying to avoid."

He handed the gun across to Chester who paused, then took the weapon. "Take care of it for me."

"Ah, sure."

Kane walked outside and stood on the edge of the lot. "Are you fellers looking for me?"

"That's him, Barrett."

Kane's gaze shifted to the young man who spoke. He recognized him as one from the alley.

"Are you the feller who beat on my brother?" Barrett demanded.

"Seemed like a good idea at the time," Kane told him. "He figured to run me through with that knife of his."

"He was going to do no such thing," Alton lied.

Kane's icy stare bored into the young man. "I guess you had your eyes closed, huh?"

"You're a liar," Alton sneered.

"It don't matter much," Barrett snapped. "You did it. You said as much."

Barrett put his hand behind his back and retrieved his gun that he'd had down the back of his pants. Kane froze. It wasn't the first time he'd had a gun pointed at him. He just hoped it wouldn't be the last. The first words that came into his head were, "You don't want to do that."

It was weak and lame, but hell, he was trying to buy time for himself.

Barrett's eyes glittered with anticipation. "You don't get no say in what I aim to do, Mr. Tough Guy. You just get to die."

The gang leader's finger tightened on the trigger.

The sound of two blasts from a sheriff's car siren as it entered the lot, stayed the trigger-finger, and Barrett lowered the weapon and turned around. Kane searched the driver's seat and saw that it was the deputy who'd talked to him earlier.

The car stopped, and the deputy climbed out. He

placed his hat on his head as he walked around to the front of his vehicle and leaned his butt against the hood.

His gaze fixed on Kane and he said in a patronizing tone, "I knew you were trouble when I saw you the first time. I said to myself, Cleaver, this stranger is trouble. And what happens? I get a call from the emergency room saying that some stranger had beat up on young Bolt Miller. Busted his arm, his nose, his jaw. Immediately, I thought of you."

"Kid came at me with a knife," Kane said.

"That's a lie," Alton declared.

Cleaver shifted his gaze to Alton and then to Barrett. "Are you trying to make extra work for me, Barrett? Going to shoot this feller here and now? Your boss ain't going to like that much. You know how he feels about unwanted attention."

"You know what he did to Bolt," Barrett snarled. "He's got it coming."

"Not here, not now, Barrett," Cleaver warned him. "Your friend here will put the bat away, and you and your boys will turn around and go home."

"Friend, hah, he's no friend of mine. What about my brother?"

"Teach him to pick on someone his own size," Kane offered.

Alton took a step forward and snarled, "Fuck you!"

With a blur of movement, Kane's arm swept up and then down. On the latter stroke, he let the baseball bat go. It whistled through the air, and the thickest part of the bat cracked Alton between the eyes, dropping him on the spot, blood flowing from the neat cut that had opened on his forehead.

"Son of a bitch!" Barrett shouted and brought his gun up.

"Hey!" Cleaver shouted and drew his own sidearm. A Smith and Wesson M&P 9mm. However, it wasn't pointed at Kane. The deputy had a bead drawn on the side of Barrett's head. "You pull that trigger, Barrett, and I'll drop you where you stand."

The tension in the air was palpable as everyone waited to see what Barrett Miller would do. Kane stared hard into the gang leader's eyes.

Before anyone had the chance to find out, two more sheriff's vehicles roared into the lot. The first was a car like the one Cleaver drove. Behind the wheel was a grey-haired man.

The other vehicle was a Tahoe driven by a woman. Beside her was the kid Kane had helped in the alley.

Barrett lowered his handgun and tucked it into his pants. He turned away and walked off a distance and then stopped.

The older man climbed from his car, a pump-action shotgun in his right hand. He was of average height and build with his thickened waist starting to show the effects of mid-fifties.

"What the hell is going on here?" he demanded. His gazed jumped back and forth from one to the other. It dropped to Alton who was still on the ground. "What's wrong with that little shit?"

Barrett stabbed a finger at Kane. "That son of a bitch threw a baseball bat at him. Do your damned job and arrest him, Sheriff."

The sheriff stared at Kane. "Is that so?"

Kane shrugged.

"Is that what happened, Cleaver?" the sheriff asked his deputy.

While Cleaver rattled off the details, Kane glanced over at the Tahoe. The woman climbed out and stood beside the front of her vehicle, her hand resting on her sidearm.

She was in her mid-thirties, slim with short, dark hair, tanned face and like Cleaver, wore aviator sunglasses.

"Hey, I'm talking to you."

Kane looked at the sheriff.

"Was it you who put young Bolt in the emergency department?" he asked again.

"He came at me with a knife."

The sheriff nodded. "You want to press charges?"

Kane shook his head.

"All right, then," he turned to look at Barrett. "You get the hell out of here before I arrest every last one. Cleaver, make sure they keep going. I'll have a word with our friend here."

"I was going to arrest him for assault," Cleaver told him.

"Just do as I told you. I don't want these clowns coming back after we're gone."

The sheriff waited until they had left before he turned his attention back to Kane. "Right, what's your name?"

"Kane."

"Kane what?"

"Just Kane."

The sheriff eyed him cautiously. "I'm Sheriff Walt Smythe. Retribution is my town."

He turned to his female deputy and motioned her to come forward. "This is Cara. She's my right hand."

Kane nodded. "Ma'am."

She looked at him and nodded, her broad smile showing

even white teeth. "My son says you rescued him from Bolt Miller and his crew a while ago."

"He was kind of outnumbered."

"Thanks. They tried the same thing a while back, and I happened by in time to save him."

"Dangerous town."

Cara nodded.

Smythe interrupted. "Now that's over, tell me if you're staying or passing through."

"Haven't made up my mind yet."

"If I was you, I'd seriously think about leaving. Barrett Miller ain't one to trifle with."

"Yet he's still walking around free."

"He may look dumb, but let me tell you, he's as smart as they come."

Kane said, "I'll remember that."

Smythe gave him a skeptical look and said, "All right. I'm going back to the office. If you get the time, you might want to thank Chester. If it weren't for him, you'd be dead by now."

The sheriff departed leaving Kane and Cara alone. The deputy waved to the boy in the car, and he climbed out. He sauntered over to them, and Cara said, "You got something to say, Jimmy?"

The kid nodded. "Thanks, mister."

"It's OK," Kane said to him and held out his hand. "You might want to try running faster next time."

Jimmy grinned, took the hand, and shook. "I'll try to remember that."

Cara said, "Go hop in the vehicle, Jimmy, I'll be there in a moment."

The kid turned and walked off, and Cara stared at Kane. "Been a while, Reaper."

"Philippines, '09," Kane allowed, rubbing his chest. "Never thought you'd wind up in a place like this, Cara."

"Long story."

"I got time."

"I don't. How about I meet you later for something to eat. You OK with that?"

"Sure. Where and when?"

"Sally's Diner. Know it?" She shook her head. "Of course, you don't. Ask Chester; he'll give you directions. Maybe around eight."

"I'll see you there."

"Yeah."

Cara turned away and walked back to the Tahoe. She was about to climb in when she called back to him. "It's good to see you, Reaper."

"You too, Cara."

CHAPTER 4

THE SHERIFF'S office wasn't big by any stretch of the imagination. It didn't need to be to accommodate the three of them. Although, Smythe did have his own office area with a large glass window that provided him a full view of the rest of their workspace.

That consisted of two desks, multiple filing cabinets, a large counter for walk-ins, plus countless cupboards for all the other crap that they needed. The twin cells were out the back, and a large, reinforced, steel gunroom had been added which formed their armory. That was Cara's job. She was the one to maintain all the weapons.

Deputy Cara Billings had come to Retribution straight out of the Corps. Her and Jimmy both. Her husband had been killed by a street gang in Phoenix which left no one to care for the boy while she was deployed. She needed employment a little closer to home and had ended up in Retribution.

The sheriff leaned back in his office chair and stared at the map on the left wall. Saguaro County. Miles and miles of desert with four towns, of which, Retribution was the insignificant county seat. And there were only he and his two deputies to patrol it.

But, not for much longer. Twelve months from now, the county was to be amalgamated with Pima County; everything would fall under the jurisdiction of the Pima County Sheriff's Department. Then Retribution would be their headache, and he and his wife, Maureen, could get the hell out of Dodge.

With all the drugs, the violence, Barrett and his gang of no-goods, Smythe had sent countless pleas for assistance to the governor, the Marshals, DEA, and FBI. Hell, he'd even tried the ATF. All had been ignored. No one wanted to know about Shitsburg, Arizona. Or even cared.

Smythe looked through the window of his office and saw Cleaver at his desk. "Asshole," he muttered.

Of the three of them, Cleaver was the only one who would retain his job. Oddly enough, he would be based in Retribution. Maybe someone would shoot him in the ass.

There was movement at the front entrance, and Cara came in. He waved to her, and she changed direction and walked towards his office.

"Close the door and take a seat," he told her as she entered.

"What's up?"

"Is Jimmy OK?"

"Sure."

"Where is he now?"

"Missy's."

Smythe nodded. Missy was Cara's neighbor. "What do you make of our friend?"

"He's OK."

He stared at her for a drawn-out moment. "You know him, don't you?"

"Was it that obvious?"

"Let's just say I know the signs."

"I knew Kane in another world, Walt. I'll guarantee he's a good man."

"You sound positive."

"He took a bullet in the Philippines when Abu Sayyaf decided they wanted an American Ambassador to play with and attacked the embassy. I was in charge of the Embassy Guard," Cara explained. "He and his team were in-country doing some covert work when it happened."

"How long since you've seen him?"

"I haven't seen him since it happened in '09."

Smythe sighed. "I'll have to take your word for it. But he's been here five minutes and already pissed off the biggest crook in town. And Cleaver. Not that I give two shits about that."

"I'll find out more tonight. He and I are having dinner."

"All right then."

There was a knock at the door, and Cleaver entered.

"What is it?" Smythe asked in a terse voice.

"I'm taking the spare SUV out on patrol."

"Where?" Smythe demanded.

"Taking a run down to the border and then cutting back through Grissom's place. He's been complaining about someone using the old road that runs through his place again. Thought I'd take another look."

Smythe looked at his watch. Four o'clock. He rose from his seat and said, "You stay and mind the office. I'll go. I'm sick of being cooped up in here anyway."

A fleeting look of alarm crossed Cleaver's face. "Hell, Walt, I'll do it. It's my job."

"Nope. Stay here."

"But I know the area."

Smythe grew impatient. "And I don't?"

"I didn't say that."

"Then shut up and get back to your desk."

Cleaver bit back a retort and closed the door. Smythe looked at Cara. "What was all that about?"

———

Sonora

Ten minutes later in Sonora, a cell phone rang.

Montoya picked up. "Yes?"

"You have a problem."

"Why is it when you call, it is always I who has the problem?"

"It's your shipment."

Silence, and then, "I'm listening."

The cartel boss waited while the information was relayed to him. His face grew darker with every word that he heard. When the man on the other end was finished, he said, "You told me the road was good. That the *gringo* wouldn't be a problem. Yet, here he is, being a problem."

"I'm doing the best that I can."

"Obviously it is not good enough. I will take care of it."

The line went dead, and Montoya stood before a massive plate-glass window that gave him a view over the cactus and rock-strewn, copper-colored landscape from where his villa stood.

He wasn't a tall man at five-nine, however, he threw a large shadow, and the mention of his name brought fear to those in Sonora who heard it. His black hair and neatly-trimmed goatee were in stark contrast to the white suit that fitted his slim frame perfectly. And so it should; the damn thing cost him five thousand dollars. Like the other twenty. Montoya's shoes matched his suit.

The cartel boss stared down at the crystal-clear pool, surrounded by white marble tiles. Three large umbrellas were securely anchored around it to keep the harsh Sonoran sun at bay. On the banana lounges situated in the shade were three bikini-clad women. All were slender, deeply-tanned, and had long black hair. One of them was his wife, Carmella. The other two were her sisters, Rosa, and Juanita.

"There is a problem, *Jefe?*"

Montoya turned and stared at the man seated on his luxurious white-leather sofa. It matched the rest of the room, the villa really. The walls, the furniture, floor tiles, even his armored Humvee. It looked very sterile.

Montoya nodded. "I have business for you, Cesar."

The cartel boss went on to tell his man what he wanted. When he was finished, Montoya said, "Maybe leave a message when you are done."

Cesar Salazar was Montoya's personal hitman, or as they were known, *sicario*. They called him *El Monstruo*, The Monster. A name that chilled the blood of anyone who heard it.

He was a solidly-built man of medium height, in his early forties, had short black hair, and was clean shaven. Unlike Montoya, Salazar preferred to wear black, the color matching his permanent mood.

Salazar was once an officer in the *Policía Federal Preventiva* (Federal Preventive Police), also known as the *Federales*. He had been good at his job. While the cartels killed *Federales* at will, Salazar had remained alive. All those sent to deal with him had died violent deaths.

After a while, death became so ingrained that he was

unable to see the line until he'd crossed it. At which point, his bosses turned on him, and he was about to go on trial for doing his job.

Salazar would have none of it and reached out to Montoya. Now, apart from the cartel boss, he was the most feared man along the border.

Salazar gave his boss a passive stare and nodded. "I'll take care of it. I'll have to leave right away."

"Do you know where you are going?"

The *sicario* nodded.

Montoya's expression changed. "Do not disappoint me."

"Do I ever?"

The Grissom place

Cyrus Grissom sat on an old sun lounge on the veranda of his timber home and took a sip of his Coors beer. Across his lap was a Browning, 12-gauge, pump-action shotgun.

Grissom had the white hair, tired eyes, and lined face of a Vietnam Vet. He also had a limp, courtesy of an NVA bullet from his time on Hill 861A.

He checked his watch. 8.30. It would be fully dark soon, the night bringing some relief from the late summer sun. Grissom wondered if the truck would be back tonight. He knew it was a truck because of the high headlights. That and the fact the old road was only navigable by high-ride vehicles since the previous summer's storms had washed out the road in places.

But somehow, they managed to get through. He'd told the county sheriff on more than one occasion. The response was, "We'll come and check it out." No one ever came.

The truck, on the other hand, came at least once a week, sometimes twice. If they were true to form, then the truck would come that night.

Half an hour later, just as the moon had peeked over the far hills, the truck appeared, but it wasn't alone. With it was a second vehicle. They bounced over the road. Headlights bobbed wildly as the vehicles hit every hole and rut that they came across.

Grissom sat in the dark and watched their passage in the distance, the drone of the motors reaching his ears. He gripped the shotgun tighter as they slowed at the Y intersection and stopped. Then the second vehicle turned and started toward the house. The first kept going.

For the first time since he'd left Vietnam, Grissom was scared.

Tires crunched on gravel as the vehicle approached the house, its lights blazing a path through the dark. It stopped, and the black SUV's engine was switched off.

Silence.

Grissom waited patiently in the dark. Palms sweaty against the shotgun, his heart beat hard in his chest as it threatened to burst free of its enclosure.

Come on you son of a bitch, get out. Do something.

Nothing.

The tick of the cooling motor reached Grissom's ears. The low, mournful howl of a coyote drifted across the desert and sent a chill running down the old man's spine. He gripped the pump-action tighter and contemplated a possible shot at the vehicle.

But he didn't have to. The door opened, and a man

stepped out into the moonlight. Grissom pointed the shotgun in his direction.

"Who are you and what do you want?" he snapped as he tried to sound confident.

The man's calm, accented voice answered, "I'm but a lost soul trying to find my way this night, *señor*."

"You're a Mexican," Grissom said, stating the obvious.

"*Sí*, the last time I checked."

"You're a little off your range, ain't you?"

"Like I said, I'm lost."

The man moved around the door of his SUV and took a step toward the house. The sound of the pump on the shotgun caused him to stop where he was.

"You're good about right there," Grissom snapped.

"Is this the way you greet lost travelers, *señor*?" the Mexican asked. "With a loaded gun."

"Only those I don't know."

"My name is Cesar, *señor*. Now you know my name, maybe you can put the gun away."

"What are you doing on my land?"

"I told you. I'm lost," Salazar repeated.

"Where you headed?"

"Retribution."

"You know there's a road from your side of the border that'll take you right to it?"

Salazar took a step forward. "I took a wrong turn. You really need to get your road fixed, *Señor* Grissom."

Grissom frowned. "How do you know my name?"

"Oh, dear. I have said too much."

The ice-cold hand of fear touched Grissom and he froze.

The silenced gun in Salazar's hand coughed, and the bullet slammed into Grissom's chest.

Every scrap of air was driven from his lungs, and his jaw dropped from the shock of the hammer-blow. The shotgun slid from his grasp and clattered onto the uneven boards of the veranda. Both the old man's hands clawed at his chest. His actions spread blood over his shirt in vertical finger stripes.

As Grissom sat there, he heard boots on the steps which led onto his veranda. He looked up and saw the outline of the man more clearly than before, although he couldn't make out his facial features.

Salazar said in a low voice. "I'm sorry, *Señor* Grissom, but this has to be."

The gun in the *sicario's* fist spat three more times, and the old man's body jerked under each impact. When it was done, Salazar wrinkled his nose. The air was filled with the smell of copper. The job was half done.

Retribution

While Grissom breathed his last, Kane had just pushed his plate away from himself and swallowed the last of the fried potatoes which had made up most of the meal. He had to admit, it wasn't half bad.

Across from him in the small booth sat Cara and Jimmy. Cara had changed out of her uniform and now wore jeans and a red check shirt.

"You sure made quick work of that, Reaper," she noted with a smile.

"Why does Ma keep calling you Reaper?" Jimmy inquired.

"Shush, you," Cara said to her son.

Kane smiled. "It's fine." He looked at Jimmy. "It was a name I had in the Corps."

The boy looked up, surprised. "You were a marine? Were you an officer like Ma?"

Kane shook his head. "No. I was just a lowly Gunnery Sergeant."

"What did you do?" he asked excitedly.

"Hey," Cara said. "Go and see if Sally has some choc-chip ice-cream out the back. Tell her I'll fix it later."

Jimmy started to protest, "Ma—"

She raised her eyebrows and began to push him off the hard bench seat. "Go."

Once he was gone, Kane said, "He seems like a good kid."

Cara rolled her eyes and smiled. "He's a boy."

"So, what brings you to Retribution, Reaper?"

"Looking for some work."

She snorted. "Shit. No one comes here looking for work."

"You obviously did."

"Yeah, well, you got me there."

"Speaking of which?"

"What?"

"How did you end up here? The woman I knew was marine corps all down the line."

"You knew I was married when I was in the Philippines? I had Jimmy then too."

"Yeah."

"While I was deployed to Afghanistan, Jimmy's father was killed by gangbangers. I was all he had left in the world. So, one thing led to another, and here I am."

Kane nodded. "Sorry."

Cara smiled. "That's life. I'm not sorry I ended up here though. It may be the asshole of the world, but I'm with Jimmy, and that is what counts."

"From what I saw today, it ain't too safe."

"Yeah. Barrett Miller's gang of renegades. You might want to keep an eye out. He's dangerous."

"I can take care of myself. What's their story?"

"He's a cog in a chain," Cara explained. "A middleman for the Montoya Cartel. The drugs come across the border, and he takes possession of them. He cuts the produce, and then it is shipped to parts unknown where it is then distributed on the street."

"Why hasn't he been taken out of circulation?"

"We've tried. But every time we raid him, we come up empty-handed."

"What about the DEA?"

"They aren't interested in little fish. They want the biggest fish in the sea. They've sent agents undercover to try and net Montoya, but they wound up dead."

"I would have thought if they shut down this end then at least that would be something."

Cara sighed. "That's what we thought, but the DEA wouldn't go for it. They just said Montoya would move his operation and they'd lose what they've already got."

"Which is?"

"Stuff all," she snapped. "So, all we do now is try to keep the townspeople safe and whatever we can to halt the flow of drugs."

"Anything I can do to help?"

For a moment, she thought he was serious. "Stay out of trouble."

"I'll try. I start a new job tomorrow. Feller named Druce said he wanted someone to do some work."

Cara stared at him for a moment.

"What?"

"Did anything strike you as strange about him asking you to work for him?"

"You mean apart from the fact he was so snowed under with cars and stuff?"

Cara rolled her eyes.

"He said he did other things as well. Handyman stuff. Deliveries."

"That's what I'm talking about. Deliveries. Who on earth ships stuff out of Retribution? There are no real manufacturing businesses here that need to. Except for –"

"—Except for Barrett Miller."

"Exactly."

Kane stared at Cara. "Why do I have a feeling you're about to ask me to snoop around for you?"

She gave him a wry smile.

"Are you the Retribution Sheriff's Department recruiting officer now?"

She shook her head. "No, tonight was about catching up with an old friend. But when something pops up that I can use, or someone, well –"

"I tell you what, if I hear or see something, you'll be the first to know. OK?"

"Thanks, Reaper."

"And stop calling me Reaper. My name is John."

Cara picked up one of the last few fries from her plate and put it in her mouth. She smiled, and her dimpled cheeks showed. "I like Reaper."

"Whatever."

Kane slid across the seat and climbed to his feet.

"You're leaving?"

He dropped some bills on the table, and there was sarcasm in his voice when he said, "Big day tomorrow."

Cara's face grew serious. "Be careful. This is no joke. You've made an enemy in Barrett, which means you could very well have one in Montoya."

"Wouldn't be the first time I've pissed off a cartel boss," he allowed. "Or the mob for that fact."

"What?"

"Nothing. It's all good. I'll see you tomorrow. Meet me here for supper?"

"OK."

"See you then."

Cara watched him go and couldn't shake the feeling that Kane was hiding something. And what was that he had said about the mob?

———

The Grissom Place

The headlights on the sheriff's department SUV swept across the front of the Grissom home as Smythe turned and stopped near the bottom of the steps. He switched off the motor and climbed out. There were lights on inside the house, but no movement could be seen.

His boots crunched on the gravel, and with the sun gone, the chilled desert air seemed to creep down the collar of his jacket.

Smythe slammed the SUV's door to announce his arrival. He waited for a moment, but still, Grissom never showed. "Hello?"

The shout was met with silence.

The sheriff tried again. "Are you there, Grissom?"

Nothing.

The sheriff drew his .38 caliber revolver and started cautiously up the steps, pausing to listen when he reached the top. It was all silent. Then he smelled it. A mixture of blood and shit. He knew what it was because he'd smelled it many times before. There was no mistaking the putrid stench, which was impossible to forget, even after one exposure.

As he placed one foot after the other, Smythe approached the screen door. He reached out a trembling left hand to grasp the handle, his right still raised with the .38.

He eased the door back and moved into the hallway. The smell was stronger indoors. Smythe thumbed the hammer back on his gun; the ratchet noise seeming louder in the silence.

The Retribution sheriff glanced at the floor, and the light at the end of the hallway shone enough for him to see the still-tacky drag marks. His eyes followed them to the room from which the light emanated.

Smythe swallowed and took another step. And another. And another. Before he knew it, he was at the end of the hallway. He took a deep breath and walked through the doorway and into the dining room.

The .38 revolver swung around to the sheriff's right and centered on the black-clad figure seated at the head of the table. In front of the man was an FN Five-Seven handgun. Salazar had removed the silencer.

"Who are you?" Smythe snapped. "Where's Grissom?"

The man shrugged. "I'm sorry to say he died."

"Did you kill him?"

"Yes."

"Who are you?"

"Cesar Salazar."

The blood flowing through Smythe's veins turned icy, and he shivered. The gun in his hand shook. "Why are you here?" he asked hoarsely.

The *sicario's* face was deadpan when he said, "I'm waiting for you."

The sheriff frowned. "How did you know I would be here?"

Salazar shrugged.

Realization appeared in Smythe's eyes. "Son of a bitch. The bastard son of a bitch."

"Before you pull the trigger to kill me, *señor*, you might want to listen to what I have to say. Juan Jesus Montoya knows who you are. If you kill me, he will send more men to your house to kill you and your wife. Maureen is her name, yes?"

Smythe paled, then anger took over at the veiled threat to his wife. "Fuck you."

"Maybe the men he sends will have a little fun with her. Take out her eyes, cut off her breasts. Maybe they all take their turns with her while you watch. First, they might cut out her tongue, so she can't beg, too much."

The sheriff wanted to shoot this animal so bad, his hand shook. But he didn't, couldn't. "What if I don't kill you? What then?"

"I will kill you, and your wife will be left alone."

Smythe looked for the lie in the killer's dark eyes but couldn't see one.

"Is that your word?"

Salazar nodded. "*Sí.*"

The gun in his hand seemed like a lead weight, and

Smythe lowered it to lay along his right thigh. He closed his eyes.

"It is a wise choice, *señor,*" Salazar said. He then scooped up the Five-Seven and shot the Retribution sheriff between the eyes.

As the bullet punched through the back of the lawman's skull, it released a thick spray of blood and gore which splattered across the wall behind him.

Smythe collapsed into an untidy heap on the floor, his .38 clattering on the boards beside him.

Salazar rose from his seat and placed his gun into the shoulder holster inside his coat. He reached down to his left side and withdrew a razor-sharp, long-bladed knife from its sheath. Then he went to work.

CHAPTER 5

"REAPER, we got Tangos coming through the east gate. It looks like they've taken out the marine guard. Am I clear to engage?"

"Wait one, Hammer."

There was a drawn-out pause as Kane stared at the ambassador. The grey-headed Bernard Travers seemed to be fighting some inner battle. Maybe he hoped it would all go away.

Once more Kane heard the voice in his ear. "Reaper, am I clear to engage?"

"Wait one, Hammer."

"Shit."

Kane stared at the man seated at the desk before him. "Mr. Ambassador, we have Tangos inside the compound. We need your permission to engage if we're going to keep you safe."

Silence.

"Mr. Ambassador?" This time it was Cara who spoke. Her voice went up a notch. "Damn it, Mr. Ambassador!"

The U.S. Embassy was a large, two-story mansion on the

outskirts of Manila. Surrounded by high steel fences, from the outside it appeared to be a fortress. The night Abu Sayyaf knocked, however, they were taken by surprise. There had been help provided by a rogue faction in the Philippine military. The Philippine soldiers that were normally stationed outside the embassy had been called away, which left only the small marine guard detachment, along with Kane's four-man recon team.

A gunshot sounded from outside. "Tango down."

Kane shook his head. "Christ. Lieutenant, get him and the others to the safe room. This has just gone hot."

Kane stormed from the office and out onto a tiled area near a large pool when the evening erupted with violence. His communications seemed to go crazy for a brief time as his men called in targets. The night sky lit up with tracer rounds as automatic gunfire rang out across the compound. The difference between the attackers' AKs and the American weapons was noticeable.

"Reaper? Grinch. I got four Tangos with RPG's inside the perimeter to the west, headed for the house."

Kane said, "On my way. Hammer, you see them?"

"On it."

Hammer was the team sniper. When the trouble started brewing outside the compound, Kane ordered him to the roof of the embassy, providing a full field of fire. He heard the crack of the M110 sniper rifle as he ran toward where Grinch had set up a post in a raised gazebo.

Another crack and Hammer's voice came to him. "Two Tangos down. Lost the other two behind one of the hedges."

"I got them, Hammer," Grinch said. Then, "Shit!"

An almighty explosion was followed by an orange ball of flame that rose from behind a large clump of hibiscus.

"Grinch, sitrep."

Kane heard a cough followed by, "Son of a bitch blew the top off the gazebo."

"Where are they?"

"Moving toward the—"

Another explosion. This time the embassy had taken a hit. "Damn it!"

Kane came to a sliding halt as two Abu Sayyaf terrorists materialized from the gloom in front of him. He brought up his Colt M4 Commando and stroked the trigger twice. Both attackers jerked and dropped to the ground. Another terrorist appeared, and before Kane could fire again, the sound of Hammer's rifle rang out, and the third attacker was blown off his feet.

"You owe me a beer, Reaper."

"I'll keep that in mind."

Kane moved again towards the gazebo. All over the compound, he could hear the marine detachment engaged with their attackers. Another explosion roared to the north.

"Reaper? Cowboy. A bunch of these crazy fuckers just blew a hole in the fence on this side," there was a pause and gunfire rang out. Then, "I got me upwards of ten Tangos now infiltrating the compound."

"What about the marines?"

"I got one with me, and the rest are at the main gate where we thought they were going to break through."

"Hammer, you copy that?"

Kane heard the M110 fire two fast shots, and then Hammer's calm voice came over the net. "I'm kind of busy at the moment, Reaper."

"I got it," came a familiar voice.

"Lieutenant Billings? Where are you?"

Cara said, "On the roof. I can provide cover for your guy."

"Roger that."

When Kane reached the gazebo, he found Grinch extracting himself from the rubble where the roof had collapsed on top of him. He had a torn shirt and a line of blood running down the side of his face.

"You OK?"

"I'm fine."

"Reaper? Hammer. There's movement along the street leading to the front perimeter. You might want to check it out. I think they're getting a car ready to ram the gate."

"Shit! On my way," he glanced at Grinch. "Are you right to go?"

"Fighting fit and ready to rip, boss."

"I'll send a couple of marines over there to back you up."

"Roger that."

Kane whirled about and hot-footed it towards the front gate. As he ran, he said, "Lieutenant? Reaper. I want you to designate a couple of your men to back up my guy over on the west side. Copy?"

"Roger that."

"And find out how long before we get reinforcements in here?"

"Wait one."

He was almost to the main gate when Cara came back to him. "Reaper? Billings. Word is thirty minutes. Abu Sayyaf has thrown up roadblocks, and the Philippine Army are trying to break through."

Kane cursed under his breath.

He circumnavigated the large fountain in the main driveway and almost walked into a hailstorm of lead as the terrorists outside opened fire.

One of the marine's waved to him. "Over here, Gunny!"

Bullets ricocheted off the fence and the large concrete

pillars on either side of the gateway. Kane took a knee behind one of the concrete bollards beside the pedestrian gate, and the soldier joined him.

"What's up, Corporal?"

He started to speak when a round spanged of the bollard and caused him to duck. He gathered himself and tried again. "About a hundred and fifty meters along the street you'll see a car."

Kane rose just enough to see and then lowered himself back down. The car was an old Toyota.

"What about it?"

"We think they're getting ready to ram the gates with it."

"You think it has explosives in it?"

"Yes."

"Hammer? Reaper. Can you see much of that car?"

"Wait one."

"Reaper? Billings. I've just got a report from my guys at the house. They've got some Tangos trying to breach."

"Roger."

"Reaper? Hammer. There are three Tangos around the car. I can't see inside it, but I'd bet my left nut it's packed with explosives."

"Any chance you could put a couple of rounds into it and make it blow?"

"You know the answer to that."

"Yeah."

"We got that AT 4, Reaper, in case you've forgotten."

Through the firing, Kane heard the roar of the Toyota. He looked over the top of the bollard and saw it coming along the street. "Too late. Corporal, pull your men back to the embassy. Grinch, Cowboy, fall back on the embassy. Lieutenant, get your men to do the same."

"Copy."

"Hammer, put some fire into that damned car."

They fell back towards the embassy. Gunfire ripped through the compound. When they reached the main entrance, there were two marines already there. The two terrorists who'd broken through with the RPG were dead at their feet. Smoke poured from a hole in the wall on the second floor where an RPG had blown through it.

A sudden roar tore the night apart, and a giant ball of fire rose into the sky. The concussion from the explosion buffeted the soldiers.

"Reaper? Hammer. Gate's gone, and there must be about thirty Tangos rushing for the breach."

"Copy that, kill as many as you can," Kane replied and then looked at the two marines and asked, "Is anyone dealing with the fire?"

They shrugged their shoulders.

"Christ. Get up there and see what you can do. If there's nothing, we'll have to evacuate the building."

Cowboy emerged from the darkness outside the glow of the lights, marines trailing along behind him. He was a big man from Texas and his voice matched. "I see you all beat us here."

"Set up here," Kane snapped.

"Roger."

A burst of automatic fire blazed out of the blackness, and one of the marines went down. He howled in pain from a bullet buried deep in the muscle of his upper thigh. Kane and Cowboy were the first to react when three terrorists appeared to their front. They fired with precision and dropped them on the driveway.

Kane indicated to the wounded man. "Get him inside."

Two of the fallen marine's comrades dragged him through the door.

"Right, set up a perimeter around this building. Cover all entry points. Not one damned Tango gets into this building."

The sound of gunfire to the west grew in intensity. "Grinch? Reaper. Where the hell are you?"

"We're pinned down, Reaper."

In the background, Kane could hear the rattle of weapons. "Hammer? Reaper. You got eyes on his position?"

"Wait one."

"I'm coming up."

Kane ran inside and made for the internal staircase. He took them two at a time until he burst out onto the roof. "Sitrep, Hammer."

Heavy fire sounded from down below in the large drive area. He saw Cara using one of the other sniper rifles like a pro as she picked her targets and dispatched them with surety.

"Grinch and the few from the guard are pinned down by the tennis court. They've got Abu Sayyaf assholes crawling all over them."

Hammer fired at an unseen target, and chips flew from the concrete when a fusillade of bullets slammed into the rooftop.

"What's the time on the relief force, LT?" Kane asked Cara.

"Fifteen minutes."

"Grinch ain't got fifteen minutes, Reaper," Hammer said.

"Fuck!" Kane snarled.

Suddenly, an unfamiliar voice came over the net.

"United States Embassy, this is Eagle two-niner, how copy? Over."

"Roger two-niner, read you loud and clear, over."

The sky above the embassy roared to life as a Blackhawk

swooped in low over the compound. The voice came back over the net. "Someone down there holler for a Marshal? Over."

A smile split Kane's lips. "Mighty happy to see you, two-niner. Things are starting to get mighty sporty down here, over."

"Roger that. You have multiple targets converging on your position from various points. If you can light up your positions, we'll take care of the rest. Over."

"Wait one, two-niner."

"Roger."

"Grinch? Reaper. You still with us buddy?"

"Only just."

"Do you have a strobe on you?"

"Roger."

"Light it up."

Then, "Two-niner, this is Reaper, over."

"Go ahead, Reaper."

"Two-niner, do you have eyes on a strobe to the west of the main building? Over."

"Roger that, Reaper."

"We have men pinned down in that area. The rest of us are in a defensive perimeter around the embassy. Anything outside of those zones is all yours. Be aware, some of the hostiles have RPGs, over."

"Roger that. Sit tight, Reaper, and enjoy the show. Two-niner, out."

Kane would learn later that the Blackhawk was Australian, in-country on special exercises.

"Grinch? Reaper. Keep your heads down. Things are about to get loud."

"Copy that."

There was a loud brrrrrrp as the Blackhawk door-gunner opened-up with a mini-gun. Sparks flew from its rotating muzzles, and a line of tracers lit the night like the Fourth of July. From where he was positioned, Kane could hear the rounds impact whatever they hit.

Screams from the dying pierced the night, only to be drowned out with each sweep of the helicopter. It was an awesome display.

"How are we looking, Hammer?"

The sniper never took his eye away from the night-vision scope mounted on his M110. "Tangos are pulling back."

"Two-niner? Reaper, over."

"Reading you, Reaper, over."

"Hostiles are on the run, over."

"Roger that. We'll give them a few more bursts to make their night complete. Two-niner, out."

Twice more the Blackhawk swooped down over the compound and unleashed a leaden fury that ripped apart whatever it touched. Once they were finished, the pilot's voice came over the net. "Reaper? Two-niner, over."

"Copy, Two-niner."

"Looks like your visitors have left the area, over."

"Copy that. Thanks for your assistance, Two-niner. I owe you a beer. Over."

"I'd say more than one, Reaper. Two-niner, leaving station."

"Reaper, out."

Kane walked to the edge of the roof and looked out across the compound. "Grinch, Cowboy, sitrep."

Cowboy was the first to answer. "Still breathing, Reaper."

"I need a medic," said Grinch. "We got a marine down, over."

"Copy that."

Kane turned to face Cara who stood ten feet from him, the sniper-rifle she'd been using canted across her chest. Kane was about to say something to her when Hammer's voice cut across him.

"Shit! I got movement two hundred meters out. Get down, Sniper!"

Before Kane could move, a bullet slammed into him. His tactical vest was designed to stop bullets, but not all bullets were created equal, and occasionally, one got through. This one just happened to be his.

As he fell, Kane could hear the voices on the net. "Sniper down."

"Reaper's hit."

"Shit! How bad?"

"How the fuck should I know?"

Bad, he thought.

He lay on the roof, pain-free at first because the shock of the bullet's impact had numbed him. His vision swirled, and Cara's face swam into a blurred focus. Hers was joined by Hammer's as he started to strip the tactical vest off him.

Hammer's lips moved, but Kane couldn't make out what he said. Cara too was talking but still no joy.

Deep down he could feel the pain begin. A deep, burning agony unlike any he'd felt before. Kane struggled to breathe, each breath seeming harder than the last.

Then his hearing started to come back. He heard Hammer shout, "Medic! Get a medic up here!"

He looked into Cara's eyes. "Hang in there, Reaper."

Nothing came out when he tried to speak.

"Come on, Reaper, stay with me, buddy," Hammer pleaded. "You ain't dying up here tonight. And you sure as shit ain't leaving me alone with Cowboy."

Kane's vision started to darken. "Chip," he gasped.

"I'm still here, Reaper."
"Chip—"

———

Retribution

"—Chip?"

Kane sat up, his naked torso bathed in sweat. He realized it was only a dream and lay back down. Somewhere in the room, he heard the low buzz of a fly, while outside, the desert heat was already climbing, even though it was only just after six, and the sun was still low in the sky.

He rubbed at the puckered scar on his chest and then at another lower down on his side. Remnants of another war. He'd spent a month in the hospital after the embassy incident. The doctor told him he'd been lucky. Once he was fit enough, Kane re-joined his team, and they were sent to Africa where they'd lost Cowboy to a brainwashed child soldier in the Central African Republic.

It was only after Grinch had been killed that he and Chip decided they'd had enough and opted out. And now he'd run into Cara. Who would've thought?

Kane rose from the bed and walked into the bathroom. He showered and then found some fresh clothes in his pack, even if they were a little scrunched. He had a coffee and was out on the sidewalk before six-thirty. He knew that Druce had said six, but he figured that there wasn't much happening.

When he arrived at Arno's, the first thing he heard was raised voices coming from the back room where he figured the office to be. Kane walked through the workshop and halted just outside.

"Barrett said for you to be ready to go in two days," the first voice said.

"How many more times am I going to have to do it, Buck?" Kane heard Druce whine.

"You'll keep doing it until Barrett tells you otherwise."

"I've had enough," Druce said. "I paid him back the money I owed. That should be enough."

"You're in it all the way, Elmore. There is no out. Unless you'd like a visit from El Monstruo. Is that what you want?"

Druce mumbled something that Kane couldn't make out. Then he heard Buck say, "All right, so you be ready in two days."

Two men who Kane recognized from the incident at the motel the day before, emerged from the office. They stopped and stared at him. One had a tanned face and a singlet top. The other wore jeans and had long hair.

"What the fuck are you doing here?" challenged the man with the tanned face.

Kane stared at him. "I work here."

"The hell you do."

"I – I hired him yesterday when he got off the bus," Druce stammered.

Buck whirled on him and snarled, "You stupid shit! Fire him." Buck looked back at Kane. "You're fired, get the hell out of here."

Kane didn't move. "Ain't your call."

Buck took a step towards him, and Kane debated whether to pull the gun from behind his back or not, then decided against it. The gangster jabbed a finger into Kane's chest.

"Listen to me, asshole," Buck snarled. "I told you to get ... Argh!"

With swift movements, Kane grabbed the offending finger with his left hand, and his iron grip broke it like a dry twig. His right swept up like a claw and powerful fingers wrapped around Buck's throat.

"You listen to me, *asshole*," Kane hissed as he stared into the bulging eyes of the gangster. "I've had enough of you and yours. You think you can be badass? I know I can be badass. If you fellers keep coming for me, one of you won't be going home."

"Am I interrupting something?"

They turned to see Cara standing in the doorway, dressed in her deputy's uniform. Kane pushed the injured Buck away from him.

"These fellers were just leaving," Kane informed her.

Buck cradled his sore hand and growled, "You broke my finger."

"Be thankful that was all I broke."

"All right, enough," Cara said in a raised voice. "Get out of here, Buck."

"This ain't over," he snarled.

"I won't be too hard to locate," Kane informed him as he walked out of the garage.

Cara stared at Kane. "You're just making friends everywhere you go, aren't you?"

Kane smiled. "I'm a friendly guy."

"What was that about?"

"I'll tell you later."

Cara nodded.

"Ah, Kane," Druce said.

"Yeah."

"It may be ... ah ... best if you ... ah, if you don't work here."

"Are you going to let them buffalo you?"

A pained expression came across his face. "You don't understand."

Kane opened his mouth to say more, but Cara cut him off. "Reaper! On me."

He turned his head and asked, "You didn't just get all military on me, did you?"

She shrugged and gave him a smug look. "Got your attention. Besides I want a word. It's the reason I'm here."

Kane gave Druce a dark look and followed Cara outside. "All right, what is it?"

"The sheriff's gone missing."

———

The Desert

The Tahoe bounced over yet another hole in the deeply-rutted road, and Kane lurched in the seat. He'd only just righted himself from that one when the SUV hit another.

"Christ, Cara. You trying to kill us before we get to wherever it is we're headed?"

"This is the good part," she pointed out. "The rest of the road past the Grissom place is full of washouts and holes you'd lose a house in."

"Tell me about this Grissom feller."

"He's a vet. Vietnam war. Lives out here on his own. Owns a whole lot of desert that's good for nothing."

"Is he stable?"

"Never had cause to doubt it before. The only time we ever heard from him was when he called to complain about people using the old road that ran through his land. Cleaver used to check it out because this was his patrol route. Said he could find nothing. He thought Grissom was starting to lose it."

"So that's why the sheriff was out here?"

Cara nodded. "He decided he'd take this one. His wife, Maureen, called me this morning and said he never came home."

"Radio?"

"Silent."

They drove further in their own silence as Kane's mind ran through numerous scenarios that may have befallen the lawman.

Negotiating the landscape of low ridges, rocks, and cactus, the Tahoe threw up a plume of dust behind it into the mid-morning sky. Some of the ridges were dotted with copper-colored rocky crags that looked more like giant walls.

Dropping down into a wash, the Tahoe rumbled across a layer of rocks, then spun its wheels up the other side until it crested, and the terrain leveled out a bit

Ten minutes more of rugged punishment found them topping a ridge that overlooked a flat expanse about a mile square. In the center of it was the home of Cyrus Grissom. Beside the house sat the sheriff's SUV.

Cara brought the Tahoe to a halt, and they both climbed out. All was quiet, and immediately the hair on the back of Kane's neck stood up. He studied the ground while Cara checked the sheriff's vehicle.

"There was another vehicle here, Cara," Kane called out to her and motioned to the marks in the dust.

She walked over to where he stood and looked down.

Kane stared at the front of the house. The screen, as well as the main door, were open. There was no sign of movement. He started to wish he'd brought his H&K.

"Have you got a spare gun in that SUV of yours, Cara?" Kane asked.

The mention of the word was enough to cause her to drop her hand to the sidearm at her hip. "I've got a Smith and Wesson M&P in a lockbox in the back," she reached into her pocket and tossed him the keys. Kane returned to the Tahoe and found the lockbox. He opened it, took out the gun and checked its load. Then he closed the box, locked it, and joined Cara.

"How do you want to play this?" he asked her. "You want me to go around the rear?"

Cara shook her head and drew her own sidearm. "I want you watching my back."

They walked forward at a steady pace and up the stairs. Once they reached the top Cara paused. "Look there."

Kane glanced to where she was pointing and saw the dried blood. His eyes followed the trail in through the door. Cara brought up her gun and said, "Moving, Reaper."

It was like someone had flicked a switch. Suddenly, Kane was a marine again, and he was at a house which had to be cleared. He reached out, touched Cara's shoulder, and set her on her way.

As soon as they entered the hallway, the stench of death assailed their nostrils. Cara halted and brought up a hand to try and block the smell. "Shit!"

"Keep going, Cara. We'll clear these front rooms first."

Cara moved past the first door on her left and stopped. Kane tried the doorknob and felt it give. He entered the room, gun raised. Apart from a messed-up bed, it was empty. "Clear."

They moved to the door on the right. Again, it was empty. "Clear."

That left the room at the end of the hall.

Kane touched Cara once more, and she moved on. She entered the dining room and gasped. "Oh, Christ."

When Kane saw the two bodies, a shiver ran down his spine. Both corpses were seated at the table. Their arms outstretched on the scarred surface. Flies buzzed thickly in the air and swarmed over the posed bodies. The scent of already-rotting flesh filled the room.

"Who would do this?" Cara breathed, horrified.

Kane stared at the body of Sheriff Smythe. His uniform shirt was coated in blood. His hands were a mottled blue color, fingers swollen like fat sausages. Grissom's body was much the same way, except for one notable difference. It still had a head.

Cara swallowed hard. "I have to radio this in."

"It might pay to leave out some of the details," Kane pointed out.

She nodded dumbly. "I'll be right back. Don't touch anything."

A normal man would probably have followed her. But Kane had seen horrors that no ordinary man had. The battlefield was a brutal place.

Kane walked around the room but saw nothing out of the ordinary. Then he walked through to the kitchen. That was where he found the head.

It sat on a plate on the kitchen bench. The eyes had been gouged out and stuffed into the mouth. The ears had been removed and lay next to the head like some bizarre side dish.

The sight left Kane with a bad taste in his mouth and made him want to spit. He hawked and was about to let it go on the floor when he realized that it was probably a bad idea. He glanced about and saw a closed door at the rear of the kitchen. He walked over to it and turned the knob.

The door opened, and Kane walked through. He stomped down steps that led out the back and breathed in deep gulps of fresh air.

"Shit," he muttered and spat into the dirt.

He raised his head and sucked in another deep breath through his nose. That was when he saw it. On a ridge about a mile and a half from the house. A flash, a brief glint of sunlight off something shiny. In another world, Kane's immediate thought would be of a sniper. But this wasn't that world. This was different.

The breeze sprang up, lifting a small cloud of dust and grit from the desert floor. It peppered his face, and when he wiped the troublesome stuff from his eyes, he saw the flash was gone.

However, it didn't mean that the person or persons who'd been on the rock-strewn ridge were. Casually Kane turned and walked back towards the house. He climbed the steps and returned to the kitchen where he found Cara. She had a horrified expression on her face as she stared at the head.

"Bastards," she spat, venom lacing her voice. "Fucking bastards."

"Cara?"

Her stare never wavered.

He tried again. "Cara?"

She never even glanced in his direction.

"Lieutenant!"

Her head snapped around, and he could see the anguish

in her eyes. "I know this isn't easy, Cara, but you need to compartmentalize this. Someone is watching the house. Watching us."

Cara's gaze flickered. "What? Where?"

"There's a ridge about a mile and a half southwest of here. Whoever it is has found a home in the rocks about halfway up it."

"Did you see them?"

Kane shook his head. "All I saw was the flash of sunlight on something metal or glass. My guess is field glasses. How far to the border from here?"

"About five miles."

"How long before someone arrives?"

"Cleaver was coming straight out. The ME will be with him. I also told him to inform the border patrol and have them send people out here as well. There'll possibly be State Troopers or even the FBI."

"You think it was illegals who did this?" Kane asked.

"It's possible. It could be a Coyote," Cara said, using the term for the guides who brought illegals across the border.

"I would have thought once the Coyote's job was done, he'd have slipped back over the border. Not taken the time to do something like this."

Cara shrugged. "I guess we won't know until it's been investigated thoroughly."

"Come on, let's get outside. I've had enough of the stink."

They walked out to the Tahoe, and Kane asked her, "Will you be all right here on your own?"

For a moment, she looked alarmed but gathered herself and said, "Are you going somewhere?"

"About a mile and a half."

"The hell you are," Cara snapped when she realized what he intended to do.

"I'll be fine. I just want to go and look around, see what I can find. Whoever was there will probably be gone anyway."

"I'll come with you."

He shook his head. "I said I'll be fine. Remember, this is what I do."

"Used to do," she pointed out.

"I've still got it."

She sighed. "OK. But wait one."

Cara turned away and walked around to the back of the Tahoe. She opened the rear door, found what she wanted and closed it back up. When she reappeared, she carried a Heckler and Koch 416 carbine and three spare magazines complete with 5.56 NATO rounds. On top, it had a red dot sight. She also had a tactical vest and a bottle of water.

Cara held the weapon out. "Here, take this."

Kane was impressed. "You guys in Retribution are well-armed."

"Being in charge of the armory has its perks. You should see the sniper rifles the county bought us."

He checked it over and put the vest on. He kept the Smith & Wesson and said to Cara, "I'll be back."

"Try not to get yourself killed."

CHAPTER 6

Kane

The walk was dry and hot. The breeze though negligible, still carried a fine grit that seemed to work its way into everything. Kane didn't mind the heat; that he could deal with. Throughout his career as a recon marine, he'd been in hotter places.

His path to the ridge was of his own choosing. Kane had left the road not long after the three had intersected. However, he did note that the tire tracks going southward matched the ones near the house.

Finding a dry wash, he slipped down into it and followed it for a piece before climbing out into a mess of cactus, rocks, and other brush useful for concealing his approach.

Kane paused in the shade of a large boulder and drank some of the water Cara had supplied; by now tepid, but it was wet. He replaced the cap and checked the HK for dirt.

The last thing he needed was for grit to get in and jam the weapon in the middle of a firefight.

Sweat ran down Kane's back between his shoulder blades and seemed to pool at the base of his spine. While having a breather, he took a few minutes to look at the ridge and plot the next stage of his course.

Near the top stood some large saguaros and a rock formation that looked like giant, grey steps. Above the rocks were small bits of brush and a gravel-laced crest.

There was no sign of movement or of the flashes he'd seen earlier. Kane cradled the 416 across his chest and began to move again.

It was slow work. He had learned quite early on in the corps, that to rush could lead to death. He remembered a time in the Congo where he and his team had moved a total of five-hundred yards in a day. They'd been surrounded by Congolese Rebels and had to extricate themselves before being found. It was a slow, excruciating process but by dark, the four-man team was out of harm's way.

Kane was halfway up the slope when the burst of gunfire came.

———

Salazar

The gringo was good, Salazar had to give him that. Watching Kane from the moment he'd left the house, the *sicario* knew that if he didn't kill this man now, he'd become a problem later.

So, he waited.

Salazar had been waiting ever since leaving Grissom's.

He knew that someone would come eventually and was very surprised when the woman and man had shown up as early as they did. He was even more surprised to see Kane start out on foot for the ridge.

How the *gringo* knew he was there, Salazar had no idea. Once he was certain that Kane was coming for him, he hurried to his SUV and took out a Mexican made FX-05 Xiuhcoatl complete with a scope.

Salazar then returned to his position amongst the rocks just below the crest and waited for Kane to show himself again.

The FX-05 was tucked into the *sicario's* shoulder, and he stared through the scope. Sweat ran from his brow and along the bridge of his nose. Ants were running up his legs and a fly settled on his face, but Salazar didn't move. He sat stock still, waiting for the gringo to appear, his finger on the trigger.

When a head appeared, Salazar fired.

Kane

The burst hammered into the boulder next to Kane's head, and the impact showered him with slivers of rock. A cut appeared on his cheek, his flesh stinging as the sweat invaded the wound, mixing with blood to run down the side of his face.

"Shit!" Kane cursed. The bastard had been waiting for him all this time; watching his approach and almost killing him with the first burst of fire.

He ducked back behind the boulder as more 5.56

caliber slugs shattered pieces from it. He leaned out and fired his own burst from the HK in the shooter's general direction.

Up the slope, the *sicario* ducked as the snapping sound of the bullets passed close by him. He then fired another two bursts at the *gringo*.

Kane had pinpointed Salazar's position with the last burst and now traversed up the slope. He used some of the dense brush and boulders for cover but was halted when the *sicario* saw his movement and emptied the rest of the FX-05's thirty round magazine into the brush where Kane had stopped.

The bullets snapped and cracked as they scythed through the vegetation. When they erupted out the other side, they showered Kane with debris. He dropped flat onto the rocky ground, more rounds slicing through the air above him, and one buried into the earth near his right shoulder.

"Keep moving, Reaper," Kane muttered.

He rolled onto his side and dropped out the magazine from the HK. He slapped another home and prepared to move.

The gunfire came to an abrupt stop, and Kane got to his feet. He began to press forward towards the rocks where the shooter was. He kept up a steady cycle of bursts and could see the puffs of dust and rock from the bullets impacting around the would-be killer's cover.

The magazine ran dry, and with practiced skill, Kane dropped the empty one out and replaced it with his penultimate one.

In the rocks above Kane, Salazar was suddenly under a superior and accurate rate of fire. Rock splinters filled the air and peppered his exposed skin. A bullet passed close enough for him to feel the heat on his face.

The *sicario* rammed home a fresh magazine and commenced firing again, but this time, the FX-05 was on auto, and he sprayed the area below with careless abandon. He could see the spurts of dirt and sand leap from the ground about the advancing figure's feet.

Salazar burned through the fresh magazine in no time flat. He cursed under his breath and patted his pockets for another. There was none. He swore vehemently and threw the gun to the ground. Then he did something he'd never done before in his life. He turned and ran.

Down below, Kane saw the figure leap to his feet and run up the ridge and disappeared over the top. He climbed the rest of the way at a steady pace, the 416 raised and ready, remained silent.

When he reached the shooter's hide, Kane found the discarded FX-05. He bent and picked up the still-warm weapon, examined it, and found it empty.

"That's why you ran," he muttered.

Kane kept on going until he crested the ridge. In the distance, he could see a black SUV bouncing over a rough trail headed south where it would intercept the road on Grissom's land.

Kane stared at the retreating vehicle and then down at the FX-05 in his hand. He shook his head. "Coyote my ass."

The Grissom Place

Cara couldn't help but breathe a sigh of relief when Cleaver and the county medical examiner arrived. They had traveled together in a Chevrolet with the words 'Medical Examiner' on both doors.

First out was the M.E. He was a short man with a wrinkled face. His name was Grover Cleland.

Cleaver casually climbed out of the passenger side, carrying another HK 416 and wore a cream-colored Stetson. He reminded Cara of a gunman out of an old western movie. Strutting towards her he asked in an authoritative voice, "What have we got?"

"Two dead inside," Cara informed him. "Did you inform State and Border Patrol?"

There was arrogance in his voice when he asked, "Why would I do that?"

Cara rolled her eyes. "I don't know. Maybe because I asked you to. Or maybe because one of the dead is the *fucking* sheriff! Christ, Art!"

Cleaver grew defensive. "Fuck you! Maybe you should have told me that in the first place!"

"Yeah, right. Just announce it over an open channel? I asked you to do it, and you didn't. Now ..." Cara's voice trailed away as she flung her arms helplessly into the air.

"I guess that puts me in charge then, doesn't it?" Cleaver said.

Cara gave him a bewildered look and was about to say more when distant gunfire erupted on the ridge that Kane had left for.

"Shit!" she cursed. "That's all we need."

"What the hell is that?"

Cara started to run for the Tahoe.

"Where are you going?"

"Just call State and Border, Art!"

Thirty seconds later, the Tahoe was careening over the dirt road in the direction of the gunfire.

———

Kane

Kane heard the Tahoe from a long way off. He stared towards the gravel road and saw the vehicle bounce wildly as it hit numerous holes and ruts. It hammered along, at one stage appearing almost out of control, a large plume of dust following.

"Damn, Cara," Kane muttered and started down the slope headed for the road.

He was waiting for her when she pulled up at the base of the ridge. The Tahoe locked all four wheels as it skidded to a stop. The trailing cloud of dust caught up and washed over the SUV, briefly obscuring it from view. When the dust cleared, Cara was out of the vehicle with her sidearm in her hand.

"What the hell happened?" she blurted out.

Kane held up the FX-05. "Your Coyotes are well armed."

She frowned. "Is that what I think it is?"

"Yep, a Mexican made FX-05."

"But only Mexican armed forces –"

"Yes."

"Which means –"

"Which means he wasn't a Coyote. My guess is he was Cartel. He lit out of here in a black SUV."

Cara thought for a moment as she digested the information. It made sense, the brutal way the bodies were displayed. She said, "Come with me."

"Where are we going?"

"For a drive."

"What about the crime scene?"

"Cleaver can do it."

They climbed into the Tahoe and had traveled around two miles when they found something unexpected; a dry wash which had been loaded with rock and leveled to make the crossing easier.

"Someone has been busy," Kane pointed out.

"For a road that is said to be almost impassable, it's not bad. No wonder Grissom was complaining about the activity."

They kept driving and found another four the same. Deep channels which had been fixed and made useable. All had been filled with rock and compacted. When they topped another ridge, Cara stopped the Tahoe.

"That's the border down there," she informed him.

"What? No fence?"

"That's how easy it is. I'll let the border patrol and the DEA know about it. Maybe they will be able to do something."

They sat in silence for about five minutes and stared at the desert before them when Cara said, "Let's get back."

Kane nodded. "Yeah."

The Grissom Place

"What do you mean they aren't coming?" Cara asked in a savage tone. "You told them what the hell was going on, didn't you?"

Cleaver nodded. "I did. State and Border said because of where it was, to call the DEA. They said that if it has anything to do with the Montoya Cartel, which by the way you're eluding to, that we are to stay away from it as far as possible."

"But they murdered Walt!"

"Don't you think I know that! I saw his head for Christ sakes. They said to investigate the murder, but if it leads over the border, we drop it."

"What about the FBI?"

"I thought about that too. I called their Phoenix office, and I'm still waiting for the agent in charge to call me back."

"That's a load of horseshit," Cara snapped. "Walt was law enforcement. They should be falling over themselves to get down here. I'm going to try again."

"Leave it, Cara. I got it."

"The hell I will."

Cleaver's voice took on a hard edge. "I said leave it. With Walt gone, I'm in charge." He glanced at Kane. "Take Rambo here and head back to Retribution. Break the news to Walt's wife. I'll finish up here with Grover. I'll log every-thing. Going by the crime scene, there won't be much. Maybe a few prints."

"Here," Kane said and tossed the FX-05 to him. "Get some prints from that."

Cleaver stood and watched them leave, wondering how the hell he was going to clean up this mess.

He walked across to the Medical Examiner's truck and took out a satellite phone he'd brought with him. He stared at the number pad for a few seconds and then dialed.

———

Sonora

. . .

Montoya picked up after two rings. "Yes?"

"What the fuck did you do?"

The cartel boss turned and stared out his large windows. "Careful my friend or I can get Salazar to turn around and complete another job."

"You didn't have to kill the sheriff too."

"With him gone, you will be the boss, yes?"

"Yes."

"Then what is the problem?"

"I still have to clean up this fucking mess your man made. Once the State Troopers and the DEA get wind of this, they'll be crawling up my ass in no time. And then there's the other deputy."

"Get rid of her."

"What?"

"Get rid of the bitch. If she is a problem, then kill her. It is simple."

A muffled, "Christ," came through the phone.

"Is there a problem?"

"That's all I need. Another dead body in a uniform."

"I can send Salazar to do it if you do not have the *cajones* to do it."

"No! He's done enough. I'll fix it."

"I knew you would," Montoya said and hung up.

He stared out at the desert for a few moments and sighed. "Now, where was I?"

Montoya stuffed the cell into his pocket and turned to face the bloodied form seated on the chair in front of him. "I'm sorry for the interruption, *Señor* Garza. It was a business matter. But I promise you shall have my full attention from now on."

He reached across to a table, which, like the floor, was covered in clear plastic. Atop it were various tools which

Montoya was adept at using. The one he selected was a cordless drill with a large, rusted bit inserted into the chuck.

Montoya held it in the air and squeezed the trigger. It made a high-pitched whirring sound that seemed to mesmerize the cartel boss. Then, "Oops, I almost forgot."

He gave his victim a mirthless smile as he grabbed up a blood-spattered apron. "My wife would be most upset if I got blood on my white suit."

Garza watched him with pain-filled eyes. Sweat beaded on his brow, and his nostrils flared as fear surged through him. Across his mouth was a white strip of tape to muffle the high-pitched screams.

The chair was a timber one with high armrests. Garza's arms were lashed to these, his right hand missing all its fingers, now a mass of bloodied stumps. His left was only shy two. So far.

With the apron secured, Montoya took the drill back up and moved in close to the terrified man.

"You should have taken my offer, Directorate General. It would have been so much easier," Montoya surmised, using Garza's Drug Division title.

The cartel boss shrugged, and the drill began to whirr.

Retribution

Cara stopped the Tahoe outside the driveway of the motel for Kane to get out. He looked across at her and said, "Are you sure you want to do this on your own?"

Cara hesitated and then nodded. "I'll be fine."

"Meet you for a drink tonight?"

Cara shrugged. "Depends on what we're doing, I guess. If I can, I will. I'll probably need one."

"OK. If I see you, I see you."

"That's about it."

"Just yell if you need help with anything."

"Sure."

Kane climbed out and watched her drive away. It was one task he didn't envy her in the least.

He didn't worry about going back to his room. Instead, decided to call on Druce to see if he could get the job back. He walked along the street until he reached the gas station and went inside.

He found Druce out the back in his office. The man had been beaten and lay on the floor in a pool of blood. Kane placed a hand on his shoulder and said, "Druce, can you hear me?"

The man moaned.

"What happened?"

"They ... came back."

Kane muttered a curse. "I'll call for a paramedic."

"No," he groaned and tried to sit up.

Kane ignored him and reached for the phone on Druce's desk. He got the operator, and within moments help was dispatched.

"Who did it, Druce?" Kane asked.

"Barrett ...," he moaned as a wave of pain washed over him. "It was him."

"Why?"

"To teach ... a lesson."

Kane ground his teeth with anger. "Don't worry. He won't get away with it."

Druce clutched at his arm with a feeble hand. "No law. You can't."

"That suits me," Kane hissed. "Where can I find them?"

"N – No, he'll kill you."

"Where?"

"His gang usually hangs out most nights at Sully's. That's the other bar in town. If you go there, watch your back. They're a rough crowd."

"I can take care of myself."

Ten minutes later the paramedics arrived to tend to Druce, swarming over him with their paraphernalia. While they began to work on him, Kane slipped out the door.

———

Kane returned to his motel room, showered, and put on his last set of clean clothes. Instead of bothering to find a Laundromat, he hand-washed the dirty ones, wrung them out, and spread them about the room, draped over various pieces of furniture to dry.

Then he lay on his bed and waited for night to fall.

The sun had been down approximately two minutes when Kane opened his eyes and swung his legs over the side of the bed. He retrieved the H&K from under the pillow and stood up. His stomach growled a protest and, he realized he'd not eaten for most of the day. He'd have to remedy that later.

The surprise came when he walked outside and found Cleaver in the parking lot waiting for him.

The night air was still hot, and moths, along with other night creatures, were starting to swarm the nightlights.

"Going somewhere, Rambo?" Cleaver asked, sarcasm dripping from his voice.

Kane let it slide. "Going to go have a drink. Hot night. I

thought you'd still be tied up looking for the feller who killed the sheriff."

Cleaver ignored his words. "I heard about Druce. Bad thing to happen. He'll be all right though, so I'm told. Shame the gas station will be closed a few days while he recuperates."

Kane nodded. "Yeah. Any idea who did it?"

Cleaver shook his head. "He didn't say. Maybe an unhappy customer."

"Maybe."

The deputy motioned to the vehicle he was leaning against. "Climb in; I'll give you a ride to the Rose."

"I'll walk."

Cleaver's voice changed. "*Climb in!*"

Kane paused and then gave a slow nod. "OK."

"Wasn't too hard, was it?"

The acting sheriff's ride smelled like upholstery polish, and it was obvious that he took a lot of pride in cleaning his car. The radio chirped, and then Cara's voice came over the radio.

"Are you there, Art? Over."

Cleaver climbed in and reached for the handset. "Yeah."

"They're putting a rush on the fingerprints, and we should have something by tomorrow or the next day. If it's what we think, then it might get the DEA's attention."

Cleaver muttered a curse. "Even if it does, they'll just tell you to leave it be. Don't waste your time. Out!"

"Art –"

He turned the radio off.

"Right, let's go."

The vehicle pulled out of the motel and turned right. They drove along the main street towards the edge of town.

Kane knew something was wrong when they passed Arno's and kept going.

"I think you might be going the wrong way, Deputy," Kane pointed out.

"Nope. This is the way."

They were a mile out of town when Cleaver pulled the car over to the side of the road. He stopped it on the shoulder and turned to face Kane. "This is where you get out."

Kane thought, *who does this guy think he is?*

"There ain't no bar out here."

"Exactly. I knew you were going to be trouble the moment I met you. My hunch was proved yesterday and again today. So, it's time for you to move on."

"What about my stuff?"

"When you reach the next town, have Cara send it to you. Get out."

Kane opened his mouth to protest, but Cleaver stopped him with the drop of his hand to his sidearm. "Out!"

He climbed out and shut the door. The car did a U-turn, spun its wheels, and headed back to Retribution. Kane was still standing there contemplating his next move when the taillights disappeared. *What did Rambo do?*

He turned and started back to town.

CHAPTER 7

RETRIBUTION

Kane found Sully's Bar without any problems. It was a rundown joint with a flashing neon sign of a topless barmaid with the back of her skirt lifted. Even in the dark, he could tell what the inside was going to be like.

Music filtered out through the closed doors as he approached them. Kane did a quick recce outside, checking his options should a hasty exit be required, then returned to the entry. He placed his hand on the right-side door to open it when someone coming the other way beat him to it. A drunk staggered out and almost cannoned into him.

He stared at Kane through blurred vision and said, "What the fuck are you looking at?"

Kane stepped aside, and the drunk kept on walking.

When he entered through the doors, the first thing that hit him, apart from the heat, was the stink; tobacco smoke, stale beer, and human body odor. Behind the bar, he saw a thin bargirl who wore a singlet top that barely covered her large breasts. She had short, black hair and one sleeve of tattoos on her left arm. She chewed gum and looked Kane up and down before she said, "Are you in the right place?"

Kane stared around the barroom. There was no doubt in his mind that this was a rough establishment. The wire cage surrounding the stage where the band played attested to that. An empty beer bottle smashed against it and someone shouted, "Play something else other than that shit! Don't you know any Rascal Flatts?"

Suddenly the room was in an uproar, and more bottles flew. This time, however, they were directed at the offender.

Kane turned back and looked at her. "How do you stop the riots?"

"Got me a pipe under the bar."

"Use it much?"

"All the time."

Kane nodded. "I'll have a beer."

She smiled at him. "Your funeral."

Two minutes later, Kane stood at the bar with a cold bottle of Coors. While he sipped it, he ran a practiced eye over the room. From out back a tall, broad-shouldered, bald man emerged. Like the young woman behind the bar, he too had tattoos. Only his covered almost every visible bit of skin.

He saw Kane and then spoke rapidly to the young woman. She glanced over at Kane then looked back at the man who was obviously her boss. She shrugged and went back to pouring drinks.

The man, on the other hand, made his way along the bar to where Kane stood. He stared at him for a moment and then asked, "Are you lost?"

"Who wants to know?"

"I'm Sully. This is my bar."

Kane placed his beer on the bar and said, "You're the second person in a few minutes to inquire as to whether or not I was in the right place. I'm fine, thank you."

"Don't go causing any trouble in here."

Kane heard a curse and the sound of glass breaking. He said, "I'd say I'm the least of your problems."

Sully swore and hurried to deal with the scuffle. He strode up to the offender, said a couple of words which the patron didn't like, and then clipped him under the jaw. No fuss, problem solved.

Kane sipped his beer and scanned the smoke-filled room for Barrett but couldn't see him. After a while, however, he noticed a steady flow of human traffic from the room where Sully had emerged.

He finished his beer, and the young woman came to get him a fresh one. She put the open bottle of Coors in front of him and started to pick the money off the bar when Kane said, "Busy tonight."

She gave him a curious look. "About normal."

"What's your name?"

"Why?"

"Just curious is all. Being sociable."

"If you're looking for a quick lay, stranger, I ain't it. Besides, I'm too much woman for you."

Kane smiled at her.

"What?"

"You just remind me of someone."

"Who?"

"A lieutenant I once knew when I served in some far-off country. She was like you. Tough breathed fire."

"You a soldier?"

"Was."

Her eyes widened. "Hey, our deputy was a soldier."

"So I believe."

"My name is Brenda. Folks call me Butch, or ..."

"... Hey Bitch!"

She rolled her brown eyes. "... that. Excuse me."

Brenda turned to face the man who'd called out and raised her middle finger.

"Butch, customers are waiting," Sully yelled. "If you want to rattle his bones do it on your time, not mine."

She rolled her eyes once more. "Asshole."

Brenda froze, her gaze fixed over Kane's shoulder. He glanced about and saw five men entering the bar. One of them happened to be Buck whose finger he'd broken earlier that morning.

"Are you OK, Brenda?" Kane asked her.

She seemed not to hear.

"Brenda?"

Her eyes flicked to him. "Hmm?"

"Are you OK?"

"I wish they would go somewhere else."

They never noticed Kane and walked through to the back room. He watched them until they were gone. "What do they do out there?"

"Nothing."

Brenda went to walk away, but he reached out and grabbed her arm. "Wait. Is Barrett in there? Do they sell drugs in that room?"

She tried to wrench her arm free of his grip but found she couldn't. "Let me go. I don't know who you are, mister, but I know nothing."

"How many of them in there?"

"Let me –"

"How many?" Kane's voice was full of menace which made her rethink her stance.

"Two before they walked in."

"Is Barrett one of them?"

She nodded.

He let go of her arm. "Is Sully in this with them?"

Brenda shook her head. "Yes."

Eight all told. How do you want to play this, Reaper?
Frontal assault!

"Give me your pipe."

Alarm flitted across Brenda's face. The tough façade had fallen away. "What are you going to do?"

"I've got unfinished business with Barrett. The pipe."

Brenda bent down and came back up with a piece of silver pipe about two-feet long. She gave it to Kane, and he tested its weight. It was thick and solid.

He nodded. "Thanks."

Kane strode with purpose towards the door that led to the back room. Sully happened to glance up and saw him coming. He walked out from behind the bar to block Kane's path.

"Where do you think you're going, Slick?" he growled. "Out back –"

It was as far as he got. The pipe in Kane's grip drove forward, and the end rammed hard into Sully's middle. The big man doubled over with a loud grunt, and the air in his lungs expelled with a whoosh.

The pipe rose and fell, it caught Sully across the back of his head, split the skin, and drove him to the floor. He lay there unmoving.

An onlooker cursed at the sudden violence. He called for someone to do something, and a nearby thickset man tried to rise and meet the challenge. With one swing of the pipe, he lost two teeth and lay on his back, out cold.

The door to the back room opened at the uproar. Kane

saw one of the gang members standing there, a shocked expression on his face.

Kane closed the distance between them in a couple of swift steps and swung the pipe hard at the man's knee. There was a sickening crunch as the pipe found its target, and the leg gave out beneath him.

A high-pitched scream of pain filled the barroom. Kane ignored the writhing figure and stepped over him into the back room.

Six left.

"What the hell?" came the cry of surprise from a gangster as Kane's presence in the room was detected.

They were all spread out around the room. Barrett sat behind a desk piled with money and drugs.

A man on Kane's right moved, but not fast enough, for the pipe smacked him across the bridge of his nose. The cartilage gave way and blood flowed. The man reeled back and collapsed against the wall.

Five.

With another swing, the pipe came around and took down the man on the left. He held up a hopeful right hand to stop the blow. It was pitiful to see. The pipe hit him above the wrist and snapped both bones in his arm.

His scream was cut short when Kane dropped him as though poleaxed with another well-placed blow.

Four.

A similar fate befell the man who came at Kane with a large-bladed knife. Two swats of the pipe and it was over. He lay on the floor in a bleeding heap with his friends.

Three.

"Kill the son of a bitch!" Barrett screeched.

A well-muscled man in the far-right corner moved, his hand dived for the handgun in his waistband. He started to bring it up when Kane threw the pipe at him. The metal object helicoptered through the air and impacted his chest with enough force to break two ribs.

Kane's right hand went behind his back and emerged with his H&K. It snapped into line with Buck's chest as the gangster with the broken and bandaged finger fumbled to get his own sidearm out and working.

The H&K crashed, and Buck's right shoulder was smashed back. Blood sprayed the wall behind him. Kane fired again, and Barrett's Segundo fell to the floor with a bullet in his leg.

Two.

Kane's glance darted back to the man he'd thrown the pipe at, who was doubled over in pain and unaware that his attacker was closing the gap between them. The H&K fell, the barrel impacted him just behind his left ear, and he was out before hitting the floor.

One!

Kane's icy gaze settled on a stunned-looking Barrett.

"Your turn, asshole!" he snarled and launched himself at the gang leader.

Kane hit him between the eyes with the handgun. Barrett was flung backward, and his chair tipped over. Kane tucked the handgun away and grabbed a handful of the gang leader's hair. Dragging him to his feet from behind the desk, he drove a brutal right fist into his face.

"Next time you want to teach someone a lesson, think again."

Kane delivered two more crunching blows to Barrett's jaw and then let him go. The gang leader fell to the floor, groaning and turned his head to look up at Kane. He spat blood on the floor and spoke with a thick voice, "You're fucking dead."

Kane hit him again. He leaned down and hissed in his ear, "Listen close, Barrett. If you or your crew come anywhere near me, I'll kill them. Most of all, I'll come after you and put a bullet in your head. Got it?"

"I won't come after you; he will."

"Who?"

"*El Hombre*. He'll come for you," Barrett laughed. "When he does, you'll wish you were dead."

Kane hit him again. This time Barrett didn't move.

A moan drew his attention to the other side of the room. Buck was in pain from the two bullet wounds and bleeding all over the floor.

"If I was you," Kane said to him, "I'd get those looked at. I bet they hurt like a bitch."

Through gritted teeth, Buck snarled, "Screw you."

"You heard what I told your boss. You come after me; I'll kill you. Those two were just a warning. I could have killed you anytime I wanted to."

"Like Barrett said, *El Hombre* will come for you. We won't have to."

Kane picked up the pipe, turned and walked from the room. The stares he received when he emerged were ones of disbelief. He held up the pipe to return it to Brenda when the bar doors flew open, and Cleaver appeared, holding a pump-action shotgun.

He stared at Kane, his eyes cold and menacing. For a moment, he thought he was seeing things, then once he'd gathered himself, snapped, "You've caused trouble for the last time in my town, you son of a bitch. You're under arrest."

Barrett staggered out from the back room. His bloodied face pulled up into a snarl. "Shoot the bastard, Cleaver."

"Shut up, Barrett!" Cleaver snapped. "I'll do this my way."

Barrett spat blood on the floor. "The new-found power gone to your head, Sheriff?"

Cleaver ignored him. He pointed the shotgun at Kane and ordered, "Get your hands up."

"He's got a gun, Cleaver," Barrett warned him. "He shot Buck."

Cleaver's face remained unchanged. "Kill him?"

"Nope, just wounded."

"Pity. Get the gun."

Barrett moved forward and took the gun from behind Kane's back. He tucked it into his own pants.

"Give it to me, Barrett."

The gang leader looked about the room at everyone watching with bated breath. He shook his head and approached the deputy. As he handed the weapon over, he said in a low voice, "You'd best remember your place, Art."

"What's going on here?"

Heads turned to see Cara in the doorway. She was dressed in jeans and a loose-fitting T-shirt but in her right hand was her service weapon. Kane felt almost relieved to see her.

Cleaver said, "Your boy here is a one-man riot. Took down Barrett here and some of his boys. Even Sully didn't escape his wrath."

Cara looked across at the big bar owner and saw him hunched over, a towel held to the cut on his head.

Cleaver continued, "And if that wasn't enough, he shot Buck."

Her eyes fixed on Kane, an alarmed expression on her face. "What? Why?"

Kane shrugged. "They're selling drugs out of the back room. I don't like drugs. Bad stuff, tends to kill people."

"Shut your mouth, you son of a bitch," Barrett snarled and lunged at Kane.

Kane was ready, and when Barrett was in range, his right hand blurred and pulled him up cold with a punch to the jaw. The gang leader staggered back and cursed aloud. He made to rush Kane again, but Cleaver stopped him.

The shotgun discharged into the ceiling, and dust and debris rained down. The sound within the enclosed space made ears ring.

"Hold it!" Cleaver shouted.

Who the hell does he think he is? Kane thought. *Wyatt Earp.*

"Cara, get your boy the hell out of here. I'll deal with the rest of it."

"But —"

"Just do it. With the sheriff gone, I'm in charge. I won't have you question every damned thing I do."

Beneath the surface, Cara fumed. She stared at Kane and said, "Come on."

"Put cuffs on him."

She was about to protest again when Kane said, "It's OK, Cara. Put them on."

"I don't have any."

Cleaver tossed her his. Cara caught them and put them on Kane. She glared at Cleaver one last time and escorted her prisoner out to the Tahoe.

The deputy fixed his gaze on Barrett. "Out the back."

As they walked towards the door, Cleaver said to Brenda, "Call for a paramedic."

"No!"

The deputy looked at Barrett and shrugged. "OK. Have it your way."

"And Buck ain't pressing charges against him either."

Cleaver raised his eyebrows. "What was that?"

"You heard."

"It's a good thing I don't need you then, isn't it?"

"He won't testify, and it'll get thrown out of court."

Cleaver shook his head. "Christ."

Out in the back room, Cleaver stared at the mess of drugs and injured gang members. He fixed his stern gaze on Barrett. "Get this cleaned up."

"What about the drugs?"

"What drugs? Like I said, get it cleaned up."

———

Sonora

For the second time that day Montoya received a call from Cleaver. "Yes?"

"We have another problem."

"It seems that problems are all you bring me. What is it this time?"

Cleaver told him about what had happened.

There was a long silence as Montoya digested the news. Then, "What is it you wish for me to do?"

"I thought you might be able to make them both go away."

"Can you not do it?"

"No. They need to disappear and never be found."

Montoya sighed. "OK. Keep him in jail and have the woman watch him tomorrow night. You will receive a text before it happens. The team will be in and out and leave no trace."

"Tell them to be careful. He's no ordinary man."

Montoya looked at Salazar who sat on the white sofa across from him. "This I am aware of."

Montoya disconnected.

Salazar stared at his boss. "More problems?"

"Sí. The *gringo* you tell me about. It seems he is a bigger problem than we can afford."

"I will go."

"No. I have something else for you to do. Pick four men and send them to me. I will tell them what is to be done."

The *sicario* nodded. "*Sí, El Hombre.*"

———

Retribution

Cara pounded the steering wheel with the palm of her right hand. "Fucking asshole!"

"Who me?" Kane asked innocently.

"No, that other son of a bitch, Art," then she glanced sideways at him. "Yes, and you, damn it. What on earth were you thinking, Reaper? You were meant to meet me at the Rose for a drink. Then I get a report about a damned riot over at Sully's when I was on my way home because you stood me up."

"Sorry about that," he apologized.

"You want to tell me what happened?"

Kane told her about finding Druce and calling for the paramedics.

"That was you? Why didn't you call it in?"

"He didn't want me to. He was scared."

"So, you took it upon yourself to deliver justice to those responsible?"

"Kind of."

"Shit, Reaper. You can't do that. Look what happens when you do."

The Tahoe pulled into the parking lot outside the jail. Cara ripped the handbrake on and climbed out. She walked around to the other side and opened the door for Kane to get out.

He gave her a wry smile. "Why, thank you, ma'am."

"This is serious shit, Reaper. You're looking at hard time."

Once inside, she sat him in a chair at her desk. She took the cuffs off and grabbed a pad from her drawer to make notes. Cara slammed it onto her desk and stared hard at him. "OK, Gunny, start from the beginning."

Kane had only just finished telling Cara about finding Druce when Cleaver arrived back. On his own.

"Where are the others? Barrett?"

"There was no need to arrest them."

"What about the drugs?"

"There were no drugs. Your friend there was trying to save his own skin."

"Horseshit!" Kane snapped. "There was a whole desk covered in it. People were marching in and out of the back room to buy them."

"If they had been, they weren't when I went to check it out."

"What about the gun and knife they tried to kill me with. It was all self-defense."

Cleaver shook his head. "Nothing. And there is one other thing. Buck isn't going to press charges for you shooting him. But don't get too excited. There will be charges of some sort, count on it. Until then, you will be locked up in the cells."

"Can't get rid of me one way so you'll try another, is that it?" Kane snapped.

"What the hell are you on about?"

Kane turned to Cara. "Your boss here tried to run me out of town. Took me for a ride and dropped me about a mile from town and told me not to come back."

"But you did come back, didn't you," Cleaver pointed out. "And look what happened. You're trouble, and you'll get what you deserve. Lock him up, Cara. I'm going home."

Once Cleaver was gone, Kane said to Cara. "There were drugs there, Cara. One of Barrett's men tried to knife me, and Buck tried to shoot me. Hell, if I'd wanted to kill them, they'd all be dead."

She nodded. "Then what happened to them?"

"How well do you know him?"

"Cleaver? I've known him ever since I started to work here. You aren't saying that he's up to his neck in this, are you?"

"He wouldn't be the first to go bad."

Cara shook her head. "He may be a stubborn, mule-headed, chauvinistic son of a bitch whom I can't stand, but I don't think he's bad."

"Well, what about the drugs? He should have found them right where they were."

"I'm sure if they were there he would have, Reaper."

"Don't you believe me?"

"I'm a deputy sheriff. I have to believe the evidence."

"Damn it, Cara. Go back and check. Look for yourself. You'll see. Talk to Brenda."

"OK. I'll do it on my way home. First I have to make a call to get someone to babysit you."

"Good. Thank you. You'll see."

Thirty minutes later a large man with a thick white beard walked in.

"Where's this desperado you want me to keep an eye on?"

"Out in the cells, Bear," Cara informed him. "He won't give you any trouble."

Bear was a special deputy. Smythe had called on from time to time if he needed a hole filled for whatever reason. Even though he was retired, Bear was always willing to lend a hand.

Bear nodded. "OK. I'll see you in the morning."

"See you then."

"By the way, I'm sorry about Walt. I liked him."

"Yeah. Me too."

———

Sully's place was empty when Cara returned. She walked inside and wrinkled her nose at the smell of fresh puke. Brenda was behind the bar cleaning up. Of Sully, there was no sign.

She crossed to the bar, her boot-heels making a loud clunking sound on the timber floorboards. In the background, the jukebox played a slow Martina McBride song she'd never heard before.

"You get the good job, huh?" Cara said as she leaned on the bar. "Smells like someone puked a wet dog in here."

Brenda nodded. "Thanks to your friend, things kinda dried up around here, so we shut up early. Sully had a headache, so he left me to do the shit."

"Can I ask you some questions about that?"

The look of apprehension on Brenda's face was obvious when she said, "I ain't sure I can help you any."

"Can you tell me what happened?"

"The feller came in, we talked, and then he went crazy."

Cara nodded. "What did you talk about?"

"Not much. Just about how he used to be a soldier. Hey, you don't suppose he has that PTSD shit, do you?"

Cara shook her head. "What else, Brenda?"

"Not much. He saw some of Barrett's gang come in and flipped out. He grabbed the pipe we use to keep the rowdies under control and stormed off into the back room. Sully tried to stop him, but he got put on the floor as quick as spit."

"Where was the pipe he took?"

Without thinking about her answer, Brenda pointed under the counter. "Down there."

"So, he got it from down there?"

"That's right."

"How?"

"What do you mean?"

"Kane was on this side of the bar, and the pipe is on the other. How did he get it?"

"He leaned over and took it."

"Uh huh."

Cara jumped up and leaned across the bar top. She gazed down at the other side and said, "Show me where?"

Brenda pointed at a shelf close to the bottom. "We keep it there."

Cara let her arm dangle down, but it came up short.

Too late, Brenda realized her mistake. "Ah – no, maybe it was this shelf." She pointed at the one above it.

Cara pushed herself off the bar and stared into Brenda's eyes. "He didn't take it, did he? You gave it to him."

Brenda's head shook furiously. "No, no. He took it."

"No, he didn't. It was you."

Her face fell. "Ok, I did it. I thought he might be able to get rid of Barrett and his gang. Please don't tell Sully. He'll kill me."

"Were they selling drugs from the back room?"

The anguish on the young woman's face told Cara what she wanted to know.

"Is there anyone out there now?"

"No."

"Good. Come with me."

Both women went out to the back room. Brenda turned the light on, and the first thing Cara noticed was the prominent bloodstains on the floor. Brenda saw her looking at them. "I tried to get rid of them, but it's in the timber."

Cara walked the room and looked it over with a practiced eye. She stopped, went down on one knee, and touched the floor with her finger. She pulled it back and stared at the traces of fine white powder stuck to it.

"How long have they been selling out of here, Brenda?" Cara asked.

"I don't know what you mean."

The deputy came to her feet and asked again, "How long have they been selling drugs from here, Brenda, and don't give me any shit about you not knowing."

"Months."

"Is Sully in on it?"

"Yes."

Cara hesitated, then asked, "What about Art Cleaver? Does he know about it?"

Brenda nodded.

A million thoughts rushed through the deputy's head as she tried to process it all. It looked as though Kane was right, and Cleaver was in it up to his neck.

"I'll come by your place in the morning to pick you up," Cara said.

"What? Why?"

"Because I'll need you to testify against Art. The only way I can be assured of that is to keep you safe. You'll be fine until I come back."

She gave her head a furious shake. "No – no way!"

Cara wasn't about to take no for an answer. "Yes, you will. And don't try to run. If you do, I'll put the word out that you talked anyway, and they'll come looking for you."

"You can't do that."

"Can and will. I'll see you around eight."

Before Brenda could protest any more, Cara was gone.

Brenda walked back out to the bar and started cleaning where she had left off when Cara came in. Her mind reeled as she tried to think of what she could do. She dropped the rag and bent down to pick it up. Hearing the door open, she called out, "We're closed."

Footsteps got closer, and she straightened up. "I said –"

Cleaver gave her a mirthless smile. "Hello, Brenda. How about you tell me what Cara wanted."

———

The Desert

The Saguaro County sheriff's SUV slid to a stop in the desert ten miles from anywhere, surrounded by a silvery landscape of giant, unrecognizable shadows.

Cleaver climbed out and stomped angrily towards the back of the vehicle and opened it up. He reached inside and dragged Brenda out by her hair. Muffled screams sounded from behind the tape he'd placed across her mouth. Her hands were tied behind her back, and she hit the ground hard. Tears ran down her cheeks from terrified eyes.

It hadn't taken Cleaver long to extract the information he wanted. A few well-placed blows and she'd told him everything, and in doing so, had become another problem in the equation that seemed to be unraveling before his eyes.

This one, however, he could fix.

Cleaver dragged Brenda around to the front of the SUV and placed her in the beam of the headlights. She stared up at him, eyes begging him to let her go. He took out his sidearm and placed the cold barrel against her forehead.

Cleaver hesitated.

She closed her eyes.

He pulled the trigger.

CHAPTER 8

RETRIBUTION

For the fifth time, Cara pounded a clenched fist on Brenda's door. It was eight o'clock, and already hot which meant the deputy was losing patience fast.

"Come on, Brenda. Open the damned door!"

The bartender from Sully's lived in a small, rundown, L-shaped, timber-built home with a tin roof and fallen down carport on the left side. It had once been white but was now a dirty light-grey color from years of neglect.

Cara banged again. "Brenda!"

"She ain't home, deputy."

Cara turned and stared at the elderly man who stood on the other side of a half-fallen down wire fence which separated his property from the one Brenda occupied.

"Are you sure?"

"The door."

"Pardon?"

"The door," he said pointing at the rusted gate type

screen Cara had been pounding on. "Screeches like a bastard every time she goes in and out of it. I may be going deaf, but even I can't escape that thing. I didn't hear it last night, nor again this morning. Which means she ain't home."

Cara looked at the door and then back at the man. "Thanks."

"Is she in trouble or something? She may look a little rough around the edges, but she's a nice girl."

Cara shook her head. "No, she's fine." Then softer, "At least I hope she is."

"What?"

"Nothing, I was just talking to myself."

He raised his hand and turned away from the fence. Cara stood on the doorstep for a few moments more and then walked back to the Tahoe. She climbed in and turned the vehicle around. Two minutes later she was outside of Sully's Bar.

———

"Get out! We're closed!" Sully said without turning around.

"I'm looking for Brenda," said Cara, looking at the bloodstained plaster on the back of his head.

Sully turned and frowned. "It's you. What do you want with her?"

"I want to talk to her."

"Me too," he growled. "The bitch never finished cleaning up last night."

Cara frowned. "Does that happen very often?"

"Never."

Where the hell is she?

"If she shows, let me know."

"Yeah. Right. Are we done?"

"Yeah. You might want to clean up the drug residue you left out in the back room."

Sully stared after her as she strode from the room.

―――――

The Desert

The large, black birds circled lazily in the sky above the desert floor. Already, there were some on the ground, and they walked around, waiting. One moved in close and then backed away. Another did the same.

A dark shadow seemed to fall from the sky and landed heavily. Two of the vultures already on the ground moved in closer to the new arrival to chase it away. But the bird would not be moved. It was bigger than the others.

It moved forward and climbed onto the tattooed arm. The vulture studied the body. The exposed flesh was a mottled color, the tape was still in place, and the hole in the forehead was dried and crusted. The large eyes that had been brown, now milky and staring sightlessly upward.

The bird walked along the arm and up onto the corpse's chest. It stopped and looked down at the exposed flesh of the midriff, the piercing at the navel. Its head came down, and the wicked curved tip of the beak picked at the shiny metal.

Nothing happened.

It tried again. This time the object came away. It dropped it in the sand beside the corpse and turned back.

Suddenly startled by something, it flew away, while beside the body a cell vibrated in the dust.

———

Retribution

"Shit!" Cara cursed and slammed the phone down on its cradle.

"You have a problem, Deputy?" Cleaver asked.

She glared at him and shook her head. "Nope. No problem."

"Any news from the M.E. at all?"

"Nope. Shouldn't one of us be out there doing something, Art?"

"Do what? The culprit got away. There are no witnesses, and I'm still waiting to hear back from the FBI. The rest don't want to hear about it because it is cartel related."

"We don't know that."

"So, we're going to do nothing?"

"We shall wait for results and go from there."

Cara climbed from her seat.

"Where are you going?"

"I'm going to check on our prisoner that *you* haven't charged yet."

"That won't be far away."

Cara walked out through the back door to the cells. The department had two of them, and Kane was their sole prisoner. She opened the door to his cell and walked in. It consisted of a cot, four walls painted an institutional gray, and a door.

Kane studied her face and said, "Morning."

"Have you eaten this morning?" she asked.

"Nope."

"I'll see that you get something."

"Did you check out my story?"

Cara nodded. "I did. You were right. I found traces of the drugs. And I also had a witness who was going to testify to Art's involvement in whatever it all is."

"Had?"

"She's disappeared. I swung by her place this morning, and there was no answer. The neighbor said she never came home. So, I went to Sully's ..."

"It was Brenda?"

Cara nodded. "She never even finished cleaning the bar last night."

"Do you think she ran?"

"It looks that way. Yet I'm not sure. I warned her that if she did, I would put the word out that she helped us."

"Meantime, I'm stuck here."

"Yes. Art doesn't seem in any hurry to cut you loose or charge you."

"What about the sheriff's murder?"

Cara shrugged. "Nothing new. Although I get the feeling, now I know Art is dirty, that something isn't right there too. If he hasn't charged you by tomorrow, I'll let you out myself."

"What do you plan to do?"

"About Art or the case?"

"Both."

"I don't know about Art. If Brenda turns up, then I will be able to do something right away. If not ... I'll have to dig something else up."

"And the other?"

"Art says he's still waiting for the FBI, and since it looks like it is the cartel, we should leave it to the DEA. We'll know more once the prints come back."

Kane gave her a puzzled look.

"What is it?"

"You said yesterday that Art would answer the complaints from the Grissom place, right?"

"That's right."

"Is that part of his patrol route?"

"Yes."

"So why did the sheriff go out there?"

"For the drive, I think, more than anything else."

"How did Art take that?"

"Not great. What are you getting at, Reaper?"

Kane shrugged. "It may be nothing. But it seems odd to me that the sheriff and the cartel show at the Grissom place around the same time. If Art is involved with the drugs like we think, then who is paying him to keep things in check?"

"You think he's tied in with the cartel?"

"It's only an assumption."

Cara went quiet as she ran things over in her mind. Then, "What do I do?"

"You need to phone the DEA division office in Washington. Ask for a guy named Ferrero, Luis Ferrero. He was one of the top men we worked with in Colombia. Tell him you want some agents out here and why. OK?"

Cara nodded. "I'll do it first chance I get."

"Be careful, Cara. If he is cartel, he'll be dangerous."

———

Washington

Luis Ferrero hated being a desk jockey. Twenty years in the

DEA, most of it as a field agent, and now the powers that be saw fit to put him behind a desk.

He was a solidly built man of average height, and his hair was more gray than anything else these days. But shit, he wasn't a damned invalid just yet. Hell, he'd mixed it with some of the toughest cartels in Colombia and Mexico.

The more he thought about it, the angrier he became. Penned up in a small eighty-one square foot office with a pile of paperwork on his desk even Vashti Cunningham couldn't jump over. Great start to the morning.

The phone rang. "Thank God."

He picked it up. "Yeah?"

"Sir, I have a call for you from a deputy sheriff in Retribution, Arizona."

"What's it about, Lizzy?"

"She says that a former marine named John Kane told her to call you."

"Kane? There's a name I haven't heard in a while. Put her through."

"Yes, sir."

The line clicked, and a voice came through. "Hello."

"You got Ferrero, who's speaking please?"

"Agent Ferrero, my name is Cara Billings, deputy sheriff in Retribution, Arizona. John Kane told me to call you. He said you worked together in Colombia and that I could trust you."

"He was right. How is he?"

"Locked up in our jail at present."

Ferrero frowned. "OK. What seems to be the problem?"

"The Montoya Cartel."

Ferrero sat forward in his seat. His face grew serious. "You better tell me what's going on. All of it."

Cara filled him in on everything. From Kane's arrival to

the death of Walt Smythe, and what she'd learned about Art
Cleaver.

"I don't know how much of what he's told me is true.
He says that if it is Montoya that the DEA has said to stay
away from it. He says he's waiting to hear back from the FBI
and that state law enforcement don't want anything to do
with it because it is DEA related to the cartel."

"He's right about the cartel thing. Local DEA would
probably jump down your throat if it is cartel related and
you interfered, maybe turn their investigation to shit.
However, if FBI and State Troopers knew about what had
happened to your sheriff, they'd be crawling up every
known orifice around the place. I think your man is lying.
But we can use that." Ferrero frowned. "Wait one, Deputy,
I need to check something I saw on my computer a while
back."

He tucked the phone in beside his cheek and tapped
some keys on the keyboard in front of him. Stabbing at it
with a clumsy precision, he kept going until he found what
he wanted. "Shit. Damn it. We got a red flag this morning
about a hit on some prints your office ran."

"Really? We've heard nothing back yet."

"Well, I'm looking at it. The prints scored a hit to one
Cesar Salazar. He belongs to the Montoya Cartel."

"Damn it!"

"That about says it all. Listen, there'll be someone there
tomorrow to help you out. In the meantime, I suggest you
try to find your witness."

"All right, thank you."

"And tell Reaper he'll owe me."

"Yes, sir."

Cara hung up, and Ferrero thought for a moment. He
hit a button on the phone panel, and Lizzy answered.

"Lizzy, tell Traynor to get his stuff together. We're leaving for Arizona in half an hour. Also, I want you to find me all you can on a Cara Billings and Art Cleaver from Retribution."

He replaced the handset and opened his desktop drawer. He reached in and took out an old-school Smith and Wesson 1911. "Time to go to work."

———

New York

Colin O'Brien was eating a lunch of fettuccini carbonara when he got the call. The dark interior added to the ambiance of the small and cozy Italian restaurant on West 57th Street. Seated in the plush upholstered booth across from him was Bannon.

The restaurant was near to full. A popular place with many of the locals, O'Brien seemed to blend in with all the other suits.

A cell rang, and O'Brien reached into his coat pocket and withdrew it. He pressed the button and put it to his ear.

"Yes?"

"We got a hit."

"Are you sure it's him?"

"Yes. Someone did a database search from a place called Retribution in Arizona."

"Thank you."

The call ended, and O'Brien stared across the table at his enforcer. "He's been found."

"Where?"

"Arizona."

"I'll take care of it."

"Take three men who can get the job done. I want him alive. Make sure they understand that," his gaze turned to granite. "I want the bastard alive."

———

Retribution

The sun had gone down by the time Cara got back to Kane. After a hot day of searching for Brenda and coming up empty, she wasn't in the best mood or frame of mind.

Cleaver was at his desk when she walked through the door with a takeaway meal for their prisoner.

"What are you doing with that?" he demanded.

"Food for the prisoner."

He grunted and went back to what he was doing.

"Have you charged him with anything yet, Art?"

"Nope."

"Then let him go."

Cleaver sighed and leaned back in his chair. "Tomorrow. He can walk then. Maybe a little extra time in the cell will make him think twice about causing trouble. I still don't like it. He should have the full weight of the law thrown at him for attempted murder."

Cara rolled her eyes and turned away. "Whatever, Art. I'm sure it would have been a huge loss."

She found Kane lying on the cot and passed him the food which consisted of two ham and pickle sandwiches and a cola.

"I talked to your friend in Washington," Cara told him. "He said someone will be here tomorrow."

Kane nodded from the doorway. "Good."

"Cleaver said he's going to let you out tomorrow too."

Kane nodded. "What else?"

"Ferrero said that they got a red flag on our fingerprints. Came back as belonging to Cesar Salazar."

"Never heard of him."

"*Sicario* for the Montoya Cartel. He's called *El Monstruo*. Word has it he was a *Federale* who changed sides. As you've seen, he lives up to his name."

There was a moment of silence, and Kane noticed the look of concern on her face. "What is it?"

"I spent most of the day trying to find Brenda but found nothing. I checked bus timetables and known associates and came up empty."

"What do you think?"

"I don't want to. Every time I do, I get a bad feeling."

"Cara! You there?" Cleaver's voice echoed through the cells.

"Yeah."

"I'm going out to get some milk. I'll be back shortly."

"OK."

Cara looked at her watch and snorted. "Dick."

"What's the matter?"

"He's going out to get the milk, and the damn stores are all shut. It's after nine."

"You'd think he'd know that," Kane surmised.

Cara's eyes darted back and forth as her mind started to work overtime. "I'll be back."

She rushed from the cell without even bothering to close the door. Kane placed his food on the cot and eased to his feet.

Out in the office area, Cara went to the fridge and

opened it. There sitting on the second shelf was a three-parts full container of milk. "What are you up to?"

She hurried across to the window and peeked out through the venetian blind, just in time to see a black SUV pull up.

"What is it?" Kane asked from the doorway.

She whirled about, a look of apprehension on her face. "I think the Montoya Cartel is about to knock on our door."

Kane hurried across to the window and looked out. The doors on the SUV opened, and four men alighted, dressed in black, and carrying automatic weapons.

"Break open your armory, LT. This is about to go loud."

————

Ramon Conteros tucked the phone into his pocket and checked home a full magazine into the FX-05. He, like the three others in the SUV, were cartel men. The expendables, the meat for the grinder. They were expected to get the job done or die trying. In case of such an eventuality, their families would be taken care of. Their loyalty was bought and paid for.

Each was covered in tattoos. Arms, legs, chest, even face, and head. Nearly all told a story.

Conteros was in charge. This wasn't his first kill mission for the cartel. Five skull tattoos on the right side of his neck were his running tally.

The phone in his pocket buzzed, so he removed it and checked the screen.

"All is ready," he told the others.

"We kill them all, Ramon?"

Ramon looked across at the driver. "Sí. When we stop,

you will go around the back. We will go in through the front. There are only two. We kill them and then go home."

"Just in time to fuck the *chicas* at the cantina, huh, Ramon?" came a voice from the back seat.

Ramon whirled in the seat. "Get your mind on the *misión*, Chico. If you fuck it up, I will kill you myself."

The SUV with its headlights turned off pulled into the lot of the jail. They climbed out, and Ramon gave them directions by hand signal. In a couple of minutes, their surprise would be complete, and they would be on their way back to Sonora.

The driver, Juan, disappeared around the side of the building as the others, led by Ramon, approached the front door. Conteros eased the door open and held it while Chico and Ruis moved inside.

Across the street, hiding in the shadows, Cleaver watched Ramon enter the sheriff's office. His heart hammered loudly in his chest as adrenaline coursed through his body. He expelled a long breath that he didn't realize he'd been holding and stared at the front lot of windows, waiting.

Then the inside of the jail lit up.

CHAPTER 9

RETRIBUTION

"Here!" Cara snapped and tossed Kane an HK 416. "There's a few fresh mags there too."

Kane gave the carbine a once over and racked a round into the firing chamber. He took three magazines and stuffed them into his pockets.

"I saw four," he told her. "One of them looked to be headed around the back."

"He'll be trying to make sure we can't escape that way. He won't get in there because the door is locked."

Kane stared at the flimsy furniture placed about the room. Damn bullets would pass right through them. Then he saw the filing cabinet. "Give me a hand."

Within thirty seconds, they had it lifted onto Cara's desk. It wasn't great, but the metal-framed cabinet was all they had.

He gave Cara a mirthless smile. "Just like old times, LT?"

"Shit, Reaper. I thought I gave this all away."

They crouched behind the cabinet, facing each other. They listened intently for tell-tale signs of the cartel shooters entering the office area.

The harder Kane listened, the louder his heartbeat sounded in his ears.

Damn it, Reaper, calm down.

He closed his eyes and drew a deep breath in through his nose and released it slowly from his mouth. He felt the tension ease in his body.

There was a tap on Kane's knee, and his eyes snapped open. Cara was staring at him and mouthed, "What are you doing?"

Kane never answered. Instead, he brought the HK to his shoulder and rose up behind the cabinet. The three cartel men were standing inside the door, surprised to see him waiting for them with his own weapon.

His first burst nailed Chico full in the chest. The bullets punched through the cartel man's torso and out the back in a bright spray of crimson. The soldier cried out and staggered back with spasmodic jerks. His finger squeezed the trigger on the FX-05 in his hand, and it went all the way back.

The selector on the weapon was set at full auto and bullets sprayed across the room and hammered into the back wall, shattering the window in the sheriff's office. As the soldier fell backward, the slugs stitched a line of jagged holes up to the ceiling and rained plaster down onto the floor.

By this time, the other two cartel men had recovered enough to cut loose with their own weapons. Again, they too were on full auto and sprayed the room with careless abandon.

Bullets beat a staccato drum against the metal cabinet. More plaster dust filled the room as the 5.56 NATO rounds from the FX-05s ripped into the walls. The sound of the gunfire bounced around the small space in what seemed to be one continuous roar. Kane glanced at Cara who was crouched low, biding her time.

Two shots drilled through her desk and erupted from the timber in a shower of splinters which passed between the two hunched figures, hitting the wall behind them.

The thing about a weapon on full auto is that the ammunition in the magazine is expended rapidly. Which is exactly what happened.

One moment the room was full of deafening noise, the next there was an eerie silence as the rounds from the FX-05s were depleted.

Kane glanced at Cara who nodded. They rose smoothly at the same time, and as the two Mexicans fumbled with a magazine change, they shot them in the chest with bursts from their carbines.

Both the tattooed soldiers' shirts flickered, and red splotches appeared as the NATO rounds slammed into their chests. They were hurled backward, and their weapons clattered to the grey, linoleum floor. The top half of one man's body ended up out the interior doorway, his legs inside the room, still twitching. Kane and Cara moved forward from behind their cover, boots crunching on the debris which had fallen, their carbines still aimed at the bodies on the floor.

"There's still one more," Cara pointed out.

Kane nodded. "You want him?"

"I'll leave that up to you while I check these guys over."

Kane put the HK up to his shoulder and walked towards the door. He pushed out into the darkness and dropped to his right knee. He swept the area to his front and then rose. Turning left, he moved stealthily for the corner of the building. He eased his head around the side, and an accurate burst erupted from another FX-05 in the hands of the final cartel soldier.

Bullets chewed gouges from the corner of the sheriff's office and ricocheted out towards the street. Small chunks of the brickwork were sprayed from the building. This killer was more restrained with his shots, and his weapon's selector was set to burst.

Kane leaned around the corner and fired his own burst at the soldier who made for the cover of a large, disused dumpster in the alley. The bullets missed, and Kane fired again, the rounds hammering into the metal-sided receptacle just as the Mexican made his ground.

The FX-05 rattled off another burst, and the bullets slammed into the brickwork once more.

Kane took two full magazines from his pockets and held them in his left hand; then switched the selector on the side of the HK to auto and took a deep breath. He stepped away from the corner of the building and squeezed the trigger.

The HK's rate of fire came in between 700-900 rounds per minute. Which meant that Kane blew through what remained of the magazine in seconds. With practiced hands, he dropped out the empty and slapped another full one home.

Before the cartel soldier could open up again, the HK emptied another magazine into the dumpster with a deafening noise.

Kane slapped home the second magazine and brought the weapon up to his shoulder. He switched the selector back to semi.

The constant fire had been too much for the Mexican,

and he jumped up and began to run as fast as he could, trying to get away.

Kane brought the HK into line with the fleeing figure and shot him in the back of the head. The hammer-blow propelled the man forward, and he went down in a tangle of arms and legs. His weapon bounced and then skidded along the alley when his lifeless fingers released it.

As the echo of the shot rolled away into the desert, Kane moved forward to check on the killer. He instinctively knew that the man was dead, but his training forced him to make sure.

He knelt beside the body and checked for a pulse. Climbing to his feet, he was about to turn around when a voice snarled, "Drop the weapon, or I'll put a bullet in your fucking head."

———

Cleaver had watched the fight unfold from across the street and cursed inwardly when he saw the plan all go to shit. The constant staccato sound of the Mexicans spraying bullets couldn't be contained within the jail, and from outside, it sounded like fireworks at Chinese New Year.

Then he saw Kane emerge from the jail and knew it was all bad. The only hope left was that Montoya's last man could finish the job. That too did not go well.

"Christ," he cursed and drew his own Smith and Wesson then started across the street.

He approached the alley while Kane had his back turned. Raising the handgun, he momentarily contemplated shooting Kane from behind. Then, just as he was about to squeeze the trigger, Cara emerged from the front door.

Cleaver said, "Drop the weapon, or I'll put a bullet in your fucking head."

Kane turned to face the deputy but retained his grip on the HK.

Cleaver licked his lips. "Do it! Now, damn it!"

"Lower the gun, Art," Cara told him. "He helped out with these assholes who tried to kill us."

The deputy hesitated.

"Lower it, Art," Cara said again.

Cleaver holstered his gun.

"Where's your milk?" asked Kane.

"What? Oh, the store was closed."

"Convenient."

"I'll go and phone the M.E. Get these fellers on ice. I'd say the DEA will want to check them over when they arrive tomorrow."

They both noticed the change in Cleaver's face. "What DEA agents?"

"Oh. I forgot to tell you. I called the DEA today. They're sending agents out here. It appears that Walt's killer was none other than Montoya's *sicario*, Cesar Salazar."

"Damn it, you should have told me."

"I'm telling you now."

Cara disappeared inside, and Cleaver stared at Kane. "You might as well get out of here. We can look after this mess."

Kane's face remained passive. "I might hang around. Montoya could have another man on this side of the border. You never know."

———

Sonora

The cell rang.

"What is it?"

"Your crew screwed up. They're all dead."

Montoya ground his teeth together. "What happened?"

"Somehow they knew."

"Impossible."

"Yeah, well. I think they know about me too."

"You were told to be careful."

"I was, damn it."

"Obviously not enough."

"Forget about that. You'll love this. There are meant to be DEA agents arriving tomorrow. Your boy left fingerprints, and they red-flagged. And you want to lecture me about being careful?"

There was a long pause.

"Another thing. I did some digging into our friend Kane, and guess what I found? He's an ex-marine. Not just any marine though, special forces. Him and that damned woman took your men apart like they were damned children."

More silence.

"Well? What the fuck are you going to do, Montoya? The way things are, it's all going to turn to shit."

"I will fix it!" Montoya snarled and hung up.

"Another problem?" Salazar asked.

Montoya glared at him, his eyes sparked with anger. He looked at his gold Rolex and then spoke to his *sicario*, "*Señor* Cleaver has outlived his usefulness. I want him dealt with."

"Tonight?"

"Can you do it?"

Salazar looked at his own watch. "Can I use the helicopter?"

"Yes."

"Then yes, I can do it."

"Good."

"What about the other problem?"

"No. Leave them for the moment. The DEA will arrive in Retribution tomorrow. They cannot touch us. However, we'll need to shut down our operation for the time being. Tell that *gringo* Barrett I want my money delivered tomorrow night."

Salazar reached into his pocket and took out a cell. He hit speed-dial one and put it up to his ear.

———

The Desert

The Sikorsky S-76 touched down on the gravel road to the south-west and three miles outside of Retribution. The downdraft from its rotor wash blasted dirt and grit in all directions which formed a large cloud. Salazar waited until the rotors had slowed considerably before climbing out.

Bent low, and carrying a large duffel bag, he hurried towards the beat-up Ford F-150 where Barrett was awaiting his arrival. He dropped the bag in the back and climbed into the truck before closing the door.

Now that he was clear, the pilot inside the helicopter powered up, ready for the quick hop back across the border.

The inside of the truck smelled of stale beer and sweat.

Salazar wrinkled his nose then looked across at Barrett and asked him, "Do you ever bathe?"

Barrett nodded. "Sure, twice a week."

"Maybe you need to try three."

Barrett took offense to the remark. "Do you want to fucking walk wherever it is you're going, Mex?"

Salazar moved with speed, and before Barrett knew what had happened, the *sicario* had a Five-Seven pressed against the side of his head.

"Be careful what you say, *gringo*."

"OK, OK. Keep your shirt on."

"You would do well to remember this."

"So, what brings you this side of the border, *mi amigo*?" Barrett asked hurriedly.

"Cleaver."

Barrett chuckled. "What? Oh shit. What did he do to piss off the big guy?"

Salazar remained silent.

"It had something to do with the shooting earlier, didn't it?"

The *sicario* turned to stare at Barrett. "Drive."

The helicopter was disappearing into the darkness when Barrett dropped the clutch and spun the F-150's rear tires. The beat-up vehicle bounced over the gravel road for a mile before finding the tarmac and then turned left towards Retribution.

When they reached the outskirts of town, Barrett asked, "Do you know where he is?"

"I would say the jail."

"That's where I'll take you then."

"No. Take me somewhere high with a clear field of fire."

Barrett thought for a moment before saying, "There's the water tower."

"That will do."

Two minutes later, the Ford stopped at the base of the tower. In the headlights, Salazar could see clumps of weeds and what appeared to be wild blackberry brambles surrounding the old, disused steel-framed structure that looked as though it might collapse at any moment. But Salazar didn't complain. He climbed out of the truck and grabbed his duffel, then put on a head-lamp and went to work.

When the rifle was fully assembled, Barrett stared at it in awe. "Whoa. Holy shit. What kind of gun is that?"

Salazar switched off the light and looked at him. "It is an L115A3."

"A what?"

"Arctic Warfare Magnum. British-made sniper rifle."

"Uh huh."

Conversation over.

Salazar scooped the weapon up and walked towards the tower.

———

Retribution

Kane watched the M.E. drive away with the four bodies. He turned back towards Cara and said, "What now?"

She shrugged and looked at the gathering crowd of onlookers. "This is getting way out of control. I'm calling for extra law enforcement."

"No!"

Cara turned to see Cleaver approaching them. "In case

you hadn't noticed, Art, we've got a damned war starting here."

"The DEA will be here tomorrow, leave it up to them."

Kane shook his head. "You're full of shit."

"What's that supposed to mean?"

"It means, you crooked son of a bitch, that you're on the cartel payroll and set us up to die."

Cleaver snorted. "I know what happened to the drugs from Sully's. You've been using them. Stupid asshole."

"It's true, Art," Cara said. "I didn't want to believe it but tonight proved it."

Cleaver's face screwed up. "Not you ..."

There was an audible slap followed by a loud grunt escaping Cleaver's lips. He buckled at the knees and sank to the ground.

"Sniper!" Kane exclaimed. "Get the hell down!"

He took cover behind Cleaver's SUV which was parked beside the Tahoe. Cara joined him, and they helplessly scanned the dark for a shooter.

Kane gripped his HK and lowered himself back down.

"That came from a fair distance," Cara observed.

"Where though?"

Cara shrugged.

"The shooter would need to be up high with a clear field of fire. Everything around here is too close."

She thought for a moment. "The old water tower. It's the only place."

"Where is it?"

She told him.

"Give me your keys. I'm going after him."

Cara gave them up, and Kane, keeping low, opened the driver's door on the Tahoe. He leaned in and put the HK on the passenger seat. He was about to climb in when Cara grabbed his shoulder. "He still could be up there."

"I guess we'll find out."

With swift movements, Kane climbed into the driver's seat and engaged the key. He gave it a turn, and the engine started first go.

Once it was running, he engaged reverse and mashed his foot on the accelerator until he was far enough out onto the street then stopped and selected drive, bracing himself for the expected impact of another round to shatter the windshield.

When it didn't happen, he slammed the pedal to the floor once again, and with a screech of tires, the Tahoe shot forward up the street. The Ford was gone by the time Kane reached the water tower. The Tahoe skidded to a halt, and he flung the door open. Taking the HK when he exited, Kane moved around the door to take cover behind the engine compartment.

No shots came, and all he could hear was the tick of the SUV's engine. With the HK up to his shoulder, Kane drew a bead on the top of the tower and tried to see if anyone was there. He doubted it.

Still, no shots came, and Kane was about to climb back into the Tahoe when the faint thumping sound of helicopter rotors reached his ears, and he scanned the sky. Far off in the distance to the south-west, he could just make out the flash of navigation lights.

"Gotcha."

Kane bundled himself back into the Tahoe and floored it. The back end fishtailed and gripped when he hit the blacktop again. He pointed it out of town, and the vehicle topped out at a hundred along the straight road.

Off to his two o'clock, he could see the lights of the helicopter a lot brighter now. It was much lower too, almost down to pick up the shooter.

Suddenly Kane jammed his foot on the brakes, and the Tahoe's anti-lock braking brought it to a shuddering stop. He slammed the shift into reverse and backed up around fifty yards until he came level with the gravel road he'd overshot.

He turned to the right and once more the Tahoe was careening along at a reckless rate.

Kane seemed oblivious of the road corrugations as the vehicle rattled and shook violently, drawing ever closer to the helicopter. The navigation lights shone brightly as the helicopter began to lift from the ground, its rotors beating out a steady whop-whop-whop.

The headlights on the Tahoe picked up the back of the Ford as it disappeared behind a combination cloud of dust created by both the vehicle and the rotor blades.

The SUV slid to a stop, and Kane leaped from the cab. He brought up the HK and cut loose with a stream of bullets at the helicopter.

The Sikorsky did a one-eighty in the air, and although it took some hits from the HK, seemed untroubled and flew off into the darkness.

Kane stopped firing and cursed out loud, "Shit!"

He turned and stared in the direction the Ford had gone but saw nothing. He kicked the dirt. "Damn it."

———

By noon the following day, it seemed like the sky had opened and rained law enforcement. State Troopers, FBI, ATF, all had been dispatched with the utmost haste. As suspected, Art Cleaver had never even contacted them after the death of the Retribution sheriff.

When Ferrero and Pete Traynor arrived, the town looked like a damned circus in the making; cars everywhere, news trucks with their satellites on top. The sheriff's office had been taped off, and there was a one block exclusion zone where no one but law enforcement was allowed to tread.

"Christ, Pete, what the hell have we got here?" Ferrero growled when he saw the throng before them.

Pete Traynor was a tall man with broad shoulders and an unshaven face. Before he'd been transferred to the Washington office, he had served time across the border as an undercover agent.

That was before he'd been sold out by an agent on the cartel's payroll. He'd been lucky to get out alive. If it hadn't been for Ferrero going off the reservation and coming into Mexico to pull him out, he'd have died under the torturous intent of a psychotic cartel boss.

Ferrero stopped the GMC just shy of the cordon when they were approached by a state trooper. "You can't go any further this way, sir."

Ferrero flashed his credentials. "What's going on?"

"There was an incident here last night."

"What kind of incident?"

"Had some cartel action here. Four of the cartel were killed, plus a deputy."

"Wouldn't happen to be a female, would it?"

"No, sir. You'll find her over at a temporary command post at a diner just around the corner."

Ferrero gazed out the windshield at the crime scene techs who were going over the site with a fine-toothed comb.

He nodded. "All right, thanks."

He put the GMC in drive and moved on around the corner that the trooper had indicated and parked next to an SUV with an ATF sticker on the side.

Inside the diner was a bottleneck of agents. Ferrero shook his head and stood up on a chair.

"Hey!" he shouted at the top of his voice. "Who's in charge of ... all this?"

A bald man stepped forward. "I am. Forest, FBI. Who are you?"

Ferrero ignored the question. Instead, he said, "You and me, outside."

Kane and Cara stood off to one side and watched both men leave the crowded diner, a man wearing a jacket with ATF stenciled on the back, trailing along behind.

"Is that your friend?" she asked.

"Yeah."

Ten minutes later they returned. This time it was the FBI man who stood on the chair and spoke. "Listen up. All FBI and ATF, we're done here. State will process the crime scene and DEA is taking over everything else."

And that was it. Done and dusted.

Once the room cleared, only Cara and Kane, along with the two DEA agents were all that remained.

Ferrero said, "What a fucking fiasco."

He turned to Kane. "Once again, Reaper, we're hip deep in shit, and you're at the center of it."

"Good to see you, Luis," Kane greeted and held out his right hand.

The agent took it in a firm grip and patted him on the shoulder. He looked at Cara. "You'd be Deputy Billings?"

"That's me. Cara."

"Call me Luis or Ferrero."

Cara nodded.

Ferrero said, "All right, let's get right to it. Tell me what happened last night."

They told him about the cartel men, about how Cleaver had set them up, the sniper, and the escape in the helicopter.

"What about the drugs that are coming through here?"

"They're being distributed by a criminal named Barrett Miller," Cara said. "We've raided him time after time and come up empty. But with Art giving him information, we were up against it from the start."

Ferrero was quiet for a moment before he said, "Just give me a few minutes. I want to make a couple of calls. I won't be long."

They waited patiently while Ferrero went outside and did what he had to do. Twenty minutes later he was back. He said, "Reaper, how would you like to come and work with the DEA for a few days?"

"Doing what?"

"Whatever I tell you to do."

He glanced at Cara. "I don't know."

Ferrero said, "You too, Cara. I want you on this as well."

"What about my job?"

"It now falls under the jurisdiction of the Pima County sheriff. So, you're out of a job. If all this works out, I might even offer you a full-time position."

Cara was stunned. "Why? You don't know me."

"I did some digging on you. Impressive military record. Also, read where you were mixed up in that embassy fiasco. Same one as Reaper. That's good enough for me."

"What are you going to do?" Kane asked.

Ferrero smiled. "You remember when we were in Colombia? What was the best way to piss off a cartel?"

"Steal its money."

"And that's what we're going to do."

"How?" Cara asked. "We don't even know where it is."

"Your boy Barrett. He's selling the product, which means he has the money somewhere."

"You want to raid his place? When?"

"No time like the present. How about tonight?"

They nodded.

"Good, we'll do it then."

CHAPTER 10

RETRIBUTION

"Cara, you and Traynor take the back door, Kane and I'll go in the front."

"Do you think they're expecting trouble?" Kane asked, making a point about the four, armed guards that roved the perimeter.

"Too bad if they are. They'll get no quarter from us. Shoot to kill anything with a weapon. Ready?"

They all nodded.

"Let's go. Reaper, you lead. Cara, you follow. Once the guards are down, we split up."

Kane led out, the silenced HK 416 raised and ready. Behind him, Cara did the same. They walked side by side to keep each other's line of fire clear.

Kane's HK fired once, and the guard on the right of the house jerked and then dropped without a sound. "Target down."

Cara followed suit, and the other guard did the same. "Target two down."

They kept moving across the dead grass until they reached the house. There were lights on inside, and they could hear noises from within. Kane used hand signals to direct Cara around to the left while he worked his way to the front door. He was almost there when he heard Cara's voice, "Target four down."

He and Ferrero paused for a few heartbeats. Kane used more hand signals to direct the DEA agent to watch the corner of the house. He took an M84 stun grenade from his tactical vest and readied himself to breach.

Cara's voice came to him again. "Team two ready to breach."

"On my mark. Three, two, ..."

Suddenly Ferrero opened fire. "Target three down."

"Shit. Go, go, go."

Kane kicked the door open, pulled the pin on the M84, and threw it down a long hallway.

At the far end, a gang member appeared. He was holding what looked to be an AK or something similar. Kane ducked back to shield himself from the blast about to occur.

The M84 exploded, and he heard the man at the end of the hall screech. Without hesitation, he moved through the doorway and shot the gangster in the chest.

Kane started along the hallway until he reached a closed door on the left. Trying the knob, the door sprang free of the latch. He pushed it and moved into the room. It was empty, so he reversed and continued along the passage.

Ahead of him on the right was another door. This one opened, and a redheaded man without a shirt emerged holding a handgun. The HK fired again, and the wall beside the doorway looked as though some bizarre abstract artist had created an overpriced masterpiece from splattered red paint after the NATO round blew the back of his head out.

"Reaper? Cara. You got a Tango headed for the front door."

"Roger."

A figure with a handgun appeared in the hallway. The gun was quickly brought up ready to fire at Kane but not fast enough. Another shot from the HK, another kill.

The commotion from the rear of the house carried to him as Cara and Traynor cleared the rooms back there. When Kane reached the door from which the redhead had emerged, he burst through it and found a young woman sitting there naked, terrified, with her hands over her ears.

"Stay there," he barked.

Backing out of the room Kane kept moving. He turned the corner at the end of the hall where it opened out into a large living area.

Suddenly a gang member appeared with an automatic rifle in his hands. He depressed the trigger, and the weapon burned through a full magazine in zero time.

The slugs ripped through the plaster walls where Kane had been only moments before. Had he not ducked back behind the corner he would have been killed.

The weapon stopped firing, and he heard the gang member curse loudly. Moving forward again, Kane leaned around the corner and shot him in the head.

The dead man fell back across a glass-topped coffee table. It shattered on impact under his weight and sprayed glass across the living room.

"On your right!" Ferrero snapped.

Kane pivoted and saw the woman dressed in jeans and

singlet top. She wasn't armed and seemed terrified of the situation.

"Get on the floor!" Kane shouted. "Do it! Get on the floor! Put your hands behind your head."

The woman didn't hesitate. She dropped to her knees and fell to her face. Her hands went behind her head, and she lay there trembling.

Then Buck emerged. Limping, arm in a sling, and a small Steyr TMP in his good hand, he brought the weapon up and pointed it in Kane's direction.

"Fuck you, you son of a bitch!" he howled and fired.

Kane and Ferrero dived behind the sofa as the weapon roared to life. 9 mm bullets tore ragged holes through the material and with each shot, the barrel rose. Before long, the Steyr had stitched a row of holes up the wall and into the ceiling.

"Asshole," Ferrero cursed and rose. He fired and put two slugs from his handgun into the crazed gangster's chest.

Buck staggered back and crashed into the television, knocking it to the floor. The screen shattered, and he fell across it, a load of black glass shards lodged in his back, and never moved.

"You know him?" Ferrero asked.

"Yeah. I shot him."

"Hell, no wonder he didn't like you."

They climbed to their feet and cleared the rooms off the living room. There was no one else left. After moving into the kitchen, they found Cara and Traynor there with four gangsters sitting around the dining table. Three men and a woman. Another male was dead on the floor.

Kane's eyes settled on Barrett. "We meet again."

"Fuck you."

Traynor gave him a solid smack on the back of his head. "Language, asshole. Ladies present."

"Fucking where?"

Traynor hit him again.

There were two more rooms that ran off the kitchen. Cara and Traynor had cleared those. The DEA agent indicated the second door. "Have a peep in there, Luis. You'll think it's Christmas."

Kane and Ferrero walked through the doorway and found the table stacked with small packets and larger keys of dope.

Ferrero gave it a satisfied nod and turned away. Back in the kitchen, he looked at the group sitting at the table and said, "I'm going to cut a deal with the first one of you who sings. Those who don't should be looking at a long stay in the big house."

No one spoke.

"All right, I'll make this a little easier. I'll tell you what I want to know, and you can decide. Now, where's Montoya's money?"

Barrett chuckled.

"What's so funny?"

"We ain't got his money."

"You sell the stuff for him, so you must have the money. Where is it?"

Barrett looked Ferrero in the eye and smirked. "We don't have it on account he already took it. You're too late, Agent Dick."

"Shit!"

"Yeah, and you're standing right in it,' Barrett gloated.

Ferrero's fist shot forward and smashed the gang leader in the mouth. Barrett's head snapped back, and then it lolled forward. Blood ran from the unconscious man's slack mouth and down onto the top of his white singlet.

"There," Ferrero said, "that's better."

"What are we going to do with them?" Cara asked.

"You still have a jail, don't you?"

"Kind of."

"Then that'll do until we work something out."

———

Chester saw four men dressed in black suits get out of the SUV, and for some reason, his mind immediately thought of the movie, *The Godfather*.

He grew nervous as they approached the door, and two of them entered while the others remained outside.

"Ah ... something I can do for you gents? A room?" Chester stammered.

The larger of the two men said, "We're looking for a feller."

"Plenty of them in town," Chester said, trying to lighten the mood. When the man didn't respond, he continued, "Yes, sir, plenty ... of them ... around ... ah, what's this feller's name?"

"Kane."

Chester stared past him and made out he was deep in thought. His gaze came back, and he shook his head. "Nope. Can't say I recall that name."

The big man held out his hand. "Register."

"What?"

"Give me your register."

"I don't have one."

The big man stepped forward and grabbed the closed A4 book on the right of the counter and turned it around.

"Oh, that ... register ..." his voice trailed away under the stare of the second man.

The big man opened the ledger and flicked through the pages until he found what he wanted. Then he ran a finger down the column. It stopped when it reached Kane's name and ran across the page until it located the room number.

The big man looked up. "Is he there?"

Chester shook his head.

The big man opened his coat to display a shoulder holster with a gun nestled in it. Chester paled. "He's not, honest. I ain't seen him all day. Ever since the shootout and the deputy got killed. And the DEA and a whole heap of others turned up afterward; it's just been crazy."

"What other law enforcement?"

"FBI, ATF, State Troopers. But they've all gone now. Well, most of them. The DEA and a few State Troopers are still here."

The big man thought for a moment and then said, "We're going outside to wait for him to come back. If you warn him, or I even get wind that you tried, I'll come back here and kill you. Do you understand?"

Chester nodded.

"Good."

They turned and left.

"Shit," mumbled Chester. "Shit, shit, shit."

———

"Man, I ain't seen a building with the crap shot out of it like this since I was last in Afghanistan," said Ferrero as he walked through the sheriff's office. Every one of his steps brought a crunch to his ears.

"You should have been in here when it was going on," Kane said. "It wasn't the most joyous experience."

"I'd love to get that son of a bitch on U.S. soil," Ferrero said.

"He'd need a good reason."

"If we could have got his money, that would've done the trick."

"Maybe we still can," Traynor put in.

Ferrero frowned. "How?"

"I still have a few contacts south of the border. One of them might know where he keeps it."

"And then what?" Cara asked. "Steal it?"

Ferrero shook his head. "It's too risky."

"Just think about it, Luis," Traynor said.

"If I let you go, it would be off the books," Ferrero pointed out. "There would be no backup. It would be a recon mission, nothing else."

Traynor nodded. "OK."

"I'll think about it."

"Good enough."

"Now, who's going to sit on the criminals for what's left of the night?"

Traynor said, "I'll do it."

Cara sighed. "Good. I'm out of here. I can hear my bed calling me."

———

When Kane awoke, he forgot where he was for a moment. The sound of the ceiling fan brought back memories of countless helicopter rides and insertions.

Half asleep he mumbled, "Check your gear."

"I said what are you doing here?"

Kane cracked an eyelid at the sound of the strange voice and turned his head. He stared at Jimmy with the same eye and said, "It was too far to walk to the motel."

Jimmy shrugged. "Could be worse I suppose. You could be in her bed."

Without thinking, Kane shot back, "Depends if you were me or not."

The kid gave him a look of disgust and shook his head. "You want coffee?"

"Sure."

"Black? No sugar? Strong?"

"You're good."

"Not really. My mom was a marine too, remember?"

Kane nodded. "Yeah."

He sat up and looked around the living room. It was small and sparsely furnished. The walls showed cracks and another part had a giant stain of some sort on it.

Cara entered the room. She'd obviously just gotten out of the shower. Gone was the uniform, replaced by jeans and a white T-shirt. Her hair was still damp and combed straight. She stared at him and gave him a wry smile. "Depends if you were me or not?"

Kane turned red. "Oh, crap."

"Thin walls, Reaper. Old house. Not that it wasn't flattering to hear that I've still got it, but my kid?"

"Yeah, sorry about that. Just kind of slipped out."

"How did you sleep?"

Kane straightened out another kink. "You need a new sofa."

"I need a new damned house."

"I've slept in worse places."

"Thanks a lot. Tonight, you sleep in your motel."

"That's one of them."

They laughed.

Cara asked, "How serious do you think Ferrero was about giving me a job after this is all over?"

"If he says he will, then he will."

"I hope so. I'd love to get Jimmy out of here."

"Yeah, I don't blame you."

"You want some breakfast?"

"Sure, why not."

"Pancakes?"

"Sounds better than MREs."

"Anything's better than MREs."

They walked through to the kitchen, and Kane pulled up a stool to the breakfast bar. Jimmy was just finishing with the coffees.

Taking the mug he was offered, Kane took a sip. It was hot and bitter, just the way he liked it.

"This is good."

The pancakes were even better. Kane was halfway through his meal when there was a knock at the door.

Cara answered it and found Ferrero on the step. "Come on in. You're just in time for breakfast."

They came back to the kitchen, and Cara made the agent some breakfast. He started to stuff his face when Kane asked, "What's up, Luis?"

"Why does something have to be up?"

"You came here for a reason."

Ferrero glanced at Jimmy. Cara saw the look and said, "Jimmy, give us a moment, can you?"

Once he was gone Ferrero said, "I have news."

Kane said, "About what?"

"After everything that has gone down here, I made a call to one of the higher-ups. Bottom line, I've been given the

OK to put together a small team to do whatever it takes to put a stop to Montoya."

"I thought you guys already had Special Response Teams?"

Ferrero smiled. "Have you ever seen that show on television, Strike something or other?"

"Strike Back?" said Cara.

"That's it. Well, consider us the DEA's version of Section-20. Traynor has already left for Nogales. You two will be my *strike* power."

Ferrero paused and focused on Cara. "If you say yes, your job here is done. We'll use Retribution as a base until it's time to take it across the border. Well?"

Kane could see that she wanted to say yes, but there was one thing that stopped her. "What about Jimmy?"

"Do you have any other family?"

She shook her head.

"I guess we'll have to work something out."

"Before you say no, Cara," Kane said. "I might know of a place that could take him when you're not around."

"Good," Ferrero said before she could speak. "What about you, Reaper?"

Kane hesitated as he remembered what had brought him to Retribution in the first place. "Before you sign me up, I need to tell you something."

Ferrero smiled at Cara, "Sounds serious."

"A while back, I worked for a firm called The Gilbert Foundation. We, Hammer and me, were sitting on a couple in West Virginia in a safe house."

Recognition registered in Ferrero's eyes. "You were mixed up in that?"

"In what?" Cara asked.

Kane continued. "The people, a husband, and wife

were meant to testify against Irish mob boss, Colin O'Brien. The man we worked for betrayed us. Sold us out for money. A team of British mercenaries came in to kill the witnesses and us too. When the dust had settled, I was the only one left."

"Hammer?" Cara asked.

"Yeah, Hammer."

Cara gave him a sorrowful look.

"Anyway, I knew it was Gilbert because when I tried to call him right before they hit us, the phone had been disconnected. I went to his house and found out all I needed to. Just as I finished with him, O'Brien's enforcer showed up. Tidying loose ends."

"Was it them who shot Gilbert?" Ferrero asked.

Kane stared at Cara. He shook his head. "That was me. He gave O'Brien files on us all. He found out I had a sister."

"What did you do?"

"I went after him."

Ferrero snorted. "That's the Reaper I know."

"O'Brien had a place in New York. He liked to take his victims down into the basement. When I was there, he had a feller strapped to a chair. He was already dead. I ended up shooting O'Brien, his son, and his enforcer. There were a few others too."

"It was a pity you didn't kill the son of a bitch," Ferrero said.

Kane's head snapped about. "What?"

Ferrero nodded. "He's still alive."

"Shit! That means he'll be looking for me and Melanie."

"Where is she?" Cara asked.

"I found a place for her in Maine. I hid her up there before I went after O'Brien. I was going to suggest Jimmy go there when you're working. The man who runs it is an ex-marine surgeon. I'll have to call to let him know about O'Brien."

"You don't believe in having normal enemies, do you?" Ferrero commented.

"Now that you know, do you still want me on your team?"

"Hell yeah. That ain't no reason to cut you. After this is all done, you'll most likely have killed a lot more scumbags."

Kane stared at Cara. "What about you?"

"I'm good."

Ferrero wrung his hands. "There you have it. Welcome to Team Reaper."

———

Chester looked up from what he was doing and saw them there. The scary part was that they'd made no sound, so he'd never even heard them. They'd been out there for hours, and now it was morning, they didn't look happy.

"Where is he?" the big man asked.

"I – I don't know?"

"You warned him, didn't you?"

With a furious shake of his head, Chester said, "No, no."

The big man took out his gun and then reached into his pocket. His hand came out with a cylindrical tube which he screwed to the end of the weapon.

"Did you warn him?"

"No, no."

"Put your hand on the counter."

Chester never moved.

The big man nodded to his friend who walked around the end of the counter and drew his own gun. He placed it against the side of Chester's head and with his left hand, grabbed Chester's right and placed it on top of the counter.

Once more he placed the end of the silencer against flesh and repeated his question, "Did you warn him?"

There was terror in the motel owner's eyes and sweat formed on his wrinkled brow. He shook his head, unable to speak.

The gun fired.

Chester screeched as the bullet smashed through bone and flesh, the heavy timber of the countertop retarding its downward motion. Reflexively, he dragged the wounded hand back and cradled it against his chest. Blood ran from the wound, leaking between his fingers, and dripped onto the floor at the motel owner's feet.

He gasped in pain and tears ran from his eyes. Fear took hold fully now, and his bladder let go, and he pissed himself.

"The other hand," the big man said in a calm voice.

Chester took a step back and shook his head. "No. Please, no!"

The other man drove the barrel of his gun up under the frightened motel owner's chin. Through gritted teeth, he said, "The other fucking hand. Now!"

The hand went up onto the countertop, and Chester felt the splinters from the previous shot dig into his palm. The end of the silencer touched the back of his hand, and he tried to pull it back. The other mobster, however, prevented him from doing so.

"Where is he?"

Chester opened his mouth to answer, but nothing came out. He knew that if he said what he was going to, the man would shoot him again. He clamped his jaw shut.

"I'll ask you once more, and then I'll shoot you. Where is he?"

"I don't ... No, wait. The female deputy, Cara. She might know."

"Where do I find her?"

"Maybe her house."

"Where?"

Chester told him. When he was finished, he blurted out, "Please don't kill me."

The big man stared at him for a moment with a contemptuous look and then shot him in the head.

———

Kane hung up from the call and placed the cell back into his pocket.

"Is she OK?" Cara asked.

"Yeah. No one's been there asking."

"That's good."

"I asked him about Jimmy. He said there would be room for him there anytime you wanted it."

"That's something I guess."

Ferrero appeared. "All right, I have a mobile team that will be here day after tomorrow. They'll bring with them vehicles, armaments, and a few other odds and ends that we'll need."

"How many in this team?"

"Three."

"Big team."

"Big enough. What we do need, however, is a place to house us for the duration," he turned to Cara. "Any ideas?"

"There are a lot of abandoned buildings about the town. Take your pick."

"The old furniture store across the road from the motel I'm at," Kane said. "It looks big enough."

Ferrero nodded. "Let's see, shall we?"

They agreed, and Cara turned around. "Jimmy?"

He appeared in the doorway, a wireless PlayStation controller in his hands. "Yeah?'

"Yes."

He rolled his eyes. "Yes."

"I'm going out for a bit. We'll be back soon."

"Kay."

"Yes, ma'am."

Another eye roll. "Yes, ma'am."

———

The black SUV parked along the street, and the four men in it watched them drive off. The man behind the wheel said, "You want me to follow, Bannon?"

"No."

"Why not?"

"Look at the front yard of the house. What do you see?"

"Junk?"

"What kind of junk?"

"Kid's junk."

"Now you're seeing it," Bannon said.

"What's a bunch of kid's junk got to do with it?" the driver asked.

The man in the seat behind clipped him in the back of the head.

"Ouch, what did you do that for?"

"Because you're stupid. What Bannon means is that there's a kid that lives here. Instead of us going after them, we make Kane come to us."

"Oh. I knew that."

"Putz."

"Get us over to the house."

The driver turned the key, and the engine started to purr. He eased it into drive, and they pulled away from the curb.

A minute later Bannon knocked on the door. After about twenty seconds, Jimmy opened it and looked up into the face of the big man in the suit.

Bannon smiled. "Hi, kid."

————

They pulled up in the lot across from the motel and climbed out of Ferrero's vehicle. Standing in front of the building, they cast a cursory eye over it. There was a main entrance door at the front and a large roller-door on the right side.

The building itself was wide and long.

They walked around to a side door and tested it. It remained closed.

"Locked," Ferrero said.

Cara pushed past him and kicked it next to the mechanism. The door sprung back, and Cara stepped aside. "After you."

Inside was much like the exterior, rundown and dirty and had that unused smell about it. The main floor was open plan and stairs ran up to a mezzanine office area. Out the back where the storage area would have been, all the shelving and such had been removed, and it was like the front portion, open and empty. However, it would comfortably accommodate quite a few vehicles.

Ferrero nodded. "This'll do. We can set up in the building, have a place to park the vehicles; our people will slot right in."

Kane walked to the far end of the building and looked out the rear window. The building took up the width of the block and a street ran along behind it. Weeds grew from a seldom-used footpath that had cracks and dips in it.

He turned away from the window and walked back to the center of the warehouse area where Cara stood. He was about to speak when her cell buzzed in her pocket. She took it out and looked at the screen, frowned, and then answered.

"Hello?"

"Put Kane on."

"Who is this?"

"If you want to see your kid again, you'll do as I say. Put him on."

Cara's eyes opened impossibly wide, and Kane could tell that something was very wrong.

She snarled into the phone, "If you hurt him, I'll kill you, asshole!"

"Put him the fuck on!"

There was a moment of hesitation before she handed the cell to Kane. Anxiety was etched on her face, and she began to wring her hands. "They've got Jimmy."

"Who has?" Ferrero snapped.

Kane put the cell to his ear. "Kane."

"We've got the bitch's kid. Who we really want is you. We'll trade, you for him."

"Who are you?"

"You know who I am."

Kane thought for a moment. "You're not O'Brien. That makes you Bannon. Am I right?"

"You'll have to come to find out."

"Where?"

"Edge of town. The place called Arno's, you know it?"

"Yeah."

"After dark. Come alone."

Kane passed the cell back to Cara. "Who are they? Who has Jimmy?"

"They're muscle for O'Brien."

She gasped.

"What do they want?" Ferrero asked.

"Me. They said to meet them at Arno's, after dark. They said they'll trade."

"And you're entertaining the idea?"

"Nope."

Ferrero's eyes shot across to Cara. She said, "They won't let him go. He'll have seen their faces. The only chance to get him back alive is to take him by force."

Kane looked at Ferrero. "We'll need communications and weapons."

The DEA agent nodded. "I can do communications."

"I can get the weapons we'll need," Cara told him and held up a set of keys.

Kane said, "Let's do it."

They'd only just gone outside when the first of the stationed deputy's cars pulled up at the motel, siren howling.

Kane growled. "I think I know where they found out about Jimmy."

CHAPTER 11

RETRIBUTION

Kane felt nervous. Not about the impending action, but the fact that there was a kid in the mix. Cara's kid, and he'd be damned if he was going to let anything happen to him.

He'd waited for an hour without any sign of Bannon. The temperature had dropped significantly as it did in the desert at night. Especially with no cloud cover.

Arno's was shrouded in darkness, the only illumination, the quarter moon which had started its arc across the sky.

Cara and Ferrero had set up earlier, before dark. Ferrero was inside the gas station in tactical gear and armed with a Colt M4 carbine, while Cara was on a ridge, hidden in a clump of boulders some three hundred meters out. Her right eye stared through a night scope perched on top of an M110 semi-automatic sniper rifle. It had a range of eight hundred meters and fired a 7.62mm round.

Even though it was dark, with a clear field of fire, she would hit anything she aimed at.

Kane was the only one not wearing tactical gear. All he had were his communications, and the H&K USP tucked into the back of his pants.

"Zero, we've got a vehicle inbound, maybe a mile out."

With everything that was at risk, Cara was being a consummate professional. Kane heard Ferrero answer. "Copy, Reaper Two. Reaper One, you copy that last?"

"Roger, Zero. Reaper Two, just one? Over."

"Roger, Reaper One. Only one vehicle."

"Copy," there was a pause. "Cara?"

"I'm here."

"Don't miss."

Kane remained beside Ferrero's SUV and waited. Suddenly the lights on the approaching vehicle appeared, followed by the sound of the engine.

"Here we go. I'll buy the beers when we're done."

The SUV with the kidnappers in it pulled off the road and did a full circle on the gravel around Kane's position before it stopped in a cloud of dust, headlights still on.

Kane waited for them to emerge. He said softly, "Reaper Two, you got a clear line of sight?"

"Roger."

"Wait for my signal."

Four doors opened, and men disembarked from each. He recognized Bannon who walked to the front of the vehicle. The driver moved out to the left while one of the men who'd climbed from the back moved out to the right. The fourth man stayed beside an open left rear door. All were armed with handguns.

"You look a mite better than the last time I saw you," Kane said, as a way to break the silence.

Bannon said, "So does my boss."

"Pity that."

"Did you come alone?"

"Would you expect me to? I mean, did you? You don't think I'm a total moron, do you? Ferrero, come out."

"Reaper, what are you doing?" Cara asked hurriedly.

"Easy, Reaper Two," Ferrero said. His voice was calm and professional. If Kane's action had taken him by surprise, he didn't show it.

The door to the gas station opened, and Ferrero walked out, the M4 cradled across his chest.

Bannon wasn't happy. "You were told to come alone."

"What? And have you kill me and the kid. Not how it works. Where is Jimmy?"

Bannon waved a hand at the man by the rear door. He said a few words to someone inside and then stepped back.

Jimmy climbed out and went to walk forward but was stopped by his guard.

"Are you happy now?" Bannon asked.

"Bring him closer. I want to see if he's all right."

The mobster and Jimmy came closer. "Are you happy now?" repeated Bannon.

"Are you OK, Jimmy?"

"Yes, sir."

"It'll all be over soon. Just walk to me."

The man with Jimmy placed his handgun against the boy's head.

"That ain't how this works," Bannon threw his own words back at him.

Kane nodded. "It's OK, Jimmy. If you're scared, just close your eyes."

"What are you up to?" the man with Jimmy snarled.

Kane ignored him. "Just close your eyes."

"He's up to something, Bannon," the man said, his voice starting to crack. "He's fucking up to something."

"Take it easy," Bannon cautioned.

Kane's right hand edged around behind his back. "That's it, keep them closed."

"No! No! It ain't right, Bannon. It ain't fucking right!" the man screeched, and he took the gun from Jimmy's head and began to point it at Kane.

The 7.62 NATO round whistled out of the night. There was a sickening wet sound as it punched through the mobster's head and blew his brains out all over the gravel. There was no sound to the shot because the weapon Cara had used was silenced.

Before the rest of the mob men could react, another round slapped into the mobster on the right, and he dropped without making a sound.

After the first bullet impacted the man with Jimmy, Kane wrapped his right hand around the H&K's grip and brought it forward and up. Once the foresight settled on Bannon, Kane squeezed the trigger. The slug hammered into the enforcer's chest and made him stagger. He fought to bring up his gun, but before he could, Kane fired three more shots in quick succession. All of them grouped about the first.

Bannon jerked under the impact of them like an epileptic drunk. Then his legs refused to hold his weight, and he sank to his knees, head slumped forward onto his chest.

Off to his right, Kane heard Ferrero open fire with his M4. A line of bullets stitched the last surprised mobster from crotch to throat. Their force threw him onto his back in the dirt where he spasmed and died.

With the echoes of the shots fading across the desert, Kane moved forward, his progression swift, his H&K still trained on Bannon. When he reached the enforcer, there was no movement. The man just knelt there, arms limp at his sides, head resting on his chest, blood dribbling from his slack mouth.

Kane said, "We're clear."

He checked Bannon's coat while Ferrero checked on Jimmy. In the inside top pocket, he found the enforcer's cell. He pushed a few buttons and found only numbers. He started to try them.

The first belonged to someone named Michael. The second, a woman named Francis from some business in Manhattan. He struck gold with the third.

It rang twice, then, "Did you do it?"

"They're all dead."

Silence.

"Is it you?"

"Is it me what?"

"Are you the bastard who shot me and killed my son?"

"Yeah."

O'Brien's voice grew cold. "I will kill you."

"Piece of advice for you, Paddy," Kane growled. "If you keep sending men after me, I'll kill them all and then come after you. However, if you're not some chickenshit asshole, come after me yourself, and we'll have it out. It might save a few of your subordinate's lives."

"I'll cut your fucking heart –"

Kane hung up. "Yeah, yeah, whatever."

He looked up to see Cara jog out of the darkness. She carried the M110 in her right hand, and when she reached Jimmy, laid it on the ground to have her arms free to wrap the boy up.

"Oh, Jimmy. Are you OK?"

"I'm OK," he said, more than a little shaken.

"Did they hurt you?"

"No."

She hugged him again.

Kane walked over to them and tossed the cell to Ferrero. "You might find something useful on there."

Jimmy noticed the rifle on the ground and stared at the body of the man who'd held him. "Was that you, Ma?"

Cara hesitated. "Yes."

He looked at her, his eyes as wide as saucers. "Wow! You are shit hot!"

"Jimmy Billings!" she scolded. "That was not shit hot. That was me keeping you safe. It is something I hope you never have to do in your life."

"Is he all right?" Kane asked.

"Yes, thanks to you."

He shook his head. "It was because of me that he was in this mess."

Cara stared at her son. "Jimmy, I need to keep you safe. You can't stay in Retribution. I have a place for you to go where you'll be safe."

"OK," he said, which took her by surprise.

She patted him on the shoulder. "Agent Ferrero has a way to get you there. I need to finish the job here."

"I understand."

Cara hugged him again. "I knew you would."

"I hate to break up the party," Ferrero said. "I think we need to do something about this mess."

Kane glanced at Cara and then at Ferrero. He said, "I'm sure you can sort that out."

They began to walk away, Jimmy in tow.

"Hey, where are you going?"

No answer.

"Hey!"

They kept walking.

"Shit!"

———

Nogales, Sonora

Pete Traynor wandered into the stinking backstreet bar and stopped. It had changed some since he'd been there last. It certainly wasn't just a bar anymore, that was for sure. The premises had been extensively renovated with the bar pushed back, new lighting, large mirrors against one wall, stripper poles, and armed men were strategically placed around the large room. Cartel men.

Nogales was the newest center for the cartel drug wars. On one side was the Sonora Cartel, on the other, the Nogales Cartel. And in the center, Montoya had driven a deep wedge between them both.

The resulting bloody war had claimed a staggering ten thousand lives over the past five years alone; not all those cartel members. That wasn't factoring in the deaths on the Arizona side.

Nogales law enforcement drove the streets in armored vehicles for their own safety. Although, with all the illegal arms that the cartels could get hold of, every now and then someone would pop up with an RPG-7 and blow the car to hell and gone. Weapons were the one thing there was never a shortage of.

It wasn't uncommon to see members of various drug task forces on the streets, wearing balaclavas to hide their identity. But hell, they were far from bulletproof, and hardly a day went by without some kind of blazing gunfight on the deadly streets of Nogales.

If you represented the law in any way, shape or form, you were a target; from the judges and lawyers, right down to the very lowest of the low on the law enforcement ladder.

Judging by the tattoos that these fellers wore, Traynor guessed they were Sonora Cartel.

Like the bar, Traynor had changed too. Gone were the clothes he'd worn in Retribution, replaced by torn jeans, a shirt with the sleeves ripped out, and a jacket which had the same done to it.

Being sleeveless exposed his muscular arms with tattoos, most of which he'd had done when he'd worked as an undercover. In his right ear was an earring in the shape of a cross. And with the cowboy boots, he resembled a biker more than a DEA agent.

A young woman approached him, her only attire being a black thong, high-heeled shoes, and a stoned smile. Her dark-tipped breasts jutted out firmly from a bony chest.

"Hey, *hombre*," she slurred, "you here to drink or fuck? Manuela do both for you, *si?*"

He ignored her and made to step around when she blocked his path. Her face screwed up. "Am I not good enough for you, *gringo?* Is that it? You want some other *puta?*"

Traynor stared into her glazed eyes. In another life far away from here, Manuela would have been quite attractive. Most likely she'd been forced into the life she now led. He said, "I'm here to see someone."

Manuela didn't budge, and the pair had now drawn the attention of some armed cartel men. Traynor cursed under his breath and was about to leave when a voice said, 'Frig off, Manuela."

Traynor turned his head and saw a slim, blonde woman

in the same state of undress as the olive-skinned one
before him.

Manuela looked at the interloper and then threw her
arms in the air, her breasts jiggling with the action. She let
out a string of curses, turned, and stormed off.

"Thanks," Traynor said.

"If I was you, cowboy, I'd turn and leave. This ain't a
place for *gringos* if you know what I mean?"

"I'm here to see someone. He owns ... used to own this
place. His name is Rodrigo."

The woman nodded. "He's still here. You'll find him
behind the bar. But don't say you weren't warned."

"Thanks ..."

"Candy."

Traynor cocked an eyebrow. "Really?"

She gave him a tired smile. "Shit, every white whore in
here is called Candy."

"OK, then. Thanks ... Candy."

"If you want a good time after, I won't be too hard to
find."

He watched her walk off, then became aware of eyes
upon him. He turned his head and saw one of the armed
men staring at him. Traynor looked away and walked to the
bar. Standing behind it were two other mostly naked
women. And a man; Rodrigo, who looked as though he'd
seen a ghost as soon as he spotted Traynor.

Rodrigo's face paled, and he hissed, "Are you crazy?
What the fuck are you doing in here?"

"I came to see an old friend."

The Mexican nodded towards the end of the bar. They
walked along it until they were out of earshot, and Rodrigo
whispered. "You need to get out of here. If the cartel works

out who you are, they'll cut your balls off and feed them to you. Then they'll do the same to me."

Traynor ignored him. "I like what you've done with the place."

"*Mierda!* What do you want, *agente?*" Rodrigo growled impatiently.

Traynor's face hardened at the veiled threat. "Is that any way to speak to a friend?"

"We are not friends anymore," the Mexican shot back. "Not now that I have the cartel looking over my shoulder. Tell me what you want and then leave."

Traynor nodded. "I want information."

"No! Get out!" spittle flew from Rodrigo's lips.

"Nope. Not until we talk."

The Mexican stared into Traynor's eyes and could see that he was determined to get what he'd come for.

"You are crazy, you know this?"

"It ain't my first rodeo, *amigo.*"

"Wait here."

Rodrigo hurried along the bar and grabbed a bottle and two glasses. He waved at Candy and then came back and said, "We go to a booth."

"I don't want a girl."

"Listen, *amigo*, men come here for two reasons, tequila and girls. The Sonora men already watch you."

"All right."

They found an empty booth in a darker area and sat down. Candy slid in beside Traynor and started to rub the top of his thigh. As she did, she snuggled in close and started to kiss the side of his neck.

Traynor pushed her back, and he said, "I told you, I don't want a girl."

"The girl or death. The choice is yours. If it doesn't look

real, then they will get suspicious and then kill you. Now, tell me what you want and get out."

The DEA agent glanced at Candy and then back at Rodrigo. He said nothing.

Rodrigo nodded and said, "Candy, under the table."

Candy rolled her eyes. "What the hell do you want me to do under there?"

"I don't care, just make it look good."

She slid under the table, and within seconds, Traynor could feel her fumbling with his pants button. He slapped her hand away, but she came back for more.

Rodrigo guessed what was happening and said, "Tell me?"

"I –" Traynor cleared his throat as Candy took his breath away with the warmth of hers. "I need to know where Juan Montoya keeps his money."

For the second time, Rodrigo's face grew pale and fearful. He leaned in close and whispered in a harsh tone, "Are you fucking crazy? Get out! Get out and don't come back."

"I need to know, Rodrigo."

"If they find out, they will kill me."

"What does it matter? You don't work for them, and you're under the watchful eye of the Sonorans."

"It doesn't matter."

Suddenly one of the cartel men appeared around the corner of the booth. He ran a suspicious eye over them and then noticed Candy under the table. He watched her head move up and down and then smiled at Traynor. He asked, "*La puta chupa Buena?*"

Traynor nodded. "Yeah, she sucks real good."

The Mexican smiled again and moved on.

"You must go now," Rodrigo blurted out.

Under the table, Candy started to work on his cock with

more vigor. His toes began to curl in his boots, and it took all his concentration to stay on task.

"I'll leave when I have what I came for."

"Well, you're out of luck, *hombre*. I have no idea."

"Come on, Rodrigo, you and I both know that's horse-shit. You've heard something. People talk, they can't help it."

There was uncertainty in Rodrigo's eyes, and Traynor knew he had him. "Where, Rodrigo?"

"In a bank."

"Bullshit."

"It's ..." he lowered his voice. "It is true. Not a normal bank. There is an abandoned one in southern Nogales."

"Why hasn't anyone stolen it?"

"Because it is in a vault under the floor. There is an alarm that is triggered if it is disturbed. *El Hombre* can have fifty men there within minutes of it going off."

"What about guards?"

"He has none. Why would there be? Only the *estúpido* would try to steal it."

"What else?"

"That is all I know. If there is any more, you will have to find it out for yourself."

Traynor nodded.

"Now will you go?"

"Yes. In a ..." the DEA agent stopped mid-sentence as a wave of pleasure washed over him. Once he'd gathered himself, he continued, "I'll leave now."

Traynor fixed his pants and slid out from the seat. He dug into his pocket for a roll of bills, peeled a hundred off and tossed it on the table. Candy had crawled out and smiled at him. He pointed at the money and said, "There, that's for making it look good."

She took the money and walked away. Traynor stared at Rodrigo and said, "I'll be seeing you, *amigo*."

"Not if I can help it. Stay away. If someone recognizes you, they will hang pieces of you from the border fence."

Outside, the moon was rising, and the heat of the day had dissipated somewhat. Moths attracted by the bar's neon lights seemed to fill the air like a swarm of bees. Traynor looked left and right along the sidewalk but saw no one.

Tomorrow he'd find the bank used by Montoya and do some surveillance on it. For now, his room at the motel seemed a good prospect. He stepped down off the curb and started to cross the street. Behind him, standing in the shadows of the doorway was the cartel man who'd spoken to him in the bar, who waited until Traynor had slipped from view and began to follow him.

———

The sound wasn't much but was sufficient to make Traynor's eyes spring wide, and he was instantly awake. A dull orange light from the street outside shone through the holes in the curtains and gave the small room a limited illumination.

He lay there listening. Two heartbeats, three, four, fi –

The door crashed back and ripped the chain from the wall. Two tattooed men armed with automatic weapons pushed in through the opening and split up to either side of the room. They brought the guns up to fire, but Traynor was ahead of them. As soon as the DEA agent had come awake, he'd retrieved his Smith & Wesson 9mm M&P handgun from beneath his pillow.

Traynor fired twice, and the Mexican on the right

jerked as two rounds hammered into his chest. He switched his aim and brought down the second man.

Each gunshot sounded unusually loud in the confined space, and the noise only grew worse when the second Mexican squeezed the trigger on his AK-103 as he collapsed.

The bullets plowed into the ceiling, smashing the fan that hung from it. Large chunks of debris fell onto the bed, narrowly missing Traynor. He rolled to the side and onto the floor, the bed shielding him from the next intruder.

Another AK roared to life, and a jagged pattern of bullet holes appeared in the wall behind him. More debris rained down, and Traynor crawled along on his belly to the end of the bed to allow him visibility for a shot. He took a deep breath and lunged forward while the shooter fired at his last known position.

Traynor brought the Smith & Wesson to bear and fired three times. The first two slugs hit the last shooter in the chest; the third opened a grisly wound in his throat. Blood sprayed up the side wall as the cartel soldier fell back and landed with a thud on the bloody carpet.

Now that the shooting had stopped, all Traynor could hear was the sound of his labored breathing.

"Shit!" he cursed and scrambled to his feet.

There was no time to lose. People would come to see what the commotion was, maybe more cartel men. He needed to get out of there.

Hurriedly, Traynor slipped the S&W into his belt, gathered his things, slipped out the door before anyone appeared, jumped in his SUV, and roared off into the night.

———

Retribution

Ferrero was dragged from his slumber by the annoying sound of his cell ringing. He looked at the bedside clock, and the glowing red numbers on the display showed two-thirty.

Ferrero sighed heavily. "Good Christ. Who the hell rings at this time?"

He picked up the phone and pressed answer. He growled into it, "This better be damned good."

"Would you like me to call back later?"

"Shit, Pete, what's up? It's half-two."

"I just had me a visit from the Sonoran Cartel. Shot the shit out of my room while they tried to do the same to me."

Ferrero sat up. "Are you all right?"

"For the moment. I've just got to keep moving for the time being."

"How'd they get onto you?"

"Who knows. Listen, I need to tell you this just in case something happens to me. Montoya keeps his money in a bank in south Nogales."

"You're shitting me."

"Nope. That's what my contact says. I'm going to verify it tomorrow, sorry, today."

"Fuck that, come on home."

"No, we need to know. I'll be a couple more days."

Ferrero contemplated ordering him to cross back over. Instead, he said, "OK. Just keep your head down. The rest of the team should be here tomorrow."

"Roger that. I'll contact you when I know more."

"Stay safe, Pete."

―――――

Nogales

The front of the old bank looked more like a replica of the Alamo than an establishment where people had once kept their money. It was built from stone, had an arched door-way, and four windows in its façade. The main body of the building ran back along its block for perhaps twice the length of its frontage. Two tall trees stood on either side. The sign fixed above the entrance was splintered from being shot up on more than one occasion, and every panel of glass in the window frames had been shattered. Then there were the bullet holes. The façade was pockmarked with tiny craters where lead slugs had gouged them out.

Traynor watched it for most of the day and into the night. No one came. No one went. If Rodrigo hadn't told him what was there, he would have figured it to be just what it looked like. Abandoned.

The moon came up shortly after nine pm, and the only living thing the DEA agent had seen was a cat. It was as though everyone knew not to go anywhere near the build-ing. He remembered what Rodrigo had said. Armed men could be there in minutes. The thing was if the team was going to knock the bank over, he needed to know just what to expect for a response time. Traynor smiled at the thought of DEA agents robbing a bank.

He reached into his coat and took out his S&W. He checked its loads and put it back. Then Traynor climbed from the driver's seat and walked around to the rear of the SUV. He opened the back, lifted the carpet and unlocked a compartment in the floor.

Leaning in, Traynor withdrew an M84 stun grenade. If the sensors were sensitive enough, then it should do the job. There was no point in taking too much of a risk.

He relocked everything and from where he was parked, walked a hundred meters to the old bank. Once close enough, Traynor pulled the pin on the stun grenade and tossed it, so it pitched against the wall.

Then he turned and ran.

By the time the grenade blew, the DEA agent was well out of harm's way. While he jogged, he counted. He climbed back in the SUV and continued to count. Then he sat, waited, counted.

Traynor had rattled off three minutes when the first of the armed men appeared. Ten of them ran out of the darkness, armed with AKs. Six of them set up a small perimeter around the front door while the rest went inside.

"So, you ten guys are the QRF," Traynor murmured, using the abbreviated term for a Quick Reaction Force. He raised his cell and filmed them. He said, "It took these guys three minutes to arrive."

The men emerged, and one of them, obviously the leader, threw his arms around, and the cartel men started to search the exterior of the building. That was when they spotted his vehicle.

A cartel man stopped and stared into the shadows where the SUV was parked. He must have made the outline because he said something to the man in charge and pointed in Traynor's direction.

He murmured, "Time to go."

The DEA agent tapped a few icons on the cell and tossed it on the passenger seat. By the time the vehicle was started and in drive, the footage had been sent to Ferrero.

The SUV's movement signaled the start of a furious few minutes that seemed to go on forever.

The cartel men opened fire as soon as the vehicle started its U-turn. Bullets slammed into the SUV and made a sound like Traynor had driven into a severe hailstorm. The rear driver's side window shattered and when the vehicle was finally rear-on, the back one disintegrated too.

"Shit!" Traynor exclaimed when he felt a bullet embed itself into the headrest behind him.

He floored the accelerator, and the SUV's tires slipped and then bit. It shot forward and into the night. Traynor cursed loudly knowing that Ferrero wasn't going to be happy about this.

CHAPTER 12

RETRIBUTION

The rest of the team arrived mid-morning in two semi-trailers and another SUV. The first truck was pulling an expandable unit full of all the tech gear they would need. On the roof sat a satellite dish, while a front compartment held their own personal armory.

The second vehicle carried two DPVs, or Desert Patrol Vehicles. They were modeled on the ones used by U.S. forces in the First Gulf War and could carry mounted armaments.

"Where the hell did you get those dinosaurs?" Kane asked Ferrero as the vehicles rolled off the truck inside the warehouse.

He slapped Kane on the shoulder and smiled broadly as he said, "Wait until you drive it before you call it names, my friend."

"Uh huh. What's with the extra SUV?"

"That baby is fully armored. The only thing that'll stop it is a missile."

"Or an RPG."

Ferrero nodded. "Or that."

"What else have you got?"

Ferrero said, "Let's gather everyone around, and we'll get to know each other."

Stepping forward he raised his voice, "All right everyone, gather around."

They all stopped what they were doing and closed on the DEA agent.

"OK," he said, "for those who don't know me, my name is Luis Ferrero. I'm the man you come to if you have a problem, want something, or have a question regarding this team. You were all hand-picked by me because each of you has a set of skills that this team requires. From now on, we are to be known as Team Reaper. Field team call-signs will be such. Base call-signs will be Bravo."

Ferrero paused. "This guy here on my left is John Kane, the original 'Reaper'. Work with him long enough, and you'll find out why. Reaper is in charge of everything we do in the field. To his left is Cara Billings. She is his number two. She'll also be our armorer. They will do most of the heavy lifting when it comes down to the bad guys, along with agent Traynor, who isn't here right now. The fourth person on Reaper's field team is Conrad Hawkins or Hawk. He's done time in Colombia and a few other places that your mother would never let you vacation in."

Muffled laughter rippled throughout the small gathering.

Ferrero went on, "Brooke Reynolds."

A tall, athletic woman with long black hair stepped forward.

"Brooke is a computer whiz who will double in the field if required. She is also drone qualified and will be our eye in the sky," he turned to Kane. "Be nice to her, Reaper. A time may come when she is all you have between you and the bad guys."

Kane nodded.

"You can rely on me, sir."

Kane shook his head. "Call me Kane or Reaper. I ain't a sir. On this team, we're all equal. Right, Luis?"

"Right up to the point where I start chewing on someone's ass for screwing up."

More muffled laughter.

"That leaves Sam Swift."

"Swift by name and slick by nature," the tall thirty-something with red hair said. He flashed a broad smile.

"Sam is another computer tech as well as a mechanic. Every single one of us will work in the field if required. As I have said, if this happens, Reaper is in command."

"Would you like to tell us exactly what we're doing here?" Hawk asked.

Ferrero stared at him. "For a long while now, I've been at the higher-ups about forming a task force that can take the fight to the cartels. And for that very same length of time, they've just sat on their side of the fence and laughed at us. No more. A few days ago, the Saguaro County Sheriff was killed by a man known as *El Monstruo*. His real name is Cesar Salazar. He is the personal *sicario* of Juan Montoya of the Montoya Cartel. The thing is, he didn't just kill the sheriff but decapitated him. If that wasn't enough, he then sent a kill squad across the border, and they attacked the jail and tried to kill Reaper and Billings."

He paused and ran his gaze over them all. "As soon as I informed them of what had occurred here in Retribution, those in command finally said that enough is enough. They also said that I could have whatever I needed to succeed. We have a blank cheque if you like, using our discretion of course; to cross the border and shoot that little fucker between the eyes if need be, to do whatever it takes to stop the endless bloodletting along the borderlands. Montoya is where we start."

"Is that what we're going to do?" Swift asked.

Ferrero shook his head. "I'd prefer to lure him across the border and do it then. But if it comes down to it, I'll send a team to do just that."

"How do you intend to do it? Get him across, I mean."

"I have someone looking into that," Ferrero said. He shifted his gaze. "Can you get me some pictures of Montoya's compound? Satellite stuff, drone footage, whatever?"

"How soon do you want it?" she asked.

"Just as soon as."

"Can do."

"Slick, I have some footage which was sent through to me last night. I want you to download it so Reaper and Billings can look it over."

"Sure thing."

Ferrero looked at Kane. "It's from Traynor. Apparently, Montoya keeps his money in an old bank."

"No shit?"

"That's what I thought. I need a way of getting it out of there. The killer thing about it is, the place has sensors, and once they are disturbed, cartel assholes are onsite in three minutes."

Kane nodded. "I'll see what I can come up with."

"What do you want me to do?" Hawk asked.

Ferrero smiled, a sarcastic look on his face. "You get the

good task. I want you to run some surveillance on Montoya's compound. We'll have photos of the place, but I want to know the rest of it. If we have to get into that place and kill him, I want to know the best way to do it. Take one of the DPVs. Reynolds will set you up with any other kit you need."

Hawk nodded. "Roger that."

"One more thing. If any of you get into trouble, fall foul of any situation, I shall move heaven and earth to help you out. I will have your back no matter what. For that, however, I demand total loyalty. If you can't give me that, the door is over there, don't let it hit you in the ass on the way out."

No one moved.

The underlying tone was unmistakable. Kane said, "Are we deniable?"

"If something happens to you on the Mexican side, or any other place for that matter, your government will not be of any use to you whatsoever. I, on the other hand, will be your best friend. This is a chance to do something about it all. However, it isn't without danger."

"What if it's you that ends up in trouble?" Hawk asked.

"Then we're all in the shit."

No one laughed.

"All right, you've got –"

A noise from outside stopped him short.

"What the hell is that?"

They all moved to the door and passed through it. Outside, Traynor was climbing from the battered SUV which had smoke coming from beneath its hood, bullet holes in every panel, and missing glass where each window had been shattered.

Kane heard Ferrero mutter something under his breath before he said louder, "Don't tell me, you got too close?"

Traynor leaned against the vehicle. "They shoot a lot better than they used to."

"That's because most of them are ex-military." Ferrero shook his head. "Next time I'll send you out in a DPV."

"I got you what I said I would."

"Yeah. Now you can help Reaper devise a plan to get the money out of there."

————

Kane shook his head after they'd watched the vision and heard Traynor's description of the area where the bank was located. "It can't be done."

Traynor said, "I agree."

It was Cara who came up with an alternative. "What if we can make him move it and steal it in transit?"

The two men looked at each other.

"Might work," said Kane.

"*If* we knew where they were going to take it," Traynor added.

Cara said, "If you were Montoya and you thought a fair haul of your money was going to get stolen, where would you take it?"

Traynor said, "I guess I'd be wanting it close so I could keep an eye on it."

"Exactly. So where can he do that?"

"At his hacienda," Kane concluded.

Cara nodded. "That's what I figure."

Kane called Reynolds over. "While you're getting those pictures of Montoya's compound, could you also get us some of the roads between – shit, I need a map."

Reynolds turned away, and a few heartbeats later, she was back with what Kane wanted.

"You're good," he said.

"I aim to please." She flashed him an even-toothed smile.

He unfurled the map, ran an index finger over it and stopped when he found what he was looking for. "Can you get us some pictures of this spot here?"

Reynolds leaned over the map. "Yes, no problem there."

"Cool. How soon?"

"Should have something for you tomorrow."

"That'll be fine."

Reynolds turned and walked away.

"Now," said Kane, "let's work the rest out."

"There's a good chance that all of the vehicles will be armor-plated," Traynor pointed out. "They'll have a heavy guard too."

Kane nodded. "We need a Pred."

The MQ-1 Predator, UAV (Unmanned Aerial Vehicle), capable of carrying two AGM-114 Hellfire missiles, was perfect for the job that was required.

Cara and Traynor gave him a look as though he was crazy. Kane turned and looked for Ferrero. "Luis, you got a moment?"

The DEA agent walked across the room to them. "What is it?"

"How bad do your bosses want Montoya?"

"Deadly, why?"

"Do you think you can get us a Predator armed with a couple of Hellfires?"

Ferrero snorted and waited for Kane to laugh at his own joke. It never happened.

"You're serious?" he asked.

Kane told him about luring Montoya into transporting the money and then hitting it in transit. "They'll have armored vehicles. We'll need eyes on to tell us which one the money is in when they leave Nogales. We can use the UAV for surveillance and the attack."

Ferrero nodded. "If it's possible, I'll get one. I don't know where from, but hell, I'll get it anyway."

"You should be able to get one from Davis–Monthan Air Force Base in Tucson," Cara told him.

"Fine, but that still leaves a body to fly it," Ferrero pointed out.

Kane called across to Reynolds again. "Reynolds!"

"Yo!"

"Can you fly a Pred?"

"Right up Montoya's ass if you want me to," she answered without glancing up from the computer she was working at.

"From here?"

That got her attention. Her head snapped up, and the chair she was sitting on rolled back. She stood up and as she approached the group, asked, "What do you mean, from here?"

"I mean control it from here if the boss gets you one from Davis-Monthan? It'll fly out of there," Kane explained.

"Sure. I've used them for surveillance before."

"This won't be just for surveillance. It'll have two Hellfires attached to it."

Her eyes lit up. "Damn! Always wanted to shoot something with one of those. I'll need a second man though."

"What for?"

"Sensor operator."

Kane turned to Ferrero. "Good enough?"

"All right. I'll get the Pred. But I want a detailed plan before I tick off on anything."

"You'll get it."

For the next hour, Kane, Traynor, and Cara bounced ideas around until they had nutted out a plan they thought best suited.

"And if it doesn't work, or Montoya doesn't do what you expect, what then?" Ferrero asked.

"We do it another way," Kane told him.

"When do you want to make your plan operational?"

"We'll need to execute the first part tomorrow night."

Ferrero's eyebrows knitted. "What first part?"

"We're going to attack the bank."

"Whoa there! You said it couldn't be done."

"It can't. The aim of it is to make Montoya think that it's possible. Once he does, then he'll be more likely to shift the money."

"You realize that once you do, there'll be cartel assholes swarming the place, don't you?"

"That's the idea. Can't bake a cake without cracking a few eggs."

Ferrero shook his head. "All right then. Consider the first part of the plan OK'd."

"We'll take one vehicle. Once we clear the area, we'll head out to the ambush site and dig in. Hawk will meet us there. If Montoya decides to move the money, it'll be within twenty-four hours. We can use the UAV to watch over the bank, so we know when that happens. It can then track the shipment to where the target area is. There is one other thing."

"What's that?"

"I'll need some explosives."

Ferrero rolled his eyes. "You don't want much, do you? Maybe a ballistic missile?"

"C-4 will do."

"I'm starting to regret this already."

———

Hawk
The hills above the Montoya compound

"That's a sight you don't see every day," Hawk muttered aloud.

"Get your mind back above your belt, Reaper Four," Reynolds' voice came over the radio.

Hawk gave a wry smile and lowered his high-powered field-glasses. "Always wanted an angel on my shoulder, Bravo One."

"Keep your mind on the mission, Hawk, or your mama will spank you."

Hawk raised the field-glasses back up and peered through them at the bikini-clad ladies around the pool. "Right now, Bravo One, spanking don't seem all that bad."

Hawk had been on station since the previous day. Now it was mid-morning, and once more the temperature was climbing through the roof. The Reaper team member had set up his observation post on a ridgeline high enough to see down onto the compound as well as a fair view of the surrounding area.

He'd been filled in on the operation by Ferrero and knew that the first phase would happen that night.

Hawk lowered the field-glasses and looked out along the dirt road which led to the compound's fortified front gate.

Around two kilometers out, he could see a dust cloud rising from the desert.

"Bravo One? Reaper Four. We have movement to the east about two klicks. Are you picking it up? All I can see is a dust cloud."

"Wait one, Reaper Four."

Back at the Reaper Team base in Retribution, Reynolds worked the joystick from her station. By some miracle, Ferrero had managed to get not one, but two Predator UAVs, so the team could have one in the air and the other on standby. If needed, the drone could stay on station for around twelve hours. Seated beside her was Master Sergeant Pete Teller, a big, broad-shouldered man assigned to the operation for the duration.

"Pete, can you zoom in, so we can get a better picture?"

"Yes, ma'am."

The screen in front of her tilted as the Predator's camera turned to the east. It might have been 15,000 ft in the air, but the camera made it seem like a hundred.

The camera stopped when the cloud of dust came into sight, and he worked the focus to get a closeup view of what was at its base.

"Reaper Four, Bravo Three. I'm looking at a two-vehicle convoy making good time."

"Copy that, Bravo Three."

"Both are black SUVs."

"Black SUVs, copy, Bravo Three."

Hawk shifted his gaze back to the compound and saw movement as the guards there swung open the tall, steel gates.

"Bravo One, Reaper Four. Looks like our visitors are here to see Montoya."

"Copy."

Hawk watched as the vehicles passed through the gates and stopped in the large courtyard. Montoya and another man appeared from within the large house; the cartel boss dressed in his customary white, the man beside him wearing black.

"Talk about yin and yang," Hawk muttered.

"Say again, Reaper Four."

"Sorry, Bravo One. Just talking to myself."

Two men climbed from the first SUV while three emerged from the rear one. Two came from the front of the vehicle while the third from the rear door. It was this man that Montoya walked towards and greeted.

He, like the rest of the men, was dressed in a black suit but carried a briefcase. Closing the distance to Montoya, he held out his right hand, and they shook. The cartel boss then placed his hand on the new arrival's right shoulder in a friendly gesture.

"Are you getting this, Bravo One?"

"Roger, Reaper Four."

Suddenly the man's face swam into view. "Shit! Bravo One, zoom in on our friend and inform Zero he'll need to see this."

"Copy."

Reynolds ordered Teller to zoom in tight on the new arrival and saw what had Hawk concerned. "Christ!"

She punched a few buttons, placing the Predator on autopilot, then rose from her seat and hurried across to where Ferrero was talking to Kane as the field team made final preparations to leave.

"Luis, you need to come see this," she interrupted.

He frowned at her, but both he and Kane followed her back to her station.

Once she was seated again, Reynolds said, "Bring it up, Teller."

The master sergeant punched a couple of keys, and the image popped up on a large monitor to his left.

"Son of a bitch," Ferrero hissed when he saw the face.

Kane stared at the picture. The man was clearly in his fifties, with grey hair. He looked at Ferrero and asked, "Who is that?"

"That, Reaper, is Senator Mac McCarthy from the great state of Texas. The son of a bitch has been against us performing operations outside of the U.S. for years. Now we know why. The bastard is in bed with the cartels. I bet they pay for a fair chunk of his campaigns."

"What do you suppose he is doing there?" Kane asked.

"Who knows? Picking up his next payment maybe?"

"Who are those fellers with him?"

"Zoom in on the detail and get some pictures of them. We'll see what crops up."

"Roger."

Reynolds went to work getting some screen captures of the senator's security team. Before long, they too were on the screen. Kane studied them. He frowned and leaned in closer. When he drew back, he turned to Ferrero and said, "They're military contractors. My guess is either Protection Services or Stay Safe."

Ferrero nodded. "Makes sense."

"What do you aim to do?"

"After I have a talk to him, I'm going to pass on what we have to the FBI. They can sort the mess out. We'll stay on mission."

"You're going to let him know that we know? Hell, he might tip our hand."

"Once we have him and any information he has, I'll pass him off to the FBI."

"OK. I hope it works out."

"It will, have faith." He turned to Brooke. "Reynolds, tell Hawk to keep an eye on them."

"Yes, sir."

"Reaper, finish getting ready. You need to be over the border before dark."

Kane nodded, and once Ferrero was gone, he asked Reynolds, "Did you guys get some shots of the terrain around the road I asked about?"

"Sure did. I gave them to Billings to look over a while back. Those and an aerial shot of the old bank and its surrounds."

Kane said. "Thanks."

He went to turn away, but she stopped him. Without taking her eyes from her screen, she asked, "How does it feel?"

"What feel?"

"Being back in the saddle, so to speak."

"I'll tell you once the mission is over."

Reynolds turned to face him and gave him a serious stare. "Take care out there."

Kane gave her his best smile. "We'll be fine. After all, we'll have our eye in the sky."

———

Inside the Montoya Compound

Senator Mac McCarthy sat on the sofa opposite Montoya, with Salazar seated in a large chair to his left. There were only the three of them; McCarthy's protection squad were outside in the courtyard.

The Senator toyed with his half glass of whiskey and then took a sip.

"What brings you across the border, Senator?" Montoya asked. "Such visits from you are quite rare."

His lined face grew hard. "I heard from one of my many acquaintances in the capital about a new team being formed to target you especially, Juan. I figured you would like to know about it."

Montoya waved the information away. "Your government has tried many times to come after me. I am still here."

"Not like this, Juan. This time it is different. After what happened with the sheriff from Retribution, they've hand-picked a team especially for the job."

Montoya studied his face and could see that the senator was genuinely troubled. "Tell me about this team."

McCarthy reached for his briefcase. "I can do one better. I have files on them. It's not much but should be enough."

He opened it up and passed a couple of manilla folders across to the cartel boss. Montoya studied them in silence and after he'd finished with each file, passed it over to Salazar.

Montoya looked up and stabbed a finger at the file on his lap. He said, "Tell me about this Ferrero."

"He's a good operator. Career DEA. Worked in Colombia for years. One of the men in his team worked with him there as part of a covert marine recon team. Kane."

Salazar flicked through the files Montoya had given him until he found Kane's. He opened it and stared down at the picture. He said, "I know this man."

Montoya's head swiveled, and he gave the *sicario* a questioning look.

"He was there. At the *gringo* place where I killed the sheriff. He came with the woman deputy."

Salazar paused and riffled through the files again and found the one on Cara. He held it up. "This is her."

Montoya still showed nonchalance. "Why should I worry? I am here in Sonora. They cannot touch me."

"You still don't get it, Juan. They've been given the green light to cross the damned border anytime they want."

Montoya's voice grew harsh. "If they cross the border to come after me, then I will bury them here. Who do they think they are to come to my country and try to stop me? Don't they know that I am untouchable?"

For a moment, McCarthy saw the flash of craziness in the cartel boss' eyes, and it made him nervous. He leaned forward and placed the glass of whiskey onto the coffee table. "I'll be going. I only came to warn you about what was happening."

Montoya stood erect. He held out his hand. "Thank you for this information. I will be sure to put a little extra into my next donation to your upcoming campaign."

"My campaign thanks you."

They all went outside, and McCarthy and his entourage climbed into their vehicles. Montoya turned to Salazar. "I want you to find out more about this team the *gringos* have sent against me."

"*Sí, Jefe.*"

The SUVs pulled out of the compound and started their rough passage over the corrugations in the gravel road. Dust spewed from their rear, and the one carrying McCarthy lurched over a deep hole when the cell in his pocket began to buzz. He reached inside and checked the lit screen. Frowning when he didn't recognize the number, he pressed answer.

With the cell up to his ear, McCarthy spoke with a hesitant voice, "Hello?"

"Hello, Senator McCarthy, how's your day going so far? All is well I trust?"

"Who is this?"

"Someone who wants to chat with you in person."

McCarthy snapped impatiently, "Make an appointment like the rest of my constituents do."

"It is rather urgent. I don't think it would be too far out of your way to come visit me."

The senator's voice was brusque. "I'm sorry. I'm not in Texas at the moment."

"Neither am I, Senator. How about when you cross back over the border from your visit with Juan Montoya, you swing by Retribution, Arizona so we can have that chat."

McCarthy's blood ran cold. "Ferrero," he breathed.

"That's good, you know me. Saves on the introductions. Just so you understand, if you don't comply with what I've asked you to do, or if you try to turn around and run, there is a Predator drone above you this very minute, armed with two Hellfire missiles. I will not hesitate to use them."

"You wouldn't dare," he snarled, the venom in his voice thick. "I'm a fucking United States Senator."

"And I don't give two shits what you are. You've got ten seconds to make up your mind. After that, you won't have a mind left."

McCarthy's jaw set firm. "Go ahead."

"Five seconds, Senator."

"Fuck you!"

With McCarthy listening on, Ferrero said, "Bravo One, bring the first Hellfire online."

"Copy."

Then a female voice said, "First missile coming online now."

"Let me know when you're ready."

"Target acquired."

McCarthy's eyes started to roll in his head as fear gripped his heart and began to squeeze it in a vice-like grip. The son of a bitch was actually going to do it.

"Fi—"

"Wait! All right! All right, I'll do it."

"I'll be expecting you, Senator. I think you know where to find us."

When the line went dead, he threw the cell onto the floor of the SUV and shouted, "Fuck!"

"Is everything all right, Senator?" asked the man in the front passenger seat.

"No, it damn well isn't!" he snapped. "We're making a detour. Take us to Retribution, Arizona."

———

Retribution

"Would you really have done it, sir?" Reynolds asked Ferrero.

"Damned straight, Reynolds. One thing I can't stand is a turncoat, corrupt son of a bitch like that."

"Yes, sir."

"Get me the FBI Phoenix office. I want them here before McCarthy shows."

CHAPTER 13

RETRIBUTION

The two dust-coated SUVs screeched to a stop outside the old furniture store late in the afternoon. The orange sunset had spread itself across the Arizona desert and turned it a luminescent copper color, the sky streaked with purple. Within the hour, the sun would be gone, and the desert chill would fill the air.

The protection detail stepped out first, followed by the senator himself. Ferrero walked outside, and the detail immediately drew their sidearms.

The DEA agent held up his hands. "Now, gentlemen, how about you put your guns away. I only want to talk to your boss."

They glanced at McCarthy, and he nodded. The four men holstered their weapons.

Ferrero grinned. "That's better. Follow me, Senator."

McCarthy stepped forward and was followed by the

four-man detail. The DEA agent raised his hand. "Not you, gentlemen. You stay here."

The senator stopped almost mid-stride. "They go where I go."

Ferrero shook his head. "Nope."

"Then we're done here," McCarthy snapped. "Shoot him."

"I'd take a look at this before you do anything untoward, Senator," Ferrero said and held out the cell in his hand.

McCarthy stepped forward hesitantly to where the agent waited and took the cell from his grasp. He stared at the picture on it. One of himself and Montoya in the court-yard of the cartel leader's compound. Without a word, he passed it back.

"Shall we try again, Senator?"

McCarthy motioned for the escort to stand down and followed Ferrero inside the building. He was amazed at the setup that the small team had. Computer panels, multiple monitors. One of which had a FLIR, (forward-looking infrared radiometer), picture on it with telemetry changing constantly and crosshairs at its center. The picture itself showed a large building in a semi-populated area. Seated in front of the monitors were a man and woman.

"Where's that?" McCarthy asked curiously.

"Nogales," Ferrero said.

"I presume that what you are doing is sanctioned?"

"You knew who I was, and where I was, Senator. Work it out for yourself."

"May I ask what you are doing with a drone over Nogales?"

"Sure. We've got a team on the ground, and we're going to steal Montoya's money that he keeps in the building on screen."

Shock appeared on McCarthy's face. "You're going to commit a crime on foreign soil?"

"We aim to do more than that," Ferrero stated.

"I can't believe that Washington would give you permission to do such a thing."

"The war on the cartels has just escalated thanks to your friend Montoya, Senator. Quite frankly, the leaders in Washington have had enough. What we are doing here is a test case. If it proves successful, then I assume that we'll be unleashed on the rest. Now, let's get to you. What is *your* relationship with Montoya?"

McCarthy thought about lying but shrugged his shoulders and said, "He's donated millions to my campaign fund over the past few years."

"What does he get in return?"

"Information basically. A man in my position hears things."

"Such as?"

"Intelligence on upcoming missions and such. Only those who would directly affect Montoya."

His comments gave Ferrero pause for thought. After a few heartbeats, the DEA agent said, "That was why you were there, wasn't it? You were passing on information about this team."

McCarthy shrugged.

"Who else knows about you and Montoya?"

"Only the escort I use."

"Who are they? Stay Safe?"

McCarthy nodded. "Is there anything else you want to know?"

"Nope, I think that'll do. You can leave now."

The senator frowned. He stared at Ferrero and asked, "Just like that?"

Ferrero nodded.

McCarthy took a hesitant step. He looked back at Ferrero who ushered him towards the door. The senator kept walking, the DEA agent behind him. They exited the building, and McCarthy came to an abrupt halt. Standing before him in the manmade light was a gaggle of FBI agents. Handcuffed against the black SUVs stood the senator's security detail. He turned back to look at Ferrero. "I knew it was too easy."

The agent in command of the FBI detail came forward and put cuffs on McCarthy. He stared at Ferrero and nodded.

"You get all that?" the DEA agent asked.

"Sure did."

"Good. I've got work to do."

"Thanks, Luis."

"Just get him the hell out of here."

————

Nogales

"Bravo One? Reaper One, how copy? Over."

"Read you five by five, Reaper One," Reynolds confirmed.

"What's our eye in the sky see, Bravo One?"

"All clear, ready to start the mission when you are."

The night was quiet. It was after one a.m., and the cool desert air was well and truly upon them. The sky was a cloudless, moonless blanket above them, and Kane checked his silenced HK416 to make sure it was in full working order.

"You ready, Traynor?"

"As I'll ever be."

Both wore tactical vests and night-vision gear. Like Kane, Traynor was armed with a silenced HK416.

"Reaper Two? Reaper One, are you set? Over."

"Roger, Reaper One," Cara came back.

Cara had picked the rooftop of an abandoned building to the northeast of the target to set up her sniper nest. It gave her a clear field of fire to the front of the building that housed Montoya's money. She was armed with an M110 with a night-capable scope mounted on top.

"Reaper One, this is Zero."

"Go ahead."

"Remember, engage only those with weapons. I don't want any civilians getting shot by accident."

"Copy, Zero." There was a short pause, and Kane said, "Reaper Two, commence."

"Copy, Reaper."

Suddenly, in quick succession, the only two streetlights were blown out, shattered by 7.62 bullets from the silenced M110, cloaking the street in darkness. Glass fell to the street like rain, the tinkling sound reaching Kane's ears.

Kane dropped the night-vision goggles over his eyes. Everything turned green. Before he moved, Kane said, "Bravo Three? Reaper One. How are we looking?"

"All clear, Reaper One."

"Copy. Moving."

Kane raised the silenced HK and moved towards the rundown bank. Behind him, Traynor moved with silent strides. They kept to the shadows, and once they reached the building, the DEA agent took a knee to cover the street while Kane placed the C-4.

As Kane set the charge, he said, "Sitrep, Reaper Two."

"All clear."

"Bravo Three?"

"All clear."

Once the charge was set, Kane said, "Charge set. Reaper One and Three moving."

"Copy."

When they were out of range, Kane stopped, and they both took cover behind a crumbling adobe wall. He retrieved the detonator switch from a pocket in his tactical vest and armed the C-4 charge. "Fire in the hole."

The blast rolled along the deserted street while a gout of orange flame shot across it from the explosion. The charge ripped the old door from its rusted hinges and blew it into the building.

"That'll get their attention," Kane muttered. Then louder, "Call when you see them coming in. Switching on strobes."

The strobes would make them visible to the team back at base. If things got confused on the ground, Reynolds and Teller would be able to pick them out.

"Copy."

"Strobes on, Bravo One. We are moving."

Kane and Traynor moved forward once more to the wrecked doorway of the bank. "Copy, we see three strobes."

"Reaper One? Bravo Three, copy?" Teller said.

"Copy, Bravo Three."

"We're starting to see movement at your twelve o'clock. Three armed Tangos closing your position."

The two men settled in the doorway and prepared to meet the cartel men. "Copy, Bravo Three. Have you got them, Reaper Two?"

"Copy."

Through her night-vision scope, Cara could see the

three cartel men running towards the old bank, unaware of the waiting danger. When they reached the front of the building, Cara fired her first shot.

The bullet hit, and the cartel man gave a violent shudder before slumping to the ground without a sound.

"Target down. Shifting aim."

The M110 fired again, and the second cartel man dropped. "Second Tango down."

Before Cara could move her aim again, Kane's laser sight centered on the last man, and he squeezed the trigger. One shot, one kill. "Last Tango down."

"Reaper One? Bravo Three. You now have multiple Tangos inbound your position."

"Call them out, Bravo Three."

"Targets inbound at your twelve, two, and six o'clock," Teller instructed.

"Traynor, take the targets at six," Kane ordered.

"Copy. Bravo Three how many Tangos? Over."

"Reaper Three, you have two, repeat, two armed Tangos at your six o'clock."

"Copy."

"Reaper Two? Reaper One. Do you have eyes on the Tangos at our twelve?"

"Copy, Reaper," Cara confirmed. "So far, I count six, confirm Bravo Three?"

Teller's voice came over the comms. "Confirm, Reaper Two. The count is six. Reaper One? You should have two more appear at your two o'clock in three ... two ... one."

Kane's laser sight settled on the first cartel man who appeared from behind a building along the street to the right. Through the NVGs, it appeared as a ramrod straight beam like in some sci-fi movie. As soon as it touched the chest of the first cartel man, Kane fired.

The target dropped, and Kane shifted aim and fired again. This time, however, when the mortally wounded narco stiffened he squeezed the trigger of his weapon, and it rattled off a full magazine of ammunition before he hit the pavement.

The bullets sprayed into the air, some hammering into the building adjacent to the one past that they'd emerged. Behind him, Kane heard Traynor open fire at the ones at their six o'clock.

"Six is secure, Reaper," he said in a monotone voice.

"Reaper One? Reaper Two. You copy?"

"Go ahead, Cara."

"Two more Tangos down at your twelve. But they're still coming. You should be able to see them shortly."

Suddenly the night erupted with the staccato sound of AKs. To the trained ear, they were unmistakable.

"Reaper Two, are you taking fire? Over."

"Negative."

"Bravo Three to all Reaper callsigns. You now have multiple, repeat, multiple targets converging on your positions. Estimate twenty-plus Tangos. Looks like that burst of fire woke them up."

"Reaper One, copy."

"Reaper One? Zero, over."

"Copy Zero."

"Reaper, it might be time to pull out while you can. You don't want to get cut off where you are."

"Copy. We'll start now. Bravo Three, how's our path of egress? Over."

"You have four Tangos between you and your egress point, Reaper One."

"Copy. Reaper Two, you copy?"

"Roger."

"Give us two minutes and then meet us at the rendezvous point."

Kane heard the M110 fire as she said, "Copy, Reaper One. Two minutes."

"Come on, Traynor, let's go."

"Wait!" Traynor snapped. He brought his HK416 up and loosed a burst of gunfire at a group of cartel men. They returned fire and bullets slammed into the front wall of the old bank.

Kane swiveled and loosed his own burst. They struck the chest of one of the cartel men and brought forth a savage hail of bullets. A round whined close to Kane's ear, so close he felt the heat of the displaced air.

"Come on, Traynor, move."

Up on the rooftop, Cara watched on as the pair broke cover. She shifted aim with the M110 and fired. Another narco dropped in his tracks when a 7.62 caliber bullet blew through his chest.

The good thing about the M110 Semi-Automatic Sniper System was just that, it was semi-automatic, and took either a ten or twenty-round box magazine. Right now, Cara was using the twenty-round version.

She fired twice more as the cartel shooters emerged from cover. Two more dropped, and she watched the others fire wildly in hope rather than aiming. With the suppressor on the end of the M110, the muzzle-flash was non-existent; therefore they had no idea where Cara was.

"Reaper One? Reaper Two. Are you and Reaper Three clear yet? Over."

"Almost there, Reaper Two," Kane said. "Time for you to pull back, Cara."

"Copy, Reaper One. Pulling back."

Cara came to her feet and moved swiftly across the

rooftop and climbed down into a dark alley. Once her boots hit solid ground, she checked left and right. When she was sure everything was clear, Cara walked to the mouth of the alley. She was about to exit when a man appeared; not a cartel soldier, a civilian.

Confronted with a figure which seemed to have climbed out of the bowels of hell, he threw up his arms, screamed, and staggered backward.

Cara flicked up her NVGs and put a finger to her lips. "Shh. It's OK. I'm friendly. I won't hurt you."

The fear-stricken man babbled something in Spanish and fell to his knees, hands clasped in front of him as he begged for mercy.

Cara cursed. "I don't have time for this shit."

She dropped the NVGs back down and went to step around the blubbering civilian when a man with an AK appeared. He shouted and swung up the weapon in his hands. Cara arced her own up but knew she would not be in time. Her blood ran cold, the M110 grew leaden. The AK in the cartel man's grip opened fire before it had snapped into line with her body.

Five shots ripped through the air to her left and slammed into the wall of the building that formed that side of the alley. The last one, the sixth, tore a hole in the fabric of her sleeve. After that, the magazine in the AK ran dry.

The M110 finished its track, and Cara fired two shots in quick succession. Both smashed into her attacker's torso and flung him back.

"Shit!" she breathed, casting a glance at the man who still knelt on the ground, and hurried out of the alley.

"Reaper Two? Bravo Three, are you OK? Over."

"I'm good, Bravo Three."

"Sorry about that one, he just suddenly appeared."

"Copy," then she muttered, "Fuck!"

———

"Reaper One, be advised that your four Tangos are now three."

"Copy that, Bravo Three. It might be a good idea to tell us where they are, over."

"You should be seeing them now, over."

On cue, three armed men appeared before them and opened up with their weapons. Bullets cracked as they passed close to the two Americans. Kane dropped to his left knee and calmly settled the laser sight upon the first of the three attackers. With the HK set to semi-auto, he squeezed the trigger twice. The carbine kicked back against his shoulder, and the target was dead before hitting the ground.

Without waiting to see the result, Kane had already shifted targets. He noted the laser from Traynor's HK had already settled on the second Tango, so he kept traversing until his was aligned on the third.

Traynor's weapon coughed a fraction of a heartbeat before Kane's. Both Tangos jerked, then spasmed as another 5.56 round finished what the first had started.

Before they moved, both scanned the surrounding area for any more threats.

"Clear," said Kane, followed by Traynor.

Kane rose to his feet and said into his comms, "Bravo Three, copy? Over."

"Copy, Reaper One."

"How is the path to the egress point? Over."

"Path looks clear, Reaper One."

"Copy."

The two moved once again through the darkness until

they reached the armored SUV. Waiting there for them was Cara.

"Are you OK?" Kane asked her.

"I had an issue, but it was sorted."

"You two want to catch up later?" Traynor asked.

They ditched some of their gear in the back before climbing in. Traynor drove, and as they were leaving, Kane called in their sitrep.

"Zero, this is Reaper One, over."

"Go ahead, Reaper."

"We've reached egress and are on the move."

"Copy, you're on the move."

"Reaper One, out."

———

Retribution

Ferrero placed his headset on the desk and said, "That's the first stage down. Ought to piss Montoya off bad enough."

"Sir?"

He stared at Reynolds. "What is it?"

"The Predator is getting low on fuel. We need to get it back to Tucson."

The DEA agent nodded. "If he starts to make a move, we'll have plenty of time to get a bird back up, yes?"

"More than enough time, yes, sir."

"OK. Land it and get some rest."

"Yes, sir."

Ferrero shifted his gaze to Teller. "Master Sergeant Teller?"

Teller turned his head. "Yes, sir?"

"You did great keeping my people safe. Glad to have you aboard."

"Thank you, sir."

Ferrero took one last look at the screen before he turned away. He had a call to make.

———

Washington

The phone rang twice before United States Deputy Attorney General, Mike Turner picked it up. "Yes?"

"It's Ferrero, sir. The first phase is done."

"Any problems?"

"No, sir."

Turner slumped back in his red-leather chair and loosened his multi-color striped tie. He removed his wire-framed glasses and placed them on the polished top of his hardwood desk.

"What's next, Luis?" he asked.

"It's wait and see, sir. We'll monitor everything with the UAVs, and hopefully, Montoya will do what we expect him to."

"I'm not too sure about using Hellfire missiles on foreign soil, Luis. When you first came to me with this idea, I must admit I was hesitant. Now, the more I think about it, the more reservations I have. If the Mexican authorities find out, it could be construed as an act of war."

Ferrero hesitated before asking, "Do you want us to cancel the operation, sir?"

There was a long pause before Turner answered, and the DEA agent thought he was about to say yes, when, "No, keep it going. But if something goes wrong, it can't be traced back to this office."

"It won't be, sir."

Turner stared at the picture of his daughter on the desktop. It had been taken at her graduation. The photo showed a happy young woman, her broad smile split her face and her eyes sparkled as her mother's had done. Now they were both gone. His wife, Mary, to cancer. Amy, to the vile stuff that killed so many young people; Cocaine.

"Tell me, Luis. If this doesn't work if you can't draw him out, what will you do?"

"I'll send a team across the border, and they will kill him wherever they find him."

Another moment of silence, then, "I'd rather he faced the legal system, Luis. But if you can't manage that, then, do what you must. He can't be allowed to hurt any more American families."

"Once we get his money, sir, he won't be able to help himself. He'll be hopping mad."

"I hope you're right."

"Couple more things, sir."

"Yes?"

"Have you given any more thought to my proposal?"

"You mean about this becoming a permanent task force?"

"Yes, sir."

"You get Montoya, Luis, and I'll see you get your task force and all the funding you need to run it. I'll take it to the president myself if need be, but you'll get it."

"And the other?"

"Your man, Kane?"

"Yes, sir."

"Taken care of."

"Thank you, sir."

"Good luck, Luis."

"Goodnight, sir."

Hawk
Sonora

It seemed as though every light in the compound came on at once. One moment the desert was dark, quiet. The next, it was illuminated by floodlights for half a kilometer in every direction.

"Shit," Hawk murmured. "Looks like someone got the news."

He took up his field glasses and scanned the compound. Men were starting to move about like a colony of ants after a crumb.

"Reaper Four to Bravo. Anybody up? Over."

"I wish I wasn't, Reaper Four," a tired-sounding voice came back.

"Is that you, Slick?"

"Roger."

"You'd best wake the old man up. We got a whole lot of movement out here."

"Copy, wait one."

A few minutes later the radio-silence was broken by Ferrero. "Reaper Four? Zero. What do you have, Hawk?"

"Looks like our boy just got the news about our little show. They took their time about it, probably too scared to tell him. Anyway, the place is lit up like a Christmas tree, and he's got fellers running about everywhere. In the last minute or so, he's had a couple of vehicles lined up ready to go. It looks as though the plan is working."

"So far. All right, Reaper Four, keep an eye on them and let me know if anything else develops. If not, wait until they're gone and move out to link with Reaper One."

"Copy. Reaper Four, out."

"Zero, out."

Ferrero paused before he tried Kane. "Reaper One? Zero. Copy? Over."

"Copy, Zero."

"Reaper Four just informed me that our friend is marshaling his troops. Over."

"Copy."

"What's your position, Reaper One?"

"We're about ten minutes out from our destination."

"Copy. Keep me informed if anything changes. Zero, out."

"Reaper One, out."

———

Montoya
   Sonora

"You find the *puta* who tried to steal my money, and you cut his fucking balls off, so I can feed them to him!"

Flecks of spittle flew from Montoya's lips as he raged at Salazar. When the call had come, the Cartel boss' screams of anger were heard throughout the whole house.

"And another thing. The one who was supposedly in charge of watching over the money, *my money!* Kill him!"

Salazar's voice was stoic. "He is already dead."

Sarcasm replaced the anger in Montoya's voice. "Then kill his family. Kill someone, anyone. I don't care!"

"*Sí*," Salazar said, but he knew he wouldn't do it. There was no point.

"I want all of the money brought back here," Montoya said, his voice somewhat calmer.

"The vehicles will be ready soon. Romero will take care of it."

The cartel boss shook his head. "No. You do it. I want someone in charge that knows what they are doing."

"*Sí.*"

Salazar was about to leave when Montoya asked him another question, almost as an afterthought. "Who do you think it was? The Sonorans or Rafael?"

Rafael Martinez was the head of the Nogales Cartel.

"It is hard to say."

The cartel boss' voice grew cold, eyes flared with bright sparks, and he hissed, "Find out."

"*Sí, patron.*"

CHAPTER 14

Nogales

Salazar stood on the rooftop, sun at his back, and stared towards the bank where his men were loading a small Isuzu refrigerated truck with the money from the in-ground vault. Five others stood guard with AKs.

There were no worries about *Federales*. They never came to this part of Nogales, hence the reason why Montoya chose it to house a portion of his money. He refused to keep it all in one place, said it was safer that way. Besides, who would be fool enough to steal money from a cartel?

When Salazar had arrived, all the bodies were gone, taken away by the ones who'd survived the gun battle. All that remained were bloodstains and spent ammunition cases. He stared down at those in his right palm. 7.62 shells he'd picked up from the rooftop where he was.

Someone had set up position here and picked off the responders as they'd appeared. Almost twenty men had fallen. Not all were dead, but a good number were. Whoever had done it was good, well trained. He frowned.

Salazar's gaze dropped to the rooftop. It was covered with dust, debris, bird shit. Then he saw it. The imprint of a boot. He walked over and knelt beside it. His fingers traced over the ridges and bumps of the tread pattern.

The *sicario* had seen a pattern like it before. They were Danner RAT (Rugged All Terrain) Boots worn by U.S. armed forces.

Why? Why would American armed servicemen be in Nogales trying to steal Montoya's money? A Special Forces operation, maybe? That would explain the sniper nest.

He shook his head. It still didn't make sense. So, who? Salazar came to his feet once more and stared back out across the way. Surely someone must have seen something.

He walked to the edge of the building. He estimated the distance for the shooter to be around two-hundred and fifty meters. In the dark. They had skills. Military? Ex-military? Either way, Montoya wasn't going to like it.

He reached into his pocket and took out his cell. He punched in a number and then waited for the man on the other end to answer.

"S*i*?"

"Take some men. Find me some witnesses."

"S*í*."

Salazar disconnected the call and replaced the cell back into his pants pocket. Then he looked up.

———

Retribution

. . .

"Shit! Has the son of a bitch made us? Did he see the UAV?" Ferrero snapped, afraid their surveillance had been blown.

"Negative, sir," Teller assured him. There is no way he could see the Predator at this height."

"Damn it! Are you sure?"

"Teller is right, sir. He couldn't see the UAV."

There was an element of relief in Ferrero's voice when he said, "Thank Christ for that. Did we get a facial shot of him when he looked up?"

"Yes, sir," said Teller.

Ferrero nodded. "Good. Send it across to Swift for him to run facial recognition on it."

"Yes, sir."

"Whoever he is," Reynolds said without turning her head from her screens, "he's no amateur. He found the nest that Cara used, and studied the rooftop as well."

"He also policed the brass that was left behind," Teller put in.

"It would only have raised more questions than answers. Keep watch on them to see what they do next."

"Holy shit! Mother fucker!" Swift burst out.

"Something you would like to share, Slick?" Ferrero called across to him.

He spun on his chair. "Sorry, sir. But I got a hit on the picture."

"Already?"

"Yes, sir. Didn't have to dig too far at all."

"I presume you're going to tell us who it is?"

"Ah, yes, sir. It's him. It's Cesar Salazar. *El Monstruo* himself."

Nogales

Salazar's men rounded up nine witnesses. Eight of them weren't worth much at all. They told him what he already knew. There were two would-be robbers with automatic weapons. The last witness, however, proved to be quite helpful.

At first, he seemed to be confused and kept saying, "*Ojos verdes, ojos verdes.* Green eyes, green eyes."

The *sicario* thought the man was touched in the head until he remembered his theory about the American Special Forces.

Eventually, Salazar extracted, under intense questioning, that what he had seen was a person with night vision goggles on. And not just any person, a woman. The sniper was a woman!

She had killed one of the responders while the frightened man had been present. So, there were only three in all. Three highly skilled attackers who blew open the door and then killed a sizable number of the responders.

Still, they had been driven away.

Once again, Salazar reached into his pocket and withdrew his cell. He dialed in the number, and it was picked up straight away.

"Yes? What did you find out?"

"I questioned several witnesses and checked things for myself. It looks like the ones who did this were professionals."

"What makes you think this?"

"There were three of them. They blasted their way through the wooden door. There was a sniper with them, a woman. I found where she set up."

"That doesn't mean they were professionals."

"They had night vision."

"So?"

"They shot almost twenty men, they wore American combat boots, they had automatic weapons. I tell you, they were professionals. Maybe even special forces."

Silence. Then, "I will contact the senator and have him find out if there are any special forces in Sonora."

"What about the taskforce he told you about?"

"You think it might be them?"

"*Sí, Jefe.*"

"What do you know about them so far? I asked you to find out."

"If it is them, they are well organized."

"Bring the money back here. I will think about what to do next."

"*Sí.*"

———

Retribution

"They're moving out now, Zero," Teller called across to Ferrero.

On the monitor, the four vehicles had dropped into column formation and were now making their way through Nogales.

"Reynolds, do you have enough fuel in that bird?"

"Yes, sir. Just."

"All right. Radio ahead to Kane and give him a rundown on the situation."

"Roger, sir."

A few moments later Reynolds called up Kane.

"Reaper One? Bravo One. Copy?"

Nothing.

"Reaper One? Bravo One. Copy?"

Dead air.

"Do you copy, Reaper One? Over."

When Kane's voice finally came over the net, it sounded to be no more than a hoarse whisper. "Just wait." That was it, no more.

Reynolds frowned. "Reaper Two? Copy?"

"Copy, Bravo One. What's up? Over."

"Cara, is Kane OK? I just tried to give him a sitrep, and he sounded weird."

"I think so, Bravo One. He's on overwatch at the moment. Would you like me to check on him?"

"Yes. Something isn't right."

"Roger, Bravo One. Wait one. Out."

Reynolds glanced at Teller who gave her a quizzical look. She shrugged.

There was a long silence, and then suddenly Cara's voice came. "Shit!"

"Reaper Two? What's the problem? Over."

Silence returned.

"Reaper Two? Bravo One. Repeat your last."

Nothing.

Then came the gunshot.

"Reaper Two, come in."

Nothing.

"Reaper Two? Bravo One. Come in."

Still nothing.

"Christ! What is going on out there?"

———

Sonora

It was closer to five feet long than four. Thicker than a man's forearm, and curled back in an S-shape, ready to strike.

Large beads of sweat started to trickle down Kane's face as the rattle at the end of the cold-blooded beast's tail seemed to reach fever-pitch. He felt it imminent that at any moment the Western Diamondback Rattlesnake would strike and sink its long fangs into the flesh of his face.

"Reaper One? Bravo One. Copy?"

Fuck!

"Reaper One? Bravo One. Copy?"

Kane stared into the animal's beady little eyes.

"Do you copy, Reaper One? Over."

"Just wait," he said in a hoarse whisper without moving his lips.

He hadn't noticed the reptile until it was too late. He'd been belly down on the ridge, watching the road, under a damned hot sun when movement to his left drew his attention. When he turned to see what it was, he was face to face with this brute.

How the snake hadn't struck out when he first moved, he'd never know. After all, it was no more than three feet from him. More than ample distance for a strike.

Now, all Kane could do was wait and hope that it slithered away. Although he'd spent countless hours in the jungle with many poisonous reptiles, even encountered the world's deadliest serpent, an Inland Taipan, while on training maneuvers in Australia, there was something about being face-to-face with a rattler that nothing else compared to.

A droplet of sweat dripped from the end of Kane's nose and fell to the burning sand. No sooner had the moisture touched the granules than it was quickly sucked up by the parched ground and disappeared leaving no trace that it had ever existed.

Then he heard the other sound. The one made by boots crunching on sand and gravel. It was soft at first but gradually grew louder with its approach. When whoever was coming was almost right on top of him, they stopped, and he heard the sharp intake of breath. Then, "Shit!" followed by the sound of fumbling.

Then the shot rang out, and the Diamondback's head disintegrated. Left behind was the writhing body and the bloody stump where it had once been.

Kane rolled onto his back and breathed a sigh of relief.

"Are you OK?" Cara asked.

"I am now. Thanks."

In the background, radio chatter sounded. He said, "Bravo One? Reaper One. You copy?"

"Copy, Reaper One."

"What on earth is going on out there?"

"Local wildlife problem."

"Is it sorted?"

Kane glanced at Cara. "It is now."

More heavy footfalls sounded as Hawk and Traynor came running up the back of the slope. Hawk had joined them an hour before.

"What the hell was the shot all about?" Traynor growled.

Cara pointed at the dead Diamondback not far from where Kane lay on his back. Traynor's mouth formed a perfect O as he stared at it. Then he shivered as the prospect of what could have happened went through his mind.

"Are you still there, Reaper One?"

"Go ahead, Bravo One."

"The convoy is headed back your way. As before, there are three SUVs and the truck. Except there has been one development. In the lead SUV is Salazar."

Kane stared at the others who were now logged into the net. Traynor smiled. "Good, we can drop a Hellfire on the son of a bitch."

"No," said Kane and shook his head. "We stick to the plan. Use the missiles on the escort cars either side of the money truck. If we get a shot at Salazar afterward, then we take it. He's not the mission. The money is."

"Correct, Reaper One," Ferrero's voice came over the net. "If you get the chance, take it. Otherwise stay on mission. Do you all understand?"

They nodded under Kane's gaze. "Copy, Zero."

"Zero, out."

"Right," said Kane. "Traynor, you and Hawk take up position on the other side of the road. Cara will set up her M110 on the crest of the ridge this side. Once it kicks off, push forward. I want the survivors to panic and run. Anyone who presents as a target, kill. No matter what, we secure that money. Got it?"

Cara smiled. This was the Reaper she knew. The combat soldier from the embassy raid. Professional, confident, hard as nails.

"What are you smiling at?" he asked.

"Seeing you this way reminded me of the embassy and what a damned good soldier you were."

"You want to hope this don't turn out the same way,"

Kane said, and turned and walked down the slope of the ridge towards the vehicles.

"What happened?" Hawk asked.

Cara's face grew grim. "He got shot. Nearly died."

"What embassy are you talking about?" Traynor asked.

"Philippines."

Hawk realized what she was talking about. "He was there?"

She nodded. "We both were. I was in charge of the security detail, and Reaper was in-country with his recon team. They were actually at the embassy waiting for a ride home when the shit went down."

"I heard you lot kicked some terrorist ass defending the joint."

"That was all Reaper. He organized the defenses. Called the shots. But if it hadn't been for an Australian Blackhawk, we'd have been overrun. So, if there were any real heroes that night, it was those guys. He was shot by a terrorist sniper not long after."

"And you guys kept in touch ever since?" asked Traynor.

"Nope. Never set eyes on him again until he showed up in Retribution."

"What makes you think he hasn't changed since you last saw him?" asked Hawk.

"He had the chance to walk away from all this, but he stayed. He's still the same."

Hawk nodded. "Good enough."

"Reaper One to all Reaper callsigns. When you're finished with the mother's meeting you're having on the ridge, how about we get ready for this mission."

Cara said, "Reaper Two, copy."

Then she looked at Hawk and Traynor. "Still the same man."

―――――

Kane studied the small laptop screen and in real-time feed watched the small column's progress across the rough gravel road. It kicked up a large plume of dust, and Kane thought they were making good time.

"Bravo One? Reaper One. Do you have the number of Tangos in the lead SUV and in the truck? Over."

"Copy, Reaper One. Bravo Three tells me there are two Tangos in the truck and another four in the lead SUV. That includes Salazar."

"Copy. How far out are they now, Bravo Three?"

Teller came on the air. "Reaper One, the target is ten klicks out from your position, repeat, ten kilometers, over."

"Roger, ten kilometers from my location. Don't miss, Bravo One. I'd hate to have a lap full of Hellfire."

"Have no fear, Reaper One. I've never missed a target before. Never fired at one before either."

"You instill me with faith, Bravo One. Reaper One out."

"Good luck, Reaper one. We'll keep you updated. Bravo, out."

Kane closed the laptop and removed it from the hood of the SUV. He placed it in the vehicle and turned to face Cara. "You got all you need?"

In her hands were the M110 and a small case with a laser target designator. Not that they'd need it, for the MQ-1 Predator had its own inbuilt system. But you never could tell. About her head was a sandy colored bandana, and she wore yellow-tinted glasses.

Her tactical vest held spare magazines and had a holster

attached by Velcro low on the left with a Smith & Wesson M&P handgun in it.

"I'm good."

"If you get a shot at Salazar, take it," he said in a firm tone.

"If I get half a chance, I'll shoot the son of a bitch, Reaper."

Reaper nodded. He dropped out the box magazine from his HK416 and checked the loads and the breech mechanism to make sure it was all free of sand and grit. Then he reloaded it.

Like Cara, his tactical vest was loaded with spare magazines, and he also had his handgun in a Velcro holster.

Both wore tactical headsets with the mic on an arm around the front and the push to talk module attached to the front of the tactical vest. Kane reached up and keyed his. "Reaper Three? Reaper One. Confirmation on target. Ten klicks out, copy?"

"Copy, Reaper One. Ten klicks. Out."

He stared at Cara. "Let's do this."

Salazar stared out at the gravel road before him, deep in thought. The SUV hit a deep rut and lurched to the left. The driver corrected the partial skid, but the *sicario* didn't seem to notice.

The troubled expression on his face said it all as he dwelled on what he'd found in Nogales and the conclusion he'd drawn. American special forces had tried to steal the money. The question was why?

"You are worried, *Jefe*?" the driver asked.

"Tell me something, Raoul. What did you make of the attempted robbery?"

Raoul used to be Mexican army before he worked out that he could make more money working for the men he had sworn to stop.

He shrugged. "I'm not sure what you mean."

"You were military. You must have an idea."

"Whoever did it was well trained."

"Why do you say that?"

"There were three of them, and they shot almost twenty men. They had a sniper and night vision."

"Yes, there is that. Anything else? Anything you thought strange?"

"Why did they not bring more men? They knew what they were doing. They knew that *El Hombre* would have men close by. All they did was blast the door open, and there was no sign that they tried to open the safe. It would take three minutes for anyone to reach the old bank, and yet if they had explosives, why did they not try to blast open the safe in that time?"

Salazar nodded but remained silent.

"That is what bothers me, *Jefe*. They never even tried."

"But why, Raoul? Why would they not try?"

"If it was to kill *El Hombre's* men, then it worked. Or ..." his voice trailed away as the thought inside his head silenced his voice.

"Or what?"

"Or we are doing what they want."

To Salazar, it was like being hit between the eyes with a brick. Of course! That was why they never tried to break into the safe. They already decided that it couldn't be done. They wanted Montoya to think it could be done and force him to shift his money. Which was what the cartel men were now doing. They'd played right into their hands.

"*Madre de Dios*," Salazar breathed.

He reached into his pocket to get his cell. But the realization had come too late. Behind them, the first SUV exploded in a giant ball of fire.

————

"Reaper One? Bravo Three, copy?"

"Reaper One, copy."

"Reaper One, you should have a visual on the target shortly, over."

"Roger, Bravo Three, we see the dust. Estimated time of arrival? Over."

"ETA five minutes, Reaper One. The second Hellfire should impact within thirty seconds of the first. No one moves before that. Copy?"

"Copy. Give me real-time updates, Bravo Three."

"Roger."

"All Reaper callsigns, copy?"

"Copy."

The minutes seemed to drag by like a three-ton weight at the end of a chain. Then Bravo Three came back to him. "Bravo Three, to all Reaper callsigns. Thirty seconds until Hellfire release, over."

The missile would be fired from a height of five thousand meters. At its optimum speed of four hundred-fifty meters per second, the first laser-guided Hellfire would take approximately ten seconds to reach its target.

"Target acquired," Teller's voice was calm, methodical.

Reynolds said, "First missile away."

Kane counted the seconds off in his head until he

reached eleven. At that point, two things occurred. The small convoy drew level with their position, and the second SUV in the line was decimated. The high-explosive charge in the Hellfire was designed to knock out a tank. The armored SUV stood no chance.

Kane watched as a large orange and black ball of flame shot skyward. Debris by way of razor-sharp shards of metal and glass blew in all directions.

The truck carrying the money skidded to a halt a heartbeat before it slammed into the blazing wreck. The driver threw it into reverse and started to back up.

Kane toggled his push-to-talk. "Reaper Two, take out the tires on the truck."

He heard Cara say, "Copy."

The truck started to move and backed into the front of the rear SUV. That vehicle, in turn, began to back up in a hurry and shaped to turn around.

Kane heard, "Missile two away."

Ten seconds later, the Hellfire had the same devastating effect on the half-turned SUV; flames, debris, the shattered, scorched remains of those within.

The money truck stopped dead in its tracks. The near side tires were shot out, and Cara had just tested the passenger's window with a 7.62mm NATO round. It punched through the glass with ease and slammed into the passenger. Through the scope, she saw him slump over.

"Reaper One, moving," Kane said and rose to his feet. He raised the HK and moved down the slope. In his ear, he heard Traynor say, "Reaper Three and Four, moving."

"Reaper Two, keep an eye out for threats from the lead SUV."

"Roger."

Kane immediately heard gunfire erupt from the far side

of the truck. The driver had emerged and began firing at the two Reaper men as they approached.

"Reaper One, we're taking fire from the truck and the lead SUV."

"Reaper Two?"

"On it," Cara said. Then, "Tango down."

Kane looked and saw the doors open on the black SUV. On the near side, a cartel man lay in the dirt. Another had taken shelter at the front of the vehicle, while one or two more were on the off side.

The team leader saw movement under the truck where the remaining occupant had squirmed for cover. He heard the staccato sound of an AK as the Tango fired at Traynor and Hawk.

Bullets hammered into metal above the man's head as he kept firing. Kane swept his HK around and went down on one knee. He sighted on the man's boot and squeezed off a shot.

The foot jumped, and the wounded man howled with pain. His firing stopped, and he went still after a bullet from either Reaper Three or Four smashed into his head.

Kane shifted his aim to the SUV and tried to find a target, but they were masked by the vehicle.

He toggled his push-to-talk. "Reaper Two, can you get a clear shot at any of the remaining Tangos? Over."

"Negative, Reaper One."

"Put some fire into the damned thing anyway," Kane snapped.

"Roger."

"Reaper Three, sitrep."

"These fuckers are dug in behind a large rock, Reaper," Traynor said. "We can't advance because they're laying down too much fire."

On cue, the gunfire seemed to crescendo and then drop away. Kane heard a muffled, "Shit!" as Traynor still had his mic open.

"Do what you can, Reaper Three. Keep them busy."

"Roger."

Crouched low, Kane made a bee-line for the truck. When he reached it, he dropped to his belly and started to crawl beneath it.

"Reaper Three? Reaper One. I'm under the truck, don't shoot me."

"Roger, Reaper One."

As he moved past the dead cartel man, he saw a gruesome hole in the top of the head where a bullet had punched into it. The eyes were wide, the face covered with tattoos.

Kane slithered out from under the truck and came up on one knee. He saw Traynor and Hawk, both on their bellies behind a rock which was hardly sufficient to provide enough shelter for a rabbit, let alone two grown men. The fire from the cartel people was tremendous. Bullets ricocheted all around them. Puffs of dust spurted upwards like small geysers with every bullet strike.

He turned to his right and saw them sheltered behind the large rock that Traynor had told him about. They were armed with more modern weapons, which, from a distance, looked to be FX-05s.

Kane glanced back across at the two men who were pinned down. There would be no assistance from that quarter.

"Reaper Two? Reaper One. Can you give me a sitrep on the third shooter? Over."

"Still same as before, Reaper."

"Roger."

He closed his eyes and took a deep breath. "Shit!"

Frontal assault.

Kane came to his feet and raised the HK416 to his shoulder. The red dot sight fell upon the closest shooter who'd caught his movement. The cartel man began to turn but only made it halfway before Kane put two 5.56 slugs into him.

The man jerked under their impact and fell to the ground. His companion was quicker than his dead friend had been and whirled. His finger depressed the trigger and held it. Hot rounds from the FN-05 tore through the air about Kane as the man sprayed them with careless abandon.

The one-time MARSOC Recon marine kept his cool, and as soon as the red dot sight landed, he squeezed the trigger twice.

The shooter jerked like a rag doll and fell back. His boots kicked in the dust, and then he died.

That left Salazar, who suddenly appeared from around the front of the SUV. The two locked eyes immediately before the *sicario* opened fire with his weapon.

"Fuck!" Kane snarled and threw himself sideways as angry lead hornets filled the space he'd just occupied. Salazar was not a cartel soldier. He was the real deal, a professional.

By the time Kane rolled and came back up, he caught sight of the *sicario* disappearing into the SUV.

The door started to swing closed, and Kane let loose a burst of gunfire which ricocheted off the armored exterior. No sooner had the door slammed shut when the engine roared to life, and the vehicle lurched forward.

A rooster-tail of dirt and gravel spurted out from beneath the rear tires. It fish-tailed side to side, trying to gain purchase on the loose surface, straightened and then disappeared in a cloud of dust.

"Damn it!" Kane cursed. "Reaper team, call in."

"Reaper Four, OK."

"Reaper Two, OK."

"Reaper Three, OK."

"Bravo One? Reaper One. We've secured the money, but Salazar got away, over."

"Copy, Reaper One."

"Reaper One? Zero. Are your people OK? Over."

"Roger, Zero."

"Load the money and come home, Reaper. Forget about Salazar. We'll leave the UAV in the air until you're ready to leave. Good job. Zero, out."

"Reaper One, out."

CHAPTER 15

Montoya

"I want them all fucking dead! Do you hear me? Dead!" Montoya raged. He stabbed his finger into his own chest. "How dare they think they can steal *my* money and get away with it. I don't care who they are, Cesar. They must all die."

"Why worry?" asked Carmella. "You have plenty more."

Montoya's eyes flared as he whipped his head around so fast that he almost gave himself whiplash. Carmella sat on the white sofa, working on her nails. She cared not that her husband had lost close to twenty-million dollars. Like she said, there was plenty more where that came from.

However, Montoya was in no mood for her flippant attitude. In two strides, he was at the sofa, and his right hand shot forward and locked around her throat and squeezed hard.

Carmella's eyes bulged, and her tongue started to

protrude between her lips. He raised her, kicking and lashing out with her arms, from the sofa, so she stood before him, fear and pain in her eyes. His eyes, on the other hand, showed only the glowing embers of red-hot rage. Through gritted teeth, he said, "When I want you to fucking speak about business, I'll tell you. Until I do, shut your mouth, *puta*."

He shoved her roughly back down onto the sofa. She rubbed at the deep marks her husband's hand had inflicted. Carmella gathered herself and looked up at him. All the fear was gone, replaced now by anger.

She spat, "Fucking asshole! You do not touch me like that. I am not one of your *imbécil soldados* you can treat any way you wish. Save it for them or your whores. If you do that again, I will kill you!"

Salazar froze. He'd never heard anyone speak to Montoya in such a way before. Even the beautiful, hot-headed Carmella. Then the cartel boss surprised his *sicario*. He smiled. Laughed even. He said, "*Cariño*, I do believe you would. My apologies for the way I treated you. It will not happen again."

"It better not, Juan. I will not stand for it."

"Leave us. Cesar and I have things to discuss."

With her anger still plain to see she rose from the sofa, stared hard at her husband, then turned and walked out of the room.

Montoya turned to his *sicario*. "You see that, Cesar? She may be afraid of me, but she still has the courage to speak her mind."

"What do you want me to do about the Americans?" Salazar asked, changing the subject.

The cartel boss' eyes hardened. "They dared to attack

me in my country, and they stole my money. So, we will do the same. We will attack them."

"But what will stop them from attacking us again?"

"We will let the Mexican government do it," Montoya explained. "I will reach out to one of my many contacts inside their corrupt castle, and he will then do our work for us."

"It must be someone important for the *gringos* to take any notice of them, *Jefe*."

Montoya smiled. "It will be, Cesar. It will be."

––––––

Washington, The following day

There was a knock at Secretary of State Frank Muir's door before it swung open, and a tall, slender woman in a pantsuit filled the void. He removed his glasses and asked in a tired fashion, "What is it, Wendy?"

Wendy gave him a wan smile. "Sorry to bother you, sir."

"It's OK. I was going to sleep reading these papers anyway. So, how can I help?"

"There is a call for you from Mexico's Secretary of Foreign Affairs, Ferdinand Morales, sir."

"Any idea what it's about?"

"No, sir," she winced. "But he doesn't sound overly happy."

Muir sighed. "OK, I'll take the call. Thank you, Wendy."

She turned and left, the plush carpet absorbing her footfalls. The door snicked shut, and Muir stared at the large bay window to his left. Outside it was a grey, dismal day.

Rain fell steadily from leaden clouds, a sure sign that the conversation he was about to have would be unpleasant.

Oh, well, might as well get it over and done with. He picked up the phone and put it to his ear.

"Ferdinand, my friend. To what do I owe the pleasure of this call?"

Muir had been right, the voice that erupted from the earpiece was anything but pleasant.

"Don't call me a friend," the voice snarled. "Friends don't send their armed forces onto foreign soil and attack their citizens!"

OK, this had started well.

Muir said, "I'm not sure I know what you are talking about."

"Do not lie to me."

"I assure you, Ferdinand, I know nothing of American forces in your country. Tell me what happened, and I shall get to the bottom of it. I assure you."

Morales took a deep breath and said, "I have been informed that yesterday a party of farmers in Sonora suffered an unprovoked attack by some kind of task force that is being run by your Drug Enforcement Administration. You know that sending armed forces onto sovereign soil constitutes an act of war!"

"I can honestly say that I know nothing of such a task force. Was there anyone hurt?"

"I was told twelve men were killed. Some died when missiles were fired upon them. Can you believe it? Missiles! The rest of those who died were shot by your damned special forces!"

Muir frowned. "Farmers, you say?"

"Yes, farmers."

Alarm bells rang in his head. Even if they were farmers,

surely, if indeed it was an American task force, they would have been able to positively identify them. Still, it didn't explain the fact that they were there in the first place.

"I'm very sorry, Ferdinand. Please, leave it with me, and I'll look into it. I promise you that those responsible will pay for what they have done."

"Make sure that you do. My president will be in contact with yours shortly to protest this unprovoked aggression. My source says that you will find them in Retribution, Arizona."

The phone call was disconnected abruptly from the other end.

"Wait! How do ... Christ," Muir muttered and pressed a button on the intercom.

"Yes, sir?" came Wendy's voice.

"Get me Horton over at the DEA, now!"

———

Drug Enforcement Administration Administrator Rich Horton knew about as much as Muir did. The news was just that to him. News!

"I can honestly say, Mr. Secretary, we have no operations, covert or otherwise, happening in Sonora or any other part of Mexico. Mind you, I'd like to. Whoever is heading up this task force is obviously rattling some cages. I'd bet my left nut that they weren't farmers who were killed."

"That was my thought too," Muir confided. "I'd say they were cartel and some corrupt official in the Mexican halls of power has twisted it all about. Still, we can't have a damned war erupting along the border with Mexico."

"No, sir."

"Tell me something, Rich. Who do you think would set

up a task force without telling you and run it under the auspices of the DEA?"

"It could only come from higher up. Attorney general."

"Or the Assistant AG?"

Horton nodded. "They have the power."

"OK. I'll head on over there right now. Get to Retribution, find out what the hell is going on."

"Yes, sir."

———

Assistant Attorney General Mike Turner had not long hung up from another call when Muir appeared in his office an hour later. Right away, from the look on the Secretary's face, he knew what it would be about. Before Muir could open his mouth to speak, Turner picked up the phone and said to his secretary, "Helen, could you see if William is free and have him come to my office, please. Tell him that Frank Muir is here."

He hung the phone up and stared at Muir. "William will be with us shortly."

"Before he gets here, Mike, you want to tell me why I got a call from the Mexican Secretary of Foreign Affairs earlier today telling me that a DEA task force is operating on their sovereign soil? And what I tell the president after he gets off the phone with the Mexican president? Who has probably already called him, by the way."

"I wondered how long it would be before it came back to here."

"So, it's true?"

"Wait until William gets here, and I'll explain everything."

Muir shook his head. "Damn it, Mike. This better be fucking good."

A few minutes later a tall, grey-haired man entered the assistant attorney general's office.

"Hi, Frank, what brings you into our illustrious company?"

"Frank received a call from the Mexican Secretary of Foreign Affairs about a DEA taskforce on their sovereign soil."

"Oh."

Muir's eyes flared. "Yes, oh. Someone better tell me what the hell is going on before the Mexican government starts telling the world we fired the first shots in a damned border war."

Bell looked at Turner. "This was your plan, fill the man in."

Turner nodded. "A while ago, a DEA agent approached this office about setting up a taskforce to take on the cartels, answerable only to this office. He wanted to handpick those in it so he would get people he trusted. Also, he proposed that the team be allowed to cross borders to hit them in their own backyard. We said no. I said no."

"So why has it gone ahead?" Muir demanded.

"Some new developments occurred, and I revisited the idea. After all, this office can run operations at its discretion."

"Like firing missiles at farmers on the Mexican side of the border?" Muir seethed.

Turner glanced at Bell before he said, "That is troubling. Who told you that?"

"Fernando Morales."

"They weren't farmers," Turner explained. "They were men from the Montoya cartel. They were shifting a load of money from Nogales to his compound when their escort was destroyed by a UAV armed with two Hellfire missiles."

Muir's gaze snapped back to Bell. "Holy shit! You let this happen?"

"Mike is in charge of this operation. Anything that happens, he has the final say. With my full support."

"You're both crazy. You shot the shit out of a drug lord's convoy, risked starting a war, just to destroy his money?"

"Not exactly. We stole it."

Muir's eyes almost popped from his head. "You what?"

"Our team stole the almost twenty million he was shipping."

The incredulous look on the secretary's face said it all.

"Maybe you should go back to the start and fill in some of the blanks, Mike."

Turner nodded. "I was telling you about the new developments that changed everything. Montoya sent his *sicario* across the border, who killed the sheriff of Saguaro County. Cut his head off and left it for the deputy to find. Montoya was using the town as a line to traffic his drugs. He even had one of the deputies in his pocket."

Turner paused.

"That deputy was later killed. When a call came in to one of the DEA agents, he decided to check it out. After which he then called me, again to pitch his taskforce idea. This time he was given the go-ahead and all he needed to get it done."

"Including armed UAVs and permission to cross the border and start a war?"

Turner ignored the sarcasm. "Their primary target is Juan Montoya. The theft of his money is to draw him out onto American soil so we can sweep him up."

"And if that doesn't happen?"

"Then the team will kill him."

"Christ Jesus!"

"That isn't all," Attorney General William Bell put in. "While the team had the Montoya compound under surveillance, they picked up Senator Mac McCarthy paying him a visit. He had given Montoya a file on each member of the task force. How he found out about it, I don't know. There's only a select few in this office who knew about it. They are all being questioned about it as we speak."

Muir held up a hand. "Whoa, hold up a moment. You are talking about Mac McCarthy from Texas, right?"

Bell nodded. "That's right."

"Son of a bitch. Where is he?"

"The FBI has him under lock and key at a secure facility until this is over. Now I have a question for you."

"Go ahead."

"Morales. Did he say who his source was? How he knows about the taskforce?"

"No."

Bell sighed. "I think we can assume that he was tipped off by Montoya."

"That wouldn't surprise me at all," agreed Muir.

"Frank," said Bell, "we need you to convince the president not to shut this operation down. If it works, we'll take down one of the worst cartel bosses of our time. On top of that, if it *does* work, we want to continue the task force and use it against other cartels and drug distributors. It's time to fight back. Convince him that it could well be his legacy long after he's gone."

"I don't know. He's not going to like the department conducting covert operations on foreign soil."

"Then convince him to reserve his judgment until we've

finished this operation. After that, I'll talk to him myself," Bell said. "Or hand him my resignation if it fails."

"We both will," Turner said.

Muir stared at the assistant attorney general and asked, "Does this have anything to do with your daughter, Mike?"

"No!" he snapped.

The Secretary studied his face for a moment before he nodded. "OK, I'll do what I can. But I'd advise you all to get some good results."

"How about twenty-million dollars' worth?" Bell asked.

"That's a start," Muir said. "There is one other thing. I ordered Rich Horton down to Redemption to see what was happening."

"I'll take care of it," said Bell.

Muir shook his head. "I sure hope you fellers know what you're doing."

———

Sonora, That night

"I have been assured, as has the president, that there are no American forces on Mexican soil," Morales told Montoya over the phone.

"They are liars," the cartel boss hissed.

"We both know that," the Secretary of Foreign Affairs said. "We need to prove it beyond any doubt."

Montoya stared at the crystal tumbler in his left hand. It was full of amber-colored liquid. He raised it to his lips and drank. When he lowered it, only half remained.

"Are you still there?" Morales asked.

"I am still here."

"We need proof to take to the president."

"If it is proof you want, then you shall have it."

"Where will you get it?"

"From where they least expect it."

"Don't do anything foolish, Juan," Morales cautioned.

Montoya's voice turned cold. "I am never foolish."

He hung up and stared at his reflection in the large windows, helped by the pitch-black night behind them. He shifted his gaze so he could see Salazar's. "Will your men be ready tomorrow night?"

"Are you sure you want to go to war with the Americans, *Jefe*?"

Montoya turned and gave Salazar a harsh look. "They came to my country and stole my money. It was they who declared war, the *gringos*. Now they will understand what real power the cartels have. Morales says he needs proof that the Americans were on Mexican soil. While you are in Retribution tomorrow night, I want you to bring back a prisoner. Before we are finished with him, he will tell the whole world that the Americans were here."

Salazar didn't like it. In the short time since the theft of the money, Montoya had changed. All he could think about was revenge. He was sending a chainsaw to do something better suited to a surgeon's scalpel.

"Let me go on my own, *Jefe*. I will bring you the proof that you need. Don't let what has happened cloud your judgment."

"Do you think that is what is happening?"

"*Sí*."

Montoya was silent with his thoughts. He stared at Salazar and nodded. "Do it. But do not let me down."

"I will see to it, *Jefe*."

———

Retribution, *Same time*

Kane and the others, with the exception of Traynor, were seated around a circular table, drinking beers when Rich Horton arrived. Ferrero knew that he was on his way, but the DEA Administrator never bothered to announce his arrival, he just barged on in.

Behind him were three other agents, all sour-faced men who looked as though they'd woken up for breakfast and found that someone had shit in their cereal.

Horton screwed up his face and hissed, "I should have known this would be you. Of all the people in the department it could have been, I fucking get you!"

Ferrero lowered his beer to the table and stood. "How about we don't do this here."

"Why? You scared your people will find out how much of a fucking asshole you really are?"

Kane held up his half-empty bottle. "You want a beer? Nice to meet you, by the way."

Horton's eyes snapped to Kane's smiling face. "Who are you?"

"Kane. Field commander."

"Shut the fuck up, Kane. This doesn't concern you."

"Yeah, you're probably right." He nodded, then switched his gaze to the other agents. "What about you fellers?"

They ignored him.

"Suit yourself."

"How about we take this outside, Rich?" Ferrero suggested.

"The hell we will. You know, you could have come to me with this idea of yours instead of going over my head."

Cara and the rest of the team vacated the table and walked away. But not Kane. He wanted to see how this played out.

"And what would you have said, Rich? You'd have shut it down."

"Damned straight. You're taking armed men onto Mexican soil. Not to mention using UAVs with Hellfires."

"Did you talk to the AG, Rich?"

"You damned well know I did. And I told him the same thing. It seems to me he'd rather listen to low-level shit-kickers than anyone with an ounce of sense. Just remember, when this all falls flat on its ass, and it will, neither you, nor your people will ever get another job with the U.S. government again."

"Well, what the fuck are you doing here then?" Kane snapped.

"Excuse me?"

Ferrero gave him a slight shake of the head.

Kane went on, "If you knew all of this before you arrived, then why are you here?"

"I don't have to damned well answer to you."

"In case you haven't worked it out yet, we don't answer to you either. And just so you know, it's working." Kane pointed to a tarp-covered mound in the corner of the warehouse. "See that? Under there is the money we stole from Montoya to lure him out."

Horton frowned. "How much?"

"Almost twenty million dollars."

The surprise was unmistakable on the DEA Administrator's face. "I guess the AG forgot to mention that, huh?"

"Maybe."

"He's right, Rich," Ferrero explained. "At the moment, we're waiting to see what Montoya will do next. The guys at Davis–Monthan Airforce Base have a UAV in the air right now keeping an eye on things. Normally we would do our own, but tonight is about the team having a rest. They've earned it."

Suddenly, it seemed that all the bluster had gone from the administrator's sails and a calmness settled upon him. He stared at Ferrero and said, "I might hang around for a day or so if it's all right. Maybe you can catch me up on what's happened? Show me around?"

Ferrero nodded. "Done."

Horton turned to face Kane. "I've heard of you. The whole embassy thing in the Philippines. My wife happened to be on the embassy staff when it all went down."

Kane nodded. "Small world."

"Small world."

Kane held up an unopened bottle of Coors. "Beer?"

"Why not?"

———

Kane walked outside into the skin-prickling cool of the night. The moon was full, and stars seemed to fill the sky. An old farm truck rattled along the street, spewing out smoke that was visible even in the darkness.

He saw Cara as she finished a call on her cell, and he walked over to her. In the false light, she smiled at him. "Jimmy says hi."

"How's he doing?"

"He's good."

"How are you doing?"

Her gaze dropped. "I miss him like hell but in saying that, I'm glad he's not here."

Kane touched her shoulder. "Doc will look after him. Once this is over, you'll be able to go visit. How are you dealing with the other?"

"You mean being part of the task force? Being under fire and all the shit that comes with it?"

He smiled. "Something like that."

"I've missed the buzz," Cara told him honestly. "Is that bad? I love my son and all that, and being a deputy was great because I could be with him every day but doing this makes me feel alive."

"I'm hearing you."

"What do you think he'll do?"

"Who?"

"Montoya."

Kane shrugged. "The longer it takes, the worse it'll be, I'm thinking."

"They call it the war on drugs, but it isn't like that, is it?" Cara commented.

"Nope. They say there are no rules in war. The cartels have taken it to a whole other level. I saw things in Colombia that no one should ever see. We were covert, but still, it is hard to miss. Judges assassinated, along with politicians. Police officers constantly wore balaclavas for fear of being recognized and their families being butchered. Their reach is at times unbelievable."

"And this bastard Montoya has files on us all," Cara pointed out.

"I tell you right now, Cara, if you get a chance, you kill him. We don't want him left alive. He's too dangerous."

"But the AG's office ..."

"I don't give two shits what they want. If you get your

crosshairs lined up on his head, you blow his brains out. I'll give the others the same instructions. OK?"

Cara nodded. "OK. After this is all done if Ferrero gets his taskforce, are you going to stay?"

"Are you?"

Cara smiled. "I asked first, Reaper."

"Maybe. I've no one except my sister to worry about. Frankly, the more distance between us, the safer she'll be."

"O'Brien," Cara breathed.

"Yeah."

"You sure have pissed a lot of people off lately, Reaper. It's a wonder you still have any friends left."

"I've got you."

A brief silence hung between them before Cara stepped closer to him and touched his arm. "Yeah, you've got me."

Her voice was soft, alluring. Coupled with her touch, small sparks of electricity surged through him. Suddenly, he no longer looked at her as a team member, but as a woman. She came into his arms, and their lips met. He pushed away from her.

Cara was confused. "What's wrong? Don't you want to?"

"Yes. Hell yes, but not yet, not now. Maybe after all this is done. I need to have my head in the game. You understand?"

She stared at him, not knowing whether to be hurt, angry or relieved.

"Can we revisit this at a later date, please?" Kane asked her.

Cara nodded. "OK. But make sure you do."

"I promise."

CHAPTER 16

RETRIBUTION

"Zero, we have movement at Montoya's compound," Reynolds called to Ferrero.

He looked around from where he sat discussing several operational options with Horton and nodded. "Be right there."

The shout drew Kane and Cara's attention, and they arrived at the station at the same time as Ferrero and Horton.

"What are we looking at?" he asked.

Teller said, "Salazar is about to leave in one of the SUVs."

"On his own?" Kane asked.

"Yes."

"No sign of Montoya?" Ferrero asked Teller.

"None at all, sir."

Reynolds turned her head. "Do you want us to follow him?"

"No. Stick with Montoya. I don't want us off chasing one asshole and have the other give us the slip."

"Yes, sir."

"Do we know how he gets his drugs in?" Horton asked. "Where he stores them?"

"Not as yet," Ferrero allowed. "Although he does have a helicopter as you will see. Sergeant, pan to the rear of the compound."

"Sir."

The camera on the UAV zoomed out to the rear of the house where a helicopter sat on a concrete helipad.

"I doubt it is big enough to ship much at all," Ferrero pointed out.

Horton nodded. "And there are too many ridges and not enough flat areas for a landing strip."

Teller suddenly frowned, deep in thought. He turned to stare at Kane. "Reaper, could you get me the aerial photos off the desk behind you, please?"

"I've got them," said Cara.

"What is it?" Ferrero asked.

Teller took the pictures from Cara. "It may be nothing, but the other day we did a broad sweep of the area and ..."

He flicked through the pictures and found the one he wanted. He handed it off to Kane. It was a picture of the desert country with its copper sands, large rocks, and any amount of cactus you could want. Towards the center of the print though, were two small adobe buildings. Alongside them was a gravel road.

"Reynolds, how long would it take for you to reposition the bird over this area?"

"Ten minutes."

Kane turned and stared at Ferrero, who nodded.

Kane said, "Do it."

"Copy. Repositioning now."

"What did you see?" Horton asked.

"My question, exactly," Ferrero put in.

Kane handed the picture to Horton and asked Teller, "Can you put the picture up on this big screen here?"

He motioned to the thirty-six-inch monitor to his left.

"Sure."

His fingers danced across the keyboard in front of him, and the picture appeared in front of the group.

"What do you see?" Kane asked them.

"A road and some old buildings," Swift spoke for the first time.

"Take a closer look at the road."

"I see it," said Cara. "The section of road that runs past the buildings is straight."

Horton took a pair of glasses from his pocket. He went to put them on and almost poked himself in the right eye. Once they were in place, he leaned forward and squinted. "So it is. The road is straight. But that doesn't have to mean much."

Kane nodded. "Granted. But look beyond the road itself."

They stood staring at the picture, but nobody expressed an opinion on what they were supposed to glean from what lay before them. Finally, Kane said, "Teller, I know you see it."

The air force man nodded. "If you look at the end of the straight piece of gravel road, you'll see that all of the desert plants and rocks are closer to the roadside. However, along the straight piece of road itself, you'll notice that it is fractionally wider, and the desert has been cleared back some."

Teller turned back to his monitors and worked the keyboard again. A live picture appeared which was much like the shot they'd been looking at. "Now, here's the kicker. If I do this —"

They all watched the telemetry change on the screen as Teller worked his magic. He turned back, a broad smile on his face. "The measurements of the road come in at just under eight-hundred meters. Just long enough to land any drug smuggler's light aircraft of choice."

"Damn it, you could be right," Ferrero allowed. "Can we get in closer on those buildings?"

Once again, Teller's fingers did the work. The buildings grew larger on the screen. They looked just like normal rundown buildings. Nothing special, a hole in one of the rooftops, tufts of desert plants growing around them.

"How big are those buildings, Teller?" Kane asked.

"About fifty by fifty; both of them."

"I doubt they're much use for anything," Horton observed.

Then, on cue, just to prove the DEA Administrator wrong, an armed man emerged from the building closest to the road.

"Well, I'll be," Ferrero murmured.

"I guess there might be something to it after all," Horton conceded.

Kane said, "There's only one way to find out."

"You want to go and have a look, Reaper?" Ferrero asked.

"It's the only way to know for sure."

"Who do you want to take?"

"Me, Cara and Hawk," Kane said.

"What about Traynor?"

Kane shook his head. "Truth be told, I'd rather just go with two of us. But in case there is something unexpected there, I'll take one extra."

"I don't mind," Traynor said. "I've been shot at too much lately, anyway."

Ferrero let out a long, slow breath, then he nodded. "All right, Reaper. Go and have a look. Be aware, you won't have any direct air support. I intend to leave it where it is. If the need should arise, then I'll redirect it to you. It's the best I can offer. Other than that, if something happens, you're on your own."

"It won't be the first time. If we leave in the next hour, we can be there before dark. Once the sun goes down, we'll go in and take a peek."

"What do you want to do if you find something?"

"Can I make it go bang?"

Ferrero glanced at Horton who said, "This is your show, Luis, I'm only here as an observer."

Ferrero nodded. "Make it go bang, Reaper."

———

"You two all good?" Kane asked Cara and Hawk as they finalized their equipment.

Hawk nodded. "Sure."

"Cara?"

"All good," she acknowledged as she placed some spare magazines in a large duffel.

"You both have extra ammo, silencers, flash-bangs, night-vision kit ..."

"... and extra batteries for comms, maglite," Cara continued.

"What weapon did you pull from the armory?"

"The M110."

"Grab yourself an HK416 with laser sight instead. Up close and personal tonight. Both of you be ready in twenty."

"Copy."

———

Sonora

"Zero? Reaper One. Reaper team moving in."

"Copy, Reaper One."

"Cara, on me. Hawk, cover our six. Only fire if you need to."

"Copy."

Kane moved forward through the darkness. With his night-vision goggles down, the desert turned from a burnt-orange arid landscape into a green-hued moonscape. Above them, the dark cloudless sky was full of stars. He raised his silenced HK, and immediately the laser sight's beam reached out across the desert.

Somewhere out there amongst the rock and cactus, a coyote howled, a low, mournful sound that would send a shiver down anyone's spine.

They were all decked out in their tactical vests, pockets filled with spare magazines. Each carried a flash-bang grenade and, in a holster strapped to their thigh, they carried an HK USP also with a laser sight.

All three wore combat helmets with the NVGs fixed to them, and each had their own personal cameras.

Before he moved off, Kane toggled the radio. "Bravo Two? Reaper One. All cameras should be up. How are they looking? Over."

"Reaper One? Bravo Two. Confirm all cameras are up and operational," Swift came back.

"Copy. Reaper One, out."

They had two miles to trek to reach their target. It was all over rough terrain. Dry washes, rocks, gravel, cactus, even rattlesnakes. It was a harsh and merciless landscape that could kill the careless.

The team traveled in silence until they were no more than three hundred meters from their target where Kane stopped them.

"OK, listen up. This is my world. We don't know what we're walking into or how many Tangos we'll find on the inside. If possible, they won't even know we're there until it is too late. However, if things go hot, pick your targets and put them down the first time. Any questions?"

Hawk said, "Yeah. Can I go home?"

"Just make sure you don't go home in a body bag, Hawk. That would inconvenience me somewhat. Because I ain't humping your dead ass out of here. Come on, let's get it done."

Kane toggled his comms. "Zero, Reaper One, copy? Over."

"Copy, Reaper One."

"We're moving in. Out."

"Copy, you're moving in. Zero, out."

———

Retribution, *That same time*

The black SUV rolled slowly into Retribution, its tires crunching on the intermittent layers of gravel which had been used to fill potholes. Its headlights swept across the facades of darkened stores each time it turned a corner.

Behind the wheel, Salazar's face was lit a luminescent

green by the dash lights, his eyes darting left and right as they looked for any sign of trouble. He took a left-hand corner and from his mental notes, knew that one more right a little further on would have him close to his destination.

He squinted as the headlights from an oncoming car filled his windshield. When it passed, he could see that it was a state trooper's cruiser.

Salazar tensed, and his eyes flicked to the rear vision mirror as he watched it start to recede into the distance. It kept going. Fifty yards, a hundred, one-fifty, two-hundred, then the brake-lights came on, and it did a U-turn.

"*Mierda!*" he spat caustically. "Shit!"

The green glow on the *sicario's* face changed to red and blue when the cruiser's rooftop light bar started to flash, the reflection from the mirror beaming it onto his skin.

Salazar's mind began to work overtime as he tried to figure out what to do. Then he saw an alley up ahead on the right and turned into it. He parked far enough along so the trooper would pull his car in behind and be out of sight from the street.

The *sicario* reached inside his jacket and took out a silenced FN Five-Seven handgun and lay it by his thigh. Then he waited.

The car pulled in behind Salazar and did exactly as he hoped. The glare of the headlights filled the mirror, and he could just make out the trooper who got out of his vehicle.

The officer rested his hand on his holstered sidearm and approached the driver's side door with cautious steps.

Salazar rolled down his window and looked up at the mustachioed man who stared down at him. He gave him his best smile and said, "Evening, officer. Did I do something wrong?"

The trooper eyed him suspiciously. Maybe because

Salazar was a Mexican driving around the streets of Retribution in the dark, or maybe because of the recent trouble with the cartels. The trooper shook his head. "Nope, just routine, can I see your driver's license, please?"

"Sure."

Salazar reached slowly into his pocket and withdrew the fake license. He passed it over, and the officer held it up to the light provided by his own vehicle's headlights. The trooper muttered something and reached down to get his small light to shine it on the license.

He examined it, and then shone the light on Salazar's face. "What brings you to Redemption, Mr. Gonzalez?"

"I am passing through to Tucson, officer. I have a seminar on irrigation systems."

Behind the glaring light, the trooper raised his eyebrows. "In the desert."

"Where else would you need water if not the desert?"

The trooper handed the license back. "You've got a point there. Have a safe trip, sir. Remember, when traveling at night, if you get tired, pull over and have a rest."

Salazar smiled. "I'll do that."

That was it. The trooper turned and went back to his car.

Salazar watched him go all the way back and climb into the car. It then reversed and disappeared.

The *sicario* placed the Five-Seven on the passenger seat and slipped the SUV into reverse. He backed all the way to the mouth of the alley and out onto the street. He reached down to place the vehicle into drive when a gun came in through the still open window and its hard barrel pressed against his head. A voice hissed, "Turn the engine off, asshole, and get the fuck out of the car!"

———

The cell in Ferrero's pocket buzzed, and he cursed at it. He reached down without taking his eyes from the live feed before him and pulled the accursed culprit from his pocket. He felt for the answer button with his thumb and raised it to his ear. "Ferrero."

Still, his eyes never left the live feed, but they changed, grew harder, his jaw set firm. Then, "Thanks."

Ferrero dumped his headset on the desk where he stood, turned away from the monitor and swore, "Shit! Fuck!"

"What is it?" Horton asked.

Ferrero had already started towards the door when he said, "Take over, Rich. A young trooper just pulled Salazar over in an SUV not far from here. They want us to take a look. Apparently, he's on routine patrol, and he's the only cop in town. They haven't manned the sheriff's office yet. All this shit going on in Retribution, and the dumb bastards only have one trooper holding down the fort."

"Wait, Luis. You're needed here. Let me go. I can take care of it."

Ferrero stopped, thought about it, and then nodded. "OK. All yours."

Horton singled out his men and snapped, "You three, on me."

"Zero? Reaper One. Am about to breach. Out," the voice was hushed.

Ferrero hurried back to the desk, replaced the headset and said, "Copy, Reaper One."

———

"I said get out of the fucking car!"

"Easy, officer," Salazar cautioned him. "I don't know who you think I am, but I can assure you, I'm not him."

"Bullshit! You're Cesar Salazar. I know who you are."

The *sicario* thought about reaching for the Five-Seven and decided against it. This *Americano* policeman was just nervous enough to pull the trigger for no reason. "OK, officer, I'm getting out. You won't shoot me, no?"

"I'll fucking shoot you if you don't get out."

Salazar eased the door open and slid from the seat. The weapon in the trooper's hand shook. Whether due to nerves or exuberance, the *sicario* wasn't sure.

"Move to the front of the vehicle and place your hands on the hood," the trooper barked.

Salazar did as directed, and his hands rested on the hood of the SUV.

"Spread your legs."

He complied.

"Now, don't move or I'll shoot you."

"I can –"

The gun was pressed hard against the back of the *sicario's* head. "Shut the fuck up."

Mistake!

With movements akin to lightning, Salazar stepped to the right and whirled around. Caught off-guard, the trooper froze and gave the *sicario* the precious heartbeats he required to commit a maneuver so graceful it was almost pretty to watch. Salazar seemed to spin around the trooper's immobile body and once behind him, placed one hand firmly on his chin, while the other wrapped around the back of his head. Then with one violent movement, the head was twisted, and an audible crack sounded.

The trooper's legs turned gelatinous, and he dropped to the street, dead. Salazar looked about to see if there had been any witnesses to the killing. When he saw no one around, his next thought was about what to do, as he was almost certain that it had been called in.

What he needed was time. He heard the screech of tires from somewhere along the road and knew he didn't have much of it.

———

When Horton and the others arrived, they found the trooper standing over a prone form on the street. He leaped from the almost stopped vehicle and swore, "Damn it! I'm DEA Administrator Rich Horton, what in Christ's name happened?"

The trooper never turned around. "The fucker tried to kill me, so I had to take him down."

"Shit! No great loss, son," Horton assured him. "He was a bad son of a bitch. Probably got what he deserved."

The trooper nodded.

One of the other DEA agents knelt beside the body to check for any sign of life. His fingers touched the neck to feel for a pulse. He then used a small flashlight to shine on the face.

The gasp was audible, and his head snapped up. His mouth opened. "It's not –"

The silenced Five-Seven appeared in Salazar's hand and coughed twice. The crouched DEA agent was slapped back, his words cut short. Salazar twisted and fired twice more. The second and third agents died without a sound.

The only man left was Horton, who reached into his coat to pull his personal weapon. He never even managed to get it halfway out before the Five-Seven snapped into line with his face.

"If you do not wish to end up like your *compañeros, señor*, I would think very carefully about drawing your weapon," Salazar warned him.

Horton left the gun where it was and raised both hands. His face screwed up in anger. "Fucking murdering son of a bitch."

A mirthless smile split the *sicario's* face. "I would like to stand here and swap insults with you, DEA man, but unfortunately for you, we will be leaving."

"The hell we are. I ain't going anywhere with you."

Salazar didn't bother to argue. He just stepped in close and brought the butt of his gun down hard on Horton's head.

Horton collapsed as though poleaxed. "I disagree, *gringo*."

A short time later Horton was bound, loaded into the back of the SUV, and on his way to Sonora.

———

Sonora

"Zero? Reaper One. Am about to breach. Out," Kane's voice was hushed.

"Copy, Reaper One."

Kane came out of the desert on the far side of the improvised runway and hurried across the open space. He stopped on the other side, short of the first building, and while he scanned the area through his NVGs, raised his left hand to wave Cara across.

Once she was by his side, he waved to Hawk and then

used hand signals to direct Cara to move to the first adobe building.

Bent low, Cara advanced, her silenced HK at her right shoulder. When she reached the building, she moved along the wall to the large opening in it. She peered around the corner and saw nothing. There was no sign that it had ever been used for anything.

Cara toggled her radio and whispered, "Reaper one? Reaper two. First building clear. Moving to the second, out."

"Copy."

There were around ten meters between the two buildings, and Cara moved like a wraith across the ground towards the second. When she reached it, as before, she eased along the wall until she made the opening. This one was larger than the first.

She peered around the side of the doorway, everything before her bathed in the green hue of her NVGs. She swept her gaze from left to right and then saw him. A lone man in the far corner of the room.

But he wasn't the only thing to catch Cara's eye. From the edge of the opening, a large portion of the building's floor sloped downward at a steady angle and continued until it reached a doorway, albeit closed, the same size as the one where she stood.

Cara edged back from her position and toggled her radio. "Reaper One? Reaper Two. I've got one Tango in the second building, Over."

"Take care of him, Cara."

"Copy."

She edged back to the doorway and looked again. The man hadn't moved. She was about to bring her HK up to shoot him when something else caught her eye. "Shit!"

Cara backed away and toggled the radio once more. "Reaper? We've got cameras."

"Copy. Wait one."

Thirty seconds ticked by, and Kane was there by her side. It felt like thirty minutes. "What have we got?"

"There is a Tango in the right far corner, and a camera above him."

"Any others?"

"Not that I saw."

"OK."

Kane eased past her to look in on the interior of the structure. Then he edged back. "I only saw the one camera. It doesn't mean that there aren't more."

"What do you want to do?"

"You take the Tango, and I'll take the camera. Once they're both down, we enter and check the corners either side of the door. You go right, and I'll take left."

Cara nodded. "Copy."

"Reaper Four, hold and watch our backs."

"Reaper Four, copy."

Kane and Cara edged up to the opening once more. "On my mark, Cara."

"Copy."

Kane took a deep breath and whispered, "Three, two, one, mark."

They both appeared in the doorway, silenced HKs up to their shoulders. The laser from Cara's weapon settled on the guard, and she squeezed the trigger twice. The cartel man jerked under the impact of the NATO rounds, and he dropped to the floor. "Tango down."

Certain he wouldn't get back up, she stepped into the room and pivoted to her right. Through her NVGs, she saw another camera and fired twice more. The first of the two bullets smashed it. The second knocked it from the wall.

Kane's first shot had disabled the corner camera. He stepped into the room and swept his weapon up to the left and found the wall bare. He heard Cara say, "Tango down," and then he heard her gun fire twice. He swung back to see the camera fall to the floor.

Kane pressed the toggle and said, "Reaper Four? Reaper One. Room clear. Come to us, over."

"Reaper Four, Copy. Coming to you."

Kane swept the room and saw the way the floor sloped down to the secondary doorway. "Jackpot."

CHAPTER 17

"Zero? Reaper One. We have one Tango down and security cameras. Also, there is a closed door I need to know what's behind. Are you able to get me a look? Over."

"Copy, Reaper One. You have a closed door. Wait one. Over."

"Don't be too long, Zero. If they see that their cameras are down, we're in trouble. If you can't, we'll breach. Over."

A few moments later and, "Reaper One? Zero. Bravo Two says we might be able to get a look in there. Wait. Out."

"Come on, hurry the fuck up," Hawk growled in a low voice.

Kane remained silent, after all, Hawk had only vocalized what they were all feeling.

―――――

Retribution

"Damn it, Swift, can we do it or not?" Ferrero's impatience had surfaced quickly.

"I'm working on it. All I'm saying is I might be able to do something."

His fingers danced across the keyboard, the frantic pace making it vibrate as he tried to work it out.

"Ask them what kind of cameras they are?" Swift said.

"Reaper One? Zero. Copy? Over."

"Copy, Zero."

"Bravo Two wants to know what kind of cameras you have there? Over."

"Tell him they're dead ones, Zero. Over."

"Did you get that?"

"Yeah," Swift groaned. "OK. I think we have a signal ... and ... we're in. Holy shit!"

Ferrero hurried across to where Swift sat. "What is it?"

"Get a load of this shit."

Ferrero squinted at the grainy screen. "Damn it, put it on the big screen."

The bigger monitor on the wall switched from the FLIR picture from the drone, to that of a camera inside what turned out to be a bunker.

"Is that what I think it is?" Ferrero asked.

"Yes. A cocaine lab of some kind. My guess is possibly the last stop for finishing it before distribution to be cut and sold."

Ferrero nodded. "Reaper One? Zero, over."

"Go ahead, Zero."

"Looks like you just won the lottery. Cocaine lab for sure."

"Copy. What are we looking at on the other side of the door? Over."

Ferrero glanced at Swift. "Well?"

The screen began to flicker as numerous other cameras came online. After a quick calculation in his head, Swift said, "Reaper One? Bravo Two. Maybe six armed men and ten or so others. Unsure if they will be hostile or not. The possibility of more Tangos due to numerous blind-spots. A vacant, well-lit hallway on the other side of the door. Over."

"Is there time to find the power and cut it?" Hawk asked.

Kane shook his head. "I wish there was, but if someone comes out here, we'll lose the element of surprise."

He toggled his radio. "Zero? Reaper One. We're going in hot. Over."

"Copy, Reaper."

Kane said, "Bravo Two, you're our eyes. If you see anything that's not right, call it. Copy?"

"Copy, Reaper."

"All right. Let's do this. Reaper One, out."

There was a long, drawn-out silence as the Bravo team watched them enter through the unlocked door. They were walking stealthily along the hallway when the bunker suddenly erupted with the sound of gunfire from an unknown source.

Over the loudspeaker, Ferrero heard Kane's raised voice call out, "Contact left! Contact left!"

———

Team Reaper
Sonora

The bullets slapped into the concrete wall all around Kane as the cartel soldier with the AK-47 emerged from an opening in the wall to his left. The snarling, tattooed-face man screeched as he held the trigger all the way back.

A hammer-like blow slammed Kane in the chest, forcing him into the wall directly behind. The air was forced from his lungs, and he couldn't breathe. Stunned, he slid down the hard gray surface. In his ear, he could hear Cara's automatic call of, "Man down!".

His vision blurred and came back in time to see two rounds from Cara's HK416 slam into the cartel soldier's chest.

"Cover me, Hawk!" she snapped.

"Roger."

She knelt beside Kane. "Hey! Reaper? Hey! Are you OK?"

Kane groaned. "Get me the fuck up."

She grabbed his hand and dragged him to his feet. "Are you OK?"

"That hurt."

"Do we continue?"

"Damn straight."

"Zero? Reaper Two. Reaper One still in the fight, continuing mission. Out."

"Copy."

Hawk fired his weapon from up ahead where the passage turned to the right. His shots were answered by a spray of automatic fire that bit chips of concrete from the walls.

Kane saw him lean back around and fire another burst, ducking back to the safety of cover before more rounds cracked through the air.

"How you feeling?" Hawk asked him when he moved to his side.

"Like I been kicked by a mule. What do we have?"

"It opens out into a –"

More gunfire peppered the wall.

"It opens out into a large room where they appear to be doing whatever it is they're doing."

"Break out a flash-bang."

Hawk pulled the pin on an M84 and tossed it around the corner. The explosion brought forth cries of pain and bewilderment which carried to Kane's position.

"Move!" he snapped, and he and Hawk turned the corner. Kane to the left and slightly behind. A man staggered about ahead of them, disoriented from the blast. Hawk dropped him with a burst that ripped into his chest.

More automatic fire sprayed at them and forced the team to hug the walls. Kane reacted first and fired a burst at the ceiling where a large light was situated. It shattered, raining glass to the floor, and the room turned black.

The trio dropped their NVGs into place, and the inky blackness suddenly became their friend. With their NVGs down, everything turned green once more. Ahead of them, three cartel shooters staggered around. Kane's first shot killed the man closest to him. Hawk's killed one to the right.

The third man screeched wildly and started to fire a broad arc in hope, but his aim was too high, and the bullets missed and ricocheted dangerously from the roof. Kane depressed his trigger again, and a small puff of powder erupted from a bag of cocaine as the bullet passed through it before hammering into the Mexican's chest.

"Move!" he snapped and pressed forward.

Kane and Hawk split up to make their way around the large table centered in the room, which held a pile of already-wrapped cocaine bricks. Hawk's gun spat again, and he put a bullet into a prone cartel soldier before moving on. Kane did the same. A live killer behind you was a dangerous one.

"Reaper, on the left!" Cara snapped.

Kane pivoted and brought his HK around in an arc. Huddled against the wall were two women. A fraction of an instant before he was about to squeeze it, he took his finger from the trigger.

"Cara, take care of the women," Kane barked.

Cara reached into her pocket and found a glow stick. She broke and shook it in a vigorous manner, creating a spooky green illumination and knelt beside the women.

"Bravo Two, Reaper One. Talk to me, over."

"Reaper, Bravo Two. Your Tangos have multiplied. The remaining ones have withdrawn to what appears to be an armory where they are presently arming themselves."

Kane cursed under his breath. "How many, Bravo Two?"

"Ten, could be as many as fifteen, over."

"Reaper? This is Zero. Get out now."

"Hawk, deploy the explosives here."

"Copy."

Hawk unslung the pack he was carrying.

"Reaper, this is Zero, get out now. I say again, get out now!"

"We came here to do a job, Zero. We do it before we leave."

"Break! Break! Reaper One? Bravo Three. We've got

movement from the compound. Three open-backed vehicles with mounted-guns. At a guess, they're .50 cals."

"Copy, Bravo Three," Kane turned to Cara. "Take the women above ground. Get ready for incoming."

"Copy, Reaper."

"Reaper One, this is Bravo Two, you have cartel goons coming your way."

"Roger."

Ferrero's voice came over the radio. "Damn it, Reaper."

Kane snapped, "Clear the frequency, Zero! Let me do my damned job! Out!"

He moved to the rear of the room and lifted his NVGs, so he could see along the second short hallway without being blinded by the light. It sloped down away from him, deeper into the earth. He raised the HK and shot out the fluorescent light. The hallway was instantly enveloped in darkness.

With that done, Reaper once again donned his night vision and fell back towards the center of the room.

"How you doing, Hawk?"

"I'll need two minutes tops, Reaper."

"See what I can do."

The first of the cartel soldiers appeared. Two shots and the threat was eliminated. A second was dispatched the same way. A third cartel man was not as brave. He poked his weapon around the corner and let rip with a long burst of fire.

Bullets slapped into the bags on the table, causing them to explode. Others slammed into the rear concrete wall after ricocheting violently from the roof. One round fizzed past Kane's face while another tugged at the material of his tunic.

All but forgotten was the throb in his chest where his

tactical vest had prevented the bullet from ending his life in the earlier ambush.

The HK jumped in his hands as he fired more shots. He heard a shout from the hallway, and the Tango suddenly appeared. The man held a hand to his head where a ricochet had grazed him, causing him some disorientation.

Kane shot him in the chest.

Then silence.

Kane frowned, finger on the trigger.

"Reaper One, Bravo Two. You have six Tangos backed up around that corner about to come your way. Over."

"Copy."

Bravo Three came on the radio. "Reaper One, the three trucks are maybe four minutes out. We've redirected the UAV to give support, but we've only got two missiles. You do the math."

"Copy. Out," then, "Hawk, talk to me."

"One minute."

"You've got thirty seconds. Reaper Two, are you above ground yet?"

"Roger, Reaper."

"Cut the women loose and dig in. We've got three technicals four minutes out."

"Copy."

After a brief shout, a handful of armed cartel men surged around the corner.

———

"Más rápido! Más rápido!" Montoya screeched at the driver. "If they get away, I will cut off your fucking *cojones* and feed them to you!"

"I am –" the truck hit a large bump in the road, and the

driver launched from his seat. Once he'd regained his composure he said, "I'm trying, *Jefe*."

"Try harder."

Someone had dared to attack his underground cocaine lab. His immediate thought was of a rival cartel, but the next one was the most logical. Americans! DEA, special forces, or that damned task force. Yes! It had to be them. Fucking *gringos*.

"*Más rápido!* Fucking move!"

The truck slid around a tight corner, gravel spraying from its rear tires when the driver stepped on the pedal and gave it more gas. The lights from the vehicle behind it bounced wildly and flickered in the mirror.

They were perhaps thirty seconds from their destination. The truck lurched again.

Twenty-five seconds. The driver wrenched the wheel to the left as a large rock rose up in front of them.

Twenty-seconds. Montoya grasped at the door handle while holding a Mexican FX-05 Xiuhcoatl in his other hand. He was never one afraid to get his hands dirty.

Fifteen seconds. Almost there.

Ten seconds.

Then his much-prized cocaine lab exploded.

———

Kane dropped the empty magazine out of the HK416 and slammed another home. He brought the gun up and fired a second burst. An additional cartel soldier dropped to the concrete floor, slumped half-across the body of another.

"Come on, Hawk! Are you done yet?"

"Almost."

"Shit!"

"Reaper, those technicals are getting close."

"Almost done, Cara."

"That's it, Reaper, all set."

"Thank fuck for that. Zero, we're pulling out."

"Copy, Reaper One."

They retreated to the hallway that led up to the ground level. Shots followed hard on their heels and slammed into the concrete corner as they disappeared around it. They ran along the next hall until they reached the doorway. Then up the ramp.

When they passed through the doorway, Cara was there outside waiting for them. "Come on, Cara. Clear the area!"

They were bathed in a sudden bright light as the first technical's headlights swept over them, the vehicle skidding to a halt. "Damn it. Hawk blow the damned thing."

"Copy."

At first, there was a low, hollow rumbling sound, then the noise grew louder, as though a train was screaming towards them. A giant ball of orange flame rocketed skyward as the roof of the adobe structure disintegrated before it.

The concussion wave knocked the three of them to the ground. It washed over them and then out into the desert.

Within seconds, they scrambled to their feet and started to run across the road towards the open desert on the other side.

The first .50 caliber machine-gun opened up. Bright tracer rounds began to chase them across the empty space of the wide road. The second gun quickly followed, spraying the ground behind them with heavy rounds. The noise became louder as the bullets got closer.

They dived into a shallow wash beside the road, and tracers ripped by above them.

Kane squirmed around and brought the HK416 up to return fire. "Everyone OK?"

"I'm good," said Cara.

"Me too," said Hawk. "That was some wild shit."

Satisfied his team was intact, Kane opened fire on the closest technical. Small sparks appeared as the bullets struck the metal of the vehicle. The front windshield disappeared and the man in the driver's seat jerked and died.

Cartel men emerged from the other two vehicles, illuminated by the orange glow of flames behind them.

Cara and Hawk joined Kane on the offensive and raked the other technicals with NATO rounds.

Kane toggled his radio. "Bravo One? Reaper One, come in, over."

"Got you, Reaper One, over."

"We could use a Hellfire about now."

More heavy caliber bullets gouged the area and a giant saguaro behind them exploded when two rounds ripped through it, pulverizing its meaty flesh, cutting it in half, and the now unsupported weight toppled to the ground.

"Wait, one."

A moment of radio silence, then, "Hellfire One away."

"Get your heads down, people," Kane shouted to the others. "We've got a hot one coming in."

They dropped their heads to the ground and wrapped arms around the back of them. Then, nine seconds later, the Hellfire impacted the furthest technical.

Once more, the night pulsed with light when a large orange cloud mushroomed outward. Pieces of twisted metal flew in the air as the vehicle blew apart. Screams could be heard from injured and dying cartel men who had been close to the explosion and were peppered with razor-sharp shards of glowing metal.

Montoya was jolted by the sudden blast. He turned to look and saw the flaming wreck and, in the fire-light, saw one of his men casually bend down to pick up his own arm.

"Motherfuckers," he hissed. "Kill them! Kill the *gringo, putas!*"

Kane heard the screeching of the cartel boss but couldn't pinpoint his exact position. Instead, he picked out one of the closer Mexicans and shot him in the face.

The two .50 caliber guns on the backs of the remaining technicals opened fire again. Tracers scorched through the air, and the staccato, whack, whack, whack, of their impacts occurred all around Team Reaper.

"Bravo One, we sure could use that next Hellfire," Kane said in a loud voice.

Beside him, Cara changed out a magazine and said, "Tell her sooner rather than later."

"Wait one, Reaper."

"We got some of them trying to flank us on our left, Reaper," Hawk shouted.

Kane toggled his radio. "Bravo One?"

"No joy, Reaper. I say again, no joy. There is something wrong with the last Hellfire. Suggest you get the hell out of there at best speed. Over."

"Copy, Bravo One."

"That's a bitch," Hawk called out. "What do you want to do?"

"Shoot and scoot. Give them a good enough burst of fire to keep their heads down and then make a run for it. Concentrate on the fifties."

"Copy."

"On my mark. Three, two, one, mark."

All three of them rose and let loose a long burst of sustained fire before Kane barked, "Now! Go! Go!"

They turned as one and ran into the desert towards the spot they'd infiltrated. Bullets hissed all around them. Kane broke to his right with Cara and Hawk following him. Behind them, in the glow of the burning technical, Montoya screeched orders while he sprayed the dark wildly.

After the three had covered some two-hundred meters, Kane stopped. The gunfire continued to rage, and the tracer rounds indicated where the fire was directed. It hadn't moved from their last known position.

"They can't see in the dark," Cara observed. "They've no idea we've pulled out."

Kane nodded. "Bravo Three, Reaper One. What does your FLIR tell you? Over."

"Your team is clear right now, Reaper One. There are no indications of pursuit. Over."

"Copy. We're falling back to the SUV. If anything changes, let us know. Reaper One, out."

"Copy. Bravo Three, out."

Kane got to his feet. "OK, let's move. Cara, you're on point. If you strike anything that ain't right, call it."

"Copy."

————

"Alto el fuego!" The maniacal screech emanated from Montoya's lips. "Stop fucking firing!"

His man was too slow in following the instruction, and the cartel boss raised the FX-05 in his hands and shot him in the head. "I said stop!"

The rattle of gunfire died away and then ceased. The glow from the burning technical illuminated the surrounding area and showed the livid look etched deep on Montoya's countenance.

He turned around and stared at the burning hole in the ground that had once been his cocaine lab. Another wave of rage washed over him. He raised the FX-05 into the air and from deep down came a rumbling sound.

"Aaargh!" the cartel boss shouted and squeezed the trigger until the magazine was empty. "Find them! Find them and kill them!"

"Sí, Jefe," one of the men said and hurried into the darkness, closely followed by others.

Montoya ground his teeth together. They would pay, someone would pay. Not only had they stolen his money, but they'd cost him millions more by destroying his lab.

Yes! They would pay.

———

Retribution, 1 hour later

Traynor crossed to the desk where Ferrero sat going over recon photos taken by the drone in the few days previous. He said, "The team is on the way back, and the UAV is headed to Davis–Monthan."

Ferrero looked up. "Any news from Administrator Horton?"

"Nothing."

Ferrero reached for his cell and punched in a number. He held it up to his ear and waited. And waited.

He pressed the button to disconnect and looked at Traynor. "Go and find out what's happening. The first report I got was that the trooper was over on Cholla Street.

Take my SUV and draw an additional weapon from the armory, along with a tactical vest."

"You expecting trouble?"

"I don't know, but I've got me a feeling, and it isn't good."

Traynor grabbed the things he required and threw them into a large duffel. He began to make his way towards the door when Ferrero called out. "Take Swift with you."

"I'll be fine, Luis."

"Take him. It's not up for debate."

He nodded. "Fine."

Five minutes later they were in the SUV. The thin voice of the GPS said, *"In two-hundred meters turn left."*

"The boss seems a little anxious about this," Swift observed.

"Yeah."

"Do you think something has happened?"

"I don't know. I guess we'll find out."

They drove on, then, up ahead they saw Horton's SUV and the State Trooper's cruiser.

"This doesn't look good," Traynor said. "Lean over the back and get my HK off the seat."

While the DEA agent eased the vehicle to a stop, Swift retrieved the 416.

"What are you carrying, Sam?"

"Just my Smith and Wesson M&P."

"OK. Watch my back," Traynor told him. "Let's go."

Before he opened the door, Traynor reached up and turned off the interior light so it wouldn't illuminate the vehicle. Then he grasped the handle.

Ding, ding, ding, came the warning alarm as the door swung open. Traynor slipped from the seat and placed the

HK to his shoulder and rested it in the V between the door and the body of the vehicle.

Swift hadn't moved.

"Are you coming?" Traynor asked him.

Once Swift was out of the car, they moved towards the DEA vehicle. The HK was kitted out with a light attachment and Traynor flicked it on. They advanced with slow, deliberate steps. Boots crunched on the road surface with each movement.

The passenger door was open and Traynor swept the interior with the mounted light but there was no sign of any of the agents, including Horton. No blood or evidence of a struggle either.

"Should we call this in?" Swift asked.

"Wait. We'll clear the area first."

They cautiously approached the cruiser and found the same. Empty, no sign of struggle.

Swift asked, "What do you think happened to them?"

Traynor remained silent and lowered the HK's light to sweep it over the surface of the road. It didn't take long to find what he was looking for.

The DEA agent walked three steps before kneeling. He shone the light on the dark patch and touched it with his gloved fingers. They came away tacky. He smelled it. Coppery. Blood.

Like an arrow, a small thin streak pointed away from the puddle. Traynor raised his eyes to follow the line which sent his gaze in the direction of the alley.

He came to his feet and headed towards the mouth of the dark alley. Hesitantly, Traynor swept the ground there with his light to discover a grisly sight. The trooper and the three agents who'd come down with Horton. Of the Administrator, there was no sign. He shook his head.

Traynor reached for the radio on the front of his tactical vest. He toggled the button and said, "Zero? Reaper Three. Come in, over."

Ferrero's voice came back an instant later. "Copy, Reaper Three, over."

"You'd better get out here, boss. This just turned into a whole shit storm."

CHAPTER 18

WASHINGTON, 30 minutes later

Beep-beep, beep-beep. Beep-beep, beep-beep.

"Christ! What now?" grumbled assistant attorney general, Mike Turner.

He rolled over in his bed and fumbled at the cell on the nightstand. It fell onto the floor with a thud.

"Shit!" he cursed and threw his arm over the side of the bed and felt around on the carpet, then picked the phone up.

With practiced fingers, he pressed the answer button and placed it to his ear. "I hope this is good."

"Quite the opposite, Mike," Ferrero said, his voice grim. "Horton's gone."

Turner sat up in his bed, all vestiges of sleep evaporating. "What happened?"

"While we were looking one way, Salazar slipped across the border, killed a trooper and three DEA agents. He took Horton with him."

"Damn it, Luis. What do you mean you were looking one way?"

"We had an op going on in Sonora."

"What op? Why didn't I know about it? Christ, Luis, you were meant to keep me in the loop."

"Yes, sir. Sorry. Horton was here when we discussed it, and he ticked it off."

"Rich Horton isn't in charge, is he? I am. From now on, nothing gets done unless I know about it. Understood?"

"Yes, sir."

"Tell me about the damned op and what happened to Horton."

Ferrero gave him a brief description about the airstrip, the cocaine lab, and the sighting of Salazar in Retribution being called in.

When he finished, Ferrero said, "Sir, I'd like to send Team Reaper back out to raid Montoya's compound to see if Horton is there."

"No. Have your people ready, but that's all. This needs to go further up the chain."

"But, sir —"

"No, Luis. You don't even know if he is there. I'll get back to you."

"Yes, sir."

Turner disconnected and glanced at the bedside clock. One a.m. It was going to be a very long night.

———

Washington
The Oval Office, *One Hour Later*

. . .

President Jack Carter was used to getting bad news in the middle of the night. Being woken during the small hours always put him in a mood but being woken to bad news did little to improve it.

The grey-haired, sixty-seven-year-old head of state stabbed a straight finger at the conference button on the phone sitting on the polished desktop.

"I'm here with Frank Muir, Bill," Carter growled in his deep voice. "Now, how about you tell me what all the damned fuss is about."

"Yes, sir, Mr. President. I have Mike Turner with me on this end."

"Fine, fine," Carter said dismissively.

"Mr. President, this is Mike Turner."

"Speak, Mike, my patience is growing thin."

"Yes, sir. Mr. President, earlier this evening, DEA Administrator Rich Horton was taken from U.S. soil by a man called Cesar Salazar."

Carter glanced at Muir and leaned forward in his chair. "What do you mean? Did this Salazar come to Washington and kidnap him?"

"No, sir. Horton was in Retribution, Arizona, observing an operation we have going there against the Montoya Cartel."

There was a spark of anger in Carter's eyes. "That's a damned name I know. This Retribution thing is quickly becoming a pain in my ass. How the hell did he manage to do something like this."

"Sir, if I may, I'd like Luis Ferrero to join us. He's the agent in charge on the ground down there. He'll be able to fill you in."

"Go ahead," Carter grumbled.

"Luis?"

"Mr. President, has Secretary of State Muir briefed you on what the task force is trying to accomplish down here?"

Carter stared at Muir. "He has. I have reservations about it. Especially after the shit storm it has already caused with the Mexican government."

"It has also flushed out a rogue senator and pointed us in the direction of a corrupt Mexican official in the current government."

Carter was at the end of his patience and snapped, "I'm also aware of that. Get on with it, Mr. Ferrero."

"Yes, sir. Early yesterday, we identified what looked to be an airstrip not far from the compound of Juan Montoya. We also became aware of a lone figure in an area that consisted of two apparently abandoned buildings. To us it seemed strange, so we sent a team in to look. It turned out to be a cocaine lab, which our team destroyed."

Carter sighed. "Some good news at least, Mr. Ferrero. Now, for the bad."

"Yes, sir. While we were doing that, a state trooper pulled over a man in an SUV whom he identified to be Salazar. He called it in for backup, but all that was available was us. Horton volunteered to go because we were in the middle of the op in Sonora. He and three other agents who had come with him answered the call. After the op was complete and I couldn't raise them, I sent out two of my men to investigate. They found the trooper and the three DEA agents dead in an alley. Horton was missing. It is presumed that Salazar has taken him and that by now he is across the border."

Carter ran a hand through his hair. "Jesus Christ."

"Are you sure it was Salazar?" Muir asked.

"We have no reason to believe otherwise," Ferrero said. Then, "Mr. President, if you give us permission, I have a team close at hand who can take Montoya's compound, and with some luck, rescue Administrator Horton."

"How can you be sure he's there, Luis?" Muir asked. "Have you seen him?"

"No, sir."

There was a drawn-out silence before the president said, "No. This time we go through the proper channels. I'll consult directly with the Mexican president, and if he gives us the OK, then I'll send a team of special forces to do the operation."

"Mr. President, the Mexican government is corrupt," Turner protested. "You can't trust them."

Muir said, "I agree, sir, they are more likely to warn Montoya than help us. I say use Ferrero's team to do the job. They know the man and how he operates."

Carter shook his head. "We do this the right way, gentlemen. I'll schedule another conference call with you at eleven this morning. Until then you do nothing. Am I clear?"

"Mr. President?" Ferrero interjected.

"Yes, Mr. Ferrero?"

"Sir, I would like to keep our UAV in the air to monitor the compound if that is all right by you?"

"Fine. While you're at it, get me some proof that he's there. But no boots on the ground, understood?"

"Yes, sir."

Carter disconnected the call and looked up at Muir. "What do you think, Frank? No bullshit, give it to me straight."

"Sir, we have a chance to get rid of a major player in the drug war. At first, I didn't agree with this taskforce idea, but shit, they're getting results, and Montoya is worried. If he wasn't, he wouldn't have taken Horton alive. If we get the chance, sir, I say turn them loose and kill this fucker before he can do any more harm."

"Frank, can you say for certain that this wasn't a retaliatory attack for stealing the son of a bitch's money?"

"It most likely was, sir."

"Why should I use them instead of our own special operators?"

"Firstly, sir, you'd be sending our troops onto foreign soil which technically is an act of war –"

"We are at fucking war!"

"—and another good reason is that Ferrero's people *aren't* military. In saying that, they are good. Their field team is led by an ex-recon marine named Kane. His second was a deputy sheriff and a marine corps lieutenant. So, while technically they aren't military, they have been. Another thing is that they have everything they need to complete the mission on hand."

Carter scowled. "All right. I want the chairman of the joint chiefs brought up to speed on this. I want to hear what he has to say if we take an off-the-books route. I want this field commander of Ferrero's at the next conference at eleven. I want to meet him for myself. And I want files on all of those involved in this team Reaper thing. Understood?"

"Yes, sir."

"Now, get me the president of Mexico."

"Yes, sir."

———

Sonora

. . .

The black SUV came to a stop, its tires crunching on the compound's gravel. In the back, Horton stirred and opened his eyes. The headache was still there, a sure sign that he had a concussion from where Salazar had hit him.

Horton's hands were cable-tied behind his back while a strip of duct-tape had been placed over his mouth.

He heard Salazar switch off the engine and open the door. The sound of footsteps on gravel filtered into the rear as the *sicario* moved alongside the vehicle. Then came the voices. They spoke in Spanish and were muffled so he couldn't understand them.

When the back of the vehicle was opened, hot air rushed in. Salazar grasped Horton by the shirt collar and dragged him mercilessly from the SUV and dropped him to the gravel drive.

Pain shot through his body when he landed awkwardly on his right shoulder. A muffled curse escaped from around the tape.

He looked up and was blinded by the early morning sunlight. There was movement beside him, and he was momentarily overshadowed by a figure which bent down and tore the tape from his mouth.

"Stand him up," the figure ordered.

Horton was manhandled to his feet and stood before a man in a dirty white suit. The face was unmistakable. Juan Montoya.

"At last we meet, huh," Montoya said. "The big American DEA man and the cartel boss. You have been trying to get me for years. Now I have you. Not to worry, though. Over the next few hours, we shall become well acquainted with each other. I for one am looking forward to our conversation."

A cold chill ran down Horton's spine as he realized that

the best he could hope for was a quick death. He stared at Montoya and then craned his head all the way back and looked at the cloudless sky above him. "I hope you're still watching."

_____

Retribution, That same time

"We've got him!" Teller burst out. "That's him, that's Horton. He knew we were watching. He looked up."

Ferrero hurried across to the monitor and saw the group of men huddled together. "Are you sure?"

"One-hundred percent."

"Play it back," Ferrero snapped at Swift. "How far out is Reaper's team?"

"Maybe thirty minutes," Traynor supplied.

The large screen went blank and then came up with the recording from the UAV. Ferrero watched it intently and then, right on cue, Horton looked up.

"It is him," Ferrero breathed. "Get this to the assistant AG, now. Then get him on the line."

"Yes, sir," Swift said.

As Ferrero watched, the group moved inside the house. Then he said to no one in particular, "We don't have much time."

But even now, he knew they were already too late.

_____

"What do we know?" Kane asked as he strode across the

room to stare at the picture of Horton on the big-screen monitor.

Ferrero stepped in beside him, as did Cara. "We know Montoya has him and that the Mexican government isn't going to allow us to mount a rescue mission with any kind of team that is American."

"So, send one anyway."

"There is a meeting with the president at eleven when I'm sure such an option will be discussed."

"Now isn't the time to be talking about anything. It's time to be doing. I can get the team inside there and have Horton out in under five minutes."

If it had been anyone other than Kane making the boast, Ferrero would have cried bullshit. But he'd worked with Kane before, and the man sure knew his own capabilities. He shook his head. "I'm sorry, Reaper, we're under direct orders from the president to stand down until a decision is made."

"Mr. Horton will be dead by then, sir," Cara said.

Ferrero turned and stared at her. His face was grim. "If he isn't already."

"Fuck!" The loud curse came from Swift who sat in front of his monitor.

"I swear that boy can be overdramatic at times," Ferrero growled. He called out, "Found a fly in your morning coffee, Mr. Swift?"

"It's Horton, sir. They're streaming him live on the net."

Kane said, "This can't be good."

They hurried across to Swift's workstation, and the picture showed Horton tied to a chair.

"Christ!" Traynor muttered when he saw the feed.

"Put it on the big screen," Ferrero snapped.

Horton still had his mouth taped over, and there was a

line of blood from a gash above his swollen right eye, which ran down the side of his face and stained the white shirt collar at his throat.

There was movement at the edge of the frame, and a figure walked into view to stand behind the restrained DEA administrator.

"Fucking Montoya," Ferrero cursed.

Montoya looked a fraction to the side and asked, "Is it working?"

An unseen male voice said, "Sí."

The cartel boss stared into the camera. "I have a message for the American special forces who come to my country and steal my money and destroy my property. You deny, *your* government denies that you have done such things. But, here is the proof."

Montoya stabbed a finger at the back of Horton's head. "This man, the head of your DEA, was caught on my land last night when he and others came onto Mexican soil and destroyed my property, killed some of my men."

"Lying sack of shit," Traynor growled.

"You can no longer deny it," the cartel boss continued. "Here is the proof my government wished for. Although I suspect that they are scared of the fascist regime that is run by President Carter, I am not. I will not stand for such acts of war against my country. I will not bow down to their fascist ways. It is time that the *gringo* dogs finally realize that the world will no longer bow down before them."

"The bastard is crazy," Kane said aloud.

Suddenly Montoya was distracted. His eyes ventured to the right of shot, and another figure moved into focus. He whispered something in the cartel boss' ear and withdrew.

"That was Salazar," Kane said with surety.

"What's going on?" Ferrero wondered.

"Sir, we have movement outside the compound!" Reynolds cried out. "Six vehicles. All closing in at a great rate. Oh, God –"

"What is it?" Ferrero snapped.

"They have to be *Policía Federal Preventiva*, sir. *Federales*."

Kane cursed. "Damn it, the bastards are raiding the compound."

Ferrero reacted instantly and barked an order as he walked across the room to see. "Damn it! Get the assistant AG on the line."

"Oh, fuck no!" Traynor blurted out. "Luis, get back over here."

With an about-face, Ferrero hurried back. When he saw what had Traynor bent out of shape, he paled. "No way. No, no, no."

In his absence, Montoya had produced a wicked-looking knife. He held it up for the camera to see clearly and said, "Let this be a warning to those who think they can steal my money and interfere with my business."

The knife lowered, and with one fluid movement, the cartel boss drew it across Horton's throat. It released a torrent of bright-red blood which cascaded across the white shirt-front and turned it a rich crimson.

Kane closed his eyes, not wanting to watch until the end. Already the image was burned deep.

When he opened his eyes, Montoya was gone, and the screen showed the slumped body of the DEA administrator. Then came the sound of gunfire and the picture disappeared.

"What's happening?" Ferrero called out.

"The *Federales* have breached the front gate and are closing in on the house," called Teller.

"Big screen! Now!" Ferrero snapped.

The picture changed to an aerial view of the compound.

Swift appeared beside Ferrero, holding a handset. "Sir, I have the AAG on the phone for you."

He took it and said, "Ferrero."

"What the hell is going on down there, Luis?" came the flustered reply.

"Montoya just killed Horton on a live internet feed."

"My God."

"We do have another issue, sir. The *Federales* are attacking the compound. We picked them up right before Montoya killed the administrator."

"I need to ring the president. Keep an eye on them, and I'll get back to you."

Ferrero looked up at the screen. "Better hurry, sir, I doubt very much that the *Federales* are going to last long."

———

Sonora

The incoming team were not *Policía Federal Preventiva* but wore the same uniforms. They were in fact, a rapid intervention force, part of the Mexican special forces group. They'd been used in the war on drugs ever since the escalation of cartel activity over the past few years.

Capitán Primero Carlos Arenas braced himself as the armor-plated SUV crashed through the gates of the compound, the reinforced steel barrier pitiful against the vehicles. He gripped the FX-05 in his right hand and spoke into his mic. "Prepare to deploy. No prisoners, kill them all."

Every one of the twenty-man team was dressed in a

navy-blue uniform. All had decked-out tactical vests, helmets, and balaclavas which covered all except the eyes.

Most were armed with the FX-05 Xiuhcoatl carbine. A few also had Mossberg 500 pump-action shotguns or H&K MP5s, while all carried a Beretta 92 semi-automatic pistol in a holster on their thigh.

As soon as the vehicles stopped, he flung his door open, and the ten-year veteran of the Mexican armed forces shouted into his mic, "Go! Go! Go!"

The rapid intervention force spilled from their SUVs and was immediately hammered by gunfire from the rooftop of the main house. A strong force of cartel body-guards had gathered there and were now pouring fire down into the ranks of the attackers.

Alarm ran through Arenas' mind. Somehow, they were obviously expecting them. It was the only explanation as to how the surprise raid was being turned back on them.

The special forces men took immediate shelter behind their armored vehicles. Four were already down and hadn't moved. Another soldier tried valiantly to drag a wounded comrade to cover before he fell victim to a bullet in the head.

"Clear the roof!" Arenas shouted into his mic. "Snipers, clear the roof! Cruz, rush the house with your men before we all die out here. They knew we were coming."

Instantly, a squad of four heavily-armed men rushed for the house while the rest concentrated their fire on the gunmen atop the roof.

Cruz and his men had almost made it when two cartel men armed with Striker 12-gauge shotguns equipped with twenty-round revolving magazines, appeared. It was a slaughter as they fired load after load into the soldiers. Their tactical vests might have stopped the lead pellets, but their heads offered no such resistance.

Arenas watched on in horror, and then anger began to consume him. He brought up his FX-05 and shot the first shotgun wielder in the head. He shifted aim and sighted on the second. He was about to squeeze the trigger when a shout from behind one of the other vehicles drew his attention.

"RPG!"

Arenas looked up at the roof in time to see a cartel man with an RPG-7 fire it. With a roar, the rocket streaked forward, leaving behind a white contrail. It hit the third SUV in line which exploded in a large orange ball of flame. Three men sheltering behind it were engulfed in the pyrotechnic display and died within milliseconds.

The special forces commander ground his teeth together. His men were dying because some fucking *puta* had betrayed them.

Another shout signaled the next RPG round. He saw it and yelled, "Shoot him before he fires it!"

Gunfire raked the edge of the flat roof, but it was no use. The RPG roared, and two more men died as the next vehicle in line exploded.

Arenas ducked down behind his SUV as bullets rattled along the far side of it. He glanced down the line. Orange flames leaped skyward from the two burning hulks. He'd brought twenty men with him. Now, he'd be lucky if there were a handful left.

"Carlos, this is Santiago, do you read? Over."

Ruiz Santiago commanded another of Arenas' squads. "I hear you, Ruiz, over."

"We need to pull back, Carlos. Before we are all killed."

"It is too late, Ruiz," Arenas replied. "Whoever betrayed us has already seen to that."

Silence.

"Break! Break! Break! This is Bravo Three calling Mexican force commander on the ground. Do you copy? Over."

Arenas frowned. Americans?

Retribution

"Damn it, Luis, we have to help them. They're getting slaughtered!" Kane demanded after the first RPG blew up the SUV.

"My hands are tied, Reaper. We were ordered to stand down."

Kane swore savagely. "Fuck that, Ferrero. They'll all die unless we do something. You've got a UAV in the air."

"Reaper –"

Kane never took his eyes from Ferrero when he said, "Teller, does that UAV have a Hellfire attached to it?"

"It has two, Reaper."

"It'll all be over in a few minutes if we do nothing, boss," Cara joined in. "They just lost another vehicle."

"Get them some help, Luis," said Traynor.

Hawk was next. "Do it!"

Kane's voice softened. "Come on, Luis. They're the good guys."

Ferrero shook his head. "Shit. Swift, can we break into their signal?"

"Already done it."

A wry smile touched Ferrero's lips. "Teller, it's all yours."

"Yes, sir."

Kane nodded. "Thanks, Luis."

"Break! Break! Break! This is Bravo Three calling Mexican force commander on the ground. Do you copy? Over."

_____

Sonora

"This is *Capitán* Primero Carlos Arenas. I read you loud and clear, over."

"You look like you could use some help there, Captain," the American voice crackled. "Tell your men to keep their heads down. We have a special delivery on the way."

"A special delivery?"

"A Hellfire missile, Captain. It should be there in eight seconds."

Arenas' eyes grew wide. He shouted into the mic. "Everybody, get down! Get down! Get down!

And then the Hellfire hit.

Montoya's house exploded outward. Those cartel men on the roof who weren't incinerated by the blast were thrown from their positions onto the ground below.

Orange flames shot through the windows after they blew out, and heat washed over the few special forces soldiers that remained alive. The concussive wave hit Arenas a solid blow even though he was behind the SUV.

Debris started to rain down on them, but what the

special forces commander would never forget was the ringing in his ears. The blast had been deafening.

It took a few moments before Arenas realized that the American was calling him again on the radio.

"Bravo Three, calling Captain Arenas, come in, over."

"I'm here," he groaned.

"You all still alive down there?"

Arenas looked around and saw the remnants of his crew trying to gather themselves. Then he realized something else. The gunfire had stopped.

"I think we are all fine, thank you. Who are you?"

"Glad you're all OK, Captain. Our indications are that the cartel men are all gone. The missile we fired took them out. Best of luck. Bravo Three, out."

"Wait –" But he was too late. Whoever had come to their rescue, was gone.

CHAPTER 19

RETRIBUTION

The video conference was up on the big screen. It was split into three sections which consisted of the two attorneys-general, the chairman of the joint chiefs, and the secretary of state, and one very pissed-off president.

"How about someone tells me what the fuck happened?" he thundered from behind his desk.

"Which part, sir?" asked Ferrero.

"Oh, I don't know. How about we start with how the DEA administrator got killed, or even the fact that the Mexicans launched a raid without our knowledge. *Or the fact that we launched a fucking missile into that compound without permission!*"

Kane said, "The first part is easy, Mr. President. Horton got killed because we were left sitting around playing with our dicks! The same thing would have happened to the Mexicans if we hadn't intervened."

Muir blanched, Assistant Attorney General Mike

Turner shook his head, and Ferrero remained straight-faced. Carter, on the other hand, turned a different shade of red.

"Who the hell are you?" he roared.

"Kane."

"You don't speak until I tell you to."

"Yes, sir. But first, would you tell me what dick decided it was a good idea to tell the Mexican government about Horton before we had a chance to get him back? Especially when their ranks are filled with men owned by the cartels."

"That *dick* would be me," Carter said through clenched teeth. But then he sighed and said, "It would seem like you're hellbent on speaking your mind, Mr. Kane. Let's get it over with."

"You told the Mexican government, sir, then you are partly to blame for Horton's death."

"Kane," Attorney General William Bell cautioned him.

Carter held up his hand. "No, let him speak."

"We had a window, sir. A chance of getting Horton back. Montoya wasn't going to kill him straight away. He wanted to make an example of it. But just before the attack, there was a phone call from an outside source. We know this because our tech guy found it. That was when he killed Horton. The call was the warning about the inbound special forces team. And that was why they were slaughtered."

For a moment, the president didn't know what to say. He leaned back in his chair, and Muir whispered something in his ear. Once they were done, he said, "Is your tech guy there?"

"Yes, sir."

Kane stepped back for Swift to move in. "Mr. President."

"Is what Mr. Kane said true?"

"Yes, sir. The call came from Mexico City."

"Thank you."

"Yes, sir."

Carter nodded. "All right. Who ordered the missile strike?"

Ferrero lifted his chin. "I did, sir."

"My orders weren't clear on that one, Mr. Ferrero?"

"Very clear, sir."

"Good. You're fired."

Kane looked as though he was about to come through the monitor, but Ferrero stayed him with a hand. "That team would have died to a man had we done nothing, sir. They arrived twenty strong. When it was over, there were five. Ask their commander what he thinks about our intervention."

Carter shook his head. "You disobeyed a direct order, did you not? You blew the crap out of Montoya's house and didn't even get him. Am I right, General Jones?"

General Hank Jones, chairman of the joint chiefs, nodded. "Our intel says that he isn't there, sir."

"We can find him, sir," Kane interjected.

"How do you propose to do that, Mr. Kane?"

"I'd like to know that myself," Muir put in.

"By going to the source of that call."

Carter raised his eyebrows. "Mexico City?"

"Yes, sir."

"You know who made the call? Is that what you're saying?"

"Yes, sir."

"Who?"

"Ferdinand Morales."

"Oh, shit!" Muir blurted out.

"This is a bad idea, Kane," A-G Bell put in.

Carter leaned forward once more in his chair and stared directly into the camera. "You're telling me that you want to go after the secretary of foreign affairs of Mexico?"

Kane's face never altered.

"Yes, sir."

"Damn, man. You've got some big balls. How do you propose to accomplish such lunacy?"

"With the help of an insider, sir. I would go and take one of my team with me. We would question him, get the information we require, and then leave."

"Just like that?"

"Just like that."

"And if you get the information you require?"

"Then, with your permission, we go after Montoya and Salazar," Kane confirmed.

Carter sighed. "I like you, Mr. Kane. You're not afraid to say what you think no matter what the consequences. All right put your plan into action. Just remember this, if it goes wrong, then you're on your own."

"One more thing, sir."

"Yes?"

"A team is only as good as the man running it."

Carter hesitated. "All right. Mr. Ferrero, you're back in. Whether or not you stay in depends on how the team performs. Hell, if they perform badly, you're all out. Good day, gentlemen."

The president's screen went blank.

The general cleared his throat. "Could I have a quick word, gentlemen, please? Ferrero and Kane, I mean."

Bell and Turner nodded. Turner said, "Keep me up to speed, gentlemen." And then they too disappeared.

"Fire away, General Jones," Ferrero said.

"First off, gentlemen, I admire what you're all doing. I

think taking the fight to the cartel's doorstep is just what this country needs."

"Thank you, General," Ferrero said.

"I also admired the way you didn't take a backward step, Gunny. Takes some balls to stand up against the president the way you did, for your commander."

"Thank you, sir."

"Now that is out of the way, I want to offer you, gentlemen, anything you need to help with your operation. Choppers, men, planes, any intel avenues you need, hell I'll give you the whole U.S. Navy if you require it. Anything at all, you call direct to me. I knew Rich Horton from a long way back. So, if you need it, just holler."

Ferrero nodded. "Thank you, General."

"I don't offer it lightly. I've done my research into your whole team. I know who did what, where, and how they went about it. Before I go, is there anything at all?"

Ferrero said, "Not at the moment, I don't think, General."

"Gunny?"

"Do you have any contacts in the Mexican military, sir?"

Jones frowned. "A few."

"Could you maybe get someone sent across the border, say, as a liaison?"

"I presume you have someone in mind?"

"Yes, sir," Kane confirmed. "*Capitán Primero* Carlos Arenas."

"Someone special?"

"He was the commander of the special forces team from the raid on Montoya's compound."

"Consider it done, Gunny."

"Thank you, sir."

The screen went blank, and Ferrero turned to Kane. "If you ever speak to the president of The United States like that again, you're out. You hear?"

Kane's face remained passive. "You're welcome."

Ferrero ignored it. "What's your plan for Arenas?"

"I figure he can get us in and out of Mexico City."

"You figure he's mad enough to do so?"

"Wouldn't you be?"

"Point taken."

Ferrero walked off, and Cara approached Kane. "Which one of us do you think is crazy enough to go with you?"

He looked into her brown eyes and smiled. "I thought you might be up for it."

She reached up and jabbed his chest with a straight finger. Her eyes flashed when she said, "I'm up for anything."

Kane returned her smile. "I bet you are."

She nodded and poked him again. "Uh huh. Unlike some people I know."

"You'd best watch that finger of yours."

"Oh yeah," it came forward again.

Before the appendage even touched him, Kane moved swiftly, and Cara found herself facing the other way, strong arms wrapped around her and unable to move.

"You're quick," she acknowledged.

"Uh huh." He was suddenly all too aware of her firm body against him. He whispered in her ear, "I need a shower."

Kane released her and headed for the door. Cara smiled to herself as she watched him go. Then she said in a hoarse voice, "Me too."

———

Cara traced a finger over the scar on Kane's chest and said, "The next time we do this we don't use your room. Your shower is too small to be doing shit like that."

"I was quite happy having a shower until you came along," he said with a smile. "Nice tattoo on your ass by the way."

Cara's face reddened. "Drunk Saturday night in Tokyo."

"Why would you get Daisy Duck?"

"It was a bet, OK?"

"I *bet* your husband loved it?"

"He did, actually."

Silence descended over the naked couple. Kane stared at the ceiling while Cara had her head resting on his chest, listening to his strong heartbeat.

Kane asked, "What was his name?"

"Byron."

He chuckled. "Was there a Lord in front of that?"

Her hand slid in a swift movement and grabbed his left nipple between thumb and forefinger. She gave it a savage twist.

"Ouch, shit!"

"You're awful, John Kane."

His face grew serious. "What happened, Cara?"

Her voice turned somber as she recalled. "We were living in Phoenix at the time. I was deployed. Byron and Jimmy were at home, and Jimmy finished the last carton of milk in the refrigerator. Byron went out to get more and never came home. It took Jimmy a long time to get over it. He blamed himself."

"Tough."

"Yeah. What about you, why did you get out?"

"Figured it was time. Saw too many good men die, good friends."

"So, you went private?"

"Seemed like a good thing at the time."

"And now you're here."

Kane sighed. "And now I'm here."

Cara rolled over and climbed out of the bed. Kane watched her and smiled to himself when he saw the way the tattoo came to life when her lithe body moved.

"You're staring at my ass, aren't you?"

"Nooo."

"Liar."

"Where are you going?"

"For another shower," she called over her shoulder.

"Wait for me."

Kane scrambled from the bed and stood up. The ripple of his taut back muscles animated the large tattoo there with each movement. The detailed artwork covered a considerable quantity of his skin, from shoulders to waist, and depicted a skull inside the hood of a cloak, smiling evilly. It held up a sickle, and the wicked blade curved around the back of its head. Bony hands held the wooden shaft of the deadly weapon while its ragged apparel seemed to be flickering in the wind.

It was the only tattoo Kane had. The one which gave him his name.

It was the Reaper.

———

Retribution, Three days later

. . .

The sand-colored military Humvee came to a halt outside the warehouse, and a young corporal emerged from the front passenger side then opened and held the rear door, waiting for their guest to climb out.

Capitán Primero Carlos Arenas slid from the seat and stood erect under the hot Arizona sun. Gone was all his tactical gear from the other day. As too were his helmet and balaclava, allowing his square-jawed face and short-cropped black hair to be exposed.

He let his brown eyes wander over the rundown building before him and wondered what on earth he'd been sent to.

Normally, after a disaster such as had occurred at the Montoya compound, there would have been weeks of inquiries to front, because blame had to be laid somewhere. More than likely with him, for he was the mission commander.

But instead, three days later, here he was, sent north of the border to act as a liaison. He snorted. Liaison to what? Perhaps this was his punishment.

The corporal dumped his duffel bag beside him, and without a word, climbed back in the Humvee, and it drove off.

"Captain Arenas?"

Arenas looked at the doorway and saw a man standing there.

"Yes."

"I'm Swift. Follow me, sir."

Arenas retrieved his duffel from the dust and followed the man inside the building. Once he'd entered, he stopped and stared at the size of the setup. Impressive.

"Over this way, sir," Swift said.

When he reached Ferrero's desk, the DEA agent stood and

stuck out his right hand. "Captain Arenas, I'm Luis Ferrero. I'm in charge of all this," he explained, waving his hand in the air.

Arenas took his hand in a firm grip. "Pleased to meet you."

Ferrero indicated to Kane, who was approaching them with Cara at his side. "This is John Kane. He's in charge of our field team. Cara here is his second in command."

They shook, and Arenas asked the obvious question. "What is here?"

"We are a task force that is currently trying to take down the Montoya cartel," Ferrero explained. "Which is why you're here. We requested you personally."

The penny dropped. "It was you the other day when my team was in trouble."

"Actually. it was Sergeant Teller over there who you talked to."

Arenas glanced over to where Teller was seated, and the master sergeant nodded.

"Thank you."

Ferrero said, "Let's get down to business, shall we?"

Arenas nodded. "OK."

"Good. What can you tell me about the other day?"

Arenas' face changed, and he hissed, "We were betrayed."

"What makes you say that?"

"It is the only answer. They were expecting and ready for us, and it cost me most of my men. I was prepared to die and were it not for your intervention, I would have."

"Any idea who it might have been?"

"Hah," sarcasm dripped from the outburst. "It would be easier to ask me who it was not. I trust no one except for those I command, and then sometimes not even those. It is why we always wear the masks. If the cartels find out who we are, they kill our families."

"What about your family?" Kane asked. He'd been studying the special forces commander while he spoke. Kane figured him to be about his own age, but the lines on his face told of the hard times he'd endured in his current profession.

Arenas became immediately defensive. "My family are my concern."

"What I mean is, are they in constant danger?"

"Sí. Yes."

"How would you like to get them out of Mexico, Captain? Yourself included." Ferrero asked.

"I would be crazy not to."

"Come and work for us, and I can make it happen."

"I thought I already was."

Ferrero grinned. "I mean work *for* us, Captain. Not be a liaison."

Arenas looked at him with suspicion. "Doing what?"

"As part of Kane's field team. He currently has four people on it, but we need an extra man with your experience. It would be dangerous work."

"And living in Mexico is not?"

"Point taken. The thing is, you wouldn't be the man in overall charge. That is Kane's job."

"And if I agree, you can make this happen?"

"You and your family will be American citizens within twelve months."

Arenas hesitated. "I think there is something you are not telling me. You brought me here for a reason. Why?"

"We know who betrayed your team, and we want your help to get to him."

The special forces captain snarled. "Tell me who it is, and I will go myself."

Ferrero held up a hand. "That isn't how it works. Tell him, Reaper."

"We need your help to get to this person in Mexico City," Kane explained. "We think he knows where Montoya is hiding, and we need that information, so we can get him. It is *not* a revenge mission. I'd prefer to do it on the quiet."

"Tell that to the families of the men who are dead," Arenas growled. "Stare into the eyes of the grieving widows and explain to them why their husbands aren't coming home."

"I've done that more than once, Captain. I know what it feels like to lose men under your command and to face their loved ones afterward. But I need to know I can trust you if you're going to be part of this team. If we go to Mexico City, and you go rogue on us, I'll put a bullet in your head and not bat an eyelid."

Arenas' voice was abrupt. "If I cannot have this man then I want Montoya."

"As long as it doesn't endanger any of the team, then he's all yours."

Arenas stuck out his right hand. "Then I will join your team."

Kane took it. "Glad to have you aboard."

"Get the man settled and kitted out, Reaper," Ferrero said. "Introduce him to the rest of the crew. Welcome to the team, Captain."

"My name is Carlos."

"Carlos," Ferrero agreed.

"You have not told me who it was that warned Juan Montoya."

"Secretary of foreign affairs, Ferdinand Morales."

————

Retribution

"Can you do it or not, Mike?" Ferrero asked the assistant attorney general.

"Seeing as you told him it would happen, then I guess it will have to. He was happy enough to come on board then, I take it?"

"Yes, sir."

"When will your team go in?"

Kane said, "That depends on the general."

Jones lifted his chin in curiosity. "How so, Gunny?"

"Carlos knows the area, General," Kane explained. "But if I were back running a recon team, we'd have nice big satellite pictures of the area, so we could plan properly."

"Consider it done, Gunny. Anything else?"

"I think that will do, sir."

Jones nodded. "If you get into trouble, Gunny, the CIA have a safe house within three blocks of the location. Just so you know."

"Let's hope I won't need it, sir."

"Let's. I'll have the pictures for you tomorrow. Good luck."

"Thank you, sir."

————

The general was as good as his word, and early the next day, the team had two large satellite pictures to plan from. One was taken in the daytime, the other at night. He'd also supplied them with smaller ones of the security detail assigned to the secretary.

The not so small mansion stood on a substantial block surrounded by considerable gardens. There were floodlights, a high fence, and double gates at the front.

The house itself was a two-story adobe building with a multi-vehicle garage, and a small bungalow was situated out the back near a rectangular inground pool. The team studied the details intently.

"I don't see any security cameras," Hawk observed.

Traynor said, "He doesn't need them. Did you see the security detail? They're packing plenty of hardware. All ten of them."

Kane moved from the daylight one across to the one taken at night. "Carlos, take a look at this."

Arenas moved to stand beside him and stared at the picture.

Kane drew a circle with his finger around a dark patch close to the fence on the east side. "We could get in here. It's dark enough. The trees create this shadow that the light doesn't penetrate."

"Someone has been careless. Once we get over the fence, we can use the shadow to make our way along here," he ran his finger across the picture, "and that will take us up to the pool area. But then there is the problem with the lights in that area. Once past them, we can get into the house," Arenas said.

"That's all well and good," Cara pointed out, "but there's still the problem with the security. Are they private contractors?"

Arenas held up a hand as an idea came into his head. "Wait."

He crossed back to the smaller pictures and riffled through them carefully. He studied them one at a time until he found what he wanted. He held it up and exclaimed, "This one. This picture."

He lay it flat on the table for them all to see. It was a picture of one of the security detail near the front gate. It was a closeup, and the facial features were relatively clear. But the special forces commander wasn't pointing at the face. He was indicating the neck.

"What are we looking at?" Hawk asked.

"There," Arenas said and stabbed his finger at the picture again. "Do you see it?"

Kane looked closer. "A tattoo."

"Yes. These are not private contractors, they are cartel."

"Son of a bitch," Hawk muttered. "What does that mean?"

Kane said, "It means, if push comes to shove, we can take them down and not feel bad about it. It's not like the secretary can scream down the roof. How's he going to explain his security detail being cartel?"

"Exactly."

Kane's face grew stern. "When we go in, we'll be dressed accordingly. Full tactical gear with balaclavas. We don't want to be recognized. If you have to shoot, shoot to kill."

Arenas spoke in a low voice, "With pleasure."

CHAPTER 20

*MEXICO CITY, **Two nights later***

Three almost indistinguishable shapes moved through the shadows with the stealth of a panther stalking its prey. Soft, rubber-soled boots created no sound, each step carrying them closer to their target. NVGs were down for this part of the insertion, however, when the team moved closer to the house, the goggles would become useless.

Kane paused in a deep shadow and waited for Cara and Arenas to close the distance. So far, so good. Cara came to a crouch beside him, and they were soon joined by the special forces captain.

"This is where it gets hairy. Carlos, watch our six. If any guard pokes his head up, put him down."

Arenas nodded. "Copy."

Kane looked down at his MTM watch. It was two in the morning. Some of the rooms inside the double-story house were still lit. The worst part was that they were going in blind. Unable to lay their hands on any plans for the place, they had no idea how many rooms there were or which one the secretary might be in.

"Listen. We clear the rooms one at a time until we find him. Copy?"

"Copy."

"Zero? Reaper One. We're about to breach, over."

"Copy, Reaper One. Good luck."

Reaper flipped up his NVGs and said, "Let's go."

They moved forward in a crouched position. Reaper had his silenced H&K USP up and ready. Its laser sight not as visible as with the NVGs down.

Behind him, Cara covered their right while Arenas covered their rear.

They emerged into the floodlit area around the large inground pool. Kane went left while Cara and Arenas circled it to the right. Under the bright lights, the clear water seemed to sparkle like a tropical oasis. The canopy of palms reaching out from either side made it feel even more so.

Cara weaved between a couple of terracotta pots planted with large, leafy foliage. Kane strode between some powder-coated aluminum outdoor furniture and suddenly stopped.

"Tango," he hissed into his mic and backed up a few paces. He was too far away from the small bungalow for it to be of any use, so he dropped behind the only cover there was for him. The outdoor table.

Cara and Arenas stepped into a small garden and positioned themselves against the wall of the main house, sheltered behind a small palm.

"Hold your fire," Kane whispered.

The guard walked along the path, part of his normal patrol route, oblivious to their presence. He was armed with an AK and had a walkie-talkie fixed to his belt. However, one thing was certain, if he held his current track, he would discover Cara and Arenas.

Kane waited until the guard was almost upon them, then scraped a chair-leg beside him along the top of the sandstone pavers.

The Mexican whirled around to identify the noise, and as he did so, Cara came away from the wall.

With swift movements, she reached over his left shoulder with her left hand and clamped off his mouth. Her right hand drove the barrel of her silenced Smith and Wesson M&P into his back and squeezed the trigger three times.

There was an audible grunt after the first shot, and he stiffened. By the time the third bullet had smashed into his body, his knees weakened, and he began to slump.

Arenas hurried forward and helped Cara drag the body into the garden, out of sight before blood went all over the paved area.

Kane whispered into his mic, "You all good?"

Cara's voice betrayed her heavy breathing when she came back to him, "Roger, all good."

"Let's keep going."

Down the path from which the guard had emerged, Kane discovered an entry point. He reached out to try the door handle, but Cara grabbed his hand. "What if it's alarmed?"

"I don't think it will be because the guards will be going in and out."

Cara raised an eyebrow. "You don't think?"

"I guess we'll find out."

He tried the handle. It moved, not locked. Kane dropped his NVGs over his eyes and swung the door open. He stepped through, his gun up, and swept the room. A bedroom. Empty except for a single bed, a dresser, a hand-tooled chair in the corner and a picture on the wall.

Behind him, Cara and Arenas entered. The latter pulled the door to behind them. On the far side of the room, a small sliver of light showed beneath another door. Kane crossed quickly to it then raised his NVGs again and cracked it a mite to look out.

On the other side was a well-lit room with large sofas and a tiled floor. He could make out the edge of a large fire-place, but that was all. The sofas were vacant, but that didn't mean there was nobody there.

With his eye still at the crack, he held up his left hand all fingers splayed apart. Then he began to drop them one at a time in a slow countdown.

Five.

Four.

Three.

Two.

One.

He swung the door wide and walked through, swept left and right. Cara emerged behind him, and he directed her to the left where he sighted another closed door. Arenas moved right.

Now that he was in the room, Kane could see every-thing that hadn't been visible from his limited aspect of the doorway. The fire, a bar along the far wall, a large television, billiard table, and a small coffee table with bottles on it.

"Shit," he breathed into his mic. "This is where the guards hang out. Cara, clear that room. We need to leave."

A few moments later Cara said, "Room's clear, Reaper."

The three of them hurried towards a doorway on the other side of the room. Kane paused before he walked through to check for cartel men. There were none, and they kept going ...

... into the largest foyer he'd ever seen. It was magnificent.

The floor was marble; white, unblemished, sterile. From the ceiling, on a golden chain hung a large chandelier. Twin, curved staircases led to a second floor, the balustrade made of fancy fretwork and edged with handcrafted terra-cotta trims.

This was obviously a small sample of the luxury that cartel money afforded you.

Kane waved Cara across to the stairs, and Arenas to the large timber front doors. He tried a door opposite, and it swung open. It was a library and study wrapped up in one. There was a large desk, and many shelves of leather-bound books, ornate furniture and fittings, and large mullioned double doors which led out to another part of the garden.

He closed the door and silently moved along to a wider opening which led into a spacious dining room. With the H&K still raised, Kane traversed the room and found the kitchen. Voices from within gave him ample warning of their presence, and he peered around the corner to see two men standing near a large island bench.

Kane backed away and retreated the way he'd come.

When he reached the foyer, he found the other two still there. "Two Tangos in the kitchen."

They nodded and followed him up the stairs.

The landing was clear. It swept around the front of the house and out onto a balcony.

A long hallway ran off the landing, with three doors

along each side and another closed one at the end. Kane figured that room to be the master and the most likely place they'd find Morales.

He situated Arenas at the start of the hallway, to watch their backs, and then he and Cara proceeded towards the door. They had almost reached halfway when the middle door on the left opened, and a woman in her forties stepped out into the hall.

Without a second thought, Kane closed the distance between them and clamped a hand firmly over her mouth. She stiffened and was about to struggle when he whispered into her ear. "If you try to cry out, I'll kill you. Do you understand?"

Not knowing that he wouldn't, she nodded.

"Good. Are you Ferdinand's wife? Ferdinand's *esposa*?"

She nodded as best she could.

"Is that your room?"

She shook her head.

"Where?"

She indicated the last room with her hand.

"Good. You walk in front. If you try anything, you know what will happen."

With his left hand on her shoulder, Kane walked her quietly along the hall until they reached the door. Once there she opened it, and they entered the room.

Ferdinand Morales must have had some sixth sense that something was amiss because he was instantly awake. He turned the bedside lamp on, and his eyes widened when he saw the black-clad figure standing next to his wife.

He rolled violently in the bed, and Kane thought he was going for a gun in the bedside dresser. Kane squeezed the trigger on the silenced USP, and splinters erupted from the front of the drawer. Morales' wife let out an involuntary half scream.

The sound of the ejected brass casing hitting the tiled floor rattled around the room. Kane shook his head. "The next one I'll put in your head, *amigo*. Get out of bed."

With great hesitation, Morales did as he was ordered.

Kane signaled to Cara. Careful not to use her name he said, "Tie his wife up and gag her."

"What do you want?" Morales asked.

Kane took a small recorder from his pocket and placed it beside the secretary. "We're here to ask you a couple of questions. If you answer correctly, then you might get through this night alive. Ready?"

"You are a *gringo*. What are you? A soldier? A hired killer? You will not get away with this. You have no idea who I am."

Kane quickly lost patience with the man's false bravado. "Shut the fuck up and listen, asshole. I know who and what you are, and I don't give two shits about it. Tell me where Montoya went."

Morales gave him a defiant look. "I don't know what you are talking about."

"Reaper One, from Arenas. We have movement inside the house. Three men so far. I heard them say something about an alarm. They're on the stairs."

"Put them down."

"Copy."

Kane let out a whispered curse and shot Morales in the leg just above the knee. The secretary screeched and grasped at the wounded leg. Reaper ignored it and turned to face Cara. "They're coming. Get out there and help our friend."

Cara nodded, hurried towards the door and disappeared.

Kane turned back to Morales. "How many guards?"

The secretary sat and whimpered.

Kane raised the USP again. Morales' eyes widened. "*Quince!* Fifteen!"

From the end of the hall, Kane heard the shots from the suppressed handguns followed by the clatter of weapons dropping to the tiles.

"I ain't got time to fuck around. Tell me where Montoya is!"

"I do not know."

"Bullshit. These are his men. He pays you, and you tip him off when things are going down. Where?"

"I do not *know!*"

"Fuck!" Kane swore and brought the USP in line with the man's head.

Morales cried out and brought his bloodied hands up in a useless display of self-defense. "Wait! Wait! Don't shoot me. I'll tell you!"

Kane could hear the muffled sobs of the secretary's wife in the background, but he ignored her. "Where?"

Morales made one last desperate attempt to stall. "You do not understand. He will kill me if I tell you."

Kane hissed, "I'll fucking kill you if you don't. Where?"

Cara's voice came through the comms. "Move your ass, Reaper. There are more coming."

"Reaper One? Zero. Get out now! Over."

"Where?" Kane snarled and made the secretary flinch.

"Reaper, do you copy? This is Zero, get, out, now!"

Morales cracked. "He is in Guatemala. There is an abandoned resort near the Pacific Coast. He is there. He has another lab there."

"Zero, you copy that?"

"Copy, Reaper. Guatemala."

Kane picked up the recorder and grasped the wounded Morales by the collar. "Get up."

"Ahhh! I am wounded. You shot me."

"Too bad," Kane snapped and dragged him to his feet.

A cry of pain escaped the secretary's lips, and Kane shoved him forward.

"What are you doing?"

"We're going to see how much your security detail think of you."

"Reaper, easy," Ferrero's voice came over the radio.

Out in the hall, more gunfire erupted. Bullets twanged off the walls and some smashed into the ceiling. AK-47s rattled out their staccato death song. Ahead of him, Cara and Arenas ducked back as another burst of gunfire hammered out.

Cara leaned forward and dropped a cartel man on the stairs. The man cried out and fell backward, only to be replaced by another more eager killer who sprayed the landing with a deadly hail of bullets.

Kane shoved Morales forward. "Tell them to hold their fire."

"They won't listen to me."

The silencer dug up under the secretary's chin. "Fucking tell them."

"OK, OK," he blurted out. He lurched forward and shouted, "*Mantén el fuego! No dispares!* Hold your fire! Don't shoot!"

Raised voices came from the bottom of the stairs, and Kane edged Morales forward. There were two men on the stairs, and another three or four below in the foyer, it was hard to tell.

Kane hissed in his ear. "Tell them to put their guns down and let us through."

"Bajen las armas. Déjalos pasar!"

Incoherent murmurings came from below. Then one of the men on the stairs snarled, *"¡Vete a la mierda! Imbécil!"*

The AKM in his hands roared to life, and 7.62 rounds cut through the air like knives, two of which ripped into the secretary's chest, killing him instantly.

"Shit!" Kane cursed.

He fell back to the hallway with the others and dragged the body of Morales with him. "I guess they said no," Cara said above the gunfire.

Kane checked the secretary for a pulse. "He's dead."

Glancing up, he saw a cartel soldier's head appear above the top step. The H&K came up, and he put a bullet in the man's forehead.

He glanced at Cara and Arenas. "Fall back to the bedroom; we're going out the window. Cara, you first, check it out."

"Copy."

"Reaper One? Zero. Sitrep, over."

"They killed Morales, Zero. We're cut-off from our exfil point and are looking for a secondary. Out."

"Copy. Out."

Suddenly a door opened behind Arenas, and a kid appeared. Kane snapped, "Get the kid back in there!"

Arenas whirled and pushed the frightened child, a boy, perhaps ten years old, back inside the doorway. He knelt in front of him. "Hide behind your bed and stay there."

He slammed the door and almost cannoned into Kane. "Come on, fall back."

More bullets lashed the air, and Arenas fired twice at another cartel man whose large frame seemed to fill the end of the hallway. After the second shot, the weapon's slide locked back with a dry magazine.

"Reloading!" Arenas said in a loud voice.

Kane fired more shots along the hall to cover the vulnerable special forces officer. Cara's voice came over the comms, "Reaper One? Reaper Two. The window is clear."

"Copy."

Kane touched Arenas on the shoulder and ordered him to fall back, then emptied his own gun along the hallway and followed him. He slammed the door shut and saw Cara leap out of the second-floor window. Arenas prepared to do the same.

From out in the hallway an AKM sounded. Bullets punched through the wooden door and sprayed splinters across the room. The secretary's wife grunted, and Kane saw that she'd been hit.

"Fuck! Go! Go!" Kane snarled to Arenas as he slapped a fresh magazine into his HK.

The special forces officer disappeared as he jumped from the ledge.

The bedroom door crashed back, and a large man filled the void. Kane snapped off a couple of shots before diving out the window.

Fuck! This is going to hurt.

Straight down. Six-feet-four of rock-hard muscle plummeted towards the ground. He vaguely remembered the window above being shattered by gunfire as he went through.

When the impact came, it wasn't the sudden, bone-jarring crunch he'd expected. It was to the snap of branches and the rustle of leaves. He'd landed in a clump of shrubs. Their tight-knit branches had broken his impromptu fall.

A familiar hand dragged him free of the tangle. "Come

on, Superman. Next time, try your underwear on the outside of your suit."

Arenas fired at the figure who appeared through the window and was rewarded with a cry of pain.

"Cara, lead out," Kane ordered. "The way we came in."

The trio started to jog along the side of the house towards the pool area. Once adjacent to it, they were stopped by shouts from cartel men. Four appeared suddenly on the other side of the pool. Cara reacted first and shot out one of the floodlights, before diving into the garden. Arenas was right behind her and bullets scythed through the air where the pair had been only moments before.

Kane brought up his H&K but realized he was going to be too late as an AKM held by a snarling Mexican centered on him.

He threw himself to his right and into the pool, as hot metal tore through the space above him.

The cool waters engulfed his body, the sound of gunfire distorted by the roiling liquid. Kane found his feet as bullets peppered the water like small, leaden torpedoes. He waited for as long as he could before he surged upward and burst free of the surface. Water cascaded from his body in a liquid sheet.

The HK came up, and he sighted on the closest gunman. He fired two shots, and both punched into the killer's chest. The guard threw his arms up and squeezed the trigger of his HKM. Bullets lashed the sky as the man fell backward to the hard pavers.

More cartel men appeared out of the darkness and this time, each of the three-member team opened fire at them. They jerked and twitched as the rounds hammered home. Two fell, but one managed to get some shots off.

Bullets ricocheted off the house, and a statue of the

Madonna lost her head as a stray slug smashed through the neck. Then the shooter was slammed back as rounds found their mark.

Arenas stuck out a hand to pull Kane from the pool. "This is not the time, *amigo*."

"No shit."

Kane climbed from the pool. "Lead out, Cara. Let's get the hell out of here before more of them come after us."

A crackle came from Kane's comms, and he cursed. "They're fucked. So much for being waterproof."

"What?"

"My comms. Move."

They slipped into the shadows and headed towards the boundary fence. Behind them, the leftover cartel guards could be heard calling to each other. Before long, they were at the fence and moments later, were over it and about to climb into the SUV.

Cara stopped Kane before he could climb into the driver's seat. "Uh uh, water boy. All fish in the back."

And with that, she relieved him of the keys and climbed behind the wheel.

Arenas chuckled at him.

"Shut up," Kane snapped. "Call Zero and tell him we're on our way home. Also, confirm with them that I want a meeting with General Jones and clearance for a mission to Guatemala."

Kane climbed into the back and closed the door. "We'll get this son of a bitch before we're done."

Cara floored the accelerator, and the SUV shot forward. Behind them, a cartel soldier watched them leave and then reached into his pocket. He took out a cell and dialed a number.

Guatemala

Montoya touched the disconnect button and stared across at Salazar, fuming. "These fucking people won't leave me alone!"

"What has happened now?"

"They killed Morales and his wife."

Salazar raised an eyebrow. "But why?"

"I don't know. Maybe they were after me. Trying to find out where I went."

"Did he know?"

"Of course he fucking knew! *Dios mío.* These *gringo* bastards are getting on my nerves."

"Are we sure it was them?"

Montoya nodded. "It was. One of the men heard them speak American."

"Then we must leave," Salazar said, indicating around with his hands. "It is not safe for you here."

"We will wait until the shipment is ready."

Salazar wasn't happy. "But that is still ten days away."

"Yes, it is."

"But, *Jefe –*"

"We are staying, Cesar!" Montoya erupted. "The shipment is worth two-hundred million dollars. I am going nowhere until it does."

Salazar nodded. "Then at least allow me to bring in some more men."

"Do it," Montoya agreed. "How many will you need?"

"Twenty should be enough. I can have them here within twenty-four hours."

Montoya turned away and stared out at the darkness. "If they come, we will be ready."

———

Washington, The following morning

Mike Turner reached across his desk, picked up the phone, and said, "Tell me it went well, Luis."

"Morales is dead, Mike."

"Damn it, Luis. What the fuck happened?"

"His own men shot him."

Turner shook his head in disbelief. "And why would they do that?"

"Because they were cartel. The whole security detail was. They were a private hire. All the Mexican government officials do it. You know that. Well, this one had cartel men from Montoya as his."

"Christ, the president is going to love this. Is there any good news?"

"We know where Montoya is."

"Where?"

"The *Tranquilidad Resort*. Or the Tranquillity Resort. It's an abandoned place on the Pacific coast of Guatemala."

"Holy shit!"

"He has another cocaine lab there. The team is on their way home, but Kane requested a meeting with General Jones when he gets back, and permission to plan another mission. This time to get Montoya."

Turner hesitated and then said, "I'm not sure about this, Luis. I'll have to kick it upstairs and get back to you."

"I expected as much."

"When will your team be back?"

"Tomorrow evening."

"OK. I'll have an answer by then. If the mission is OK'd, I'll set up a meeting with the general for the following morning."

"Thank you, sir."

"Don't thank me yet, Luis," Turner said and hung up.

CHAPTER 21

RETRIBUTION
Teleconference

Assistant Attorney General Mike Turner and General Hank Jones stared out at the gathered team from the divided large screen. Their expressions sufficiently conveyed the gravity of the situation.

Turner said, "The president has given the green light for the operation to proceed. Under no circumstances are there to be any American forces used on the ground, what-soever. The operation is deniable. I suspect you know what that means. How you get in and out will be up to you. Although, I suspect that the general has it covered. If there is anything you need, come to me or General Jones."

Ferrero nodded. "Thank you, sir."

General Jones took up the dialogue. "I have taken the liberty of organizing some satellite maps, which you should have tomorrow."

An image of one with notes and markings appeared on

the screen, and Jones continued, "Once I got word about this, I also had some of Rear-Admiral Joseph's guys take a look at this. The ones you receive will be the same."

Rear-Admiral Alexander Joseph was commander of The United States naval special warfare command (NAVSPECWARCOM).

"His boys thought the DEA was crazy sending a small team in there to extract someone like Montoya. Looking at this, I tend to agree. You'll see that they've marked out all the guard points. The larger buildings have at least one machine gun post on top. They have standing patrols along the beachfront and the marina. As near as they can figure, the coke lab is in the trees behind the lagoon. Some of the bungalows are used for the cartel soldiers that live onsite."

"How many are there, sir?" Kane asked.

"A rough estimate is forty men."

"Yes, sir."

"And I do mean rough, Gunny. They weren't able to nail it down too well."

"Yes, sir."

"The issue will be both the insertion and extraction of your team," Jones continued. "We've looked around in all of the dark closets, and we've come up with a way. The day after tomorrow, a helicopter will come and collect you all–"

"What about our equipment?" Ferrero interrupted.

"It'll be taken care of. You'll travel light."

"OK."

"From Retribution, you'll be flown to a small freighter off the coast of Acapulco. The freighter will then transport you to where you need to be."

Kane said, "I take it that the freighter isn't actually a freighter."

"It is, but on the outside only. It is maintained by the

NSA, so you can imagine all the extra bits beneath the run-down exterior."

"It's a spy ship?"

"We prefer to call it an observation platform. Anyhow, it'll be your home for as long as required. Everything you'll need, plus a few things you won't, will be onboard."

"How do we get ashore, sir?" Kane asked.

"There will be a SOC-R on the freighter with its team to do the insertion. You've got Joseph to thank for that. The admiral agreed that you were all crazy and thought that you needed all the help possible, so gave us the use of his best team."

The SOC-R stood for Special Operations Craft – Riverine. It was a fast boat used for SEAL insertions, with a top speed of forty knots. It was crewed by four and had five weapons mounted onboard, which included two miniguns and a .50 caliber.

Jones spoke again. "Insertion point will be a mile from the target. The planners seem to think that if you make your way along the coast until you reach the lagoon's inlet, you'll be fine. From there, use the inlet for cover to get you within the perimeter."

"I don't suppose they know how deep the channel is, sir?" Cara asked.

Jones gave one of his rare smiles. "No idea, Lieutenant, but the insertion is timed to be done at low tide so there won't be a lot, one would think."

"Yes, sir."

"It seems like the planning guys have thought of everything, General," Kane pointed out.

"They did it under my orders, Gunny. As you know from experience, we have many assets at our disposal that you do not."

"I'm not complaining, sir."

"I didn't think you would be."

"This is becoming more a military than DEA thing by the minute," Ferrero observed.

"All of this extra stuff is my doing, Luis," Jones assured him. "However, if this all works out for the best, and the president gives the taskforce a permanent green light, Mike and I have discussed that there will need to be some changes. But we can talk about that at a later date. And don't worry. All your jobs are safe, up to a certain point."

"You mean if we don't all get killed?" Arenas put in.

"Exactly right, Captain. Now, where was I? Oh, yes. After the insertion, the SOC-R will stand offshore and await your signal for exfil. If you run into any trouble, make for the beach. The team will give you cover while you are extracted."

"I thought you said no military?" Hawk asked.

"I said no military on the ground. There was nothing mentioned about the water."

Hawk shrugged. "I'm good with that."

"OK. That's all from me for the moment, Luis. If you or your team have any questions, let me know."

Ferrero nodded. "Thank you, General."

Jones disappeared, leaving Turner on the screen, alone.

"Keep me up to speed, Luis. Same goes for me, if you need anything, let me know."

"Thank you, Mike."

Then he, too, was gone.

Ferrero turned to Kane. "What do you think, Reaper?"

"I'd say we've got some shit to organize."

"My thoughts exactly."

———

Retribution, The next day

Kane stood in front of the satellite picture, his face plastered with a scowl. No matter how he looked at it, the answer he kept coming up with was the same.

"You look troubled, my friend," Arenas observed as he and Cara approached.

"What's up, Reaper?" Cara asked.

"Look at this," he said, running a finger over the picture. "We've all been over this, right? We infiltrate here and move along the channel. We reach this point here and split up. I take Traynor with me and Arenas takes Hawk. I do the lab, Arenas goes for Montoya. Cara, on the other hand, takes up position here."

Kane stabbed a straightened finger at the rooftop of the right-side building.

"She takes up overwatch after she takes care of those on the roof. But if the shit hits the fan, she can't cover us all. Which makes us short one shooter."

The Mexican special forces captain stared at the picture intently and then nodded. "Yes. So, we shift her."

Cara sighed. "I'm right here, guys. Should I get a say?"

They looked at her. Kane asked, "What do you think?"

"I agree with Carlos. I reckon I'd be better situated here." She pointed at the main building. "However, I agree too, that we're a shooter short. If we had another, then we could take out those on building one and then those on two and three. After which, we could provide overwatch."

Kane gave a satisfied nod. "I agree."

"Do you have someone in mind?"

"Yeah, I do," he said, then turned away and walked towards Ferrero's desk.

Cara and Arenas watched Kane and their boss discuss something before the latter picked up the phone. He spoke for five or so minutes and consulted with the Reaper team leader twice before he hung up. Both men seemed satisfied, and Kane left Ferrero to his paperwork and walked back to where Cara and Arenas waited.

"All set?"

"Who did you get?" Cara asked.

He gave her a wry smile. "You'll see."

"Uh huh."

His face grew serious again. "When we go in, I want you to take an extra weapon. Think you can handle it?"

"Sure."

"OK. Along with your M110, I want you to take an HK416 with an M203 attached. You too, Carlos. I want the extra fire-power. I'll have a 203 as well. Since you're our armorer, Cara, make sure it happens. If we don't have the gear we need, then get it. Whether it comes here or it's on the chopper, I don't care."

Cara said, "I'll get on it."

"I'll help her," Arenas said. He looked at Cara. "If that is OK with you?"

"The more, the merrier."

Off the coast
  Acapulco

"Shit, Reaper, when they told me you were leading this mission, I told them they were fucking crazy," the big man said as he took Kane's hand in a firm grip.

"If you'd asked me six months ago whether I'd be doing this, then I would have said the same, Axe."

Axel "Axe" Burton, marine recon sniper (MARSOC). As good as they come and then some. Kane had worked with him a few times over the years. He knew of only one better. Chip.

He was a tall, broad-shouldered man, in his early thirties. Single, good-looking, and would hump anything that moved. Some said that even if it didn't move, old Axe would push it.

"How's Hammer? I heard you two were working together."

"He's dead." Nothing else, no other way to say it.

Axe's face dropped. "That's fucked."

"Yeah."

Ten minutes earlier, the helicopter had dropped the team to a beat-up freighter that looked like it deserved to be in some scrapyard instead of sailing the oceans. But looks could be deceiving, and the NSA had created the nondescript look it wanted, and in fact, the ship was as sound as the next one.

The name on the stern said: **Artoro.** The script beneath it said: **Panama.**

"So, what gives, brother?" Axe asked Kane.

"Let's get inside, and you can meet the team. I'll fill you in along the way."

———

Artoro, The following day

.   .   .

Below decks in one of the converted hold spaces, Kane held the team's final briefing. He stood in front of a satellite map with a laser pointer. The thump, thump of the freighter's motors seemed to vibrate throughout the entire ship.

"OK, for those of you who haven't met yet, I'll introduce you to our escort for tonight. Chief, you guys want to step up here?"

There was movement, and four men stepped forward to position themselves beside Kane.

"This here is Chief Hunt and his men. The chief is our driver tonight on the SOC-R which will be inserting us."

Hunt nodded.

"After the briefing, get to know these guys, be nice, or he'll make you walk home."

"Wouldn't be the first time," Axe joked.

"All right," Kane continued. "We'll go over it one more time. Listen up –"

Axe gave a fake yawn. "Wake me up when you're done, Reaper."

A chuckle went around the group.

Kane smiled. "Shut your hole, Axe, and listen."

"I'm all ears, Admiral."

Kane used the pointer. "After we're inserted, we'll make our way to here."

The red dot settled on the mouth of the inlet.

"We traverse the inlet until we reach this point and then we'll split up. Myself and Traynor will go for the lab up here in these trees. Carlos and Hawk get the prize; Montoya. Axe and Cara, take the rooftop of the main building, silence the guards on the other rooftops, and then provide overwatch for us. We want to do this as quietly as possible. I'd rather we had no noise until the explosives go bang."

"What happens if it all kicks off?" Axe asked.

"The only heavy support we'll have is the M203s on the 416s we'll be using," Kane explained. "You and Cara will have one each, Carlos and I will have one as well. Use them sparingly and kill anything that isn't a friendly."

Axe nodded, satisfied.

"Teller informs me we'll have an eye in the sky for a while," Kane said, and turned to Hunt. "Is that right?"

Hunt said, "Yes, we have a Raven. Once we stand off and you guys radio us that you're in position, we'll put it aloft. You'll have ninety minutes, tops. After that, you'll lose the window."

"At least that's something," Cara acknowledged.

Kane shifted his gaze to Arenas. "If you and Hawk get inside and secure Montoya without any hassle, stay put until we're ready to extract. If not, bundle him up and head for the beach. If you need to terminate him at any point, do it."

"*Sí.*"

"Cara, you and Axe hold that rooftop. If the op goes south, we'll be relying on you to keep them off our backs. Even though we'll have an eye in the sky, the Raven can only see so much."

"Copy."

"OK. For this op, callsigns are as follows. I'm Reaper One, Arenas, Two, Traynor, Three. Hawk is Four, Cara, Eagle One, Axe, Two. Our support is Bravo, and Chief Hunt is Scimitar. Any questions?"

They remained silent.

"OK. Low tide is at twenty-two hundred. Have everything ready to go before then."

———

The inlet

"Reaper One? Scimitar. Raven is airborne, over."

"Copy, Scimitar. Raven is in the air. Bravo Three, do you have visual?"

"Copy, Reaper One. I have visual."

"Roger. Out."

In the background, the crash of waves on the broad sandy beach seemed loud in the stillness of the night. Kane tightened his grip on the silenced HK416 and scanned the other side of the channel through his NVGs. Everything seemed clear.

He said in a low voice, "Reaper Two, move out."

"Copy."

Arenas pushed past him through the stunted shrubs and eased into the salt water of the channel. Reaper followed him and was soon up to his chest. Behind him came Cara, and at the rear of the column was Axe.

"Reaper One? Bravo Three. Confirm two men on each of the main buildings."

"Copy."

"Reaper, you have a mobile patrol at your eleven o'clock. Thirty yards out."

"Copy."

Arenas stopped. Raised his left arm a fraction and then lowered it slowly. Behind him, the entire team sank below the surface.

Kane counted off the time in his mind and then resurfaced. The others followed suit.

Arenas slowly moved forward again.

Under his feet, Kane could feel the uneven bottom.

Every now and then he felt a rock and had to change stride to accommodate it.

The pace was agonizingly slow, but if they were to succeed, that's the way it needed to be. On missions such as this, to rush might lead to carelessness which could get them killed.

Up ahead the bridge loomed large. As indicated by the intel provided, a heavily-armed cartel man was stationed at either end.

Arenas never hesitated. He dropped lower in the water until everything below his nose was under the surface and proceeded beneath the bridge.

As Kane moved soundlessly under the timber construction, he could hear the pair speaking in Spanish, too low for him to make out what they were saying.

To their left, above the bank of the inlet, the last of three large resort buildings reached upward into the darkness. All ten levels of it.

The team proceeded another fifty meters before Arenas stopped again. They'd reached the location designated as the break-off point. Kane toggled his mic.

"Bravo Three? Reaper One. Over."

"Copy, Reaper One."

"We've reached Alpha, Bravo Three. Do you have eyes on?"

"Roger, Reaper One. The path to building one is clear until you reach the entrance. Two guards on the door. Over."

"Copy, out."

"You get that, Reaper Two?"

"Copy."

"Move out."

Arenas walked towards the bank and eased his way up

over the edge and disappeared. Hawk followed him a short time afterward. As Cara moved past Kane, he said, "Watch yourself."

She nodded, and when Axe moved in beside Kane, he whispered, "What about me? Going to tell me to be careful?"

"I hope a Tango puts a round between your eyes."

"Nice, brother. Nice."

Kane watched him crawl over the bank and then turned to Traynor. "You ready?"

"Copy."

———

Team 2

Arenas weaved his way through the overgrown shrubs towards the side entrance where the two guards were stationed. Above him, some large palm tree fronds caught a gentle breeze and rustled. He stopped behind a low shrub and took a knee.

Hawk came to his shoulder and did the same. "What's up?"

Arenas parted some of the growth and showed him the sentries. Through the grainy green of the night vision, he could see them on either side of the doorway. They'd reached their target building. The special forces commander whispered, "You take the one on the left."

"Roger."

Hawk and Arenas brought their silenced HKs up. The laser sights settled on the targets and Arenas said quietly, "Now."

Crack, crack.

The guards jerked from the impact of the two 5.56 rounds and slid to the ground in silence.

Immediately, Arenas and Hawk were moving forward. When they reached the fallen figures, they shot them once more at close range, then quickly dragged the corpses into the lush undergrowth.

Arenas spoke into his mic, "Bravo Three? Reaper Two. Tangos down. Need location of Montoya, over."

"Reaper Two? Bravo Three. The infrared on the Raven indicates the only heat signatures inside are on the fifth level. Suggest you try there."

"Copy. Going up. Out."

Arenas and Hawk entered the building. Behind them were Cara and Axe.

They moved silently up the stairwell like wisps of smoke on a breeze. The scent within the enclosed space was that of damp caused by the constant high humidity.

As they were passing the second floor, a door above them opened. The clang of the closing door was followed by footsteps on the stairs. Arenas waved them back.

At the rear of the small column, Axe made a call and cracked open the second-floor door. On the other side was an empty hallway with doors branching off each side at regular intervals. He brought up his HK and moved inside. Behind him, Cara and the others followed as the footsteps coming down the stairs grew louder.

The musty smell was stronger now, the odor coming from the carpet of the disused level. The four team members spread out on either side of the door and waited with bated breath for whoever it was to be gone.

Then Arenas realized something. Whoever was going down would go out the door where the guards were meant to be. On noticing their absence, they would more than likely raise the alarm. He cursed under his breath and turned to the person nearest to him. It was Cara.

"We have to stop him," he whispered to her. "If he gets downstairs, he will find those others."

Cara nodded. "OK."

Arenas let the HK416 hang by its strap and drew out a black-bladed knife. Cara took the M110 from her shoulder and leaned it against the wall. She did the same with her HK. Then she stood in full view of the doorway and said. "Do it."

Outside in the stairwell, the footsteps were at their loudest. Arenas reached out and tapped the hilt of his knife on the door.

The footsteps stopped.

He did it again.

They watched as the handle turned and the door swung wide. The cartel man's jaw dropped when he saw Cara standing there. She smiled at him and said, "Hi."

"*Mi Dios, una puta!*" he gasped in a hoarse voice.

The knife in Arenas' hand arced around and struck the gaping man in the throat; his other hand grabbed the front of the man's shirt and dragged him forward into the hallway.

The Mexican started to gurgle, blood flowing from his mouth. Arenas pulled the knife to the right with a violent action which opened the dying man's throat all the way, easing the body to the floor as Cara closed the door.

Arenas wiped the blade on the dead man's shirt and put it away.

"He's fucked," Axe observed.

The special forces officer stared at his watch. They were behind schedule. "We must keep moving."

Cara snatched up her weapons, and they all slipped back out into the stairwell.

———

Team 1

After Kane and Traynor left the inlet, they moved through the brush and large palm trees around the edge of the lagoon. Up in one of the bigger trees, the cook-cook-cook-cook sound of a Pacific Screech Owl could be heard.

Over the comms, Kane heard Arenas report the take-down of the two guards at the doorway, and that teams two and three were entering the main building.

When he and Traynor reached the first in a line of bungalows at the lagoon's edge, they stopped. Kane whispered, "The lab should be just up ahead in those trees."

So far, they'd been lucky with the roving patrols. They'd encountered one and had let it slip by. Now he needed some intel on what lay ahead. "Bravo Three? Reaper One. Copy? Over."

"Copy, Reaper One. Go ahead."

"We've reached the first bungalow. I need a count on Tangos around the lab, over."

"Copy. The count is six. I say again, six. Over."

"Roger, Bravo Three. The count is six. Out."

Kane looked at Traynor. "Let's go."

They moved forward once more with Kane sweeping left and front while Traynor covered their right and rear. Once past the bungalow, they slipped into the stand of trees. When he sighted the target building, Kane stopped again.

With the help of his night vision, he was able to pinpoint the first couple of guards. He used hand signals to indicate their positions to Traynor, then motioned their next move.

Both brought up their weapons, laser sights trained on the two men. With selector switched to semi-auto, Kane whispered, "Now."

They achieved the same outcome as had Arenas and Hawk when the two cartel men jerked and sank to the damp ground.

"Reaper One? Bravo Three. You still have one guard on either side and two behind the building, over."

"Copy, Bravo Three," he said and then to Traynor, "You sweep right, and I'll go left. There are four more."

The two separated and edged along the sides of the building. Kane peered around the corner of the lab and saw his target. The man was lazy, standing still, a lit cigarette hanging from his mouth, and couldn't have made Kane's task any easier.

Reaper centered the laser sight on the side of the man's head and squeezed the trigger. With a wet thwack, the 5.56 round blew out the side of his skull, and he fell to the ground.

"Tango down."

Kane edged along the wall until he reached the rear corner. He peered around it and saw the two remaining guards. Once more, the HK spat venom and both men died.

"Reaper Three, copy?"

"Copy."

"Both Tangos down at the rear, over."

"Roger. Mine is now singing with the angels, over."

"Copy, meet you at the front."

When they entered the coke lab, it took them a while to

comprehend what lay before them. Even when he'd been in Colombia, Kane had never seen anything quite like it. And because the lights were on, they saw it all.

Multiple barrels of chemicals, unprocessed coca leaves, two pallets of processed coke, a long row of stainless-steel tables, and on and on and on. Everything that was needed.

"Fuck me," Traynor gasped.

"Yeah. Let's get these charges set before someone comes along. It should make a nice bang."

CHAPTER 22

TEAM 2, *That same time*

Arenas and Hawk stopped on level five while Cara and Axe continued their ascent. When the special forces officer cracked the door from the stairwell to look, relieved at the silence of his action, he saw two guards, their backs turned, no more than ten feet along the hall. Just past them, the area opened out into a large room, which, from what he could see, seemed to occupy most of the floor. He closed the door quietly and turned to Hawk.

The special forces commander used hand signals to indicate his intentions and convey instructions to the DEA man. Hawk nodded his assent, and Arenas faced the door. He held up a hand, slowly counting backward to one. When the last finger dropped, Arenas pushed the door open.

The special forces officer had only moved two steps into the hallway when he fired his first burst. The guard jerked and cried out before he fell. Arenas switched his aim immediately and dropped the second guard. The spent bullet cases clinked onto the white-tiled floor, the echo seeming overly loud.

Without a missed step, Arenas continued his forward motion. Behind him, Hawk moved to the left side of the hallway, HK raised and ready.

Poking his head around the corner of where the hall opened out, a skinhead guard with facial tattoos and piercings had a heartbeat to realize that something was wrong, before Hawk killed him with a bullet to the head, the ruptured skull emitting a red shower.

A woman's scream echoed throughout the room.

Team two pushed forward into the larger room, Arenas sweeping the right of the space, Hawk concentrating on the left.

There were three more men in the opulent suite. Two were tattooed in a similar fashion to the one Hawk had shot. The other was dressed in a white suit, and when he laid eyes on the interlopers, he screeched;

"Kill them! Kill the fucking dogs!"

Both cartel soldiers tried to get some shots off, their AKMs not quite ready, but the HKs of Arenas and Hawk turned both men's white singlet-tops into bloody, red rags. They collapsed into untidy heaps, their blood spilling across the tiles in a bright-red pool.

Three women, one of whom had screamed, stood cowering in front of a long sofa, arms wrapped tightly around each other. Montoya side-stepped with urgency, placing the group of women before him, preventing the Reaper men from getting a clear shot.

"Chickenshit fuck," Hawk cursed at him. "Cowering behind women."

"Look out!" Arenas shouted.

Montoya produced a handgun and was taking aim at Hawk who had hesitated due to the proximity of the women. The gun cracked, and Hawk cried out as the bullet ripped through the fleshy part of his arm.

Arenas, with little more than a wafer-thin gap between the women to shoot through, never vacillated. The silenced HK416 cracked, and Montoya was spun around. The gun dropped from his ruined arm, and he shouted in pain. Blood began to run from his wounded appendage, staining his formerly pristine white suit.

Pain turned to anger, and the cartel boss screeched. He lunged for the fallen gun with his good hand but was a fraction too slow.

Arenas pushed his way between the women as Montoya was fumbling with his gun, then brought the butt of his carbine down on the back of the cartel boss' head. He stared down at the slumped form then spit in the unconscious man's face. "Fucking asshole."

"Did you kill the son of a bitch?" Hawk growled.

Arenas glanced in his direction and saw the DEA man still standing but bleeding on the floor. He shook his head. The special forces commander toggled his mic. "Zero? Reaper Two. We have the package, over."

"Copy, Reaper Two. You have the package. Out."

———

Eagle Team

When Cara and Axe reached the door onto the roof, they stopped. Cara whispered into her comms. "Bravo Three? Eagle One. Sitrep on Tangos, rooftop, over."

"Copy, Eagle One. You have Tangos at left and right front corners, over."

"Roger. Eagle One, out."

"Let's go kill us some bad guys," Axe growled.

When the door swung open, Cara was faced towards the guard on the right front corner of the building. All she needed to do was aim and fire. Axe had to break left and circle back to take his own target, which is exactly what he did, and approximately three heartbeats after Cara's target died, his did too.

That wasn't the end of it, however, and Cara dropped her NVGs into place and let go of her HK. It swung to her side from the shoulder strap, and she quickly unslung the M110 Sniper Rifle, looking for her target across the way on the next rooftop.

She picked him out and dispatched him rapidly with one shot, then shifted her aim, finding the next target, replicating her accuracy, one shot, dead.

Cara toggled her mic. "Building two roof-top clear."

A moment later Axe's voice came over the comms, "Building three roof-top clear."

Cara hurried to the front edge of the building and set up her overwatch post. Axe mirrored her actions at the rear, immediately spotting movement at the northside bungalows. Then came the shouts.

Axe said, "Reaper One? Eagle Two. You've got multiple Tangos headed your way. Looks like someone raised the alarm."

"Copy, Eagle Two, we'll be ready for them."

———

Salazar

. . .

The *sicario* slapped home a fully-loaded magazine into the FX-05 Xiuhcoatl and barked at the men running past him. "Make sure they do not escape! Kill anyone who does not belong!"

When the weak call came across the radio, Salazar reacted quickly. Within minutes, he had men out of their beds and moving to meet the threat.

He opened his mouth to issue an order to a cartel soldier when the man's head erupted blood and brains. The wet gore splashed across his face and took his breath away. Then he realized that the shot had originated from the top of the main building. They were up there too. And that meant Montoya was in danger.

Salazar ducked around the corner of the nearest bungalow and out of sight. He raised a walkie-talkie to his lips and spoke. "*Jefe?* Come in, *Jefe.* Are you there?"

There was a drawn-out silence before he tried again. "*Jefe,* can you hear me?"

The radio crackled to life. "We've got your boss, asshole."

The *sicario* stared at the radio for a few heartbeats before his face turned to stone, then raised the black transmitter once again and barked more orders.

———

Tranquilidad Resort
   Eagle team

"Break! Break! Break! Bravo Three to all callsigns. Bravo

Three to all callsigns," the radio transmission echoed across the net. *"There are multiple groups of Tangos converging on the lab and the main building. Estimate numbers in excess of forty. Looks like the intel was wrong."*

"You fucking think?" Axe's voice came across the net. "You should see it from where we are."

Suddenly Ferrero came over the net. "Zero to Eagle One. Over."

Cara settled the laser sight on a Tango and hit him mid-stride. "Copy, Zero."

"You have to keep them back until Reaper can blow that damned lab. A large force is converging on his position."

Cara swore. "Shit! Copy, out. Axe you hear that?"

"Hear it? I'm fucking seeing it," Axe shouted as he fired, shifted aim, and fired again. "Cara, I need you this side. They're trying to breach this building too."

Cara dropped the M110 and took up her HK. She ran across the roof to take up position to Axe's left. Gunfire rattled from the ground and rounds started to snap and whine as ricochets passed dangerously close.

Through the green haze of her NVGs, Cara saw the cartel soldiers running towards the building. Two waves of them. Upwards of twenty-five men hellbent on murder.

"Reaper Two? Eagle One. Prepare for incoming contact. I say again, prepare for incoming contact. Out."

"Copy. Out."

Cara caught sight of a smaller group that was crossing the helicopter pad. She swung the HK around and fired the M203.

An orange ball of flame exploded amongst them, and they were flung bodily from their feet. A couple of wounded men writhed on the ground while the rest remained motionless.

Cara reloaded and fired again. This one landed closer in amongst the tall palms. Cries of pain reached her ears as the explosion ripped the night. Beside her, she could hear Axe steadily firing at the approaching men.

A bullet whipped past Cara's face, and she ducked down. She loaded another high-explosive round in the underslung grenade launcher and rose again. She was about to fire when she heard Axe shout, "Fuck! RPG!"

The rocket-propelled grenade came in at three hundred meters per second, and the two team members had little time to react. Both were blown backward when the load impacted just below the lip of the roof.

Cara crashed heavily to the rooftop, the air driven from her lungs with an audible whoosh. Her ears rang from the explosion, and her vision swam in front of her.

She realized someone was tugging at her arm and looked up. Axe looked over her like some Greek Adonis. Through the ringing in her ears, she heard him say, "Come on, Cara, get up. We have to get the fuck back into the fight. Come on. Are you OK?"

Cara allowed him to help her to her feet. "That was close, huh."

"Too fucking close," he grunted, wiping at a trickle of blood running down his left arm from just below his shoulder where a sliver of metal had opened it. He also had some leaking from a cut on his cheek.

Cara winced. She too felt blood on her face, and her chest hurt from a where a block of concrete had smashed into her tactical vest. They staggered back to the edge of the roof. Some of the cartel soldiers were vanishing into the building beneath them.

Axe fired a burst from his HK416 down at them but was too slow.

"Shit," Cara cursed and toggled her mic. "Reaper Two, be aware you have Tangos in the building. I say again, Tangos in the building. Over."

Arenas came across the net with a simple, "Copy. Out."

Axe swore once more, and it sounded almost like an exclamation of despair. "Ah, fuck! They've got another one."

He lurched sideways and knocked Cara to the ground, covering her body with his own to await the explosion. This one was different to the last as the RPG used was a Chinese Type-69, loaded with an anti-personnel high-explosive round.

Designed not to explode on impact, but to hit and leap into the air before it blew, which it did, spraying metal balls outward, cutting down anything in its path.

Cara felt the heat wash over her and then felt Axe stiffen on top of her. She heard him grunt and then his hoarse voice, "The bastard got me."

Cara rolled his heavy form off her and groaned. She said, "Axe, are you OK?"

Nothing.

"Axe, speak to me."

Nothing.

"Christ," she swore and toggled her mic. "This is Eagle One. Man down, I say again, man down."

————

Team 1

Kane ducked as a bullet snapped close to his head. It flew past and burned into a tree near the lab. He fired a burst at the cartel man who'd tried to kill him and saw the man throw his arms into the air.

By the time the mortally wounded man had hit the ground, Kane had shifted targets and dropped another charging figure with a blazing AK in his hands.

"Come on, Traynor," he shouted. "Have you got that last one set yet?"

"Almost, Reaper."

"Shit. Hurry up."

A sudden explosion erupted at the top of the main building. An orange fireball leaped into the air. *RPG*, he thought. It was followed by another, and then he heard the call.

"This is Eagle One. Man down, I say again, man down."

"Damn it! Come on, Traynor, we've got to go!"

"I'm done," he called and slid in beside Kane. "They're just waiting for you to trigger them."

Bullets whipped overhead, and foliage rained down around and on them like rice at a wedding. Traynor cursed and sprayed most of a magazine from his HK at a cartel soldier. The man seemed to trip and fall on his nose. However, he'd never rise again as one of the 5.56 rounds had smashed through his chest and all but destroyed his heart.

"Easy on the ammo," Kane cautioned. "Looks like we're going to need every bit of it."

"Reaper One, this is Bravo Three. You need to get your ass out of there before you're cut off. There are more Tangos advancing from the south."

Kane glanced to his left and saw a number of figures headed towards them. They opened fire, and he and Traynor were soon taking incoming rounds from two directions. "We've gotta move, now."

The DEA agent sprayed more gunfire at the approaching horde, dropping the empty magazine out before replacing it with a fresh one.

"But where the fuck are we going to go?" he shouted above the noise.

"We can't stay here," Kane snapped. "If I blow this lab while we're still in the blast radius, we're both fucked."

Kane ducked as another round snapped close to his head. Then he saw it. The only possible route. "The lagoon."

"What?"

"Follow me," Kane snapped and was up and running.

As the pair sprinted towards the lagoon, automatic weapon fire cracked all around them. To their right, a great geyser of sand and dirt blasted into the air amid a flash of orange light. Kane felt a bullet clip the material of his pants, but he never broke stride. Behind him, Traynor swore with a deep rumble as he willed himself onward.

In front of them, the lagoon loomed large, and Kane reached into his pocket for the detonator switch. They leaped into the air and Kane pressed the button. Behind them, the lab disintegrated as the explosives ripped it apart.

———

Team 2

"This is Eagle One. Man down, I say again, man down."

Hawk glanced at Arenas and snapped, "I'll go."

"No. We wait here until we can move and take Montoya with us."

"But we've got a man down," Hawk protested.

"Yes, and before that, they said we have Tangos in the building, who will come here to check on their *Jefe*. Both of us stay."

Arenas was right, and Hawk knew it. "Shit."

On cue, the door at the end of the hall flew wide, and tattooed men spilled inside. Armed with AKMs, they started to spray the interior without fear or favor. Their bloodlust was up and at that stage, didn't care who was in the way.

Arenas cursed and pulled the semi-conscious cartel boss to the floor beside him. Hawk dived behind the sofa that the bound women were on.

A line of bullets punched holes in the couch from left to right, and with it, the three women. Montoya's wife and two sisters-in-law. Their bodies spasmed, and two of them slid to the floor, where once more, the tiles became bathed in blood.

Arenas came up to one knee and fired the HK at the first target. The bullet blew through him and punched into the one directly behind.

The special forces officer shifted his aim and fired again. Another kill.

From behind the sofa, Hawk rose and fired a burst. The 5.56 rounds drilled three holes into the would-be killer from crotch to sternum.

More tattooed killers rushed through the door and, for the first time, Arenas knew they were in danger of being overwhelmed. He flicked the selector switch on the HK416's side and burned through the last of the magazine. Shell casings rattled across the hard floor as they were ejected from the rapidly-fired weapon.

"Loading!" Arenas called across to Hawk as he dropped an empty magazine and rammed another home.

He sighted once more and shot the next man to enter the battle zone.

Behind him, the walls were peppered with shot after shot. Plaster and debris rained down throughout the room which was soon hazy with a fine cloud of dust.

"Loading!" Hawk shouted and dropped behind the sofa once again just as three bullets ripped through it, taking clumps of stuffing with them.

The DEA agent reloaded and rose up to open fire when his head snapped back suddenly, a small puff of pink mist exploding from the rear of it.

With a clatter, his HK fell to the floor which drew the attention of Arenas who could only see an arm poking out from behind the sofa, but knew it was bad. Leaving Montoya where he lay, Arenas crawled across to Hawk. One look at the bloody hole in the man's forehead was sufficient to know that the DEA agent was dead.

"*Mierda!*" Arenas swore in a harsh voice. He spoke into his mic, "Man down. Reaper Four is hit, and I'm pinned down. I repeat, Reaper Four is hit, and I'm pinned down."

Team 1

"Man down. Reaper Four ... I'm ... down. I repeat, ... Four is ... pinned –"

Kane and Traynor had dragged themselves from the lagoon and were now under the cover of a low bank. An orange glow from the burning lab still filled the immediate area and illuminated multiple targets for the water-soaked men.

Kane swore, "Fuck! Say again, Reaper Two."

"Reaper Four is hit, and I'm pinned down. I repeat, Reaper Four is hit, and I'm pinned down."

He looked at Traynor. "Come on, we've got to get to the main building."

Traynor shot another cartel soldier. "Lead the way."

"Keep your head down," Kane snapped and leaped to his feet.

―――――

Scimitar

Chief Hunt started to bark orders to his men when he heard the call from Arenas. "Man the miniguns."

"Are we going in, Chief?" Kemp asked.

"Damn straight. NVGs on and call targets before you open fire. I don't want you killing any of our own."

Hunt slammed the throttle all the way forward, and the stern of the SOC-R sat down hard as it shot forward.

"Reaper Team? Scimitar. Reaper Team? Scimitar. We're coming in hot for extraction. I say again, we're coming in hot for extraction. Get the fuck out of there now!"

The radio crackled to life. "Scimitar? Bravo Three. Zero says to hold. I repeat, Zero says to hold. Over."

"With all due respect, Bravo Three. Fuck you! We're going in. Out!"

―――――

Eagle Team

. . .

Cara grabbed Axe's collar and cursed him. "Get the hell up, you big piece of shit. You're too heavy for me to carry."

"Leave me, I'm fucked," Axe groaned.

"You will be if you don't get the hell up. Move soldier! Our men need us."

Axe groaned, "Yes ma'am."

The big man was wounded in four places. In the left leg, the left arm, a gash on his left hip, and his scalp, just above his ear.

"Come on, Axe," she said as she helped him up. "It's only your left side. You've still got your right."

He stood on unsteady legs while Cara picked up his HK416 and rammed a fresh magazine into it. She forced it into his right hand and said, "Just don't shoot me with it."

"What about the M110?"

"Leave it."

He gave her a grimace. "Let's go kill some of these motherfuckers before I bleed out."

Team 1

A cartel man loomed up in front of Kane and fired a burst from his weapon. Kane felt the heat of the rounds as they passed close. He squeezed the trigger on the HK, and a burst ripped into the man's guts.

Two more appeared as they weaved through the clumped trees on their approach to the main building. This time Kane fired first, and the killers stopped in their tracks as though they'd hit some invisible brick wall.

Suddenly, a distant Brrrrppp tore through the darkness. Red tracer rounds seemed to be everywhere in the darkness as they crisscrossed the resort grounds.

"Get down!" Kane shouted and landed on his stomach in an overgrown garden.

Traynor dived beside him and yelled, "What the hell?"

"Tracer rounds."

"Where the fuck from?"

Kane toggled his comms. "Scimitar? Reaper One. Scimitar? Reaper One. Do you read? Over."

"Copy, Reaper One."

"Tell your man to stand down. I say again, stand down. You're lighting us up."

"Christ!" Hunt's voice came back through the comms. Then Kane heard him shout, "What the fuck did I tell you guys about your fire discipline? Cease fire!"

Immediately the lines of tracer stopped, and the comms went dead.

Traynor said, "Speaking of lights if we could turn the bastards off, it would help us no end."

"You're right. Good thinking. Bravo Three, this is Reaper One, over."

"Copy, Reaper One."

"Does anyone know where the power supply to this place is? Over."

There was a moment of silence before Teller came back on the air. "Reaper One, we think that the smaller construction behind building two houses everything, over."

"Copy. Out."

"Scimitar to Reaper One, copy?"

"Go ahead, Scimitar."

"We can take care of that for you. We have a clear field."

"Copy, Scimitar. All yours."

"Wait one."

A minute later the air was torn apart again by a long Brrrp. Tracers reached out in a long stream and then as if someone had thrown a switch, the lights went out."

"Move, Traynor," Kane ordered as he dropped his NVGs down. The pair came from the garden and tracked towards the door that Arenas and the others had used to get inside.

———

Eagle Team

With Cara in the lead, they slowly traversed the stairs. They'd met a team of three coming up, but the cartel men had lasted no longer than it took for Cara to depress the trigger. The sound of the HK echoed throughout the stairwell but was drowned out by the screams of the dying.

They pushed onward until reaching the fifth floor. A furious amount of gunfire sounded from within. Cara looked at the bloodied Axe, and he nodded. She took a step forward and then the lights went out.

As Cara cursed under her breath, a voice came over the comms. "Reaper One and Three entering the building."

"Copy. Eagle Team on the fifth. Will hold. Out."

"Copy."

———

Team 2

.   .   .

Arenas was still pinned down behind the sofa and almost through his last mag. About him was so much stuffing and debris, it was a wonder the sofa still held together. Shouts by cartel men could be heard above the gunfire, and the special forces commander was thankful the fuckers couldn't shoot for shit otherwise he'd be dead too.

At one point, they'd tried to rush the sofa but had lost three men for their troubles and pulled back. Now, though, he figured there were still four of them left.

There'd been some chatter over his comms, but he'd basically ignored it because the noise of the constant firing by the cartel men of their AKs drowned most of it out.

He rose again and fired off a burst which chipped wall tiles and thudded into plaster. The killer he was aiming at ducked back out of sight just as Arenas squeezed the trigger.

He fired again, and his last magazine ran dry, so he dropped back below his meager cover, cursing. Then he stared at the M203 and gave it some serious thought. He could take some with him that way at least. He dismissed the idea and took the Smith & Wesson M&P out of its holster. Once more he rose and fired five shots at a tattooed face.

Two of them hit the Mexican in the chest while a third burrowed into the man's throat. A large gout of blood fountained from the rent in the flesh and sprayed red across the tiled floor.

Another man appeared, and Arenas shifted his aim. He was about to squeeze the trigger again when the lights went out.

Everything went silent. It was eerie in a way Arenas had never before experienced. One moment, the full cacophony of battle roared about him, and then it just stopped.

Arenas lowered his NVGs and peered around the edge of the sofa. He counted three Mexicans just standing there, confused. He was about to cut loose with the S&W when silenced gunfire rattled out, and the three men lurched and spasmed before collapsing.

Then three figures appeared and fanned out to sweep the room. The three voices said, "Clear."

The lead figure looked around the room at the carnage and said, "Arenas?"

Arenas climbed to his feet. "Here."

"Hawk?"

"He's dead."

———

"Let's get this piece of shit out of here," Kane hissed and dragged the now conscious Montoya to his feet. "Cara, he's yours. If you need to put a bullet in his head, do so."

A flashlight shone on Montoya's face, and the cartel leader spit on the floor. "Fucking *puta*."

Kane ignored him and turned to Hawk's prone figure. He took a step forward, but Arenas stopped him. "I'll do it."

"Are you sure? He's a shade bigger than you."

"I can do it. Just help me get him up."

They stripped the dead DEA agent of all his gear, and Kane helped Arenas lift him. The man was as strong as a bull.

Kane said to Traynor, "You take our six. Anything moves, kill it."

"Copy."

"Scimitar? Reaper One. Ready for exfil. We're on our way with the package, over."

"Copy, Reaper One. We'll be watching for you. The marina is clear if you want to use it. Out."

"Copy."

"All right, let's move."

The stairwell was clear, so they had no problems reaching the ground floor. All they had to do now was get to the boat. Before they exited, Kane asked, "Has anyone seen Salazar?"

"No."

"He must be out there somewhere," Kane said. "Keep your eyes open. Axe, you need to move fast. I know you're hurt, but you can't lag behind."

"Don't worry about me, Reaper," he said through clenched teeth. "I'll outrun you."

When they pushed their way outside, Kane moved to the right. The team was directly behind him. Figures appeared to his right, and the HK fired a burst and made them scatter.

When he reached the fountain, he took a knee and scanned to the right of the path. As the rest of the team passed him, he spoke in an even voice to give them encouragement. Traynor stopped beside him and said, "They're pushing in from the rear. I saw some of them using the trees for cover."

Kane nodded. "Keep going. I'll be right behind you."

As the group disappeared behind him, Kane slipped a load into the M203 and fired. An orange ball of flame erupted to his front, and he heard a man scream in pain.

He reloaded and fired again. This time a little to the left of the last.

"Reaper One? Bravo Three, copy? Over."

As he reloaded the M203 again, Kane rasped, "I'm a little busy at the moment, Bravo."

"Is that you, rearguard?"

"Copy."

"Then I suggest you get out now, Reaper One. You have Tangos on your left and right. If you stay there, you'll be cut off."

"Shit! Copy."

He fired the M203 to his right and then swung the HK to his left and emptied the magazine into the green-filled haze created by his NVGs.

Then he ran after the others who had already reached the marina and were looking to board the SOC-R.

And Kane almost made it. He was twenty yards short of the jetty when he was hit by someone to his right and knocked from his feet.

With a loud grunt, he crashed to the ground in a tangle of arms and legs. His helmet with night vision came free and bounced away. Rolling to the side, he came up on his right knee in time to see the figure lunge at him again.

"Fucking *gringo* pig," the man cursed and reached for Kane's throat.

Claw-like fingers wrapped around his neck and the attacker began to squeeze. Kane's nostrils filled with the stench of fetid breath that blew across his face; his would-be killer's mask of hatred close to his with the effort it was taking to throttle Reaper.

Kane snapped his head forward, and lights flashed before his eyes as his forehead impacted solidly with his aggressor's skull.

With a cry of agony, the Mexican reeled away. Kane stumbled to his feet. The figure before him staggered a few steps before stopping, then turned to face Kane who suddenly realized that he was unarmed and fumbled to get his USP out and working.

The Mexican brought his own weapon up and snarled at Kane. "You come here to kill my *Jefe*, but you will not ever leave here."

Salazar!

Kane knew he wouldn't be quick enough to prevent the *sicario* from shooting him. He just hoped that the tactical vest would take the impact and that he didn't get shot somewhere vital.

"Reaper. Get down!" a voice filled his comms.

Kane dived to the ground and left Salazar standing there like a beacon.

The man laughed. "That will not save you, *gringo*."

Brrrrp!

The minigun rounds reached out across the marina like flaming lances. They cut through Salazar with brutal force, and his body seemed to dissolve as chunks of flesh were blown across the surrounding grass.

Kane hugged the ground for the duration of the gunfire burst. When the noise finally died, he heard through his comms, "Are you coming or what? Taxi is leaving in thirty seconds."

Hunt!

Kane ran. Ran as fast as he could. Behind him, the ground started to erupt skyward in orange flashes as an MK19 grenade launcher attached to the SOC-R fired rounds over his head to cover his exfil. When he reached the boat, he launched himself from the marina, landing heavily on the deck of his escape vessel, and before he'd gathered himself, Chief Hunt had the craft at full throttle and rocketing away.

He stood up and looked around at his team. "Is everyone OK?"

They all nodded, but their mood was somber. They'd lost Hawk but gotten Montoya. He saw Hunt at the helm and crossed to him as the boat bumped along.

"Thanks for that."

"It's what we're here for," he said.

Kane nodded and toggled his comms. "Zero? Reaper One. Extraction complete. We're on our way home with the package."

EPILOGUE

1 week later

It was a bleak, miserable day in more ways than one. Overhead, steel-grey clouds heavy in the drab sky dumped sheets of rain on those beneath who stood around an open grave. The priest droned on in a dull monotone, almost inaudible against the noise of heavy drops falling on the numerous black umbrellas, while Kane and the others stared at the plain casket that held the earthly remains of their teammate, Hawk.

When the service was finished, they moved to one side, away from the rest of the mourners.

Axe winced and said, "Shitty day for a shitty day."

"Amen to that," Traynor agreed.

"How are you healing, Axe?" Kane asked him.

"I had more holes than this in me when I was in Africa fighting Al Shabab," he scoffed. Then his voice lowered, "I'm healing, Reaper."

Kane nodded. "Good to see you out of the hospital, anyway."

Arenas looked at the group and said, "He was a brave man."

They all nodded in agreement.

Ferrero said, "Kane, Cara, a quick word, and we'll get out of this God-awful weather."

They moved away from the others and stood beneath one of the few trees the cemetery had to offer.

"I got word yesterday that the task force now has full backing from the president. It'll still fall under the purview of the attorney general, and any resources required for certain operations, General Jones will be more than happy to provide."

Cara said, "That sounds positive."

"In a fashion."

Kane stared at Ferrero for a moment. "Why do I get the feeling you're holding something back?"

Ferrero winced. "After the debrief, I was called back into the AG's office for a meeting with him, the secretary of state, and secretary of defense. They're replacing you as commander of field operations."

"What?" Cara blurted. "What the hell for?"

"Easy. Hold up a minute. They're doing it, and that's it. I tried to talk them out of it, but they wouldn't be swayed. They don't believe that you can run field ops and be out in the field as well. I told them that it was bullshit, and the proof was in the op we just completed."

"So, what does it all mean?" Kane asked.

"You'll still be in charge out in the field and all decisions that need to be made accordingly. The new man will basically be in charge of planning and decision-making about the ops. I'll still be in overall charge."

"What about the team?" Kane asked.

"You, Cara, Arenas, and Axel."

"What happens to Traynor?"

"He'll be part of Bravo along with Reynolds, Swift, and we get to keep Teller."

Kane thought about it, mulled everything over.

"If you want out, Reaper, I'll understand."

"I'll stay. Cara?"

"I'm in."

Ferrero smiled. "All right. The team has two weeks off, and then it's back to work."

"What about Montoya?"

"He's locked away in a supermax somewhere, all safe and sound."

"Good."

"Go see your sister, Reaper. You too, Cara. Go see that boy of yours. Relax."

Kane eyed him warily. "You already know what's coming next, don't you?"

"I'll see you when you get back."

———

Chesapeake Supermax

A long, drawn-out howl echoed along the corridor. Montoya was certain it had come from the serial killer, Cliff Serrano. Or as he was known throughout Chesapeake, Cut 'em Up Cliff, because his M.O. was to dissect his victims, and leave their assorted body parts along the east coast from Delaware to Rhode Island.

From the cell next to him, Dan Trent was making loud

grunting noises; a serial rapist and from what Montoya could gather, a serial masturbator too.

Then there was George Washington Brown, of all things, a black supremacist; Sonny-Boy Walter, who'd blown up a small church in Maine because he'd figured all those who attended to be sinners that needed cleansing by the higher power. And lastly, Mikey Ferris, the cannibal from Montana.

All were bad men, but when it came to Montoya, they couldn't hold a candle to him.

The opening of a door at the end of the hall echoed loudly, then slammed shut as the approach of multiple foot-steps could be heard. They stopped outside of Montoya's six by nine cell, and a key rattled in the lock.

Montoya threw his legs over the side of the bunk and sat up.

His door swung open, and a prisoner entered the cell. Behind him, the guard slammed the door.

The newcomer smiled and spoke with a heavy Irish accent, "I believe that you and I have a mutual friend."

A LOOK AT: DEADLY INTENT

A TEAM REAPER THRILLER

AN AMBUSH BY SUPERIOR FORCES...INTER-FERENCE FROM EXTERNAL POWERS...

In book two of the fast-paced Reaper Series, the team must divide their forces before things go too far.

After Team Reaper's convoy is attacked by Cartel soldiers and American Mercenaries, Kane and Ferrero agree that the chain of command needs to be streamlined. The decision sees the team get a new overall commander, former Ranger, General Mary Thurston.

But more bad news is on the way...

Juan Montoya and Colin O'Brien escape from prison and the facility where Kane's sister and Cara's son are at is attacked and the boy taken. On top of that, the team is lured into a trap and Kane, along with a new team member, are captured.

Now the race is on to find the boy and the two team members all while Montoya is planning a devastating blow to exact revenge against the American Government.

AVAILABLE NOW

ABOUT THE AUTHOR

A relative newcomer to the world of writing, Brent Towns self-published his first book, a western, in 2015. *Last Stand in Sanctuary* took him two years to write. His first hardcover book, a Black Horse Western, was published the following year. Since then, he has written a further 26 western stories, including some in collaboration with British western author, Ben Bridges.

Also, he has written the novelization to the upcoming 2019 movie from One-Eyed Horse Productions, titled, Bill Tilghman and the Outlaws. Not bad for an Australian author, he thinks.

He says, "The obvious next step for me was to venture into the world of men's action/adventure/thriller stories. Thus, Team Reaper was born."

A country town in Queensland, Australia, is where Brent lives with his wife and son.

For more information:

https://wolfpackpublishing.com/brent-towns/

Made in the USA
Coppell, TX
19 August 2021

60715995R00229